"An extraordinary hero ... ... as it is riveting.
The ending courtroom battle sears with intense and realistic turns and
builds to an unforgettable closing scene."
—*Kirkus Reviews*

"With its singular characters, clever plotting, and focused storytelling,
Levine's punchy, well-written contemporary legal thriller will please
John Grisham fans."
—*Library Journal*

"Our hero's clashes with a phalanx of eloquent, profoundly evil corporate
types are worth rereading. Another mark of a fine novel is the treatment
of secondary characters. Levine's are articulate and sassy. A treat for fans
of the offbeat."
—*Booklist*

"Grounded in reality, Early Grave is a novel with heartfelt emotion,
flashes of humor, and high-octane excitement."
—*Franco Harris,* NFL Hall of Fame Running Back

"Fast paced, smooth and soulful. A winner!"
—*Jacqueline Winspear,* New York Times bestselling author of the Maisie
Dobbs series.

"'Early Grave' is a twisty legal drama, a moral mystery, and even an
inquiry into what the purpose of a man's life should be, all enlivened by
Jake Lassiter's bold bravado and Paul Levine's laugh-out-loud wit. The
story will keep you rooting for the good guys, both on the page and in
the world.
—*Ed Zuckerman,* Emmy and Edgar Allan Poe award winner

"Paul Levine is one of Florida's great writers, and Lassiter is his greatest creation. It's funny, smart, and compelling."
—*Dave Barry*

"Levine's prose gets leaner, meaner, better with every book...And Jake Lassiter has a lot more charisma than Perry Mason ever did."
—*Miami Herald*

"Since Robert Parker is no longer with us, I'm nominating Levine for an award as best writer of dialogue in the grit-lit genre."
—*San Jose Mercury News.*

"Another enjoyable, breathless thriller."
—*South Florida Sun-Sentinel*

"Enough courtroom shenanigans to please even the most stalwart John Grisham fan."
—*Lansing State Journal*

"Levine manipulates the expectations of the reader as skillfully as Jake manipulates the expectations of the jury."
—*Publishers Weekly (starred review)*

"The pages fly by and the laughs keep coming in this irresistible South Florida crime romp. A delicious mix of thriller and comic crime novel."
—*Booklist (starred review)*

"A thriller as fast as the wind. A bracing rush, as breathtaking as hitting the Gulf waters on a chill December morning."
—*Tampa Tribune*

"The legal excellence of a Grisham thriller with the highwire antics of Carl Hiaasen."
—*David Morrell*

"Jake Lassiter is my kind of lawyer."
—*Michael Connelly*

EARLY GRAVE

BOOKS BY PAUL LEVINE

THE JAKE LASSITER SERIES
To Speak for the Dead
Night Vision
False Dawn
Mortal Sin
Riptide
Fool Me Twice
Flesh & Bones
Lassiter
Last Chance Lassiter
State vs. Lassiter
Bum Rap
Bum Luck
Bum Deal
Cheater's Game
Early Grave

THE SOLOMON & LORD SERIES
Solomon vs. Lord
The Deep Blue Alibi
Kill All the Lawyers
Habeas Porpoise

STAND-ALONE THRILLERS
Impact
Ballistic
Illegal
Paydirt

BOXED SETS
Shattered Justice
Miami Law
3 Deadly Sins

EARLY
GRAVE

Paul Levine

HERALD
SQUARE
PUBLISHING

Early Grave
Paul Levine

Published by Herald Square Publishing
Cover design by www.Damonza.com
Interior Design by Steven W. Booth, GeniusBookServices.com
Author Photo by Doug Ellis, www.DougEllisPhoto.com

ISBN-13: 978-1-7345056-9-6

Printed in the United States of America

To the memory of Franco Harris, a legendary football player whose lifetime of accomplishments exceeded even the most immaculate of receptions.

PART ONE

"The only thing in the world worth a damn is the strange, touching, pathetic, awesome nobility of the individual human spirit."
    – *A Deadly Shade of Gold* by John D. MacDonald

"Like a bird on the wire...
Like a drunk in a midnight choir...
I have tried in my way to be free."
    – *Bird on the Wire* by Leonard Cohen

-1-
Kill Shot

I was sitting at my desk eating a crisp green salad instead of a greasy burger – doctor's orders – when Liliana stormed through the open doorway and aimed a short-barreled revolver at my chest.

"Dammit, Jake!" Her voice quivered and her arm shook. "It's all your fault."

"C'mon, Lily," I said. "Kale and carrots as my last meal?"

"You're supposed to be the smart one." The gun barrel rose and fell with her breaths. "Smarter than my husband, anyway."

"Tank's a loving father. I'm going to help both of you. And Rodrigo."

"Don't! Jake Lassiter, you don't get to say my boy's name! You're the one who turned his life to ashes."

Lily's eyes shone with tears. Her weight shifted from foot to foot, and the gun drew circles in the air. A tall, elegant dark-haired woman in her late forties, she wore a navy pants suit with a name tag on a lanyard around her neck.

Liliana Santiago-Pittman. Department of Family Services.

Just now, it was her family in need.

"Lily, I'm Rodrigo's godfather, and I love him as if he were my own son. I know what you're going through."

"You don't know jack! I just came from the hospital."

"I'm sorry, Lily."

"He's in critical condition."

"So very sorry."

"Bull! You told Tank to forge my name on the consent form."

"What? I wouldn't have..."

Is it possible I told my old buddy and teammate to risk his marriage with a stunt like that?

She looked at me skeptically. In her job helping at-risk children and cross-examining their no-account parents, Lily was a human lie detector.

"You don't remember!"

Yeah, she nailed it.

"Everyone in Miami knows you have brain damage," she railed on. "And my husband asks you for advice? The lame-brained leading the lame!"

I pushed aside the cardboard container of tasteless salad to buy a moment of time. "Let's go back to the hospital and wait with Tank."

"I won't be in the same room with that fool. As for you, I can't decide if I want you dead or just disbarred."

"If I'm disbarred, I can't get justice for Rod. If I'm dead, Keg South will be stuck with my bar tab. C'mon, Lily. Please take your finger off the trigger."

"Maybe I'll shoot you *and* Tank."

The gun must have been getting heavier as the barrel was now angled at my gut. In an autopsy, the medical examiner would note the undigested greens while the toxicologist would find a potent cannabis known as Mendocino Thunderhump.

Lily gestured at a half-deflated football on the credenza behind my desk. The score of an ancient Dolphins-Raiders game was painted on the leather, the numbers weathered with time, much like my brain cells.

"You and my husband," she said. "A couple of has-beens reliving their glory through my son. How pathetic. Tank with his limp and you losing your mind."

"Lily, I haven't lost –"

"To betray me, to put Rodrigo in harm's way." Tears flowed down her cheeks.

"Lily, please let me help."

"You don't help people!" Her arm shook. "You break things!"

Just then I saw two people coming through the open doorway. My pals Steve Solomon and Victoria Lord.

"Lily!" Victoria yelled.

"Whoa!" Steve shouted.

If this were a movie, Lily would have been distracted, and as she turned, I would have flipped over my solid oak desk without getting a hernia. She would have dropped the gun and fainted, and I would have caught her in my arms.

A man is always the hero of his own stories.

But real life, whose first act is often a comedy, generally ends in tragedy. True, Lily was startled, but she didn't drop the gun. Instead, she inadvertently pulled the trigger and put a .38 caliber bullet into my forehead, just below the hairline.

A perfect kill shot.

-2-
A Small Flutter of the Heart

One day earlier...

Dr. Rochelle Stein asked, "So, is this your first time in couples therapy?"

"No," Melissa said.

"Yes," I said.

"And off we go." Dr. Stein smiled pleasantly. She was in her sixties with a placid face and silver hair pulled back into a simple ponytail. Her office furniture was blond wood, neat and orderly, sending the subliminal message that her life was not as messy as yours.

She wore a serape in the tawny, rusty shades of desert rocks and sat cross-legged in her leather chair. No notebook, no pen. I'm used to a court stenographer taking down everything, so I hoped the shrink had a good memory when it came time to referee.

"We had one session with a therapist," Melissa said, "someone Jake suggested."

Dr. Melissa Gold, a neuropathologist, was way too smart to be my fiancée, but human beings are not rational, no matter how many Ivy League diplomas decorate their walls. Melissa specialized in chronic traumatic encephalopathy, CTE, which has struck down several of my former teammates and might be depositing sticky gunk in my brain cells even now.

Melissa was a tall, slender woman with reddish-brown hair and a dusting of freckles across her nose. She had just come from her lab and was still wearing a blue hospital smock with the University of Miami logo. Not only was she too smart for me, but too damn good looking, too. Sure, there was a time when women seeking merriment rather than thoughtfulness found a big lug like me diverting entertainment. But these days I look like what I am. A graying, aging jock with bum knees and a busted nose that never properly healed. And yet, here we were, bit players in the great cosmic mystery of love.

"All right," Dr. Stein said. "You were in your first session with…"

"With Ms. Bubbles French, LCSW," Melissa said.

"Bubbles?" Dr. Stein arched her eyebrows.

"An old nickname," I said, as the first flames of a migraine singed my skull. "It's 'Corrine French.' A clinical social worker who does psychotherapy."

"Jake had just admitted he was keeping things from me," Melissa said. "Secrets he wouldn't share. Then, Ms. French says, 'Jake, back when you used to call me "Bubbles" because I loved champagne, did you also have secrets?'"

Dr. Stein arched her eyebrows again, even higher. Maybe it's a trick they teach in shrink school. "Jake, were you and Ms. French lovers?"

"'Lovers' is a stretch," I protested. My migraine was joined by its first cousin, tinnitus, a brass band, heavy on cornets and drums, banging in my ears.

"Do you deny having sex with her?" Melissa demanded, sounding like a prosecutor with all the goods. If I denied the accusation, she might nail me with wiretaps and DNA.

"Sex, sure. But we weren't a thing. It was..."

"Casual," Dr. Stein volunteered.

"Exactly! Totally *caszhh.*" I dragged out the word, trying to sound hip, circa 1990. "I was hanging on to the last roster spot with the Dolphins. Bubbles – Ms. French – was a choreographer."

"In a strip club," Melissa added, helpfully.

"So why hide this relationship from your fiancée?" Dr. Stein asked.

"It was a zillion years ago. I barely remember those days."

"Convenient." Melissa turned to the shrink. "Jake's memory problems relate to recent events, not a 'zillion years ago.'"

"Very well," Dr. Stein said, "but let's focus on why you're in couples therapy."

"Jake never used to keep secrets," Melissa said. "Three weeks ago, after telling me his cardiologist gave him a clean bill of health, I discovered he's been taking two medications for atrial fibrillation. Also, without telling me, he went to the hospital for electrical cardioversion."

"My ticker has a little flutter. It's no big deal," I said.

"You're at a much higher risk of a stroke," Melissa fired back.

"And a heart attack," Dr. Stein said.

Tag-teaming me like the Hardy Boyz, if you're into pro wrestling.

"He also has blockage in the left anterior descending artery," Melissa said.

"The Widowmaker," the doc said, shaking her head sadly, as if I'd already passed. "Do you have heart disease in your family?"

"My father died of cardiac arrest in his forties," I said.

"So young." She spoke in an empathetic whisper. "Did he also suffer from arrhythmia?"

"Dad got in a fight, and a guy stabbed him in the heart."

"Oh my goodness!" Dr. Stein seemed stunned, which put the interrogation on hold for a moment.

"It was a long time ago," I said, hoping to end further inquiry into that dark history.

"Jake, why did you keep your heart condition from Melissa?" Dr. Stein asked.

Melissa studied me as I tried to conjure an answer. Her head was cocked to one side, her eyes probing.

She charts my moods the way Viking cartographers sketched Iceland. And she always knows when I'm off course.

I squinted through the pain in my skull and the ringing in my ears. "Melissa teaches at the med school and oversees three CTE research projects. So far, there's no cure for the disease. She agonizes over the people in her studies – the living ones, including me – and grieves over the ones who've died. Bottom line, she's carrying a ton of stress, and I don't want to add to the load."

"So, you took it upon yourself to determine how much stress your fiancée can handle?" Dr. Stein said.

"You're damn right I did! And I'd do it again."

That's what I was thinking, but not what I said.

I exhaled a long breath and pled *nolo contendere*. "Okay, I didn't handle this right. I thought I'd take my pills, and when my heart stopped hammering like Max Weinberg playing *Wipeout,* I'd tell Melissa all about it. I just didn't want to be more of a burden to her than I already am."

"You're not a burden," Melissa said. "You're the man I love!"

"And I love you back. I just hate to see you under so much pressure."

"Jake, if you were engaged to someone who wasn't your physician," Dr. Stein said, "perhaps another lawyer, would you have told her about your heart condition?"

"Why, doc? You have someone in mind for me?"

"Of course not!"

"He's joking, Dr. Stein," Melissa said. "It's Jake's way of avoidance and evasion."

Dammit! Even neurologists take psychiatry in med school.

"Ah, yes. I'm quite familiar with the technique," the doc said.

"Now that the A-Fib has come to light," Melissa said, "I have to wonder if Jake is sugar coating his symptoms associated with CTE."

"C'mon, Mel. I tell you when I have double vision or vertigo or I forget the name of our dog."

"We don't have a dog."

"See what I mean."

Melissa didn't crack a smile. She used to find me more entertaining. Locking eyes with me, she said, "You'll tell me you're fine when you're fighting a migraine, or your tinnitus is as loud as a freight train."

Actually, it's more like a hurricane, the kind that rips metal street signs in half.

"Whenever I feel like whining about the small stuff, I think about the guys who are no longer with us."

Like six Miami Dolphins from the 1972 Super Bowl championship team. Dead from CTE. Perfect season, my ass!

Turning to Dr. Stein, Melissa said, "Jake's symptoms are common in ex-football players with CTE, but no definitive diagnosis exists, short of an autopsy."

"I'm okay with spinal taps and PET-scans, but I draw the line at an autopsy," I said.

Dr. Stein sneaked a peek at a clock on the wall and said, "Obviously, we've only scratched the surface. But I'm going to make an observation that won't please either of you. Melissa, you must know how problematic it is to treat a patient with whom you're romantically involved."

"Jake and I have discussed it, and I've spoken with my colleagues both at NIH and the university. I have clearance all around."

"I'm not talking about the ethics, but rather the practical difficulties. Out of his love and concern for you, Jake is censoring himself. So, my first piece of advice is that you need to decide whether you want to be Jake's spouse or his doctor, because while you may do both, you surely can't do both well."

-3-
Kangaroo Court

After paying the shrink to enlighten us as to our deficiencies, Melissa returned to the hospital, and I aimed my ancient ragtop Caddy – a 1984 Biarritz Eldorado – south on Dixie Highway. The neighborhood is a plug-ugly sprawl of muffler shops, discount mattress stores, fast food joints, shady tax preparers, and off-brand gas stations. There is no unified look, no distinctive architecture, no sense of planning. Just a mindless hodgepodge of unrestrained, unregulated, unattractive growth.

Have concrete, will pour.

I passed Shorty's Bar-B-Q, a 70-year-old chicken and ribs joint that's about to be torn down for a huge commercial development. If you ask me, and the county commissioners haven't, Miami needs more pulled pork and fewer high-rises.

I parked the Caddy and entered Keg South, my saloon-cum-office. After decades plying my trade in the courtrooms of the sadly misnamed Justice Building, I gave up my solo practice and took a nine-to-five job with the Florida Bar, prosecuting wayward shysters.

Doctor's orders.

Fiancée's orders.

Yeah, one and the same.

I had struggled with the decision but could not resist the irresistible force that is Dr. Melissa Gold. My new gig was low stress, and I was making a meaningful contribution to society by weeding out dishonest and incompetent lawyers. Today, I was multi-tasking in the old saloon. I had an appointment with one of the pettifoggers to evaluate a client's complaint against him. I also was meeting Langston Pittman, my old Dolphins teammate, called "Tank" by his pals. We'd have a brew or two, then go to his son's high school football game.

Keg South was a place of knotty pine walls, neon Budweiser signs, and clever signage: "They Call It Almond Milk Because Nobody Wants to Drink Nut Juice." Okay, it's not the Banker's Club downtown, but it suits me.

A Black man roughly the size of a locomotive sat in a booth that might have capsized, had he not centered himself. Tank Pittman was eating chicken wings two at a time and might have been swallowing the bones, for all I know. On the table was a plaque, "Reserved for Jacob Lassiter, Esq." Some guys have reserved parking places at their country clubs. But this, too, suits me.

"Yo, Tank," I said.

"Wish you'd start calling me by my given name," he said.

"Blame Coach Shula for saying he could park a Patton tank on your butt."

Langston Pittman grew up in Joplin, Missouri, birthplace of Harlem Renaissance poet Langston Hughes. Tank's mother was an English teacher with a love of poetry. In hotels at away games, Tank would put himself to sleep by reciting, "My soul has grown deep like the rivers." In my bed, six feet away, I would listen to his booming bassoon of a voice and grow sleepy myself, once I enhanced the poetry with a liberal portion of Jack Daniels.

Tank drained a glass of Presidente, the Dominican beer, and said, "How long's this gonna take?"

"Just a quick, informal hearing. We'll get to the game in time for the coin toss."

"Can't be late. Rod's on the kickoff team, just like you in the old days."

"Except I was a plow horse and Rod's a sprinter."

A high school track star, my godson Rod would be a gunner on kickoffs, the road runner closest to the sideline.

"You're too modest, roomie," Tank said, licking ranch dressing from fingers the size of sausages.

Nah, I was the big galoot galumphing downfield, butting heads with two blockers so some dainty speedster could make an ankle tackle and get all the glory.

"You ran angry," Tank said, "and you loved knocking guys out of their shoes."

"Had to do something to earn league minimum."

Without being asked, Lourdes, my usual server, brought me an Australian Lager. She placed the bottle on the bar's logo, a screaming eagle with the notation, "Since the '60s."

I think they mean the 1960's, but it might be the Civil War.

In a moment, she returned with a Death Dog, a frankfurter covered with jalapeno, onion, horseradish, and melted cheese, and sprinkled with Tabasco. It looks more like a toxic waste dump than a sandwich, and I secretly treat myself when Melissa is in another zip code.

"So who you persecuting today?" Tank asked.

"Pro-se-cuting." I opened the file of "In re: Cecil P. Shiner." Just then, the door opened, and backlit by a beam of sunlight, Shiner walked in, and I waved him over.

"Mr. Shiner, take a seat." I gestured toward the other side of the booth, where Tank scooched over about six inches. Shiner, looking uncomfortable, sat next to him, their shoulders touching. The lawyer wore a tailored charcoal suit that did its best to hide his paunch. A sky-blue dress shirt was open at the neck and revealed a gold chain with heavy links. He was about fifty with a horseshoe rim of dyed black hair around a shiny skull.

I signaled Lourdes who brought Shiner his own beer. "My treat," I said.

"Isn't it a little unorthodox for the Bar to hold an inquiry here?" he asked.

"I guess you're the expert on Bar investigations. You had that trust account misappropriation complaint in 2011 and the missed appeal deadline in 2017."

He jutted his chin at me. "Paid my dues on those. Solid citizen, ever since."

"Except now," I said, munching the smothered frankfurter, "you have a complaint from a Ms. Luisa Revilla."

"Disgruntled client. You know how it is."

"She's a widow who says you failed to file papers to close the sale of her house so she could move to North Carolina to live with her grown children. It was a very advantageous sales price, and when it fell through due to your malpractice, she was forced to re-list the property. Interest rates had skyrocketed, and she took a lower price, $55,000 lower to be exact."

"Doesn't sound like a Bar violation to me," Shiner said. "Let Señora Revollo hire a lawyer and sue me."

"Revilla," I corrected him. "And why did you call her 'Señora'?"

"What of it? She's Cuban, isn't she?"

"Your tone of voice. Somehow you made 'Señora' sound like a slur."

"Maybe I'm just not woke."

"Yo, Cecil. I could put you into a deeper sleep," said Tank whose wife's maiden name was Liliana Santiago. "You feel me, Cracker?"

"Hey, no need for talk like that," Shiner said. "Can't we just let this go?"

"No," I said. "You're sitting next to a Black man and across the table from a white man. You're white. And maybe you're trying to say, 'Aw fellows, she's just this old Cuban lady living in Little Havana. What difference does she make?'"

"I never said that. What the hell are you up to?"

I drained half my Australian Lager, then showed him the label. "What do you see there?"

"A kangaroo," he said.

"This is my Kangaroo Court, which is now in session. You're on trial for one count of malpractice and two counts of being an asshole."

"I see what's going on here." Shiner shot a sideways glance at the mountain named Tank Pittman. "This guy's your muscle. It's a shakedown." He lowered his voice to a whisper. "How much to make this go away? Ten grand? Fifteen grand?"

"Whadaya think, Tank?" I asked. "You wanna shake down the defendant?"

"I could take him out back to the Dumpster, hold him upside down, see what shakes out of his pockets."

"Hold on. None of that." Shiner tried to stand, but Tank grabbed him by his suit collar and dragged him back into the booth. A legal tackle in the Dark Ages when we played, but a 15-yard penalty for horse-collaring now.

"When you walked in, I noticed your loafers," I said. "What are they, alligator tanned a baby blue?"

"Crocodile," Shiner said. "Dolce & Gabbana. What of it?"

Tank bent down to eyeball the lawyer's shoes. "Look like ballet slippers."

"What'd they cost?" I asked.

"Five grand."

Tank let out a low whistle.

"What size do you wear?" I asked.

"Nine-and-a-half. Why?"

I looked at Tank.

"Wouldn't even fit my big toe," he said.

"Too small for me, too, dammit."

"C'mon, you guys," Shiner said. "What do you really want?"

"A $55,000 cashier's check to Luisa Revilla will make this go away," I said.

"I'd do it. I swear I would, but I'm tapped out. Lost a bundle on Bitcoin, then got stiffed on a deal for a marijuana operation in Georgia. No can do."

"Yo, Jake," Tank said. "Did you see his watch?"

For a law-abiding owner of a chain of car washes, Tank seemed a natural for badass thuggery.

"Piaget," I said, "in rose gold. A little feminine, but nice." I reached across the table and tapped a finger on the crystal. "Take it off, Mr. Shiner."

"Are you nuts?" he said. "This is the Dancer with a diamond bezel. Do you know what it's worth?"

"More than the shoes. I'd guess maybe fifty grand."

"Seventy grand! I took it in lieu of a fee."

"And never paid taxes on it."

"None of your concern."

"Take it off," I ordered. "We're gonna sell it. First fifty-five thousand goes to Luisa Revilla. Anything above that comes back to you."

"I'll file a Bar complaint!"

"When it comes in, I'll consider it," I said, agreeably.

Again, Shiner tried to stand, but Tank pinned his forearm to the table with a bone-crushing grip. Shiner considered resisting. His consideration took about two seconds. Then, grimacing, he slid the watch off and gave it to me.

"This is extortion," Shiner said.

"It's rough justice," I corrected him, "which is better than none at all."

Shiner gathered himself, scooted out of the booth, and headed for the door, his crocodile loafers softly slapping the floor.

Tank turned to me and belly laughed, his midsection shaking the table. "You still run angry, roomie, but you stopped knocking guys out of their shoes."

-4-
The Subterfuge

Tank had taken an Uber to Keg South, so we would ride together to his son's football game, and afterward, the three of us would head out for some late-night pizza. A man cannot survive on Death Dogs alone. At least, that was our plan.

Yeah, right.

My buddy Steve Solomon taught me an old Yiddish expression: *"Mann tracht, un Gott lacht."* Man plans, and God laughs.

I waited for Tank to fold himself into the passenger seat of my old Caddy. His beer-keg butt plopped down without flattening the tires. Then he swung his left leg inside and used both hands to drag his right leg behind it. Too many knee surgeries. But he never complained, sharing my view that dwelling on pain only increased it.

We hit rush-hour traffic on the Palmetto Expressway as we headed to Powell Stadium in the north end of the county. That's where St. Frances Academy, Rod's school, would take on St. Peter's High from Broward County. Despite those saintly names, both teams could raise holy hell on the gridiron.

I had the canvas top up, and the A/C cranked full blast. Unless you're a mosquito or a bullfrog, September is the worst month of the year in Mia-muh, a continuation of the endless summer of energy-sapping heat, steam-bath humidity, and thunderous afternoon storms. Just now, ominous black clouds gathered over the Everglades, and in the distance, lightning flashed.

"Will Lily meet us at the stadium?" I asked Tank as we passed the interchange for the Dolphin Expressway.

"Haven't told her Rod's playing," he said.

"I thought that was all settled."

"Why'd you think that? Last we talked, you told me to forge her name on the consent form."

"What? No way."

"I told you there were lines for two signatures and that Lily refused to sign because she was afraid Rod would get hurt. You said to sign her name, and when she saw Rod in his uniform and how excited he was, she'd forgive all."

I remember something, a nagging itch in the back of my mind.

I scratched at the memory and found a piece of it. "The track team. I said something about the track team."

"Our cover story, Jake. If Rod came home bruised and scraped from football practice, he'd say he tripped going over a hurdle."

So I masterminded forgery and subterfuge but don't really remember the conversation. Not a good look, ethically or medically.

"Problem is," Tank continued, "I never followed through. I never told Lily the truth."

"Aw, that's not good."

"Lily's in Tallahassee at a seminar. When she comes home tomorrow, I'll have Rod in his uniform, all grass stained and muddy, big grin on his face. And like you said, she'll come around."

Traffic eased as we skirted Hialeah and approached the exit for the Gratigny Expressway, a toll road that would take us east to the stadium. The sky had turned the gray of lava rocks, and fat, juicy raindrops pelted my windshield. A moment later, the wind-whipped rain was blowing in sheets that nearly obliterated my vision.

I slowed to a safe speed as my wipers *clack-clacked.* "Have you seen any of Rod's scrimmages?"

"Coach Coleman closes scrimmages."

"Even to parents?"

"Especially to parents. I was hanging around practice in early August, helping the D-line coach get his players into the right stance. Basic stuff."

"Nobody better than you."

"One day I ask Coleman if he wants me to teach rugby tackling. You know, head behind the runner, sling him down."

"Prevents head injuries," I said.

"Exactly. But Coleman says, 'Hell no. We'll give up two more yards every play.'"

Lightning flashed, and two seconds later, a thunderclap shook the Caddy.

"Then one day," Tank continued, "the trainers erect this long, narrow tent on the practice field. On the side, someone's painted, 'Tunnel of Manhood.'"

"Sounds like a porn film. What goes on inside?"

"No idea. But Coleman made all outsiders scram. Including me. As I'm leaving, I see a couple assistant coaches go into the tent with two players, an offensive lineman and a defensive lineman."

"You think they're running the Oklahoma Drill where no one can see it?"

Meaning the ancient and now illegal pit drill where two linemen crash into each other and keep banging away until one is eating dirt. There are other names – Blood Alley, Nutcracker, Gauntlet – and other variations, all of them violent.

"I asked Rod, but he said the brotherhood was sworn to secrecy. That's what Coleman calls the team. A brotherhood."

"The us-against-them mentality. Like a cult."

"I only went back one time. I'd bought the team a dozen of those new practice helmets with the built-in sensors. Six hundred bucks each."

"I've read about them. Real time readings of G-forces from every hit."

"Even sub-concussive hits will send the player to the sideline for an evaluation," Tank said. "If Coach liked them, I was going to outfit the whole team."

"In my day, we got hand-me-down helmets. I think mine was worn by Bronko Nagurski."

"Rod told me that at the first scrimmage, the sensors were ringing like church bells, and half the players were sidelined. Coleman screamed to get rid of the helmets, and a trainer just dumped them on my front porch. Not even a thank-you note. I felt disrespected."

"I don't know, pal. When I met Coleman, he said you knew more about line play than any coach he'd ever met."

Tank snorted. "Eleven years in the league, I must know a few things."

Coach Monty Coleman had poached Rod from the track team to add speed to his lineup. Before letting his son play, Tank had asked me to size up the coach, so I'd had coffee with the guy, and he seemed fine to me. Well-dressed and well-spoken. No chewing tobacco or pot belly like my high school coach.

I eased the Caddy into the stadium parking lot, just as the rain let up. It does that a lot in South Florida. Looks like it will pour for forty days and forty nights, and boom...it just stops.

"Coleman's polite to you because you're a local legend."

"Why? Because I ran to the wrong end zone against the Jets?"

"You have access to donors, so Coleman will kiss up to you. But if you tried to teach the swim move to an edge rusher, you'd see his insecure side."

We got out of the car and headed for the stadium. I wondered just how much sharpness I'd lost. Did I miss the real guy under Coach Coleman's polished veneer?

Is my judgment failing along with my memory?

"Yo, roomie!" Tank called out.

"What?"

"You're walking the wrong way." He gestured toward a towering set of bleachers. "Stadium's over here."

-5-
Be the Hammer, Not the Nail

The stadium lights were on, illuminating a fine mist, which drifted toward the ground like silvery tinsel falling from a Christmas tree. I followed Tank into the Parents' Section of the stands. I could tell from his grimace that his knee was shooting sparks as he limped along. Moms and Dads shouted, "Hey Tank," as we moved down the row.

Puffs of steamy vapor rose from the freshly mowed field, the cool rain having sizzled the warm earth like oil on a griddle. The yard lines, painted white, glowed eerily through the gauzy mist, the field in soft focus like a nostalgic Hollywood movie. I caught the aroma of grilling hot dogs just as the St. Frances band, booming percussion and brassy brass, started up the fight song, fans cheering and stomping their feet.

Behind the team bench, players ran short bursts, high-stepping on the strip of blacktop where an ambulance was parked. Their cleats clattered on the asphalt, the sounds as familiar to me as that of marching platoon to an old soldier. Adrenaline-pumped players smacked each other's shoulder pads, which crunched like bags of cement tossed from a truck bed to the ground.

I must have had a faraway look in my eyes because Tank elbowed me and said, "Hey, Jake. You forgot what this felt like, huh?"

"Friday night lights," I said. "Pure Americana, pal."

The P.A. announcer excitedly welcomed families and friends to the opening game of the season between the St. Peter's Peacocks and the St. Frances Commanders. We were just in time for the kickoff.

"I showed Rodrigo film of you on the Dolphins' kickoff team," Tank said. "Told him to watch your form. Shoulders square, you'd bull your neck and explode at the runner's chest. Always keeping your head up."

That made me smile. "I can still hear Paterno yelling, 'Eyes to the sky!' and Shula's 'Look to the heavens!'"

On the sideline, I spotted "Pittman" emblazoned on the back of number eleven. The single digits were perfect for Rod's small frame. If he'd been ninety-nine, the numbers on the back of his jersey would have overlapped the ones in front.

My godson was a gangly sprinter playing his first football game since middle school, and I hoped he didn't feel the butterflies that were flapping in my chest. Kickoffs are practically the only time that players collide head-on at full speed. Yeah, that's why they're called the "suicide squads."

Monty Coleman, in his late thirties, tall and handsome, suntanned and fit, with an expensive haircut, paced the sideline. His assistants were in Commanders' sweatsuits, while he wore gray slacks, a blue blazer and a striped tie in school colors.

St. Frances would kick off, Rod closest to our sideline. We'd have a great view of him high-tailing it downfield.

"Go get 'em, Rodrigo!" Tank yelled.

From a few rows behind us I heard a husky voice, "Hey, Pittman! Does your kid know this is football, not track? He's gotta hit people."

I turned and saw a beefy man in shorts and a Florida State T-shirt. About forty-five with a salt-and-pepper goatee, he was standing, looking our way.

"Hey, big mouth!" I yelled back. "Sit down and watch the game."

He studied me a second, turned to the man next to him, and chortled, "Hey, ain't that Wrong Way Lassiter? I thought he was dead."

On the field, the official dropped his arm, and the St. Frances kicker approached the ball, smacking it with a solid *thwomp*.

I kept my eyes on Rod, blazing down the sideline, angling toward the middle of the field. As he approached the first blocker, he juked and weaved, sliding by him without breaking stride.

Smooth! Silky smooth.

As he ran, Rod kept his head still, and his arms had no excess motion. A dandy athlete with what coaches call "fluid hips." Another blocker came at Rod but misjudged his speed and took a bad angle. Rod blew past him.

The St. Peter's returner, D.J. Arrington, cleanly fielded the kick, which was high and deep. A top collegiate running back prospect at 6-2 and 215 pounds, Arrington didn't try any slick moves. He just ran straight at the oncoming Rod, then tried to straight-arm him. Rod's speed got him inside the straight-arm, though he had no time to bend at the hips and wrap up the runner. Instead, they collided head-on, Rod's facemask smacking into Arrington's shoulder pad. Arrington was 30 pounds heavier, and his momentum knocked Rod backward, ass over elbows, his helmet flying off.

Be the hammer, not the nail.

That's what Coach Paterno always told defensive players. But Rod just got nailed by the heavier, stronger player. Still, he'd be credited with making the tackle as Arrington lost his balance and skidded across the wet turf.

"Wow!" Tank yelled. "You see that hit! You see that, Jake?"

"He's not afraid of contact," I said. That used to be a high compliment, but these days, I wasn't so sure.

Rod slowly got to his feet and walked in a circle trying to find his helmet. It was at his feet, but he didn't see it. After a second revolution, he staggered a step, picked up the helmet and jogged to the sideline.

Is he woozy?

Then I saw the yellow flag. Offsides on the kicking team.

"Rodrigo's gonna make two tackles on the same kickoff," Tank predicted.

"Can't do it, pal. He has to sit out one play because his helmet came off."

"Tell that to the coach." Tank gestured toward the sideline where Coleman was speaking to Rod with what appeared to be last-second instructions. "Rod looks okay, doesn't he, Jake?"

"Doesn't matter. The officials have to sit him down."

But they didn't. First play of the season, and the zebras were so engrossed in the penalty, they missed it!

Coleman patted Rod on the butt and sent him back out with the kicking team. Just then my cell phone rang. I checked the screen. Melissa.

"Jake, where are you?" she said. "What's all that noise?"

"At the game. With Tank."

"You're supposed to be with Steve and Victoria. And me! At Phuc Yea."

Phuc No!

"That's tomorrow night."

"Tonight! Victoria made reservations weeks ago."

Of course Victoria Lord would like a Cajun-Vietnamese place where the cocktails have seven ingredients, including nuoc cham – fish sauce – in their dirty martinis.

Me, I'm a steak-and-baked man. A carnivore among vegans. A brew-and-burger guy in a paté-and-Chardonnay world.

Tank elbowed me. "C'mon, they're lining up for the kick."

"Jake, what do I tell Steve and Victoria?" Melissa asked.

The kicker whacked the ball a second time, and Rod raced down the sideline once again.

"Tell 'em I'm sorry. Gonna make it up to them."

"Fly, Rod! Fly!" Tank yelled, drowning out the call.

Rod juked and cut inside the frontline blocker, just as he'd done the first time. Arrington fielded the kick on one bounce and followed a blocker to the inside.

"Jake, are you there?"

"Melissa, I gotta go."

A second blocker had a bead on Rod who used his speed to nearly avoid contact...but not quite. The blocker barely got a hand on Rod's shoulder, more of a push than a block, but it was enough to knock him off stride. Either from the contact or the slippery turf, Rod lost his balance. Arms flailing, his head over his feet, he was out of control. Without thinking, I gripped Tank's massive wrist, the way you might protect a child the second before a car crash.

Rod was airborne. Bent at the waist, like a diver launching into a jackknife.

I could see the back of his neck. Meaning his head was down!

Arrington plowed straight at Rod, powerful legs high-stepping, as if stomping grapes. His right leg thrust upward as Rod's head plunged downward.

Arrington's thigh walloped the front of Rod's helmet, just above the facemask.

I heard the *thwack*. And saw Rod's head snap back and his body topple sideways to the turf. Arrington tumbled to the ground and bounced up.

Rod lay on his side, one leg on top the other, the way some people sleep.

"C'mon, Rodrigo!" Tank urged.

I watched for movement, saw none. "Get up. Please get up," I whispered, as if praying. "Roll over and get up."

"Jake, are you there?" Melissa demanded.

I didn't know we were still connected. "Shit! Gotta go, Mel." I clicked off.

The stadium was still, quiet as a funeral.

I squinted to get a better look through the moist haze. Rod's feet were twitching.

Oh, no! No, no, no!

"Let's go, Tank!"

We rushed past the parents in our row, then barreled down the steps. A metal railing separated our section from the field. I vaulted over it and fell clumsily to the ground. No way with his bum knee and excess bulk could Tank follow me. He headed for the concrete stairs 20 yards away. I didn't wait.

At the St. Frances bench, I grabbed a cooler filled with ice and two towels. Coach Coleman and a trainer jogged onto the field, and I passed them.

Out of my way! That's my godson on the ground! He's kin to me!

From the opposite sideline, a man in a suit who must have been the St. Peter's team physician hurried onto the field.

"Don't move him!" I shouted at teammates who had gathered around Rod. "Don't take off his helmet!"

I wheeled the cooler next to Rod and squatted on my haunches. I filled both towels with ice and carefully placed them around the sides of his neck. No way would I lift his head to get ice underneath.

The physician appeared and knelt next to Rod across from me, putting a gentle hand on his arm. "What's your name, son?"

"Rod. Rod Pittman." His voice wheezing, barely audible.

"Now, Rod, can you move your legs?"

Rod tried. Nothing.

"Don't shake your head," the physician cautioned.

"Your arms?" the physician asked.

"I don't...I don't know. Are they moving?"

"Not yet, Rod."

"Thanks for the ice, doctor," the physician said to me. Thinking I was the St. Frances team doctor who was nowhere to be found.

Coach Coleman leaned over us, hands on his knees. "Hang in there, Rod."

Tank joined us, falling to his knees, and I moved over as he put a hand on his son's forehead. "Rodrigo, I'm here, son."

"Dad. Please..."

He was having trouble breathing. An injury to the spinal cord could do that...and worse.

"Don't try to talk, son." Tears rolled down Tank's face.

I turned away, fighting my own tears, feeling my heart race. An ambulance rolled onto the field, leaving muddy tire tracks. Two paramedics jumped out and removed a backboard from the rear. I heard the St. Peter's physician tell them something about "spinal immobilization" and "cervical collar." Then he turned to me, and said, "Please hold Rod's head steady, doctor, so we can remove his helmet."

I knelt at Rod's head with hands on either side of his helmet. The physician unclipped the chin strap and popped off the facemask.

"Now, hold him still," the St. Peter's physician said. "I'm going to reach inside and pull out the cheek pads."

"I don't think you have to," I said. "Without the chin strap, the helmet feels loose to me."

Too loose. As if the helmet was too big.

He thought about it a moment. "Okay, then. Remove the helmet, very gently."

I held my breath and kept my body motionless as I slid the helmet off and placed it on the turf. Rod's dark eyes shot left and right. Fear clouded his handsome features.

"There we are, Rod," the physician said, warmly. "You're a brave young man."

"Am I out for the season?" Rod asked.

"Let's get you to the hospital for some tests, and we'll see."

I got out of the way so the paramedics could put the cervical collar on and move Rod onto the backboard. Tank crouched on his knees behind me, his head turned away so his son could not see him sobbing. Rod's teammates formed a circle around him on their knees and were holding hands.

The physician was on his cell phone saying his patient would need steroids for the inflammation, and after he was stabilized, an MRI. He hung up and made another call, saying they'd still be within the "golden hour" when they got to the hospital. I knew enough medical jargon to get that. A patient with a spinal injury has a much greater chance at recovery if stabilized within one hour.

Tank pulled himself together, got to his feet, and approached the physician.

"I'm Rod's father," he said. "What can you tell me?"

"Nothing yet. I just spoke to Dr. Barton Grant, the best spinal surgeon in Miami. I'm not saying we'll need him, but he's meeting us at Jackson."

"Thank you and God bless you," Tank said.

"Tank, you ride with Rod in the ambulance," I said. "I'll meet you there."

Tank nodded and went to his son's side. Rod was strapped to the backboard, ready to be loaded into the ambulance.

"I'm here for you, son," Tank said, gently caressing his son's cheek.

"Dad?" Rod's voice was a whisper.

"Yes, son?"

"Please don't tell Mom."

-6-
Give Me a Number

For 90 endless minutes, I paced in the waiting room with Tank Pittman, neither of us speaking.

What could I say beyond meaningless platitudes?

The St. Peter's team physician kept us informed. His name was Ayjay Gupta, and I told him I was Rod's godfather, not a doctor.

"Nice work on the field, whoever you are," he said.

He told us that Dr. Barton Grant, the neurosurgeon, was going over Rod's MRI with a pair of radiologists. I recognized Dr. Grant's name from television and the newspapers.

"He's not just a surgeon," Dr. Gupta said. "He's a lead researcher at the Miami Project."

Meaning the Miami Project to Cure Paralysis.

It came into being 30 years ago after Marc Buoniconti, playing for the Citadel, suffered a spinal cord injury making a tackle and became paralyzed from the neck down. Marc's father, Nick, the legendary Miami Dolphins linebacker, was instrumental in getting the Project started and helping raise half a billion dollars for research and treatment.

Nick was my personal hero, and not because he was an NFL Hall of Famer. Coach Shula used to call him the "lawyer for the defense." Meaning he'd cross-examine the coaches about every game plan. Then, later, Nick became a real lawyer. In yet another dark irony of life, both father and son were grievously wounded by the game they loved. Suffering from dementia, Nick died of CTE.

Football giveth, and football taketh away.

"I know about the Project," Tank said. "You saying Rodrigo's gonna be paralyzed?"

"No, no, no," Dr. Gupta said. "We don't even have a diagnosis of the injury yet."

The doctor returned to the innards of the hospital. I tried reaching Melissa on her cell, but the call went straight to voice mail. I thought about leaving a message but didn't know what to say.

Just then my heart started its hippity-hop, fluttering routine. Instead of a regular beat – *tu-tump tu-tump tu-tump* – it was hammering *tump-tump-tump…tu…tump-tump-tump.* A staccato beat followed by an eerie silence, then another staccato drumming.

On the brighter side, if I have a stroke or heart attack, I'm in the E.R. at Jackson Memorial Hospital.

An hour later, Dr. Gupta returned with Dr. Grant, both wearing poker faces. Dr. Grant was in his sixties with silvery hair and wireless glasses. For a man of modest height and girth, he had thick wrists and strong hands. Surgeons are like that.

"Mr. Pittman, your son is a brave young man," Dr. Grant said. "He's conscious, aware of his surroundings, and breathing normally, albeit with the aid of a respirator."

Which didn't sound too normal to me.

Tank nodded, and we waited.

Dr. Grant spoke in a soft monotone. "Rod has a fracture of the C-5 vertebra in his neck. It's a burst fracture with bone fragments we'll clean out in surgery. There's blood around the spinal cord, which is bruised, but does not appear to be severed. That's important, very important, because if it was severed..."

"I know," Tank said. "He'd be a quadriplegic."

"Barring advances that we're working on, yes, that's true at the current time."

"So what will you...?"

"I'll be performing spinal fusion surgery."

The surgeon spent a few moments explaining the surgery, and I struggled to hear as my tinnitus was clanging in my ears. One ankle was throbbing, too. I must have twisted it vaulting the railing at the stadium.

"Rod will have a long road to travel in recovery and rehabilitation," Dr. Grant continued. "The good news is that he's a strong, healthy young man. And it will be important for you and your family to keep a positive outlook so that Rod will, as well."

"I haven't called my wife," Tank said. "Wanted to talk to you first. Could you give me a number? His chance at walking again."

Dr. Grant tenderly placed his right hand – the hand that would hold the scalpel that would slice into Rod's neck, millimeters from the spinal cord – on Tank's massive forearm. "It's too early for that, Mr. Pittman. Let's get through tonight and tomorrow, and I'll keep you fully informed."

Dr. Grant pulled out his cell phone and moved to a corner of the waiting room where he awakened his office coordinator to line up his surgical team. Tank took a breath and used his cell to call Lily, waking her at her hotel room in Tallahassee. He whispered into the phone, and I heard a shriek of unimaginable pain come through the line.

I waited for Tank to finish, and we walked through the automatic doors toward Rod's compartment in neuro intensive care. Tank's limp was more pronounced than usual, and I was gimpy, too, from my ankle. He told me Lily would be on the first morning flight from Tallahassee.

Rod was heavily sedated and barely recognizable, his face swollen, the mouthpiece of the respirator bulging between his lips. Tubes and cords sprouted from various parts of his body, and machines beeped and glowed, keeping track of his vitals. Two metal prongs were attached to his skull to prevent movement and further injury to his spinal cord. It looked as if someone had stabbed him with a pitchfork, leaving two blades behind.

Tank's knees buckled, and I wrapped an arm around his shoulders. He was a load, but not too heavy for me. For tonight and all time, he was my brother.

"Jake, give me a couple minutes alone with my boy," he said, getting his feet back under him.

"I'll find some coffee," I said, leaving him there.

In the corridor, I ran into Dr. Gupta who pulled me aside. His face was grim, his words soft. "The Pittmans are going to need support from their friends."

"Whatever it takes, however long it takes," I said.

"There'll be dark days ahead, and that's if everything goes well."

I pondered that a moment. My cell rang. Melissa calling. I didn't pick up the call.

"Dr. Grant never answered Tank's question," I said. "Will Rod walk again?"

"Let's wait until after the surgery and evaluate then."

"Right. But Tank was just asking for a ballpark figure. Some metric he can hang on to. By not answering, it seems ominous. Maybe more ominous than it should."

Dr. Gupta seemed to consider his reply but then chose to remain silent. In my profession, a simple leading question on cross-examination often elicits an answer.

"He told you, didn't he?" I said. "Dr. Grant gave you a number."

Dr. Gupta leaned close to me and whispered, "Five percent. Rod has a five percent chance of walking again."

-7-

Six Syllables

I got home just before six a.m., a mockingbird noisily singing in my chinaberry tree. Home is a little coral rock pillbox on Kumquat Avenue in Coconut Grove.

I tiptoed into the house, where nothing was stirring, not even a palmetto bug. I had not spoken to Melissa since the aborted phone call at the game. Meaning we really hadn't spoken since the rocky therapy session with Dr. Stein. Melissa wouldn't be lying in wait, hefting a rolling pin, but she also wouldn't be lounging in a silky negligee with Diana Krall on the speakers whispering "Love is Here to Stay."

As it turned out, Melissa was asleep in our big bed under the paddle fan, her arms wrapped around a pillow, instead of me. I watched her a moment, imagined her warm breath on my neck.

I love this woman. And fear I am a heavy burden on her.

She denied it, of course, in Dr. Stein's office.

"You're not a burden. You're the man I love!"

But the two are not mutually exclusive.

Maybe it was my lack of sleep or the tragedy I had witnessed. Whatever the reason, I had a quiet moment of introspection. Usually, I am as sensitive as a century-old oak tree with bark as thick as armor. Now, I vowed to be a better partner and be more thoughtful about Melissa's needs. Every day shouldn't be about how I'm feeling.

My wounded brain, my erratic heart, my aching joints.

I thought about Melissa's daily routine. Peering through the microscope at diseased brain tissue all day, then coming home to what? The living manifestation of her fears and what she perceived as her failures?

I did not want Melissa to be a shattered widow, blaming herself for failing to discover a cure for CTE. Some days, I thought she would be better off without me, though I surely would be lost without her.

With those thoughts swirling, I made a pot of coffee. We still have an old stainless steel percolator, rather than some fancy barista equipment. I like the musical, gurgling sound and the aroma that wafts through the house.

I turned on the television in the kitchen, and with the sound low, watched the early morning local news. It was the usual stew. Street flooding in Miami Beach, home invasion robbery in North Miami, fatal accident on I-95. The weather would be hot and steamy with afternoon thunderstorms. The meteorologist could have mailed it in.

Then a teaser: "Local player critically injured in high school football game." My coffee sat untouched as I watched. A reporter and camera crew had covered the game, the season opener for St. Peter's and St. Frances. There was a close-up of Coach Coleman talking to Rod before the second kickoff but no audio. Rod turned toward the camera, and I hit the PAUSE button on the remote.

Your eyes, Rod. Are they glassy? Or is that just an illusion under the stadium lights?

I hit PLAY and watched the disaster unfold. Arrington fielding the kickoff. Rod dashing downfield, so fast, so smooth. The slight contact with the blocker, Rod airborne, arms flailing, head down, and the horrendous thigh to helmet collision.

I turned off the television and heard an odd sound. It took a moment to realize I was sobbing. A moment later, a barefoot Melissa in silk pajamas had her arms around my shoulders. She had been standing behind me, watching the screen.

"Oh, Jake. How awful. The news said critical condition."

I sniffled back the tears. "You come in with a broken neck, that's pretty standard. His prognosis is uncertain, but it doesn't look good."

We hugged for a long moment. With my head alongside hers, I whispered, "It's my fault."

"What?"

"I gave Tank the green light for Rod to play football. If I hadn't..."

She pulled away from me. "Stop. I'm sure you considered everything."

"I thought he'd be one of those small, quick wide receivers. Didn't occur to me Coach Coleman would use him as a gunner – the kamikaze – on the suicide squads. So, no, I didn't consider everything. And now, I need to help the family."

Melissa pursed her lips, a sign she was pondering something. "You think someone's at fault legally, don't you?"

"I have no idea. Maybe it's just a string of unrelated incidents that conspired to create a tragedy. Or..."

"Or what, Jake?"

"Why didn't the officials or the coach sit Rod down after he lost his helmet on the first kickoff? Why didn't St. Frances have a team physician on the field? A doctor would have checked Rod after he got his clock cleaned making the first tackle. Maybe put him into the concussion protocol. To me, Rod appeared dazed. But the coach eyeballed him just before the second kickoff and sent him back in. So I could be wrong."

I poured two cups of coffee and we sat down at the kitchen table. "I'm the one who slipped Rod's helmet off his head when he was on the ground. Came off real easy because it was too large."

"Would that have anything to do with his injury?"

"Again, no idea."

On the television screen, the station's entertainment reporter seemed to be giddy reporting on a trendy new health food restaurant that served charcoal mushroom lemonade.

"Let me show you something." I grabbed the remote and rewound the news to the sideline shot of Coach Coleman speaking to Rod. "This is just before the second kickoff."

We watched for about ten seconds, and when I hit the PAUSE, Melissa said, "You want to know what the coach said to Rod."

"Yeah."

"Why not ask Rod?"

"After his surgery, I will, but I'm betting he won't remember."

"Then ask the coach."

"Coleman will cover his ass and claim he said, 'You okay to go back in, Rod? Now tell me the truth.'"

"Too many syllables," Melissa said.

"How's that?"

"Whatever the coach said was six syllables long."

I gave her my big, dumb-guy look. It comes naturally.

"I watched his lips and counted," she explained. "But that's all I've got. I'm sorry I can't read lips."

I leaned over and kissed her cheek. "That's okay, Mel. I know someone who can."

-8-
A Hat on a Hat

George Barrios, wearing a yellow guayabera with black piping, was already munching a bagel with cream cheese when I joined him at the table. A small, wiry man with a suntanned, bald head, he was somewhere between sixty and infinity. His looks hadn't changed in thirty years.

He studied me a moment as I sat down, maybe checking to see if I carried a weapon under my sport coat.

Once a cop always a cop.

"You enjoying retirement, George?"

"About as much as you enjoy brain damage." He used his tongue to investigate something in the back of his mouth. "Sesame seeds get in my dentures."

We were at Zak the Baker in Wynwood, the so-called arts section of Miami, a clever marketing name to get millennials to buy overpriced condos in what had been a dangerous neighborhood before gentrification. Zak's was fine, but it lacked history. Back in the day, we'd have been bageling at Pumpernik's or the Rascal House on Miami Beach, but that day is long gone.

I scanned the menu, which helpfully informed me that cream cheese "contains dairy," as if the words "cream" and "cheese" didn't already convey that information. I ordered coffee and an everything bagel with a schmear. Living dangerously.

"So, old-timer," I began, "can you still read lips or is that the second thing to go?"

"I can, shyster. Can you still spin bullshit into gold?"

"Sure. Just takes more bullshit to get less gold."

Let's just say we have a healthy, competitive relationship as old adversaries.

I first learned George Barrios could read lips when I defended a bookie named Trey Sugarman, who came from a long line of gamblers including his grandfather, Ace, and his father, Deuce.

Barrios, a vice detective at the time, had busted Trey a few times on bookmaking charges. Hereabouts, that's akin to jaywalking, so Trey never served more than 30 days in the slammer. This time, though, he was charged with hiring a needle man to dope a horse named Romeo-Romeo at Calder Race Course. A conviction meant hard time.

Usually, at trial, the detective who ran the investigation sat next to the prosecutor. But Barrios took a seat in the front row of the wing of the gallery. Meaning he had a snoop's eye view of the defense table. I thought it was just a psychological ploy, the detective evil-eyeing me. But soon, the prosecutor seemed to sense every move we made before we made it.

I finally figured out he was reading lips, so he knew everything Sugarman – a real blabbermouth – whispered to me. I could have had my client shield his mouth like an offensive coordinator on the sidelines hiding behind a laminated play chart. Instead, I concocted a fabricated defense strategy involving a non-existent rebuttal witness who would exonerate my client. We talked about it with Barrios watching. At the next recess, the prosecutor offered a plea deal with minimal jail time, and everyone went home happy, including Romeo-Romeo who was put out to stud.

Now, I sipped my coffee and told Barrios about Rod's horrific injury, and he shook his head, sadly. Then I asked if he could tell me what Coach Coleman said to Rod before the kickoff. Before driving to Wynwood, I recorded the second hour of the local news, which had repeated the earlier segment.

"Reading lips, easy peasy," Barrios said, as I opened the laptop and found the file.

He watched it once and said, "Again."

I did as told, and he said, "Just wanted to make sure."

"Yeah?"

"The coach said, 'Put a hat on a hat.'"

Six syllables, just like Melissa said.

"That mean anything to you?" Barrios asked.

"There are two meanings. You know I majored in theater in college, right?"

"Because that's where the girls were. You've told me."

"I played Big Jule, the dim-witted gangster, in *Guys and Dolls*."

"Type-casting, even then."

I bit into the bagel and said, "As an elective, I took a comedy class."

"It worked. I've heard your closing arguments."

"Sometimes, in improv, I'd pile a second joke on top of the first one. That wrecked both jokes, and the instructor would say, 'Mr. Lassiter, you just put a hat on a hat.'"

"But the coach wasn't talking about jokes," Barrios said.

"I told you there were two meanings. It's used in football, too. It means blocking every defensive player, one-on-one, just the way it's drawn in X's and O's."

"Well, that doesn't make sense for the kickoff team."

"Right. Rod's a gunner who's supposed to make the tackle, not block someone."

Next to us, a young couple in shorts, T-shirts, and sandals sat down and studied their menus. The woman had tattoos running up both arms and circling her neck. The man was inked on both legs, from thighs to ankles. I am old enough to remember when the only people with tattoos were sailors, inmates, and carnies.

"So what the coach said is useless, and you've got nothing," Barrios said.

"It's day one. I need more time."

"You ambulance chasers always look for someone to blame. You ask me, Jake, it was just one of those freak accidents, a million-to-one shot."

"I'm not sure that's right."

"My advice? Just give all your love and support to the family and let the rest of it go."

Letting things go isn't really part of my DNA.

"You were a great detective, George. You took little pieces that didn't fit together and yet somehow you solved the puzzle. So just hear me out, okay?"

He drained his coffee and said, "Say your piece, counselor."

"Coach Coleman runs illegal contact drills inside a gladiator tent and swears the players to secrecy. He rejected Tank Pittman's offer of high-tech helmets with concussion sensors because it sidelined his players during practice. Last night, Rod was wearing a helmet that was too big for him. On the kickoff that was called back, his helmet came off, and either the coach or the officials should have benched him for a play. Instead, without consulting the team physician, who by the way wasn't there, the coach sends Rod out for the second kickoff. We have a six-syllable scrap of their conversation, but it doesn't make sense. There's something here, George. I just need to find all the pieces so I can figure how to fit them together."

"Maybe the 'hat on a hat' would make sense if you knew what the coach said before that, and what Rod said to him."

"You saw the video, George. Their backs were facing the camera for 20 or 30 seconds. No lips to read."

"You know what I learned from watching thousands of hours of surveillance video?"

"How to drink stale coffee and pee in Styrofoam cups."

"To look at every square inch of the screen. Before Rod and the coach turned to the camera, what else did you see?"

"Nothing."

"There was a hand in the bottom left corner of the screen."

"Really? Whose hand?"

"I don't know. But it was holding a microphone with the call letters, WQAM, so I assume it belonged to the radio station's sideline reporter. It was a left hand with an engagement ring, so I also assume the reporter was female."

"Show-off," I said.

"Now, I don't know if the mic was on," Barrios continued, "or if the reporter was speaking and drowning out everything else, or even if they kept a recording of a live broadcast. But Rod and his coach were facing that direction, so if you insist on chasing your tail like an iguana in a pot of boiling water, you might head over to the station and find out."

-9-
Good to Go, Dad

A short drive north on I-95 took me to the WQAM studios in Little River. It was not far from the center of Little Haiti where I've been known to eat lunch at a joint called Piman Bouk, popular for its oxtail, goat stew, and conch fritters. Usually, I do this on the down low, Melissa disapproving of my nutrition choices.

The receptionist at the station buzzed Harry Poorman, the sports director. In a moment, a rotund man about fifty in an orange Miami Dolphins polo shirt bounded out of his office and greeted me. "The Quote Machine, in my very office!"

"Hello Harry. No one's called me that in twenty years."

"Maybe you haven't said anything quotable. Say, do you remember what you told that network gal after the Wrong Way play?"

"No recollection, Harry."

That's true, but I've seen the video replay a dozen times on "NFL's Biggest Bloopers."

"She asked you, 'How'd you end up running to the wrong end zone?' And you said, 'Both end zones look alike to me.' Classic! So what brings you here?"

I told Poorman about Rod's injury, and his mood grew somber. He'd watched the grim report on television.

"Do you have a recording of last night's broadcast?" I asked.

"You're in luck. We keep the games for 48 hours so we can use clips on the sports updates."

I asked him about the station's sideline reporter who stood next to Coleman and Rod before the second kickoff.

"Stacy King," he told me. "An intern. Works for college credit."

"I need to hear the recording."

"Anything for you, Jake. Say, you ever think about doing a sports talk show?"

"And listen to nut jobs who all think they're Knute Rockne?"

"True enough, sports talk is the septic tank of broadcasting. But the offer stands."

Poorman walked me to an editing booth where he introduced me to a producer named Adam, a tattooed, pimpled pony-tailed guy in his mid-twenties.

"This is the legendary Jake Lassiter," Poorman said, and the kid gave a blank look. I took no offense, as he probably got his news from TikTok, his dates on Tinder, and thought the Tet offensive was a form of toxic masculinity prohibited by Human Resources. Poorman told him to find the digital recording from last night and make audio files of any clips I wanted.

It took about 20 minutes to find the right spot. The play-by-play announcer spotted the yellow flag and said, "Oh, look at that. Offsides on the Commanders."

"Look at that" seems an odd expression on a radio broadcast, but what do I know?

"Rod Pittman's hard-hitting tackle gets wiped off the books," the announcer continued.

"Pittman seemed to stagger a step before coming off the field," the color announcer chimed in.

Yes! That's what I saw, too.

"Let's go down to Stacy on the St. Frances sideline," the play-by-play guy said.

"Pittman's hit has fired up the Commanders." A woman's voice, barely audible over the crowd noise. "You can hear their excitement."

She paused and must have extended the microphone. That's what Barrios had spotted in the corner of the screen. I strained to hear the audio. At first, just cheering, whistling, and hooting. And then as the ruckus subsided, a man's voice:

"Helluva play, Rod."

Coach Coleman.

He spoke again, his words lost in the clamor of the sideline.

"Stop the tape," I said. "Adam, can you do something about the ambient noise?"

"Maybe." He twisted some dials, then handed me a headset. "Try this."

"Helluva play, Rod," the man said on the recording. "You good to go?"

"I'm good..."

Rod's voice! I've known the kid his entire life.

But there was another word after "good," and I couldn't make it out. "Adam, back it up again, maybe increase the volume and do whatever you can for clarity."

Adam punched some buttons, turned a few dials, and played it again.

"You good to go?"

"I'm good, Dad."

Dad! Rod thinks he's talking to his father!

"You okay?" The coach again.

"I'm good to go, Dad."

Twice! The poor kid doesn't know where he is!

"Then do it again, Rod. Be a headhunter. Stick 'em."

Did he really say that? "Be a headhunter!"

There was a pause that had to be the moment they turned away from the radio reporter and faced the television camera. The last words I heard were, "Put a hat on a hat."

But that was not the big deal. The command to "be a headhunter" was egregious. It cried out "targeting," a serious penalty. But there were other issues, too.

Should Rod have been put into the concussion protocol after the first kickoff?

Where was the team physician?

If a player mistakes the coach for his father, do you even need a doctor to tell you to bench the kid?

I had misjudged Monty Coleman when I sized him up at Tank's request, and that's on me. But Rod's catastrophic injury should never have happened. Could I prove that was on Coleman?

I can't undo what's been done. I can't heal the body or comfort the heart. My only expertise is to peer through clouds of lies and evasions and ambiguities and somehow uncover the truth. And truth is the first cousin of justice.

My quest was clearly defined. I would do everything possible by any means necessary to seek justice for Rodrigo, and no one would stop me without first putting me into my grave.

-10-
The Circus Elephant

I took I-95 south and headed to my office. Not my Keg South saloon office. My actual Florida Bar office downtown. I called Melissa from the car, and she seemed genuinely happy to hear from me. Of course, she'd just spent three hours checking the footnotes in an article titled "Phenotyping of ABCA7 Mutation Carriers," so any distraction was likely welcome.

I told her about Barrios lip-reading the video, and the radio station giving me the audio. I told her about the coach ignoring Rod's confusion on the sideline and leaving him in the game with the "headhunter" instruction.

"I'm angry as hell," I said.

"Righteous indignation. That's okay. You're engaged and focused," Melissa said.

"I'm just getting started."

"And what's the end game?"

"A lawsuit, of course."

"But you're a criminal defense lawyer."

"Yeah, before I became a paper pusher for the Bar and turned over all my cases to Roy Black and Marcia Silvers."

She was silent a moment, then ever so carefully said, "How many personal injury lawsuits have you handled?"

"In round numbers. Zero."

I heard a "hmmm" over the line. Then Melissa said, "What exactly is your theory for the lawsuit?"

"At the very least, Rod was dazed. Probably concussed. Leaving him in the game was coaching malpractice."

"Is that a real thing, Jake? Coaching malpractice."

"If it's not, it ought to be. What's with the negativity, anyway?"

"I'm just wondering what's best for the Pittman family."

"My helping them! That's what's best!"

Dammit, I didn't want to raise my voice, but I had, almost without realizing it.

"When you told me that you wanted to investigate what happened," Melissa said calmly, "I thought that was healthy."

Sounding like a therapist more than a fiancée.

"I didn't realize you were planning to take this to court," she continued.

"I wasn't sure. But now..."

"If there really is a case, shouldn't it be handled by a personal injury specialist? Why not call Stuart Grossman?"

"Why? Do you think I'm incompetent?"

"As you've never tried a P.I. case, I couldn't say."

"Ouch, that's a low blow. I'm gonna rat you out to Dr. Stein."

"How are you feeling, Jake, and be honest."

"Fine. *Sotto voce* tinnitus. A tiny two-Tylenol headache. No vertigo, confusion, or bubonic plague."

"Heart rhythm?"

Aw, Jeez, Melissa. I love you, but this is getting old.

"A lovely waltz in three-quarter time. No A-Fib."

True. None now. She didn't ask about last night.

"You took the paper-pusher job, as you call it, to reduce stress," Melissa said. "But now you want to handle a major trial. The courtroom will be a pressure cooker."

Before I could respond, I realized I was in a double-exit lane. If I didn't make a quick move, I would be heading either west to the airport or east over the Tuttle Causeway to Miami Beach. I wrestled the Caddy across three lanes to the left, accompanied by much honking, a middle-finger salute, but thankfully no gunfire.

"Is there anything you're not telling me?" I asked.

"Like what, Jake?"

"You sound so concerned about my condition. Am I on borrowed time?"

"Aren't we all? But no, Jake. Nothing's changed with your tests or lab work."

"Then try to understand. Tank and Lily and Rod are family to me. I need to do this. Myself. No one else."

"This shouldn't be about your need. It's about what's best for them."

"So you do think I'm incompetent!"

"I don't think you can be objective."

"I don't have to be. I shouldn't be. I'm an advocate, not a judge."

"But you lack perspective." She was quiet a moment, and I knew she was choosing her words with care, and some of those words might hurt. "Perhaps you think this is the only way to expiate what you perceive as your guilt for what happened to Rod."

I searched for a clever rebuttal, but it's difficult when your debate opponent is smart, relentless, and correct. Bereft of ideas, I settled for a cheap shot. "I don't know why we need a therapist when you're able to diagnose all my deficiencies yourself."

"Oh, Jake, please."

Damn, there I go again. Irritability, of course, is one of the symptoms of CTE.

"Sorry, Mel. But try to understand. All these years, I feel like I'm the guy following the elephants in the circus parade. The guy with the broom and garbage pail."

"Circuses don't have elephants anymore."

"Proves my point. I'm as obsolete as circus elephants."

"Not to me."

Just then, my cell buzzed with an incoming call. Caller I.D. said, *Langston Pittman.*

"Mel, it's Tank. I have to take this."

"Go. And please have something green for lunch."

"Moldy cheese?"

"Go! Call me later."

Fumbling with the cell phone, I was late noticing that traffic was at a standstill on the exit ramp. I hit the brakes, and my two-ton monster screeched to a rubber-burning stop a foot short of the Dodge pickup truck ahead of me. The driver shot me the bird, my second in the last five minutes.

"Tank, how's Rod?" I said into the phone.

"Out of surgery, in recovery. Waiting to hear from the surgeon, hoping for the best."

"How's Lily doing?"

"On the warpath, Jake. I ratted you out. Had no choice."

"About what, Tank?"

"Lily knows you told me to forge her signature on the consent form. She's screaming at me, screaming at you. She can't hold it together."

"I'm sorry, pal. You gotta be strong enough for both of you. Look, I'm on the way to my office, but as soon as I clear up a couple things, I'll be back at the hospital. I'll talk to her."

"Not a good idea, man. Hey, get this. A lawyer for the school's insurance company stopped by."

"What!"

"She gave me some papers to sign."

"Don't sign anything!"

"C'mon, Jake. I never signed a football contract without my agent. I'm not doing anything without you. The lawyer said they wanted to take care of all the medical bills plus some kind of annuity for Rodrigo. Didn't say how much, but something every month as long as he lives. 'Course we'd have to sign releases."

Oh, those insurance lawyers are quick and nasty. Get the parents while the kid is still in surgery. If the kid dies, there's no lawsuit because the case has been settled. If the kid lives, you're bound to whatever you've already agreed to receive, no matter the medical condition.

"She said any lawsuit we filed would be dismissed, so what she was offering was just largesse," Tank continued.

Oh, right. Just what insurance companies are known for.

"She gave me a copy of the form I signed so that Rod could play. A lot of legal mumbo jumbo, but she says we gave up the right to sue, and it's ironclad."

"Iron rusts, Tank. I'll take care of it."

Meaning I'll try to figure out what the hell's going on. I needed the precise language in the form to determine its legal effect.

We were both quiet a moment, and I pictured my old roomie pacing in the hospital corridor, praying the surgeon had performed magic. Or maybe a miracle.

"Let my boy walk again!"

The thought of it nearly took my breath away.

"I've got Rod in my heart, Tank," I said.

"I know you do, Jake."

We hung up, and I sat in traffic, still gridlocked, the Caddy's massive engine unhappily belching. When the downtown exit is backed up like this, it means the Miami River drawbridge is up. It would be a long wait.

The drawbridge pre-dates the attempted assassination of Franklin Roosevelt in Bayfront Park a few blocks away. Don't get me started about how one man in a sailboat can force traffic to a dead stop from downtown Miami to the Key Biscayne causeway. The Florida Bar office was on Brickell Avenue in a building slated to be torn down so developers can put up a 75-story condo. Two more 80-story monstrosities are on the drawing board. Traffic is already a nightmare, and the low-lying street floods with every king tide.

Infrastructure? In Miami, it's all infra and little structure.

Finally, the bridge must have come down, and my old Caddy – on the verge of overheating – crawled along another twelve minutes for the last few blocks of the ride.

Once in the office, I realized I was hungry, and because I wanted to boast to Melissa about my exemplary dietary habits – and not lie – I ordered a kale salad.

Half an hour later, Liliana Santiago-Pittman stormed into my office and pointed a .38 caliber Smith & Wesson at my head.

-11-
Kill Shot Redux

Lily aimed the short-barreled revolver at me, her hand shaking.

I tried to reason with her, but she wouldn't put the gun down.

Her finger was on the trigger when Steve Solomon and Victoria Lord walked through the open doorway.

"Lily!" Victoria yelled.

"Whoa!" Steve shouted.

Startled, Lily inadvertently fired the gun and put a .38 caliber bullet into my forehead, just below the hairline.

A perfect kill shot.

***

Let me amend my last statement for the record.

The bullet sailed just over my head, nearly parting my hair. It shattered a glass picture frame and left a perfectly round hole in my forehead...in a faded black-and-white photograph hanging on the wall. The gunshot had executed a much younger – and cockier – likeness of myself.

The photo? A long-forgotten football banquet. Three men in suits, with me in the middle, my neck threatening to burst the collar of my dress shirt. My hair – steel gray now – was the color of sawgrass faded by the sun. My nose, already broken twice, had its distinctive bump, and my shoulders – then and now – were too wide for an economy seat on Delta.

To my right in the photo was Joe Paterno, who considered me his "problem child" when he'd been my coach at Penn State. To my left was Don Shula, who parked me so far down the Miami Dolphins bench, my ass was in Hialeah.

My heroes. My mentors. My surrogate fathers.

Both great coaches and great men. Both gone now.

I would have run through brick walls for them, and my doctors seemed to think I had.

Lily dropped the gun, collapsed into a chair, buried her face in her hands, and sobbed. Victoria Lord put her arms around her and whispered, "We heard what happened, Lily. We'll do everything possible for Rod."

Steve Solomon stood alongside, hands raised, palms up, as if waiting for a punt to fall from the sky. After a moment, he said, "What the hell, Jake?"

"I screwed up, pal. Big time. And now I'm gonna make it right."

***

For several moments, the only sounds were Lily's heartbreaking sobs. I was thankful that Solomon and Lord were here, as Lily wanted nothing to do with me.

Steve and Victoria were polar opposites, which made them a deadly trial team. A grad of Key West Law School, Steve was a dark-haired prowling cat in the courtroom, relying on instincts and street smarts, barely prepping for trials.

Victoria was a tall, patrician Ivy League blonde with perfect posture, given to Gucci suits and color-coded, cross-referenced research files. When she made a representation in court, you knew it was true. If Steve took an oath, he was liable to steal the bible with one hand and your watch with the other.

Victoria wasted no time taking control. "Lily, Steve will take you back to the hospital and stay with you and Tank until I get there," she said. "I'll go food shopping and bring whatever you need. You and Tank need to eat and sleep. Jake, I assume you're looking into a civil action."

"On it," I said.

Lily, who had been staring at the floor, looked up and said, "There's no lawsuit. Tank signed away those rights."

"So the insurance company says. I haven't researched it yet," I said.

"I don't care about the money," Lily said. "We've got good insurance. So forget it."

"Lily, it's not just about money. If I can prove Coach Coleman was at fault, we can set new legal standards. Maybe we can make the game safer for others."

"Safer?" She made a scoffing sound and reached into her purse for something that I hoped wasn't a hand grenade. Out came a document that she balled in her fist and threw at me. I speared it out of the air.

"Did you even read the form Tank signed? Did you see what the school says about football?"

No. And no.

"Football can't be made safe!" she said. "They admit it!"

I unfurled the crinkled document and skimmed it.

Lily got up and headed to the door with Steve and Victoria alongside.

"Hold up, Vic. I need you to read something."

She peeled off, came around the desk, and peered at the document over my shoulder. It was the boilerplate form of the

Florida High School Athletic Association, the FHSAA. If your child wanted to participate in football at any of 750 high schools in the state, you had to sign it.

The waiver language was in all capital letters, bold face.

"YOU ARE AGREEING THAT, EVEN IF YOUR CHILD'S SCHOOL AND ITS EMPLOYEES USE REASONABLE CARE, THERE IS A CHANCE YOUR CHILD MAY BE SERIOUSLY INJURED OR KILLED BECAUSE THERE ARE CERTAIN DANGERS INHERENT IN FOOTBALL THAT CANNOT BE AVOIDED OR ELIMINATED. YOU ARE HEREBY GIVING UP YOUR CHILD'S RIGHT TO SUE FOR ANY PERSONAL INJURY, INCLUDING DEATH."

"Have you ever seen a clause like that?" I asked.

"It's practically medieval," she said, "like the sovereign immunity that protected King George III if his royal carriage crushed you under its wheels."

Victoria ran a photocopy of the form to take with her, then left to do the promised errands for Tank and Lily. Alone with my thoughts, I looked at my faded photo, torn by the bullet and shards of glass. I had the self-satisfied smirk of a callow twenty-five-year-old.

Is there any other kind?

Wholly ignorant that life would not be an endless succession of sunny skies, warm beaches, and bikini-clad women in dire need of suntan lotion.

Life, I would later learn, is a raging river tumbling over jagged rocks, most of which are never seen. There are no signs warning of broken bones or broken promises or broken hearts. Some of us get knocked off our flimsy rafts. Others cling to the straps with utter desperation. Either way, the journey's end is the same. The river surges toward a roaring falls, unforgiving and unsurvivable.

-12-
As Random as Cosmic Waves

I fired up my computer and started my legal research. It's not my forte.

There are book lawyers, and there are trial lawyers. Book lawyers find the law. Trial lawyers use the law – and the facts and their powers of persuasion – to win cases. I'm not putting down the back-office guys who can unearth an opinion from the King's Bench in thirteenth-century England, but that's not me.

I'm the guy who stands in the well of the courtroom naked, which is to say without associates, paralegals, or any research that can't fit on one legal pad. Whether addressing a judge or jury, I believe that a congenial manner and a truthful presentation are just as important as legal acumen.

It took about an hour of research to uncover the basics. If the waiver clause didn't exist and we had the evidence, we'd be suing Coach Coleman and the school in a straightforward personal injury case.

It would be a simple issue. Was Coach Coleman negligent when he failed to remove Rod from the game before the second kickoff? If so, a jury would return a verdict for Rod.

Except there's a catch. People can waive their right to sue, letting tortfeasors – I love that word – off the hook. That's why the Florida High School Athletic Association hired big-city lawyers to draft that waiver clause.

So your kid got hurt because of lousy equipment or a pot-holed field or negligent coaching? Too bad, so sad, we're drop-kicking your lawsuit out of court.

But not so fast. Courts dislike those waiver clauses and partially ignore them.

Yeah, I said "partially."

Courts basically re-write the clauses to bar lawsuits based on "simple negligence" but not "gross negligence."

The difference? Think of simple negligence as mere carelessness. But gross negligence is utterly reckless conduct. It's akin – almost – to intentionally causing harm. Two examples: rear-ending a car at a stoplight when your foot slips off the brake would be simple negligence. But if you crashed into the same car while doing 100 miles per hour, well that's gross negligence.

Could coaching mistakes ever equate with maniacally reckless driving? I didn't yet know.

I was starting to get a headache. Not a piercing migraine from my damaged brain cells, but a mini-temple-throbber from pondering how to untangle the Pythagorean knots of the law.

Two hours later, I was still thinking about the fine art of coaching and the spidery webs of the law. Just where did carelessness become something almost sinister? It's a gray area. Sometimes, the difference between "simple" and "gross" negligence depends on which side of the bed the judge got out of that morning.

My thoughts were interrupted by my cell phone chiming with the Penn State fight song. *"Vic-to-ry we predict for thee."* Caller ID told me it was Langston Pittman.

"Tank," I greeted him. "How's our boy?"

There was a pause on the line, and I feared the worst. I am not a man given to prayer, but I said a silent one.

"Out from under and doing well, thank the Lord," Tank said, at last.

I let out a long breath. "That's great, pal."

"Surgeon says he got all the bone fragments. Confirmed the spinal cord is bruised but not severed. Rod's got sensation in his hands and feet but no movement yet. The doc says it's still better than no sensation and no movement. Rod's alert and knows we've got a lot of work ahead of us."

"Can I speak to him?"

"That's why I'm calling. He asked for you."

"What are you waiting for? Put my godson on!"

"Gonna put you on the FaceTime gizmo."

It took us a couple minutes to rig the video app. Then Tank propped up the phone on the bed tray and left the room because Rod wanted to talk solo. In a moment, I saw him from the shoulders up on my iPhone, well aware that he couldn't hold the phone himself. Or scratch his nose or wipe his butt.

He had oxygen clips in his nose, and he looked groggy. His head was shaved, and a cervical halo was screwed into the top of his skull and fastened to an overhead frame. He could not move his head up or down, left or right.

"Rodrigo!" I greeted him.

"Wha-ss up, Uncle Jake?" His words were scratchy, likely from the tube down his throat during surgery.

"Hah. I remember the first time you called me that. You were nine or ten and you must have heard my nephew, Kip, say 'Uncle Jake,' so you copied him."

He spoke softly and slowly, and I strained to hear. "Don't have any uncles or aunts of my own, Mom and Dad being only children."

"I remember telling you that since you're my godson, you could call me 'God.'"

That made him smile. "And Mom yelled at me when I did." His eyes flicked toward the door, footsteps echoing down the corridor. "Dad says you were at the game, so I guess you saw what happened."

"I did."

"Says I made a tackle on the first kickoff."

"Helluva hit, standing up a guy who outweighs you by thirty pounds. Do you remember Coach Coleman speaking to you before the second kickoff?"

His eyes moved left and right, and I realized that was the substitute for shaking his head, "No." As I had suspected, the audio tape would be indispensable to the case.

"After we ran onto the field for warmups, everything is hazy," Rod said. "Dad says the officials should have yanked me for a play when my helmet came off on the first kickoff, but they missed it."

"Your coach missed it, too."

Just what good are these new safety rules if they're not followed!

"At our last scrimmage, I asked the trainer for a smaller helmet, but they didn't have the right size."

Improper equipment is negligence, too.

"I wish there'd been no penalty on the first kick," Rod said.

"Me, too. On the replay, you could see the other gunner was less than one yard offsides. A fraction of a second."

The relationship of life to death, I thought, was as random as cosmic waves. The movers drop a piano out a tenth-story window a second after you pass on the sidewalk below. But the guy behind you gets crushed. So seize every damn day as if it's sunny and warm, the air sweet with jasmine. Because sooner or later, the ground is cold and wormy and six feet deep.

"I'm sorry I let you and Dad down," Rod said.

"What? No."

"All summer long, Dad kept telling me, 'Tuck your tail, not your head. Keep your feet under you.' I messed up."

"Forget that, Rodrigo. Did I ever tell you how I ran into a goal post at full speed down at Coral Shores High?"

On the little screen, I could see him smile.

"I don't think so."

Maybe I hadn't, or maybe Rod was just being polite.

"Split my helmet in two and bent the goal post, and I saw stars, even though it was a day game."

"Did they put you into the concussion protocol?"

"Sure, if you mean a dose of smelling salts and the coach yelling to 'shake it off, lard ass, and get back in there!'"

"That's demented."

"Even worse, coach made me pay to fix the goal post. I didn't have any money, so I got my snorkel and fins and poached a couple lobster pots off Islamorada."

"You were dope, Uncle Jake."

"More like *a* dope, Rodrigo."

I heard the squeak of rubber soles from the hospital corridor and the muffled voices of people walking by the door. Over the hospital loudspeaker, a Dr. Emery was being summoned to the E.R.

"When I was in the recovery room, I dreamed about the three of us playing rundown," Rod said. "Baseball, you remember?"

"Sure do. I was the first baseman, and your Dad would play second. You were the runner caught in between. You were quick, even then. You'd slide around the tag, or we'd make a bad throw."

"When Dad was the runner, we'd nail him every time." Rod laughed, and I loved the sound. For a few moments, at least, he could feel joy.

"You father runs like a rhinoceros with bunions," I said, and Rod kept laughing.

"The dream was a sign, Uncle Jake." He cleared his throat again, the effort lifting his head from the pillow. "See, we weren't playing in the past. The dream was happening now, or maybe next year. Whatever it takes, Uncle Jake, I'm gonna walk again. And some day, you and Dad and me, we're gonna play rundown again."

I was quiet then, it being hard to speak when you're choking back tears. I looked away and bought some time and thankfully was rescued by two nurses coming into Rod's room.

"Gotta go, Uncle Jake. A very strong woman is gonna punch me in the gut."

"In the diaphragm," a woman's voice said, chuckling. "Have to clear that mucus. And it's not a punch, young man, just some firm pressure."

"They don't want me getting pneumonia," Rod said.

Just one of dozens of complications that could strike down my godson.

"Uncle Jake, I've been thinking about the future now that I'll never play football again."

"Yeah?"

"You think I could be a lawyer like you?"

"You'll be better than me." A hand appeared in the screen and disconnected the line just before I said, "I love you, Rodrigo."

I did not allow myself the luxury of crying. There was work to do.

-13-
Public Nuisance

Later at home, I received a call from Victoria Lord. "Have you come up with a clear-cut, simple theme of the case?" she asked.

I said the first thing that came to mind. "Coach Coleman puts winning ahead of player safety in an inherently dangerous sport."

"A good starting point."

A semi-compliment, if I ever heard one.

"Now, all I need is evidence," I said.

"Jake, something in the consent and waiver form puzzles me."

"What's that, Vic?"

"Lawsuits seeking injunctions aren't barred the way suits for money damages are."

"I saw that."

"But what injunctions would parents ever seek?"

"Eligibility issues. The school says a kid doesn't have the grades or lives in the wrong district. Instead of damages, the parents ask for an injunction. 'Let my kid play!'"

"Got it," she said. "Not relevant to your lawsuit."

True, but Victoria's question kicked up dust in my brain like a bull at a rodeo.

"Injunctive relief," I said, chewing on an idea.

"What of it?"

"Vic, do you remember your Remedies class at that fancy law school?"

"I remember all my courses."

"Of course you do. Here's a hypothetical situation. Let's say I open a machine-gun range outdoors in our neighborhood in Coconut Grove."

"That's fairly ridiculous."

"This is law school, which is pretty damn ridiculous itself. What's the issue?"

"Is the machine-gun range an unreasonable threat to public safety? Of course, it is. It's a public nuisance."

"Public nuisance!" I repeated. "That's what I was looking for. And the remedy?"

"A judge will issue an injunction and shut down your mythical gun range."

"Exactly. Injunctive relief."

She thought a moment before speaking. "You're not thinking what I think you're thinking."

"I think I am."

"Don't do it, Jake. You could never win."

"When people doubt me, that's when I get fired up."

"You want to abolish high school football?"

"*Tackle* football. Enjoin it, at least, until the Association can prove it's made the sport safe. Right now, they admit it's unsafe. So, until they fix it, flag football will have to do."

"Oh, please. That's like telling the SEALs to hold Hell Week at a spa in Malibu."

"Count one will be Rod's suit for damages. Count two will be the claim to shut down the sport to prevent the catastrophic injuries that are just waiting to happen. I could save lives."

"Your motives are commendable, but the lawsuit would be frivolous. Not only that, you'll be public enemy number one. A pariah or maybe worse, a laughingstock."

"I don't care, Vic. I've already had more harpoons stuck into me than Moby Dick."

"This will be worse. And you'll lose."

"Maybe," I said. "But that doesn't mean that I'm wrong."

-14-
Last Chance Lassiter

In truth, I hadn't yet decided to go to battle against high school football. I needed to consider Victoria Lord's advice. I also wouldn't commit to such a gargantuan task without consulting Melissa, who already had expressed her skepticism about my handling the much less complicated personal injury suit.

That's right. My brain trust consists of two women because I consider them, well...brainier.

I knew what forces would be aligned against me. Not just the Florida High School Athletic Association and its hundreds of schools. Not just vehement parents. But all the other state athletic associations would leap into the fray.

If Florida falls, is Georgia next?

And how about the NCAA? If there's no high school football, there would be no college football. Without college football, there's no NFL. So I wouldn't be surprised if the case attracted a bunch of *amici curiae* filing briefs seeking to toss my ass out of the courthouse.

Years ago, I developed a reputation for taking tough cases most lawyers wouldn't touch. Some of my brethren at the bar – the Florida Bar, not Keg South – started calling me "Last Chance

Lassiter." I would tell my clients, "If your cause is just, no case is impossible."

I believed it then. But life has a way of wiping the idealism off our young and guileless faces. Oh, and Victoria was clearly right when she said that I'd be subjected to vitriol. The moment I filed the case, I'd be as popular as Vladimir Putin in Kyiv.

When Melissa got home from the hospital, we sat on the back porch in Adirondack chairs and sipped Don Julio tequila while eating take-out shrimp tacos and quesadillas. As we hit the coconut flan, I told her about my idea for an injunction to put the brakes on high school football.

"Would a judge ever do that?" she asked.

"Most would say it's out of their purview. Petition the Legislature. They're the ones who outlawed dogfights and illegal fireworks and even keeping bears as pets."

"Same question, then. Would the Legislature ever do it?"

"Not a chance. Their constituents would attack Tallahassee with torches and pitchforks. Banning high school football would be like banning sunshine."

She took a dainty sip of tequila and said, "You're looking for my approval? Is that it?"

"Absolutely. You have a pretty big vote. So, yes, fire away."

"Have you examined your motives for taking on such a difficult case? Besides helping Rod?"

"What's in it for me?"

"If that's the way you want to think about it, yes."

"Okay, I need to do something meaningful. If the sun is setting, I need to cast a shadow."

"A shadow?"

"Make an impact, leave a legacy. If I can help my godson and prevent future tragedies, that will be more than enough for me."

"I get that, Jake, and I admire it." She took a moment to gather her thoughts, then spoke softly. "Are you up to it?"

"You mean physically?"

"Yes. How are you feeling?"

"Today, remarkably well."

It was true. Tomorrow? Well, who knows?

"No headache," I said, "no tinnitus, no racing heart, no urge to smack someone in the chops."

She pondered that with a *hmm*, then said, "Maybe I was wrong before."

I refilled both our glasses with the Don Julio, an anejo tequila aged in white oak barrels. "Wrong about what?" I asked.

"Thinking that additional stress would be detrimental to you. Maybe there are positives when undertaking complicated tasks, especially where the goal is deeply important to you. It could be psychological, or maybe there's a jolt of a hormone that has palliative benefits."

"So, Mel...?"

"Jake, if you think the lawsuit is the right thing to do..."

She didn't have to finish the sentence.

"Win or lose, it's the right thing," I said.

I reached over and gave her hand a gentle squeeze. "I love having your care and support."

"I'm here for the long haul," Melissa said, "and I expect the path you're taking is long and treacherous."

"And filled with potholes, blind corners, and boulders crashing down hillsides."

"Any idea who'll they'll hire as defense counsel?"

"Some deep-carpet law firm with the senior partners' portraits on the walls, old white dudes in vests with pocket watches. They'll have trial teams of lawyers and paralegals and investigators, not to mention assistants whose only job is to fetch lattes and croissants. And all Rod will have is me."

"I think you relish being the underdog."

"I accept it. And you know what evens the odds? The case means more to me than it does to them, because I love Rod and Lily and Tank. And those fancy lawyers? They don't love the insurance company that pays them. They only love the money and the status it brings."

"Wow," Melissa said. "You're really locked in."

"Whoops. I left something out."

"What?"

"I love you, too, Melissa. I know you know, but I should say it more often."

"I love you, too, Jake," she said. "And you say it plenty."

-15-
How Daunting the Task

The next morning, I was hunched over my computer at the office banging out the initial paperwork:

> *Rodrigo Pittman, a minor child, by and through his parents, Langston Pittman and Liliana Santiago-Pittman, Plaintiffs,*
> *vs.*
> *Montgomery (Monty) Coleman, St. Frances Academy, and the Florida High School Athletic Association, Defendants.*

I am a decent typist for someone with oversize hands and two knuckles that won't fully straighten. On a snowy New England day, I got my fingers jammed inside the facemask of a Patriots' tight end when I tried to rip off his nose after he stomped on my ankle the previous play.

Beneath the caption of the case, centered on the page in all capital letters, I typed: **"COMPLAINT FOR DAMAGES (COUNT ONE) AND..."**

And stopped.

There was still time to play it safe. The smart move would be to forget about the public nuisance case to enjoin tackle football and simply file the personal injury case. Then work like hell to clear the hurdle of gross negligence and settle the case for a handsome sum. With enough publicity, that should send a message to coaches and school administrators. Maybe they'd enact safety measures on their own.

Who's kidding whom, Jake old pal?

I went back to my computer where the cursor was throbbing like a telltale heart. I finished the line:

"COMPLAINT FOR DAMAGES (COUNT ONE) AND TO ENJOIN TACKLE HIGH SCHOOL FOOTBALL (COUNT TWO)."

Now, all I had to do was write the damn thing and prove every single allegation.

In count one, I sought an unspecified amount of damages for Rod's pain and suffering, medical bills, future lost income, rehabilitation, and disability. I relied on the FHSAA's concussion protocol to claim that Coach Coleman was negligent by failing to remove Rod from the game when he came off the field dazed after the first kickoff. The Association lists 15 symptoms, any one of which requires the player to be benched and tested. "Lack of awareness of surroundings" is one symptom, and mistaking the coach for your father seemed pretty damn "unaware" to me.

My biggest problem was fattening the skinny claim of simple negligence into the fat juicy claim of gross negligence. If I couldn't meet that burden, my case would be tossed on summary judgment and never reach a jury.

I alleged that Coach Coleman rejected high-tech sensor helmets, refused to teach the safer rugby method of tackling, equipped Rod with the wrong-size helmet, and failed to have a team physician on the sideline. I also believed – but couldn't yet prove – that he ran secret pit drills in his "Tunnel of Manhood," something banned by the league and the FHSAA.

Taken together, the whole kit and caboodle amounted to "coaching malpractice," a term I invented. But would it equal gross negligence?

Damned if I know.

As I worked, a vague sense of uncertainty rolled in like the morning fog. Was I out of my depth? I hadn't even filed the case, and I was filled with self-doubt.

And that's on the personal injury count. The easier case!

Am I so arrogant that only now it dawned on me, how daunting the task, how huge my responsibility?

I stood and paced, then eased back into my chair and crackled my knuckles, *pop-pop-pop,* sounding like the cap gun I had as a kid.

C'mon, what are you afraid of? Buckle your chin strap and hit somebody!

Fatigue setting in, I started banging away at Count Two:

"Plaintiffs acknowledge that high school team sports convey benefits to student-athletes, their parents, their schools, and their communities. However, tackle football stands alone as an inherently dangerous sport. Defendant FHSAA, which sets rules for nearly 800 schools in the state, admits in its Consent and Waiver that no measures can make the sport safe for minor children. As such, the risks of serious injury and death outweigh any potential benefit of the game."

I took special care with the *ad damnum* clause, where I spelled out the requested relief. I avoided using the word "abolish." Instead, I sought a temporary ban on tackle football until the FHSAA could prove that it was safe. If it could never be made safe, well then the ban would become permanent. Alternatively, I sought a lesser remedy, giving the judge an easier way out. The court could mandate rule changes as it saw fit and let the sport continue.

Between the research and the writing and the re-writing, it took all day and deep into the evening to finish the pleading. Then, I drove home to the little house on Kumquat.

Melissa was sleeping, and I was careful to pad barefoot into the bedroom, the only sound the paddle fan and my creaking knees. The bed groaned under my weight as I slid under the sheet and nuzzled Melissa's neck.

"Mmmmn," she said.

"Didn't want to wake you," I whispered.

"Ten a.m." she said, her voice groggy.

"Okay, great. Morning sex."

She turned her head to look at me through half-closed eyes. "Ten a.m. Couples therapy. Don't forget."

PART TWO

"A school without football is in danger of deteriorating into a medieval study hall."
— Vince Lombardi

"Any man who watches three games of football in a row should be declared legally dead."
— Erma Bombeck

"Nobody in football should be called a genius. A genius is a guy like Norman Einstein."
— Joe Theismann

-16-
Early Grave

At 9:05 a.m., I filed the lawsuit in the downtown courthouse, a limestone tower shaped like a layer cake. A layer cake splattered with bird shit. The courthouse was built in the 1920s and renovated many times due to mold, water leaks, and structural defects. Many years ago, bond issues were put on the county ballot so voters could approve building a zoo and a new courthouse. Only the monkeys won, which is to say the hairy primates, not the lawyers.

I expected to have a bunch of urgent messages before noon. Even with its skeleton crew, the *Miami Herald* had a reporter check court filings every day. Then there were the television and radio stations, plus courthouse bloggers and a swarm of gadflies, influencers, and know-it-alls on social media. I was ready for microphones to be jammed in my face and cameras to be focused on my good side, where my bent nose wasn't as noticeable.

All that would have to wait. At ten a.m., Melissa and I sat in Dr. Rochelle Stein's office, prepared to both entertain and enrich her. On a bookshelf behind her shiny desk was a stuffed animal, a yellow horse you might win at a carnival sideshow.

I kept my hands folded in my lap. If I crossed my arms in front of my chest, I'd either be signaling that I'm closed off emotionally or calling a penalty for delay of game. Instead of tossing a coin to see who would kick off, I took the chivalrous path of letting Melissa begin the proceedings.

"I've thought about your advice concerning the difficulty of treating Jake while being his fiancée," Melissa said. "But technically, I'm monitoring Jake's condition, rather than treating him."

"And by monitoring," Dr. Stein said, "what do you mean?"

"Testing and establishing baselines. From imaging, I've found early evidence of tangled tau proteins in Jake's brain. That's troubling, but not conclusive of CTE. I have technicians supervise Jake's neurocognitive tests so I'm removed from that equation. We're looking for any loss of mental abilities, which thankfully has not occurred."

"I can still get a C-plus in any liberal arts course you throw at me," I boasted.

"Well, if you think there's nothing problematic, I'll honor that," Dr. Stein said, yielding to the super-smart woman I love.

"I'm good with that," I chimed in, though I'm not sure I had a vote.

Dr. Stein riffled through some notes. Through her office window, I could see thunderheads forming. After a moment, she said, "Let me ask you both a difficult question. Is there any physical violence in your relationship?"

"What!" I bounced out of the chair but my right knee gave way, and I fell backward, my 240 pounds squashing the seat cushion.

"No! Of course not," Melissa said. "Doctor, why would you ask such a thing?"

"A year ago, you wrote a paper for *Neurology Today* about the epidemic of brain injuries from domestic abuse."

"Victims of repeated blows to the head often suffer traumatic brain injuries that go undiagnosed." Melissa reached out and took my hand. "But what's that have to do with Jake and me?"

"Professionals often dive into fields that affect them personally," the shrink said.

"Hey, I'm the one with brain damage," I said. "And Melissa never smacked me."

"Nor has Jake ever struck me," Melissa said.

"Then I apologize to both of you," Dr. Stein said.

"My Granny taught me that a man who hits a woman is low-life pond scum," I said. "She made me vow that if I ever witnessed a man abusing a woman, I'd do something about it."

"I hope she wasn't advocating violence."

"Granny sure as hell didn't want me to call 9-1-1."

The shrink frowned and made a *tut-tut* sound.

"One night outside a bar in the Keys, I saw a guy slapping around a woman because she'd winked at the bartender," I continued. "I butted in, and one of us ended up in the canal behind the joint."

Dr. Stein waited for the rest of the story.

"Good thing I could swim," I added.

"Oh, my," Dr. Stein said.

"I'd just turned 15, and it taught me a lifelong lesson."

"To avoid violence?"

"That you don't win a fight following the Marquis of Queensberry. You knee the guy in the nuts and end it quickly."

Dr. Stein picked up a pad from her desk, and for the first time, scribbled a note. Maybe she wanted to remember my self-defense tip for personal use.

After a long moment, she asked, "How have you been feeling, Jake?"

"No complaints."

"Have you been taking your heart medication?"

Like a good little boy? She didn't say it, but that's what it sounded like.

"Beta blockers and blood thinners," I said, "two a day, just like my tequila. And my ticker's been ticking to a toe-tapping beat."

"Your other symptoms?"

Meaning "symptoms of brain disease," but she doesn't want to say it. Maybe it's the scary new bogeyman, replacing cancer.

"Migraines come and go like afternoon thunderstorms. Tinnitus is pretty much constant."

After a moment of blissful silence, Melissa jumped into the void. "I'd like to discuss Jake's night terrors."

"Whoa, whoa, whoa!" I protested. "'Terrors' is a little strong. I have dreams. Nightmares sometimes. No big deal."

Melissa drilled me with a sideways glance. "He wakes up screaming and punching at the ceiling, startling me out of a deep sleep, and scaring me half to death."

"Once in a while, and I'm sorry about that. Jeez, do we have to talk about this?"

Dr. Stein grabbed the little yellow horse from the bookshelf and squeezed it.

"Neigh-ayyyyy," the horse whinnied.

"What the hell?" I said.

"A prop I find useful," Dr. Stein said. "Are you familiar with the Four Horsemen?"

"The Apocalypse guys? Death, famine, those dudes?"

"Not them."

"That old backfield of Notre Dame? Crowley and Layden and two other guys?"

"The Four Horsemen that destroy relationships. Criticism. Contempt. Defensiveness. Stonewalling. Right now, Jake, you're stonewalling. And I'm sure you know that straightforward communication is essential in every relationship."

I shot a look at my watch. "Isn't our time about up?"

"Not even close," Melissa said. "What's your problem, Jake?"

"I feel like the two of you are ganging up on me."

"How so?" Dr. Stein asked.

"Two women. Both doctors. Bright and quick and perceptive. And me, a dumb jock from the Keys who's lucky not to be a bouncer at a strip joint."

Dr. Stein said, "Come now, Jake. I see right through that aw-shucks patina of yours."

"I might agree, Doc, if I knew what 'patina' meant."

The only sound was the pleasant hum of the air-conditioning, without which Miami would be home only to mosquitoes, alligators, and Ponzi schemers. Finally, Dr. Stein said, "Jake, are you embarrassed about having night terrors?"

I looked away, just like a thousand evasive witnesses I've cross-examined.

"Jake?" Dr. Stein prompted me.

"I'm not embarrassed about the nightmares. But whining about them to a shrink is unmanly."

"Flipping that around, what does being 'manly' mean to you?"

"For starters, it's not a dirty word. It's not synonymous with misogynist."

"I'm not suggesting it is," Dr. Stein said.

"A guy can be manly and still be a feminist."

Dr. Stein picked up the damn horse, which bleated another *"Neigh-ayyyyy."*

"Jeez. What now, doc?"

"You're being defensive. If you were a misogynist, this strong, independent woman wouldn't be marrying you. So, again, what does 'manly' mean to you?"

For a long moment, the three of us sat still. Four, if you count the horse.

Then, I said, "Being manly means being a provider for those you love. Old-fashioned concept, I know. It means protecting your mate from harm. Standing up for your principles, even when it hurts. Stopping bullies in their tracks and generally helping those who need it. Not crumbling under pressure. Showing grit and not crying about every disappointment and setback in life."

"Is crying unmanly?"

I shook my head. "I cried at *Schindler's List* and *Love Actually*, and when Harry got together with Sally. I cry every time a teammate dies of brain disease."

"Therefore, it follows that it's not unmanly to discuss your nightmares."

"Maybe I used the wrong word. But when two men get together for a few beers, one doesn't say to the other, 'Hey, pal, let me spend 20 minutes telling you about my dreams last night.'"

"Let's spend just a few minutes, Jake. Are your nightmares generally the same or are they different?"

"Similar. A fuzzy presence floats over our bed. Human but maybe not alive. I feel a sense of dread."

"Of approaching evil, perhaps?"

"Or an angel of death coming to get me. Then the fuzzy, ghostly thing points to the ground. And sure enough, there's a cemetery."

"Do you see a headstone with your name?"

"It's blurry, but I see my own grave, and instead of a headstone, there's a goal post with yard markers on the grass. I'm being buried on a football field."

"And how do you interpret that dream?"

"Pretty apparent, isn't it? My subconscious thinks football is leading me to an early grave."

Dr. Stein was quiet while she scribbled a note on her pad. Then, she said, "We could try cognitive behavioral therapy and if that doesn't work, hypnosis. There's also biofeedback and relaxation therapy."

"Sounds time-consuming." I inadvertently looked at my watch again.

"You get out of therapy what you put into it," Dr. Stein said, a phrase they probably teach the first day in shrink school.

"I'll think about it."

"Jake, please," Melissa said. "You promised to be open to various modalities."

"Okay, okay," I said, feeling surrounded. "I'm open."

"Jake, something else I'd like to examine is your childhood," Dr. Stein said.

"Why?"

"Exploring your upbringing might give us insight into your night terrors."

"If it's just the same to you, I'd rather leave it unexplored. Like the dark side of the moon."

"But, Jake..." the doc began.

Just then, my cell rang. I was supposed to have turned it off, and maybe I forgot, or maybe I hoped to be called by anyone, even a mechanical voice offering to extend my car warranty, which expired decades ago. Caller I.D. said, "Victoria Lord."

"What's up, Vic?" I said into the cell, ignoring Dr. Stein's sharp glance.

"Did you file?" Victoria Lord said.

"First thing this morning."

"I called to get the judge assignment, and the clerk's office can't find anything on the computer," she said. "It's like the case doesn't exist."

"I'll handle it. Thanks."

I felt like the governor signed my pardon five minutes before I was strapped into the chair. "Gotta go," I said to my two inquisitors, getting to my feet. "Emergency."

Both women looked at me wordlessly, neither pretending to believe a word.

-17-
The Official Religion

Once in the parking garage, I got into my old Caddy and checked my cell phone for messages.

Nada. Not a one.

I called the circuit court clerk's office, read the case number that had been stamped on my copy of the complaint, and asked which judge would be handling the case. The blind filing system should have already made the choice.

The clerk asked me to wait a moment. In the background, I heard two female voices speaking in Spanish. I didn't pick up much of it, but then another voice said, *"Ese archivo esta sellado."*

What the hell?

The clerk came back on the line and said, "I'm sorry, sir. That file has been sealed."

"Who sealed it?"

"I would not know. The file is sealed."

She told me she was very busy and hung up. "On behalf of all taxpayers, thanks a lot," I said to the dead line.

Thirty seconds later, my cell rang.

"Jake, you rascal, this is Erwin Gridley," growled a husky voice.

"Hello, Judge. How's retirement?"

"Danged if I know. I'm on senior status. Still got a half caseload, and now I can tilt the table, choose the ones I want."

Oh, no. Not Gridley. His semi-senility didn't bother me. But his part-time job as a college football official...well, I couldn't have caught a worse judge.

"Jake, do you know what the official fruit of Florida is?"

"I don't know. Probably the orange."

"Right. By decree of the Legislature. What about the state tree?"

"The palm, I guess."

"The Sabal palm, to be precise. How about the state religion?"

"There isn't one," I said. "That would be unconstitutional."

"Wrong! It's high school football. The official religion of Florida."

"Judge, if you've caught the case I filed, it's not proper for us to talk—"

"Bullshockey!" he said, a word I'd never heard. Maybe it was the official feces of Florida.

"Judge, did you seal the court file today?"

"Damn right I did! I'm trying to save your career, fellow. If you tear down high school football, you'd be the Babylonians destroying the Temple of Jerusalem. You'd be pissing on the Vatican walls and spitting on Martin Luther's grave. You'd be the most hated man in Miami."

With Fidel Castro dead, that was probably true, I thought. But I'd already considered that before filing the suit.

"You'll get death threats, too," Gridley went on. "You know what the state power tool is, Jake?"

"Didn't know there was one."

"The AK-47!" Gridley laughed, the sound of an old hound howling.

I felt the beginning of a migraine whistling through my skull, grayish black like the scudding clouds of a coming storm.

"Maybe you played football too long without a helmet," Gridley taunted me. "Or maybe you got some delusions of grandeur. You think you can walk into the courthouse – my courthouse – and turn off Friday Night Lights?"

"Judge, this conversation is making me uncomfortable."

"Tough *scheisse*, shyster. You're part of the cancel culture. You aim to cancel football. What's next, Christmas?"

"With all due respect, Your Honor," which is something I say only when I have no respect whatsoever, "this conversation violates the rules."

"Rules? You're the Jakester. You break the rules."

"Only the little ones, Judge."

"Every time you barge into my courtroom, you're flirting with contempt."

Flirting, hell. I take her all the way. But I never ex parte a judge, and my current job is to prosecute mouthpieces who do exactly that, among other malfeasances.

"I'm just representing a family that's been devastated, Judge."

"So you say, but you're barking up the wrong goal post."

"And you're running afoul of the ethics rules. We both are."

"Ethics-shmesiks. Meet me in one hour."

"In your chambers?"

"Hell, no. The Seaquarium."

"What! Why there?"

"What's the matter? You think I'm gonna have you whacked?" He hacked up a wet cough. "Sleep with the fishes like Luca Brasi?"

"Judge, you gotta tell me why we're meeting."

"I'll explain everything. The Seaquarium. I'll be feeding the killer whale."

-18-
Who's Consorting with Whom?

Like me, Lolita is in her fifties and weighs a ton. Okay, that was both hyperbole and understatement. I weigh less than a ton. Lolita weighs more than three tons. For most of her life, she's been kept in a tank that's too small for her. No room to roam, no adventures on the open sea.

I can relate.

There have been times when the courtroom felt like a prison cell, and I have been locked into mindless rules and regulations and subject to the asininity of judges, the lies of lawyers, and the whims of jurors. Making me yearn to tear down the pillars of the courthouse like Samson at the Temple of Dagon.

But I have no right to complain. Unlike Lolita, this is the life I chose.

Lolita is a black-and-white killer whale who used to be the star attraction at the Seaquarium, the faded attraction on the causeway connecting Miami to Key Biscayne. In the ocean, killer whales eat fish, squid, birds, seals, and even other whales. In her tank, before her retirement, she performed tricks for her supper.

I parked the Caddy in the mostly empty lot. It had been years since I brought my nephew, Kip, to the Seaquarium, and I didn't remember the layout, so I inadvertently took the long way around the park. I passed the sparsely attended sea lion show, hearing a smattering of applause. Then, I stepped carefully around the channel where sharks wriggled back and forth.

I found Gridley leaning over Lolita's tank with a bucket of fish parts. The judge wore cargo shorts, which displayed his pale legs. A blue-and-orange football jersey with the name "Tebow" on the back hung down to his knobby knees and did nothing to hide his potbelly. Gridley was a University of Florida alum and a Bull Gator Emeritus, thanks to his financial contributions and many decades of jock-sniffing around the football program.

Gridley extended his arm over the tank, and Lolita popped out of the water, her head the size of a small sedan. She opened her mouth, showing off two rows of cone-shaped teeth, sharp as paring knives. Gridley dropped a chunk of fish into Lolita's maw, and she gulped it, then whistled what seemed to be a thank-you.

Gridley turned to peer at me over his rimless tri-focals. A good look for a judge, not so much for his autumn hobby as a college football official.

"Good to see you, Jake," he said, as if he hadn't just reamed me out on the phone. "How's that nephew of yours?"

"Kip's fine. He's on the esports team at Penn State. And how's your grandson?"

"Sophomore at Fordham. Redshirted last year, he's the starting tight end this season."

"Good for him, Judge."

"I would have loved to have seen him in blue and orange, but he's not Gator material."

"Better to play in the Patriot league than sit on the bench in the SEC."

"Exactly what I told him. And a solid Jesuit education from the sixth grade through college."

He lobbed a handful of fish pieces to Lolita who swallowed them whole. "Jake, do you think God intended killer whales to inherit the Earth?"

"Can't say I've ever thought about it."

"Honest animals," the judge said. "If you're food, they'll come at you straight on, rip you to shreds."

He tossed another fish part at Lolita who gulped it, then put her upper and lower jaws together and made a smacking sound.

"She's blowing kisses to me," Gridley said. "Sweet animals. No deception. Not like homo sapiens. Oh, Jake, the shit I've seen in my courtroom."

"Judge, you lost me. Are you the whale in this story?"

"Hell, no. You are. Going straight for that tasty seal if you play it smart."

"I still don't get it. On the phone, you blasted me. Now..."

"I'm trying to save your career, boyo. Your public nuisance case is laughable. Total loser. And with the waiver of liability, your damages claim is finished, too. If I keep the case, I'll dismiss your ass myself."

"Without a hearing? Without argument?"

"I've known Monty Coleman for years, and he's a damn fine coach and human being. No way you can prove gross negligence. On the public nuisance claim, have you forgotten that circuit judges run for election? Players could be dying every Friday night, and not one judge in the state would abolish high school football. So where does that leave you?"

"You seem to have figured it out. You tell me, Judge."

Lolita was splashing in her tank, irritated with all talk, no fish. Gridley reached into the pail with two hands and let fly several chunks.

"You'll voluntarily dismiss count two, and when the defense moves for summary judgment on count one, I'll bang some heads together and you'll settle it for a fair price, which will be in the millions."

"You can bang all the heads you want, Judge, but you can't guarantee they'll pay."

He raised his bushy gray eyebrows. "Oh, but I believe I can."

"How?"

"It'll be a global settlement. You'll sacrifice the count two injunction, which is no sacrifice at all because you can't win, and the defendants will cave on count one. Your clients get paid. It's justice, and you feast on some tasty fish. Caviar, if you want."

He pushed the bucket of fish guts aside, and clever Lolita, realizing lunch was over, dived and splashed both of us with a flip of her flukes.

"How'd the defense lawyers get to you?" I asked, none too politely. "The lawsuit hasn't even been served."

"The lawyers aren't involved. I'm dealing with what you might call the defendants' *amicus curiae,* not that they'll file an appearance in court."

"And who the hell would that be?"

"They call themselves the Consortium."

"I'm drawing a blank, Judge."

"They're headquartered in Detroit, but there's no listing. No phone, no office."

"Never heard of them."

"Sure you have. Budweiser. Gillette. Pepsi. Apple. General Motors. FedEx. Gatorade. I could go on but you probably get the picture."

"No, I don't."

"The Consortium came into being to provide untraceable funds to get NFL players out of jams. A player gets drunk and busts up a bar or sends the bouncers to the hospital. Then you have your DUIs, your date rapes, your paternity cases and your drug charges. The Consortium whips out its checkbook, quick as an orphan at the dinner table. Usually before any case is filed, and always hush-hush. All settlements have NDAs that shield the dollars involved and who's paying."

"I don't see what any of that has to do with my lawsuit."

"The Consortium got concerned when the high school helmet lawsuits started a few years back. Litigation could have put the manufacturers out of business. Then came the high school heat exhaustion deaths. And the suicides of college players, their parents claiming were the result of CTE. That set off alarm bells about the future of the sport, and the Consortium got involved in some class actions against Pop Warner and other youth leagues."

"What do you mean by 'got involved'?"

"Behind the scenes. They provided resources to defense counsel. The best expert witnesses big money can buy. Chief surgeons at renowned teaching hospitals. Deans of the top engineering schools. A couple Nobel Prize winners."

"So, what are you saying? They win all the cases they don't settle?"

"Every last one. I was sure they'd lose a suit against a 260-pound coach who took part in a full-contact scrimmage with junior high players. Crippled a kid, but the coach still won the case, thanks to the Consortium's help."

"Reading between the lines, Judge, you're saying they play dirty."

"They play tough. Ruthless defense lawyers. Investigators who are former Black Cube and Blackwater operatives. A tech division that's world class at computer hacking and electronic eavesdropping."

"So why settle my case? Those 'millions' you mentioned?"

"You got their attention by trying to ban tackle football."

I tried to process the information but still couldn't get a handle on it. "And just why would Budweiser and General Motors care if a trial judge in Florida puts the brakes on high school football?"

"Oh, the Consortium members don't think you'll win. But your case will get publicity, and they don't want to open the floodgates. They're afraid better lawyers than you will come after the sport with bigger guns and more ammunition. Cases could get to the appellate courts where bad opinions can harm their interests."

"What interests?"

"C'mon, Jake. Step back, focus on the big picture. What's the $15 billion a year business all those behemoths have in common?"

"I don't know. Maybe..."

Oh. There it is. Holy shit!

"The NFL," I said. "All those companies. They're the league's biggest advertisers."

"Bingo, boyo. Did you think you were just suing a Florida high school? Hell no, you're taking the toys away from the billionaires who own the teams and the corporations that love to write them checks. You're not a lawyer with a case. You're an existential threat, so if you don't take a knee, what do you think they'll do to stop you? And don't try to answer because it's real simple. They'll do whatever it takes."

-19-
Bedroom Multitasking

Lying in bed reading, Melissa wore a black silky, lacy V-shaped thingy that slid down both shoulders and was open from neck to a friendly spot three inches below her navel. The silky thingy covered about fifty percent of her small, perky breasts, though I am not a certified surveyor and might be off plus-or-minus five percent. I don't know a chemise from a half-slip from a teddy from a bustier, so let's just say it was a helluva sexy piece of lingerie.

She put down her book when I approached the bed, cocked her head, and said, "There you are. I've been waiting."

In therapy, Dr. Stein told us to listen attentively when the other person spoke, but also to be aware of non-verbal cues. "Body language, facial expressions, and a person's attire all speak to you in code, so be alert to the cues," she had said.

Thanks, doc, but I don't need the Enigma machine to decode this.

"Gonna shower and be right there," I said, already unbuckling my belt.

I had spent the afternoon futilely trying to figure out what to do about Judge Gridley. I had called Solomon and Lord and asked for advice.

"You should have surreptitiously recorded the bastard," Solomon said.

"That's a felony," I reminded him.

"Only third degree, max of five years," he said.

"Were there any witnesses?" Victoria asked.

"A three-ton whale, and she's clammed up."

I ended the call without any idea how to get out of the jam. Now, after a quick shower, there didn't seem to be a reason to put on any clothes so I slid under the sheet with Melissa. Moonlight streamed through a window, casting a soft glow across the bed. Melissa's reddish-brown hair, once released from the tie behind her head, swished softly over her shoulders. Her eyes, gold-flecked green in daylight, took on a darker, hotter hue in the moonlight. Between soft, slow kisses, she asked about my day. So for a few moments, we were kissing and talking.

I told her about the bizarre conversation with Judge Gridley. Under the circumstances, meaning under the sheets, it was probably not the most erotic of banter. Still, she let her fingers crawl south of the equator.

"Oooh," I said. "That feels good."

"What are you going to do?" she asked.

"I'm going to peel that silky thing off and have my way with you."

"Your way and *my* way. But I meant about the judge."

"I need to bounce him from the case."

True to my word, I pulled the black lingerie, flimsy as a tissue, over Melissa's head. Even though it weighed about as much as an eyelash, she had to help. A torn rotator cuff that was botched in surgery kept me from raising my left arm high enough to complete this most basic of manly maneuvers.

"Will you file a motion to recuse him and lay out everything he said?" she asked.

I kissed the side of her neck, her skin soft and sweet under my lips. "He'll deny everything, and I'll look delusional. The Consortium? Budweiser and Apple and G.M.? I might as well say Martians landed and kidnaped me."

"And probed your various body parts?"

Her hand was now filled with a body part of mine that magically began to grow. My lips began paying attention to her left breast. Her skin was warm as if sun-kissed, and her nipple stiffened. Feeling sorry for her lonely right breast, I cupped my hand over it.

I am proficient at multitasking.

Usually, I am focused while romancing my fiancée, but my rebellious brain kept replaying the conversation with Gridley. Was there something I missed?

I dropped my head lower, puckered my lips, and dispensed little kisses down her smooth abdomen. I brushed my lips on the finely manicured triangle below.

"What's that sound you're making?" she asked.

"Oh, sorry." I hadn't realized my smooching was making the *smacking* noise of Lolita blowing kisses to Gridley.

"That's okay. Keep going. More kisses, less sounds."

After a few minutes, I was stiff and she was moist, and as I entered her, she gasped, the most beautiful sound humans have ever made. We moved in unison, and a memory invaded my otherwise occupied brain.

"I've known Monty Coleman for years, and he's a damn fine coach and human being."

Yeah, Judge Gridley's voice barging in just as Melissa sighed, "That's it. Right there. Oh, yes!"

Why would Judge Gridley know a high school coach?

"Slow down," I said softly to myself, yet aloud. "Think about it."

"No thinking, Jake. Faster, not slower!"

"A solid Jesuit education from the sixth grade through college."

Could it possibly be? His grandson.

"I've got it, Mel!"

"Yes! Yes! You've got it! Don't stop."

"Could I be this lucky?" I said into Melissa's ear.

"You're lucky, big guy! That's it! That's it!"

***

An hour later, Melissa was sleeping, purring like a contented cat.

I was at the kitchen table with my laptop, surfing the internet like Kelly Slater on Oahu's north shore. How did we ever get along without Google?

The Fordham athletics department website gave me the first nugget of information. The Saint Frances Academy website added more gold, and the school's booster club site revealed the vein of treasure linking the first two.

I crawled into bed in our familiar spooning position. I kissed the back of Melissa's neck, and she sighed peacefully. I would get up early and be in Judge Gridley's chambers before his morning calendar began.

You're gonna dismiss my ass, Judge? Yeah, well I'm gonna put a hat on a hat.

-20-
The First Family of St. Frances

Judge Gridley's assistant wasn't at her desk at 7:45 a.m. when I barged into chambers without knocking or begging the court's pardon. The judge sat behind his polished teak desk, a plate of scrambled eggs and sausage in front of him. Next to his plate sat a small, stuffed alligator, staring at me, its mouth open, jagged teeth smiling malevolently.

The carpet was blue and orange with the University of Florida seal in the middle. The seal portrayed the pleasant fiction of a Seminole woman spreading flowers on the beach as a steamboat with white settlers chugged toward her. A more accurate picture would have shown General Andrew Jackson burning Seminole villages to the ground looking for runaway slaves.

Judge Gridley's fork paused in mid-stroke. "Jake, what the hell?"

"Got something for you, Judge."

In the wee hours of the morning, I had printed out several documents. Now, I tossed a one-pager onto the judge's desk. A bio and photo from the Fordham football website: "Gary Gridley, Redshirt Freshman Tight End."

The judge raised his bushy eyebrows above his tri-focals. "Good-looking boy, my grandson."

I read aloud from the website: "'A two-year starter for St. Frances Academy in Miami, big things are expected from Gridley in the coming season.'"

"What's your point, Jake?"

"I think you know, Judge. But I can keep going."

I folded another one-page document into a paper airplane and sailed it to him. It landed with one wing dragging through his scrambled eggs. He didn't unfold the paper, so I said, "The photo is from the St. Frances booster club site. A black-tie fundraiser at the Fontainebleau two years ago. You're a founding member of the club and have the title of 'Colonel.' In the photo, you're with your son Edward and your grandson Gary. Oh, yes. Coach Monty Coleman, too, with his arm around you. Your son didn't play football, but he was on the debate team and now is president of the St. Frances Alumni Association. Which brings us back to grandson Gary. He played three years for Coach Coleman. Should I go on?"

"If you must."

"The caption says, 'Meet the Gridleys, the first family of St. Frances.'"

The judge slid his cold eggs and sausage aside. "I assume this is your way of making a motion for recusal."

"No motion. You'll recuse yourself, *sua sponte,* today or I'll take you down hard and go after your pension. Unseal the court file and spin the wheel. I don't care what judge hears the case, as long as it's not you."

"You may not believe this, Lassiter, but I was trying to help you."

"Bullshockey," I said, repeating what he'd said to me yesterday. "You wanted a quick and secret settlement to protect your pal

Monty Coleman. You wanted to cover up all the crud at the school that three generations of your family call home. Sweep it under the rug. Well, sweep it under your stupid blue-and-orange Gators rug, instead."

"You have a lousy case, fellow. Two lousy cases. And you don't know what you're up against."

"The Consortium? Gotta hand it to you, Judge. That was rich. I didn't think you had the imagination."

"You're a horse's ass, Jake. And you're gonna find out just how real the Consortium is."

-21-
Hello Shit, Meet the Fan

The next morning, I was feeling chipper. Judge Gridley had recused himself; the file had been unsealed; and the case would be re-assigned later today.

I was drinking my morning coffee in the kitchen when my cell rang. Caller I.D. said it was the *Miami Herald*. Great, I expected that. And wanted it. Not publicity for me, but for the worthy cause. I'd added one sentence to my theme of the case:

"Coach Coleman puts winning ahead of player safety in an inherently dangerous sport. Now, we turn to the courts to protect our children."

"Hello Mr. Lassiter, it's Rudy Schulian at the *Herald*," said the voice on the phone.

"Long time, Rudy. I guess you're covering the courthouse these days."

"Yes, sir. Plus the Water and Sewer Board, the Zoning Appeals Board, and the Opa-Locka City Commission."

"Still shorthanded on the city desk, I see."

"Plus, South Beach nightlife. Can't forget that one."

"Never figured you for the club life, Rudy."

"Tell the truth, I've never been to South Beach. I live in western Broward."

"Okay, Rudy. Let me give you a couple quotes. 'Let's protect our children. That's what the lawsuit is all about.'"

There was a pause on the line, and I figured Rudy was taking notes.

"Actually, Mr. Lassiter, I'm just updating your obituary."

"What!"

"The last items in our files are the Thunder Thurston murder trial and the college admissions scandal. So, the city editor told me to update your obit."

"Do you know something I don't, Rudy? Like when it's going to run?"

He chuckled and said, "C'mon, Mr. Lassiter. You know we pre-write obituaries on prominent Miamians."

"I'm flattered. What's your lead?"

He deepened his voice and read in a tone reminiscent of an old newsreel, perhaps reporting the bad news from Pearl Harbor: "Jacob Lassiter, the former Miami Dolphin linebacker turned flamboyant trial lawyer, died yesterday..."

"Hold on, Rudy. 'Flamboyant' is for the skinny wide receiver who does back flips in the end zone. I was a grinder, spitting grass and mud through my facemask."

"Well, your reputation is for courtroom theatrics."

Is that true? Maybe we never see ourselves the way others do.

"What else do you have, Rudy?"

He read aloud: "Lassiter was perhaps best known for his unsuccessful lawsuit to abolish high school football..."

"What do you mean 'unsuccessful'?' The case was filed yesterday."

"I called a few lawyers around town. Most said it was a publicity stunt. Some called it deranged. Everyone agreed it was a loser. Now, if that's wrong and somehow you win..."

I ended the call abruptly, then turned on the television where the morning news anchor, a woman who appeared to be about thirteen, said: "Stay tuned for the inside story of a Miami lawyer's wack-a-doodle lawsuit to abolish high school football."

Not "abolish," dammit. Just stop play until they can prove it's safe.

I punched another channel, intending to return after the commercial. This anchor was a teenaged boy, or at least looked like one, and his voice still had an alto quality. "Channel 4 has learned that the lawyer, Jake Lassiter, has serious brain damage. Ironically, Lassiter's brain injuries were sustained playing football."

That's not ironic! Ironic would be the opposite of what we expect. This is exactly what we'd expect. What's ironic is that people who write newscasts don't know the English language.

I changed channels again. The anchor was a middle-aged man with a fine head of gray hair. I figured he had six months until he was replaced with a dude or dudette from Generation Z. "Tonight at six, our I-team uncovers the truth behind a lawsuit to destroy the morale of the American people. It's a plot by Cuba and Venezuela with a Miami lawyer fronting as their stooge."

My email beeped with incoming messages. The deluge, a shitstorm of sniping, had begun. The first few emails were anonymous. A general theme was that I was "brain dead" or a "commie" or a "shyster" or a "pussy" or a combination of two or more.

My cell rang again, Tank Pittman calling. He told me Lily was on the line, too. She and I had declared a truce, though most communications came directly from Tank. They were at the hospital. Rod had a good night, Tank said, and they were waiting for the doctors to do their rounds and perform new tests. The last few days, his responses to the pin pricks on his arms and legs had become noticeably better. Doctors had moved him from neuro intensive care to intermediate intensive care. Optimism was in the air.

"That's great news," I said.

"About the lawsuit," Tank said. "You never told us about trying to abolish high school football."

"Not abolish, Tank. Just put tackle football on hold until the Association can prove it's safe."

"Which is never, Jake. Why didn't you tell me you were going to do this?"

"Didn't I?"

I thought I had, but I didn't remember when or where the conversation took place. Had I imagined it?

"Jake, it's your strategy, right?" Lily said. "You get them to settle our damage case by dismissing the other one."

"Actually, Lily, I intend to win both cases."

Silence on the line until Tank said, "Jake, I been getting calls. Old teammates. Reporters. Some flunky in the Dolphins office asking me not to come to the reunion dinner. You put us in the hot seat."

"We're on the right side of history, Tank. You have to trust me."

"Jake, are you feeling okay?" Lily asked. "People are saying..." She let it hang there.

"No worries, Lily. I'm not drain bamaged." I said it with a lilt to my voice to make sure they knew I was kidding, but no one laughed.

An incoming call beeped. The general number for the Miami-Dade courthouse.

I told Tank and Lily we could talk later, and I took the call.

"Mr. Lassiter, Melvia Duckworth here."

"Your Honor," I said, surprised. "To what do I owe this..."

This what?

"Mr. Lassiter, I have Ms. Sandra Day on the line. She's a senior partner at Wickerham and Snoot in New York. I don't suppose you two have met."

"No, Your Honor," I said, just as a woman's voice said the same.

"Mr. Lassiter," the judge said, "that live hand grenade of yours got tossed into my division, and Ms. Day has already filed her appearance on behalf of the high school association."

"Roger that, Your Honor," I said a bit stiffly.

"At ease, Mr. Lassiter."

I nearly said, "Aye, aye," which would have been embarrassing, as Judge Duckworth was Army, not Navy. She'd been a captain and highly regarded military jurist in the Judge Advocate General Corps. Now, she was a no-nonsense state judge.

"I'm going to fast track this case. Now, you two agree to a discovery schedule and follow it. Don't waste my time with objections and motions to compel. Work it out yourselves, or I'll level costs and fees against any party not complying with the letter and spirit of the rules. Is that clear?"

"Yes, Ma'am," I said, which is the correct way to address a female officer.

"Yes, Your Honor," Sandra Day said, which is the correct way to address a judge of any gender.

So far, I liked this. We're the ones who needed answers to interrogatories and the production of documents and videos. When Tank went to St. Frances to retrieve Rod's helmet, an assistant principal told him that the request would have to go through the school's lawyers. And that was *before* I filed the lawsuit.

Feeling the wind at my back, I said, "Your Honor, I'd like to make a motion."

"Go ahead, Mr. Lassiter."

"Plaintiffs move to strike the parents' waiver of liability clause as violating the right of access to courts for the redress of wrongs. The clause is like a three-act play."

"Let's hear it, Shakespeare." Judge Duckworth's brusque tone conveyed the impression she didn't think my show would make it to Broadway.

"In act one," I said, "they admit that there are dangers in football that can't be eliminated. In act two, they say that your child may be seriously injured or killed. And in act three, they force parents to give up all rights to sue for injuries or death."

"Motion denied," the judge said. "You've got access to judge and jury as long as you can prove gross negligence."

"Thank you, Your Honor," I said, as losing lawyers are inclined to do. It was a correct ruling, and I'd simply been throwing a Hail Mary.

"Now, listen up, both of you," Judge Duckworth said. "The media are going to treat this case like it's the landing on Omaha Beach. So, Mr. Lassiter, what are we going to need?"

"Naval cannon fire and air cover," I ventured.

"Discretion and self-restraint," she corrected me. "No press conferences. No showboating. We try the case in the courtroom, not on the courthouse steps. Now, in my experience, Mr. Lassiter, it's plaintiffs' lawyers who beat the big brass drums. In criminal court, you've had a tendency to veer toward..."

The judge seemed to be searching for a word or two.

"Expert advocacy?" I suggested.

"Flamboyance," she said.

What! That word again. First Rudy Schulian and now the judge.

"To be evenhanded," the judge continued, "in my experience, it's the defense lawyers who dig trenches, blow up bridges, and plant land mines in discovery. Anything and everything to delay going to trial. I'll have none of that, Ms. Day."

"Your Honor, I'll be on my best behavior," Sandra Day said.

"Mr. Lassiter, you may not be aware, but Ms. Day is well-known nationally for her zealous representation of the asbestos and opioid manufacturers."

"Why those guys?" I asked. "Are all the Nazi war criminals dead?"

"And I'll have none of that either," the judge snapped. "Stow the sarcasm."

"Yes, Ma'am. I, too, will be on my best behavior."

"Oh, you'll have to do better than that, soldier. I advise you not to let any of your shit hit my fan."

-22-
My Little Secret

I sat in the last row of the auditorium at University of Miami Hospital, listening to Dr. Melissa Gold's lecture at her annual neurology symposium. As I tried to understand what she was talking about, I contemplated just how unfair life can be.

No, not unfair to me!

I'm a lucky bastard. The highlight reel of my life would reveal more than my fair share of joy. I basked in the love of Granny who raised me after my father was killed and my mother ran off with a roustabout from Oklahoma. Granny taught me to help underdogs fight the powerful, and to pass along values of decency and kindness to my nephew, Kip. Not that Granny was a cream puff. She pushed me to go out for football and attended all my home games. She would have agreed with the Spartan mothers who told their warrior sons, "Come back with your shield or on it." Granny's admonition was a tad more prosaic: "If I gotta wash blood out of your uniform, it damn well better be the other boy's."

Then there was my mentor, Doc Charlie Riggs, the medical examiner who taught me to pursue justice, rather than money. Charlie lost his job because he wouldn't slant his trial testimony to favor the state. Integrity was Charlie's legacy.

At Penn State, Joe Paterno taught me to be a gracious winner and a loyal teammate. Win or lose, he said, it's being involved in a common cause that brings us joy and enduring memories.

Granny and Charlie and Joe, all gone now.

But how about the pure stroke of golden luck to find the treasure that is Melissa Gold? So late in life – but so welcome – for love to barge through my door without ringing the bell.

Sure, my two careers – gladiator and mouthpiece – have had low points. I was never a star in either field, but I left everything I had on the playing field and in the courtroom. I have no complaints. Whatever the future brings, I haven't been shortchanged. But what about my 17-year-old godson? He was lying immobile and paralyzed with the prognosis, "Too soon to tell."

What kind of luck did Rod have?

A freak accident, George Barrios had called it.

"A million-to-one shot."

A reminder of the fragility of life, how slender the thread that moors us to safe ground. So many "ifs."

If the coach or the officials had benched Rod...

If the blocker had taken Rod out of the play...

If Rod hadn't lost his footing...

If his head hadn't dropped...

If Arrington's leg had been stomping downward instead of thrusting upward...

Or the biggest "if" at all.

If I had told Tank, "Listen to Lily, pal. Rod should stick to running track. He doesn't need football."

Guilt, like the past, clung to me like mud on rusty cleats.

***

Melissa stood at the lectern and, well...lectured. Three other physicians, a neuropathologist, a neuroscientist, and a radiologist sat at a table on the stage. The audience was comprised of physicians, medical students, and PhD candidates. All brainiacs – Ha! – and all of them seeking the latest developments in CTE research.

Oh, I was there, too. The guinea pig on a running wheel.

Melissa was executive director of the CTE program at the National Institutes of Health. When she got the gig, it looked as if we'd be moving to Bethesda, Maryland. But the smart folks at the University of Miami didn't want to lose her, so they partnered with NIH and kept Melissa here in Mosquitoville with a joint project.

Other speakers had presented their papers on the relationship between repetitive head impacts and traumatic brain injuries. A large screen blinked with slides of gray matter, thin slivers of brain that looked like cauliflower shaved by a mandoline blade. In her talk, Dr. Suzanne Kreisel, a neuropathologist from Boston University, used a laser pointer to show the "abnormal accumulation of lesions in neurons, astrocytes, and cell processes at the depths of the cortical sulci."

In other words, sludge on the brain.

All things considered, I'd rather watch film of Coach Shula screaming at me after I got flagged for unnecessary roughness.

I had met Dr. Kreisel at an NIH event in Maryland. She'd led the team that found evidence of CTE in the brains of an extraordinary number of deceased former NFL players. That evening, the three of us – Melissa, Suzanne, and me – were chatting over hor d'oeuvres, when Melissa walked off to greet a group of researchers from Harvard. Suzanne and I talked a while.

And now we have a little secret.

No! Not that kind of secret. Faithful as an old beagle with arthritic joints, I would never jump the backyard fence to visit a frisky Lab.

But there was something I was keeping from Melissa.

"Straightforward communication is essential in every relationship." Or so Dr. Stein had told us.

I know. I know. But Melissa will be peeved when I tell her, even more so if Suzanne Kreisel spills the news before I do. So now, listening to Melissa, I worried that I'd screwed up by clamming up. Maybe I could blame my wobbly brain.

Earlier speakers had discussed the inability to diagnose CTE in the living. One neurologist from the University of San Francisco lamented the fact that so many symptoms of the disease were present in people with no brain disease whatsoever.

Aggression. Depression. Impaired judgment. Impulse control. Memory loss. Severe headaches. Suicidal thoughts.

I checked off six boxes, but at least I wasn't suicidal. And yes, I would cite "impaired judgment" for keeping the secret from my beloved.

Melissa's lecture concerned locating biomarkers that will eventually be able to diagnose CTE in people, like me, who are still alive. "We need larger studies to establish how PET-scans and blood tests can be combined with other assessments to make a definitive diagnosis," Melissa said. "We're getting close. Other groups are working on potential treatments, and we all hope that those in charge of contact sports will do more to prevent repetitive head injuries. We seek a lot, and it's a long road. Prevention. Diagnosis. Treatment. And, of course, cure."

The audience applauded, and Melissa looked as if she were about to take her seat. But then she said, "On a personal note, many of you have met my fiancé, Jake Lassiter, who is here today."

That drew some applause, and I resisted the urge to stand and take a bow.

"A former NFL player, Jake has been a willing participant in several of our studies." She paused for effect. "And quite an eager participant in a trial involving the drug psilocybin."

Laughter from the crowd, psilocybin being the active ingredient in magic mushrooms. At the table, I saw Suzanne Kreisel taking a note. I told myself it was something technical and medical, not something about me.

***

In the lobby at a break in the symposium, I waited until Melissa was finished chatting with her colleagues. She grabbed my arm and steered me toward a corner next to the coffee machine.

"When were you going to tell me?" she demanded. "When you're dead?"

"I planned to tell you. When, I'm not sure."

"Why are you donating your brain to Boston University, care of Suzanne Kreisel?"

"Okay, here's the deal. Would you really want to be the one to dissect my brain?"

Those green eyes drilled me. "If we could do it today, sure."

"Okay, I get it. You're steamed."

"Why didn't you talk to me about this? Why so secretive?"

"It's my impaired judgment and impulse control. Maybe memory loss, too."

"Oh, horse feathers! Relationships are built on trust, and you violated it."

It corrodes my heart when I disappoint Melissa. This was yet another of those times.

"I'm sorry, Mel. I screwed up. I hate talking about my own demise. And I guess I wanted to protect you from thinking about it."

"We've been over this! I'm an adult. Please treat me like one."

"Okay, I will. I swear."

She cocked her head to one side, gave me her empathetic look, and said, "You seem troubled. What is it, Jake?"

I promised to be open about my feelings and my fears, so here goes.

"I'm on my way to see Rod at the hospital. Whenever I do, everything about the place brings home the enormity of my responsibility. The sounds of Rod breathing, the beeps of the machines, the grim reality of a place where most of the patients will never get out of bed on their own."

"Rod trusts you, and I trust you. Don't lose that old Lassiter swagger."

"Maybe I sold Tank and Lily a bill of goods about my handling the lawsuit. Maybe it was my ego talking."

"Think about it. Did you take the case for yourself or for Rod?"

"For Rod, of course. But sure, I'd like to do something on a larger scale for the greater good."

She stepped toward me and put both hands on my shoulders. "You're a good man, and you'll find the way. As for us, relationships are living, breathing things. We need to work on ours. Now, go to Rod and do what has to be done."

-23-
The Nutcracker

I ran into Tank Pittman in the corridor outside Rod's room. He carried a cup of coffee and wore a smile. A tired smile, but still, it heartened me.

"Rod's wiggling his toes!" he said.

"Freakin' great!" I said.

"I called Dr. Grant who said that even if the spinal cord is healing, it's too soon for the muscles to re-learn how to contract. He thought the movements were involuntary and didn't want me to get my hopes up. Then he came by."

"Yeah?"

"I said to Rod, 'Wiggle your toes,' and three of them did the piggly-wiggly!"

"Yes!"

"Then his ankles, Jake. Strained like hell to do it, and he couldn't actually feel he was doing it. But the doc said it was amazing and high-fived me."

Now, I high-fived Tank, and he nearly spilled his coffee. "Rodrigo's got your spirit, pal," I said.

"His will, Jake. His inner will is stronger than mine. The doc says it's a start, but it doesn't really mean..."

Tank didn't have to finish the sentence. There was still no guarantee that Rod would walk again or have use of his arms.

We entered Rod's room where Lily was sitting at the head of the bed, scratching her son's ear.

"Right there, Mom. That's it," Rod caught a glimpse of me. "Hey. Whassup Uncle Jake!"

"You look great, Rodrigo."

I meant it. His coloring was good, his eyes alert. Oxygen clips were in his nose, but he seemed to be breathing normally. He was attached to machines that glowed and beeped and buzzed but didn't wail with any sirens.

Lily stood, gave me a curt hello, and left the room.

"She's still running hot and cold on you," Tank said, "but she'll come around."

"Why don't you and Lily go for a walk outside?" I suggested. "I'll entertain Rod with tales of playing at Buffalo in a blizzard."

"Gucci, Uncle Jake."

"I think that means 'cool,'" Tank translated.

"A blizzard and fog in Buffalo," I said. "We were wearing the away jerseys. All white. They couldn't see us."

"Definitely Gucci," Rod said.

Tank clomped me on the shoulder and exited.

I sat in the chair next to Rod's bed. "If you need anything scratched, just holler. Unless, it's you know where."

Rod smiled, and I said, "Your Dad told me about your progress. Toes and ankles."

"Not only that. This morning, I could tell the difference between a pin prick and finger pressure. Seems like a small thing, but my surgeon thought it was lit. A couple professors of spine surgery were here from the medical school. I'm getting a lot of attention, like I was a star or something."

"They're going to write pieces in the medical journals when you hop, skip, and jump out of here."

"I was supposed to start guitar lessons this month," he said, a faraway look in his eyes. "Do you know gypsy jazz?"

"Django Reinhardt," I said, exhausting my knowledge of the music. Sort of like someone saying "baseball," and you say "Babe Ruth."

"The best. Plus Jimmy Rosenberg, Olli Soikkeli, and Robin Nolan, who has lessons online."

"No doubt in my mind you'll be playing a gypsy jazz guitar."

"They're transferring me to a rehab center. And that's where they say I'll be doing all the hard work."

"Your Dad worked harder in practice than anyone I've ever seen. And you take after him. Grind-it-out perseverance will take you places you didn't think you could reach."

"Dad says you did more with less talent than any player he's seen."

"We go back a long time, your Dad and me. My roomie on the road."

"Actually, Dad says he roomed with your suitcase." Rod gave a little smile, which brought me some joy. "He told me you always broke curfew, and he never saw you until the morning of a game. Said you slayed."

"I was a dawg back then. Your Dad made the All Pro team, and I was All Party. He's your role model, Rodrigo, not me."

"You both are," he said.

I asked Rod if anything had come back to him. The tackle on the first kickoff. Staggering after the big hit. And what Coach Coleman said to him before the second kickoff. But it was still a blank and probably always would be.

Sometimes our brains seem like different entities. Alien beings, deciding on their own what to remember and what to forget, what calculations to make and what ones to avoid.

"Rod, do you know why the St. Frances team doctor wasn't on the field?"

"Dr. Herlocher quit three days before the game."

"Didn't the coach have a backup in case Herlocher was in surgery or just unavailable?"

"I guess, but no one showed up. Does it matter?"

"The league requires a physician on each sideline. If St. Frances had one, you might have been checked for a concussion before the second kickoff. Do you know why Herlocher quit?"

"I didn't see it, but some of the guys said he got salty with Coach the last day in the tent."

"The Tunnel of Manhood?"

"Yeah. Doc was always inside for the drills. And the Tuesday before the game, he came out yelling at Coach Coleman. Walked off the field and didn't come back."

"What drills are run inside the tent?" I asked.

If Rod could move, he would have shrugged his shoulders. "I never did them. It's just offensive linemen versus defensive linemen, running backs versus defensive linemen and linebackers. Big guys."

A female nurse carrying an iPad came into the room and smiled at Rod. "Oh, just keep talking," she said, focusing on one of the machines. "I think we're getting a false reading on Rod's respiratory rate."

"Even though you never did the drills," I said, "you had to know from your teammates what was going on."

"Sure, but Coach told us we're fam and what happens in the tent, that's on the down low. Area 51."

"Top secret?"

"Yeah. It's like we took an oath. And to be honest, Uncle Jake, I can't think of anything Coach did that was so bad."

"I get that, Rodrigo, and I understand your reluctance to talk. But there are legal issues involved. Now, you don't have to say anything. I'm going to give you a word. If I'm wrong, blink once. If I'm right, blink twice."

"But Uncle Jake, if I never did the drills, what's it got to do with the lawsuit?"

"It's called pattern evidence. If I can string together enough separate acts of negligence, and if the judge admits everything into evidence, well, it helps our case."

Omitting the sticky legal issue of whether a bunch of separate acts of simple negligence can be combined into one big fat tort of gross negligence.

"Okay, if that's what you want."

"The Oklahoma Drill?" I said.

Rod blinked once. Negative.

A machine beeped behind me. "Oh, sorry," the nurse said, fiddling with a dial.

I ignored her and said, "Blood Alley?"

Another single blink. No again.

"The Nutcracker," I said.

Rod paused, then blinked twice. *Bingo.* It was the full-contact one-on-one, fight-to-the-finish drill, also outlawed by the league. Now, we were getting somewhere.

Another nurse entered the room, and the first one left without a word. Our new visitor was a short woman in her forties with tired eyes. "Hello, Rod. I'm hearing good things."

"Thanks, Sofia."

She turned toward the open doorway. "Who was that who just left?"

"Never saw her before," Rod said. "Her I.D. badge said 'Mary Mallon.'"

Sofia appeared puzzled. "The name rings a bell, but I don't think we have a Mary Mallon."

"Her iPad didn't have the hospital sticker on it," Rod said. "And she wasn't wearing those thick rubbery-soled shoes that you've got on."

"Rodrigo, how'd you notice all that?" I asked.

"All I've got are my eyes. I see everything in the room. You missed shaving a little spot under your nose."

"Thanks."

"If you grew a beard, Uncle Jake, it would come in gray."

"Thanks for that, too."

"You'd look dope. Like Josh Brolin."

"Mary Mallon!" the nurse said, looking at her iPad.

"Yeah?" I said. "You find her?"

The nursed pursed her lips. "Someone has a bizarre sense of humor. Mary Mallon was Typhoid Mary."

"Who's that?" Rod asked.

"A cook who spread typhoid fever in New York a long time ago," the nurse said.

Dammit! Have I lost all my instincts? A stranger waltzes into the room and says, "Oh, just keep talking." Which is exactly what I do.

Rod's eyes widened. "She came into my room to spread a disease?"

"She wasn't here to give us anything," I said. "She was here to take whatever we gave her."

-24-
The Big Daddy Caddy

Instead of waiting for an elevator, I raced down the stairs to the lobby. Moving as fast as I could, vaulting over the railing at each landing. My dismounts would not earn a perfect ten, but at least I didn't fall and break a hip.

Bursting through the lobby door, I nearly bowled over an octogenarian woman cradling a walker. I mumbled an apology and headed for the front doors that opened onto a driveway. Just as I exited, I saw the phony nurse in the passenger seat of a black Cadillac, the supercharged monster CT5-V Blackwing.

The Big Daddy Caddy. The sports sedan that can do 200 miles per hour, but why would you want to?

All I could make out of the driver was a black baseball cap and aviator sunglasses. The Caddy pulled out of the driveway with a throaty roar. I had a lousy angle and couldn't read the license plate, but saw it was white cardboard, a temporary plate.

I thought about Ms. Sandra Day, Esquire of the law firm of Wickerham and Snoot, national lawyers for the opioid and asbestos manufacturers. They had a reputation for cutthroat ethics. But if they got caught snooping like this, invading attorney-client communications, a judge like Captain Melvia Duckworth, U.S. Army, retired, would ship their asses straight to the stockade.

But what about the Consortium? I'd been certain that was a figment of Judge Erwin Gridley's imagination, not unlike his calling Florida State offsides when he mistook its mascot for a player on the line of scrimmage, the mascot being a horse and rider. Which brought to mind Gridley's last words to me.

"You're a horse's ass, Jake. And you're gonna find out just how real the Consortium is."

-25-
Pro Bono Publico et Patria

I was back in my car when my cell rang. Someone at the Florida Bar calling from its Tallahassee number. I didn't pick up.

I had left the old Caddy parked in the sun, canvas top down. The seats were scorching, and the radio dials were damn near radioactive. Gripping the steering wheel was like lifting a pail of smelted pig iron. The sky was darkening to the west, so I put the top up, and the phone chimed again. Same number. I answered with a quick, "Lassiter here."

"Jake, Larry Blackwell. How you feeling?"

Blackwell was my boss at the Florida Bar headquarters and a decent guy who had never before asked how I was feeling. Now, instead of a friendly greeting, it felt ominous.

"Tip top, Larry."

"Uh-huh."

"You sound disappointed."

"Oh, c'mon, Jake. But listen, we have a problem. That lawsuit you filed, Jesus jumping beans."

That's as profane as Larry Blackwell gets, so this isn't good.

Whoops! Just then, I noticed I was heading west on the Dolphin Expressway, instead of east toward downtown. This was happening a little too frequently.

"Our deal was that I could still handle pro bono work," I said.

"Which doesn't include multi-million-dollar personal injury cases."

"It does if I don't take a fee. My percentage goes to the Miami Project."

"To cure paralysis?"

"That's the one."

I was still heading west. To my left, looking like a giant flying saucer, was the Miami Marlins ballpark on the site of the late, lamented Orange Bowl, where I'd plied my trade. We used to pack that rusty, leaky stadium to the rafters. This twenty-first century multi-billion-dollar palace with its retractable roof sits mostly empty, regardless whether the Marlins are good, mediocre, or lousy. As Yogi Berra said, "If people don't want to come to the ballpark, how are you going to stop them?"

"Well, that's noble, Jake. Gosh darn noble. But the Bar's problem is count two. Abolish high school football?"

"Tackle football, Larry. And it's temporary, assuming the FHSAA can make the game safe."

"Which could take, what? Years? And in the meantime...?"

"Touch football. Flag football."

"We have a lot of good old boys from North Florida on the Board of Governors, some wishing the Confederate flag still flew over the Capitol. They don't even like soccer, much less touch football."

"Change is hard, I get that."

"Jeez, Jake, have you even seen how you're trending in the Twittersphere?"

"I'm not a hundred percent sure what that means."

Ahead of me, over the Everglades, bluish-black thunderheads thickened, and the first distant flashes of lightning crackled behind the clouds. The air already had that pungent aroma of a coming storm. Nitrogen or ozone or whatever.

"If Florida high school football goes down, so does college football," Blackwell said. "Darn near all the Board graduated from Florida, Florida State, or Miami. And you know what football means to those schools. It's their...their..."

"Their lodestar?"

"Yes but even more."

"Their guiding light?"

"That, too."

"Their *raison d'etre*?"

"Exactly. I knew you'd understand why we have to let you go."

"What? Fire me? Can't I just take a leave of absence?"

"Wish I could, buddy. But there are other problems."

I took the LeJeune Road exit, and instead of getting back on the expressway, I headed south into Little Havana. It would be a straight shot through Coral Gables, then across South Dixie Highway into Coconut Grove and my coral rock house on Kumquat. I no longer had an office to go to, so it was either that or Keg South.

"Other problems, Larry?" I said.

"I have a complaint here from a lawyer named..."

I heard papers shuffling.

"Shiner. Cecil Shiner. Jake, he says you stole his crocodile shoes."

"What a liar! I let him keep his crocodile shoes, but I took his Piaget watch. It was to compensate his client."

"I've warned you about this kind of thing. You show no respect for our procedures. And holding so-called hearings in a saloon. It's undignified."

He let me stew for a moment, then said, "What frosts my buns, Jake, is that I went out on a limb for you."

"I'm sorry if I embarrassed you, Larry. Truly."

"Hiring a guy to prosecute lawyers when he'd been disciplined by the Florida Supreme Court. My first and last time for that."

"Larry, I'll take a leave of absence, which I need anyway to handle the Pittman case."

"I'm sorry, Jake, but you're done."

I was quiet a moment, processing what just happened. How would I describe my feelings to Melissa and Dr. Stein?

I'm not angry. Or sad. Just how do I feel about getting sacked?

Then I had one of those epiphanies. If this were a movie, a lame movie, the music would swell, and the sun would emerge from behind those brooding, inky thunderheads.

"Thank you, Larry," I said.

"Is that sarcasm, Jake?"

"No way. You just clarified everything for me. Now, I can do what I should have been doing for years."

"Which is?"

"First, change my personalized license plate."

"'JUSTICE?' with the question mark. I always hated that."

"But I've always thought it was a good question. I'm going to change it to 'PRO BONO.'"

"Pretty sure that one's taken, Jake."

"Then I'll register the old Eldo somewhere else. South Dakota, maybe. Or Guam."

"Okay, I get it. You're going to do more pro bono work."

"Not more. All! *Pro Bono Publico et Patria.* For the good of the public and the country. Every day. All day. From now 'til the end of the line."

And then, just on cue, a bolt of lightning split the sky, and the simultaneous thunderclap shook my ancient Eldorado, two tons of rust and nuts and bolts, rocking me gently through a heavenly downpour on my way home.

THE TWITTERSPHERE

@Fax_Not_Vax
The worst injury Lassiter ever suffered was a sprained vagina.

***

@Bird_Road_Bird_Dog19
I played football from Pop Warner through JUCO and my brain is fine even after suffering five caucasians.

***

@Real_Americane1776
You know what countries don't play football? Russia. Iraq. North Korea.
   @Luv_Me_Some_Miami1 Replied
   Neither does Liechtenstein, Einstein.

***

@Montana_River_Rat38
Florida is not part of the USA. Anyone who took a geology course knows this.

***

@Truckers_For_God89
Football, Faith, and Family. Lassiter, suck my tailpipe!

-26-
The Rolling Stones

Dr. Brian Herlocher, former St. Frances team physician, was expecting my call. I knew this because when I told his receptionist my name, she immediately said, "Dr. Herlocher has advised me to tell you that, upon advice of counsel, he will not be speaking with you."

I pondered this while lying in the hammock strung between two chinaberry trees in my backyard while sipping Don Julio tequila. The rain had stopped, and the air was locker-room humid, the ground emitting earthy smells.

Why would Dr. Herlocher need a lawyer?

He wasn't at the game. He'd quit earlier in the week. No liability, as far as I could see. So maybe it's not his counsel advising him. Maybe those fancy lawyers at Wickerham and Snoot were telling the doctor to keep his mouth shut.

Swinging gently in the hammock, I used my iPad to google the law firm. Its stately website avoided the screaming headlines and overwrought claims so popular with Miami's mouthpieces. I have a divorce lawyer pal whose avatar is an animated boxer who KO's the opposing lawyer – *ka-pow!* – while his client, the wife, grabs her husband's wallet and kicks him out of their cartoon house.

The Wickerham and Snoot site was battleship gray with interior links to its twenty-three offices. The website divided the firm into "practice areas" and brought back memories of my short stint at Harman and Fox with its oppressive regulations, including one requiring committee approval for all artwork in my office. My bronzed jockstrap lost by a 7-0 vote.

I skimmed the W&S practice areas with their exhilarating names: Contract Analytics, Bankruptcy and Restructuring, Payroll Tax, and Erisa Fiduciary Duty. The yawns go on forever, including something called Qui Tam litigation.

In Complex Civil Litigation, I found Ms. Sandra Day. As chief of the division, she had several teams of partners, associates, and paralegals working for her. I chose a junior partner named Milton W. Sanborn, Jr. Judging from his photo, he was an overweight guy around thirty-five. His bio said he had played lacrosse at Johns Hopkins and had been a Rhodes Scholar before hitting the books at Duke Law.

I sipped my tequila, and with a breeze kicking up, caught the honeysuckle aroma of the lavender bougainvillea planted long ago by Granny Lassiter. Fueled by the liquor and with nothing to lose, I called Dr. Herlocher's office again, this time identifying myself as Milton W. Sanborn, Jr., attorney with Wickerham and Snoot. The receptionist put me on hold and said the doctor was with a patient and would call me back. I told her I would wait, and I listened to the Rolling Stones on the doc's Music-on-Hold system.

Ten minutes in, a male peacock, fanning his rainbow train to attract the ladies, waddled across my yard. Key West has its roosters, Coconut Grove its peacocks, and the courthouse its circling vultures...the birds, not the lawyers.

Fourteen minutes and four songs later, Mick Jagger got off the line, and the doctor came on.

"Mr. Sanborn, I've already told Ms. Day everything I know," the doctor said, sounding irritated. "She made it quite clear she would not need my testimony and indeed, did not want it."

"Of course not," I said. "Sandra Day's going to sweep you under the rug like a lousy housekeeper with a shedding dog."

"What? Who is this?"

"Doctor, this is Jake Lassiter. I apologize for the subterfuge."

"This is outrageous! The most unscrupulous conduct I've ever encountered."

"You haven't lived, Doctor."

"I'm not speaking to you, Mr. Lassiter."

"If you hang up, I'll subpoena you for deposition and maybe waste your time and mine. I only have a couple questions."

After a pause, he said, "Was that you outside my office yesterday in a black Cadillac?"

"Was it a Blackwing?"

"I don't know what that is, I drive a Tesla."

"The CT5-V Blackwing. Low slung, a spoiler on the trunk. Did it have a white temporary plate?"

"Yes! Yes, it did. It was outside my office during the day, and I saw it cruise by my house last night. What's going on?"

"I'd guess that Sandra Day and her merry band of marauders are spying on you."

"Why? They can't possibly believe I'm on your side."

"They can't be sure. It may have something to do with the reason you quit."

He didn't chomp at that bait. I watched a crescent moon seem to slide back and forth in the sky, as my hammock swung.

"You should have a security team check all your phones for bugs," I said.

"They're not criminals, Mr. Lassiter. They wouldn't do that."

"They sent a spy into a 17-year-old's hospital room. Rod Pittman's room. And I'm betting Sandra Day never shed a tear for any of the thousands of people killed by her opioid clients."

That gave him something to think about, and it gave me time for another sip of tequila, hints of caramel and citrus on the way down.

"Mr. Lassiter, you said you only had a couple questions."

"Why'd you quit three days before the first game?"

"Personal reasons."

"Care to elaborate?"

"No. That was your second question," he said.

"I probably should have said two questions with actual answers. The day you quit, you left the Tunnel of Manhood and were seen arguing with Coach Coleman."

"We had words, that's true."

"I'd like to hear some of those words."

"No comment, Mr. Lassiter."

"What exactly did you see inside the tent?"

"None of your business. Are we done?"

Sheesh. I've gotten more information from witnesses who took the Fifth, and that includes one guy who said I should read his sworn statement, which he called his "Half-a-David."

"I'm going to take a stab at it," I said. "You previously warned Coach Coleman about the risks, not to mention the illegality, of the Nutcracker Drill, but he ignored you. On this day, you saw something inside the tent that disgusted you. You came out, argued with Coleman, and quit on the spot."

I heard him sigh. "Rod Pittman was never in the tent, so I don't see what this has to do with your case."

I wouldn't disclose my theory about building my case, brick by brick, with a pattern of seemingly unrelated acts of coaching malpractice. I already had opened my big mouth with the phony nurse listening. No way I would make the same blunder twice.

"I need the big picture of Coach Coleman's coaching style," I said, keeping it vague.

"I can't help you."

"Why didn't St. Frances have a replacement for you at the game?"

"You'll have to ask Coach Coleman. He had three days' notice to get another physician on the sideline. All I can figure, it slipped through the cracks. Had I known, I would have been at the game, notwithstanding my resignation."

There was a tremor in his voice. Maybe he felt the sting of guilt.

"Did you see the replay on television, Doctor?"

"Yes."

"So you saw Rod stagger after he made the tackle on the first kickoff?"

Another pause, the only sound the conga drums of a Jamaican steel band practicing in a garage around the corner on Loquat Avenue.

"I don't know if he staggered or slid on the wet field," the doctor said. "On television, you couldn't tell."

"And you saw Coach Coleman speaking to Rod, then sending him back in."

"Yes."

"If you had been on the sideline, would you have put Rod into the concussion protocol and kept him out of the game?"

"How can I answer that?" He sounded frustrated. "I wasn't there. I didn't speak to Rod. And if I'd been there, maybe I wouldn't have seen anything. This is the problem with your legal system, Mr. Lassiter. It tries to answer with certainty questions that are unanswerable."

I couldn't argue with that. It's an imperfect system with flawed rules administered by flawed individuals, including yours truly. But it's the best darned legal system in the world, with the possible exception of trial by combat in sixteenth century Europe.

"I feel terrible about what happened to Rod," the doctor continued. "Worst football injury I've ever seen. And I feel a certain affinity for your lawsuit, the part that goes after tackle football."

"So far, you're the only one."

"I see a lot of concussions and even more sub-concussive impacts. I worry about the boys in the long term. The studies of brain disease prevalent among former players are quite alarming."

"That's my case," I said, "and it's also *my* case."

"But you must know that you're tilting at windmills. Like the banks in the financial crisis, high school football is too big to fail."

In the distance, I heard the whistle of Metrorail, commuters heading to the Gables and points south.

"If that's all then," Dr. Herlocher said, "I have patients waiting."

"Thank you for your time, Doctor."

"I don't think I helped you any."

"No, you did not."

After another moment of silence, he said, "Do you know the coaching staff videotapes every practice and scrimmage?"

"Sure. I sought copies in discovery. Defense counsel said they delete everything at the end of every week. Security against hacking into their computers by opponents."

"I think that's true."

"So why'd you ask me about the videotapes, which of course aren't tapes any more. Everything's digital."

"Exactly. What does that tell you?"

"Nothing. I'm not following you."

"When you were holding on the phone, waiting for me, Mr. Lassiter, was music playing?"

"Yeah, the Rolling Stones, why?" I asked.

"I created the playlist myself. Can you remember the songs you heard?"

"I don't know. I was half listening. *You Can't Always Get What You Want*. Is that the message you're trying to send because, trust me, I learned that a long time ago."

"Not at all. I know where that song falls in the playlist. What else do you remember after that?"

I didn't know why we were playing "Name that Tune," but I went along for the ride. "I didn't hear *Satisfaction*. Or *Sympathy for the Devil*. Wait. I remember *Jumpin' Jack Flash*."

"Getting warmer. What was the very next song?"

"I can't remember, and I'm not sure where you're going with this."

He put some *oomph* into his voice and let loose with a hearty, "Hey! Hey!"

I got it, so I sang back to him, "Get off of my cloud."

"Hey! Hey!" he repeated.

"Get off of my cloud," I sang again.

"Don't hang around 'cause two's a crowd," he finished in a sing-songy voice.

Then he waited to see if I had followed the bread crumbs he had dropped.

"The cloud!" I said. "They erased the files on their computers, but digital copies are in the clouds."

"I can neither confirm nor deny that," Dr. Herlocher said. "Good luck, Mr. Lassiter, and please don't call me again."

-27-
In the Clouds

I needed to know why Dr. Herlocher abruptly quit as team physician. I needed to prove what went on inside the Tunnel of Manhood. I needed to know everything Monty Coleman did and said that would bolster our lawsuit. And I had nothing.

All of which meant I needed the videos of practices and scrimmages. To do that, I needed to find Julian Martinez, a second generation client and a skilled computer techie, which is to say, a criminal hacker. His father, Jorge, had been both a client and my landlord when I rented an office above his restaurant, Havana Banana.

Back in the day, I kept Jorge out of trouble with the Health Department, which occasionally found vacationing cockroaches in steaming platters of *tostones lechoncita*. A few years earlier, he had gone broke with Escargot-to-Go, when he overestimated the market for fast-food snails.

I called Jorge at Havana Banana, and we reminisced about a few food-poisoning lawsuits and one unfortunate incident in which a diner's beard was set ablaze by a flaming Spanish coffee. He gave me Julian's number, telling me his son was now working cybersecurity at one of the cruise lines.

Back when he was a bored student at a private high school, young Julian got in trouble for changing the school's website homepage to read: "Biscayne-Tuttle is a diverse haven for spoiled rich kids, moron jocks, ketamine addicts, prostitutes-in-training, and fucknuggets of every race, creed, color, and gender."

I walked him out of juvie court with a sentence of community service, which he never completed, although computer records clearly indicated he had.

An hour later, with the Caddy's top down, I was cruising over the bridge that links downtown with the Port of Miami. One of the gleaming white ships, a floating hotel with three thousand fun seekers on board, blasted its horn twice, the signal it was about to leave its berth.

I found Julian Martinez in an office the size of a broom closet in the last terminal on the Government Cut side of the port. There was one window overlooking the channel where ships steamed into and out of port. The water view probably was lost on Julian, whose office was jammed with seven monitors, a morass of cables, and several panels of blinking lights and beeping machines.

"Mr. Lassiter, great to see you!" Julian bounded out of his chair to greet me. About twenty-five and already losing his hair, he was one of those skinny guys who nonetheless had a growing paunch.

"Happy to see you doing so well, Julian. I'm damn proud of you."

His job was to keep the cruise line's computers safe from hackers. If he ever became a disgruntled employee, I had no doubt that, with a few keystrokes, he could change a ship's course from Abaco to Antarctica.

"Can you reach into the clouds for me and find a high school's files?" I asked.

He gave me a tutorial. "Cloud computing is just a name. The files aren't in the sky. The data's stored in physical servers around the world. And the answer depends on what system the school uses and what cybersecurity the cloud computing firm uses. Some are like skinny padlocks on a chain-link fence, and others are impregnable."

He told me he doubted that St. Frances encrypted its files, and its firewalls probably couldn't withstand the heat he could bring. "The higher the firewall, the slower the performance. We're not dealing with a nuclear plant where security is life or death. A high school will err on the ease of performance. But the cloud storage facility is a different challenge, a great unknown."

He asked me why I wanted videos of a high school football team, and I gave him a quick summary of the case.

"That coach sounds like a real prick," he said.

"I hope to convince the jury of exactly that."

"You know the football players at Biscayne-Tuttle bullied me."

"I don't know the details," I said, "but I figured that's why you changed their grades to D's and F's."

"And added herpes and chlamydia to their medical records."

I offered to pay him for his time, but he refused. I told him to be careful. "Not to worry, Mr. L. I'll be coming at them from a server in Slovakia. And if I get busted, you know I'd never rat you out."

-28-
Not a Serious Man

"Have the two of you done your homework?" Dr. Rochelle Stein asked.

I said, "Yes," just as Melissa said, "No."

"And off we go again," Dr. Stein said, pleasantly.

No surprise that Mel and I had different points of view. If three people witness a homicide, you get four different stories.

"So, Jake, you say you've completed the love-map questionnaire?" Dr. Stein asked, opening her notebook.

"Oh, you mean *that* homework."

"The true-false exam," she said, "the one that begins: 'I can tell you in detail how I felt when I first met my partner.'"

"True! My feelings were fueled by high-octane testosterone, if you catch my drift, doc."

"I do, indeed. But what homework have you been doing?"

"I've practiced listening to Melissa, hearing every word, noting every inflection, and asking myself how she feels when she says something. Also, I've tried to be more forthcoming about my feelings."

Okay, all basically true, but I cribbed the exact words from a book called "Marriage Like a Rock, not on the Rocks."

"Jake is leaving something out," Melissa said. Then she dropped the dime on me, or maybe it's a quarter these days. She told Dr. Stein about my stupid decision to keep secret bequeathing my brain to Dr. Suzanne Kreisel. As Melissa spoke, if you listened to every word and noted every inflection, you would have thought I'd gifted our summer home in the Hamptons – if we had one – to my paramour, if I had one.

"I've apologized for that," I said. "I've learned my lesson, Doctor."

That's a line I tell my clients to use when they plead guilty. "I've learned my lesson, Your Honor."

"Relationships are built on trust, and I violated that."

Yes indeed, repeating Melissa's admonition to me.

I wasn't through yet. *"Mea culpa,"* I said with head bowed. *"Mea culpa. Mea maxima culpa."*

I cribbed that from the Holy Mass, and I'm not even Catholic.

"Melissa?" Dr. Stein said.

"I've accepted Jake's apology and his promise to be more open in every phase of our relationship. He's learning. Slowly but more or less steadily."

"Let's move on then," Dr. Stein said.

The shrink spent a few minutes giving advice about nurturing our fondness and admiration for each other. And another few minutes explaining how to turn toward each other, rather than away. Granny Lassiter would have said the advice was "just good old-fashioned common sense." Sometimes, though, it helps to hear things you intuitively know but have fallen out of practice doing. Football coaches know this.

"Wrap up the runner, Lassiter! Don't play patty-cake with him!"

"What are you thinking right now, Melissa?" Dr. Stein asked.

"That I regret not meeting Jake earlier. Much earlier. We could have raised a family together."

Dr. Stein looked toward me and hoisted those expressive eyebrows, her way of asking, *"How about it, Buster?"*

"I agree, in theory," I said.

"What does that mean?" Dr. Stein glanced at the damn horse, trigger finger ready, as she waited for my answer.

"I'm not sure Melissa would have liked me back in the day."

"Weren't you just a younger version of the man sitting here?" Dr. Stein asked.

"I was immature and cocky and full of myself. Not a serious man."

Melissa cocked her head, a sign she was pondering a puzzling thought. "I would have seen your potential."

I can still hear Granny saying: "That boy's gonna grow old having potential."

"Don't think so, Mel. I wasn't looking for a lifetime relationship. More like a relationship until checkout time. Women were great to have around but tossed aside like hotel towels. If someone said 'soul mate,' I heard 'cellmate.' It's embarrassing to look back now, but I was living the Robert Earl Keen song, *The Road Goes on Forever, and the Party Never Ends.*"

"You were a man in your twenties in a different era," Dr. Stein said. "I can't be judgmental about that. And I applaud your honesty and introspection."

Melissa said, "I can't speak to who Jake was in those days. But he's obviously evolved, and that's the man I love."

Ganging up on me again...but this time on my side!

I reached over and gave Melissa's arm a little squeeze, and she put a hand on mine.

"In the love-map questionnaire," Melissa continued, "one of the true-false statements is: 'I know my partner's hopes and aspirations.' Of course, that's true in both our cases."

"It's an important aspect of love," Dr. Stein said.

"It doesn't go far enough," Melissa said. "It should also say that each person honors the other's hopes and aspirations."

"I do, Mel." I sounded defensive, but the horse kept quiet.

"I'm not talking about you." She turned to the shrink. "It's very important to Jake to leave a legacy. And I know how much he loves his godson who suffered such a catastrophic injury. But at first, I tried to talk Jake out of taking the case because of the stress involved. And I made it sound as if I didn't think he was competent to handle it. I didn't show respect for Jake's abilities, his hopes, or his aspirations. I was out of line."

"No way. I need your input, Mel," I said, truthfully, though I rather liked her *modicum culpa*. "I respect your knowledge and your opinions. Please don't censor yourself."

Dr. Stein closed her notebook and smiled. "We're making progress. Next time, we'll talk about your emotional bank accounts."

I felt happy about that, like a guy with a million bucks in his emotional bank account.

-29-
Bad Men in the Night

I am a light sleeper. This makes me vulnerable to the neighborhood peacocks who *screech* during mating season. The Metrorail horn from the other side of Dixie Highway can be heard inside my house when the windows are open and the wind is right. And there's that amateur Jamaican steel band around the corner on Loquat with its five different sets of drums.

But I am usually a deep sleeper after sex. Tonight, in her post-coital bliss, Melissa Gold was curled up against me, sighing in her sleep.

While I was unaccountably awake.

The windows were open, the paddle fan *whompety-whomping* because that's the way I was raised by Granny.

"Air conditioning will brittle your bones!"

I listened to the sounds of the night as I tried, vainly, to drift off. Insects made their crickety sounds, and a mockingbird, somewhere in the mango tree, chattered happily.

The digital clock on the nightstand blinked to an even 2:30 a.m when I heard the first *crunch* outside the bedroom window. It could have been a big-ass peacock rooting for worms. I squeezed my eyes shut, as if that would sharpen my hearing. Silence. The mockingbird had stopped singing.

Crunch. Crunch.

The foundation of the house is surrounded by a three-foot-wide path of small river stones. Not a path for walking, just for keeping Spanish bayonet and other dagger-sharp plants away from the house. But now, someone was out there.

I slipped out of bed, pulled on a pair of boxers, and picked up my baseball bat from the corner of the room. It's a thirty-four-inch beauty made of Canadian maple, the Barry Bonds model. I don't diss the guy for using steroids. If I could have gotten away with 'roids in the NFL, I can't swear I would have been clean.

Barefoot and silent, I padded out the kitchen door onto the back porch. The footsteps had been coming from around the corner of the house, maybe 30 feet from where I stood. I gripped the bat and took a couple practice swings, as if I were in the on-deck circle. The bat felt light and whippy in my big mitts.

I took three steps from the porch into the yard, then scooted close to the house, my bare feet silent on the tiny stones. Turning the corner, bat cocked, I paused to let my eyes adjust to the glare of a streetlight on Kumquat. I thought I saw a shape next to the window of my study, but it could have been a shadow.

Until it moved.

Outlined by the streetlight, it was the silhouette of a good-size man, his back toward me, shoulder against the coral rock exterior, face pressed to a darkened window.

I suppose I could have been sporting about it. I could have said, "Excuse me, sir, may I help you?" But I just crept up behind him, close enough to see he wore black jeans, a black windbreaker, and a black ski mask. That seemed to rule out a late night visit by the FP&L meter reader.

I wiggled the bat above my right shoulder, heard my Little League coach say, "Load, stride, swing." I didn't have the angle I wanted, so I yelled, "Hey!" and as he turned, he leapt backward with surprising grace. I uncorked a swing with a powerful hip explosion. I'd aimed at his knees, but with his leap, the barrel of the bat bashed the guy's right ankle with a detonation of splintering bone that sounded like a bowling ball scattering pins.

The guy toppled sideways, screaming. I stood over him, waving the bat. "Take off your mask, asshole!" I shouted.

His screams became high-pitched shrieks and he rocked back and forth on the ground. Inside the house, the bedroom light blinked on. I reached down to pull off the ski mask, and as I did, a bolt of lightning crackled at the base of my skull.

I saw a dazzling bright light.

Then a kaleidoscope of colors as I toppled to the ground.

I tried to get to my feet but the Earth had tilted, and I went down again. I was vaguely aware of a second figure, hoisting up the guy I'd ankled, but then it all went dark, and no one made a sound, not a peacock or mockingbird, or bad men in the night.

-30-
Sugar Ray

Much like Greenland, my freezer was low on ice, so Melissa held a bottle of vodka to the back of my head. It was Finlandia, my anti-Putin brand, which she had liberated from the back of the ice-deprived freezer.

Sitting in the kitchen, I tried to keep my head immobile. Moving any direction caused several boulders inside my skull to careen into each other. Melissa seemed alarmed, and I realized that looking through a microscope at dead tissue all day was not quite the same as dealing with a living, breathing 240-pound mass of protoplasm. As I used to say to Doc Riggs, the former coroner, when he gave me medical advice, "Charlie, you never had a patient who lived."

I took four Tylenol, opened the Finlandia, found a bottle of Bloody Mary mix, and had breakfast. Melissa used her scolding tone as she warned me about the possibility of unseen brain damage and wanted to scan this, probe that, and test everything else.

No dice. I have work to do.

I also didn't want to waste half the morning with cops finding nothing and doing less. I waited until after sunrise and called two of my neighbors who have security cameras, which I do not. Neither camera focused on my property, but each picked up the same vehicle driving from the Douglas Road intersection down Kumquat toward my house. The vehicle slowly came down the street at 2:27 a.m. and then sped back at 3:02 a.m.

Good. No time to do whatever mischief they had planned.

Oh, the vehicle? A 2022 Cadillac CT5-V Blackwing, dark as death.

My next call was going to be to Raymond Pincher, the duly elected State Attorney of Miami-Dade County. But Julian Martinez rang me first. I hoped he had several dozen hours of St. Frances football practice videos for me.

"Nothing yet, Mr. L." He sounded frustrated. "I won't bore you with details, but they're deploying hybrid cloud and multi-cloud deployments. No exfiltration of data, no insecure API's. No way to phish my way in. Gonna have to wait for the school to leave a door open on its way out."

"I think I got about half of that."

"It's gonna take a while."

"That's the part I got. But you'll keep at it, Julian?"

"10-4 Roger," he said, sounding like a 1990s truck driver with a CB radio.

Then I called Pincher, the county's chief prosecutor. Friends call him "Sugar Ray" because he was a Golden Gloves boxer in his youth. We've sparred both in the ring and in court. His best punch in both venues was below the belt, and mine was a thumb to one of his eyes. We've been competitors and friends for more than twenty years.

"The Jakester!" Pincher greeted me. "The guy who took the 'shy' out of shyster and put the 'fog' into pettifogger."

"That's getting old, Sugar Ray. Why do you sound out of breath?"

"Skipping rope. Say, I don't suppose your fiancée will let you go a few rounds with me in the gym?"

"Melissa won't let me slap my forehead when I get the occasional good idea."

Sugar Ray said, "I know why you're calling, Jake, and I appreciate it."

"What?"

"You're offering to resign from my Steering Committee."

"Why would I?"

"Because it's hard enough for a Black man to run for governor without one of his prime supporters being radioactive."

"Aw shit, it's not that bad, Sugar Ray."

"Do you listen to sports talk radio?"

"Let me guess. I'm a brain-dead commie sissy."

"Last night, a caller said you were trying to abolish football to get even with Coach Shula for not playing you more."

"Coach is dead, and I'm grateful to him for not subjecting me to more concussions."

Through the line, I heard the skip-rope kissing the floor. "So Jakester, que pasa?" he asked.

I told him about my two visitors and the Blackwing that's been trailing me like a killer shark after a tasty seal.

"And you figure that deep-carpet New York law firm plays dirty?" he asked, breathing hard.

"How do you think they bought those deep carpets? Have you ever heard of something called the Consortium that's aligned with the NFL?"

Pincher said he hadn't, so I related Erwin Gridley's story. A pit full of vipers, I told Pincher, were slithering around the country fixing lawsuits. They work for the NFL's biggest advertisers and secretly pay off plaintiffs in some cases. In others, they bludgeon the opposition with fancy lawyers and high-priced experts, and if that doesn't work, maybe bribe judges and jurors, never leaving any trail.

"C'mon, Jake. All those major companies in cahoots 'cause of your lawsuit? You sound like a conspiracy nutjob."

"I'm not saying it's true. Just that Judge Gridley seemed so certain about it. Put yourself in my position. What would you do?"

"Hire private security. One team at your house, another to follow you around. Maybe a third for Melissa."

"It's a bad look," I said.

"I can get City of Miami to increase patrols on your street, knock on your door once a night, make sure the henchmen from Budweiser and General Motors haven't hung you from your paddle fan."

I ignored the sarcasm and thanked him. The skipping-rope sound ceased, and Pincher said, "I know a lot of people in a lot of places. I'll make some calls, and I'll keep my ears open. And because I know you sometimes lead with your chin, keep your guard up, buddy."

PART THREE

"In the Halls of Justice, the only justice is in the halls."
   – Lenny Bruce

"Honest people don't need to put their hand on a Bible to tell the truth, and dishonest people could swear on their mothers' lives and still lie."
   – Jake Lassiter

-31-
Blitzing the A-Gap

Several weeks went by without my being assaulted, kidnapped, or disbarred, and the Pittman case proceeded, in fits and starts, through discovery. I made multiple requests for documents, and the defense lawyers obfuscated, evaded, and delayed.

Judge Melvia Duckworth had been serious about not wanting to referee discovery disputes. When I complained about the defense being uncooperative, she ordered that all the lawyers get together and hammer it out. Or, as she put it, "Call a cease fire, crawl out of your foxholes, share your rations, and find some common ground."

After our meeting, we were to report to the judge for a status conference. Or, as she said, "I don't expect an armistice, but I don't want to hear any sniper fire in my courtroom either."

All of that would come later today. Now, I was walking into the Southeast Spinal Cord Rehabilitation Center on my way to visit Rodrigo. Released earlier than expected from the hospital, this would be his home for several months, at least.

My godson continued to make swift progress, surprising his doctors and delighting his parents and me. He was getting physical therapy and electric stimulation treatment, and he could sit upright in a wheelchair. He had recovered more sensations in his limbs and was attacking rehab with the same grit his father had shown on the football field.

"The doctors can't make up their minds," Tank told me. "One said he was cautiously optimistic that Rod fell into the minority of people with the same injury who will walk again. Another said he didn't want to give us false hope."

I was walking down the corridor to Rod's room, my mind drifting to the case, when someone called out, "Mr. Lassiter?"

I turned and saw a teenage girl with caramel skin and dark hair that fell to her shoulders.

"Kiara, right?" I recognized Rod's girlfriend from his last birthday party. Kiara Parsons was an honor student and cheerleader who spent her spare time helping build houses for Habitat for Humanity. She had told me that Government was her favorite subject, and she hoped to have a career in the State Department.

"I just came from Rod's room," she said, her large, luminous eyes brimming with tears that had not yet started flowing.

"His Dad says there's reason for optimism," I said, trying to buck up her spirits.

She nodded and bit her lip, "I know, but it's so hard. Rod stays strong, and I...I just break down."

"That's okay. You're here for him, and he knows that."

"He told me to move on without him, but we've been in a ship since junior high."

"Ship" meaning "relationship," not the Queen Mary.

"No way will I abandon him now," she continued.

"I'm sure that's what he really wants, Kiara. Bless you for that."

She dabbed her eyes with a tissue and said, "A detective called me. Mr. Barrios. He said you asked him to. But I didn't know if I should talk to him."

"A retired detective who's helping with the investigation. I should have called you first."

"Anything I can do, I will."

"Barrios can't get anyone at the school to talk. I expected as much from the coaches and trainers, but the kids, too. Everyone is zipped up tight."

"You have to understand St. Frances," Kiara said. "There are cliques. The Anglos, the Blacks, and the Hispanics. Then there's Rod and me. We both have Black fathers and Hispanic mothers, so we don't really fit into a group."

"I get that, but isn't the football team a mixed stew of all the tribes?"

"Yeah, except the team is a cult of bros," she said, echoing what Tank Pittman told me the night of the game. "And Rod never went out for the team until this year. He was a track star, and the football players always threw shade at the track team. Making fun of their shorts, their legs, all kinds of sheisty stuff. You know how stupid boys can be."

Do I ever? I'm the guy who won 20 bucks betting I could throw a Coke machine over the third-floor railing of an Islamorada motel. Fortunately, juvenile arrests don't count.

"Anyway, Rod never got tight with his teammates. This was his first game, and now they're blaming him for ruining their season."

"What?"

"Coach Coleman spread the word that Rod was to blame for the injury. He wasn't coachable. His form was bad. And because he screwed up, the school made them eliminate full-contact scrimmages. Then they lost three of the next four games, and it's all Rod's fault."

"Blame the victim," I said. "Oldest trick in the book."

Monty Coleman, I want to get you under oath. Or in a back alley.

"Once you filed the lawsuit," Kiara said, "no one on the team visited Rod. Not the players or the coaches. That's so totally trash."

"The defense lawyers almost certainly told them to stay away."

"I get that, but is it the right thing to do?" she asked, tears dripping now. "The moral thing?"

I waited for her to dab her eyes again. Then I said, "I think Rod has himself quite a girlfriend."

Those moist eyes looked at me, waiting.

"A girl who values morality over expediency. Someone who isn't afraid to buck the crowd. Kiara, your possibilities are endless, your future as bright as the stars."

She smiled through the tears and said, "Thank you, Mr. Lassiter. You're a total zaddy."

"Thank you," I said, totally clueless.

***

I gave Tank and Lily a break by handling wheelchair duty. When I entered Rod's room, he was already in the chair with earbuds in place, eyes closed, nodding his head in time to music.

"Yo, Rodrigo, ready for a ride?"

He wriggled his ears, and I took it as a sign to remove the earbuds.

"September Song," he said. "Django Reinhardt."

"Gypsy jazz. I remember."

He lifted his right hand from the armrest and wiggled his fingers, as if playing an air guitar. The fingers moved slowly, but still, his progress was amazing.

"Wow! That's terrific, kiddo!"

This had to be the purest form of pleasure, I thought, a visceral feeling of warmth and gratitude for a blessing bestowed on someone else. I wheeled Rod down the corridor, and we passed the open door of a rehab gym.

"See that contraption." Rod pointed with a bent arm to a harness attached to the ceiling and dangling over a treadmill. "I'm working my ass off to get into that as soon as I can. I'm gonna walk, Uncle Jake."

"Damn right you are," I said. "Just keep doing what you're doing."

We exited a door at the end of the corridor onto a balcony decorated with potted palms. A cooling breeze came from the ocean, and the sun was thankfully shielded by a light cloud cover. Rod sucked in the fresh air and smiled.

After a moment, we both heard a *pop-pop-pop*, the unmistakable sound of a basketball pounding pavement. Several floors below, two hospital workers were playing one-on-one on a makeshift court in the parking lot adjacent to the loading dock. I sensed Rod's mood deflate as he saw the men.

Oh, damn, what he must feel seeing them running and jumping. Hearing their shouts and taunts and laughs.

I turned the wheelchair a different direction and did my best to brighten his spirits. "Did I ever tell you about the time in Buffalo I was blitzing the A-Gap and sideswiped your Dad's big butt?"

Rod chuckled. "I've seen the photo. You were both on the ground, eating grass, and the Bills' quarterback hopped over you."

"The *Herald's* caption read, 'Pittman and Lassiter take a nap during Dolphins' blowout loss.'"

"That's so fire!" Rod said, which I interpreted to mean "cool," strange as that seems.

Once back inside, pushing the wheelchair down the corridor, I told Rod about running into Kiara. "She's a keeper, kiddo."

"I don't want to ruin her life," he said, sadness draped over every word.

"Not your call, Rodrigo."

"What I mean is, I don't want to be her charity case."

"Not the way she sees it."

He didn't respond, and I said, "Rodrigo, sometimes, I feel guilty because I think I'm a burden to my fiancée."

"Dr. Gold. She's lit."

"In my day, we would have said, 'She's a peach,' but you're right. I started pulling back from Melissa because I didn't want my medical condition to become the primary focus of her life. Do you get that?"

He arched his neck to look up at me. "Better than anyone else could."

"But I love Melissa, and she loves me, so as long as she's good with the long and twisty road, so am I. What I'm saying is, don't push Kiara away. Okay?"

He nodded. "Okay for now, Uncle Jake."

On the loudspeaker, they were calling a Dr. Kornspan to meet a van at the rear ramp. We passed the open rehab gym again. This time, two therapists were hoisting a middle-aged woman into the contraption that hung over the treadmill.

"Mrs. Truby," Rod said. "Car accident. Her husband was killed. Guy who hit them was going the wrong way on I-95."

Another reminder, in case we need it, of the fragility of life and the randomness of death.

When we got to Rod's room, I said, "Hey Rodrigo, what's a zaddy?"

He laughed. "It's an old dude who's not bad looking."

Oh, good. I guess.

"Dad's bringing in pizza," Rod said. "Can you stay, Uncle Jake?"

"I'd like to, but I've got to get to court."

"On my case?"

"Only one I've got."

"What's going to happen?"

"I'm gonna blitz the A-gap, Rod, but I'm sure as hell not taking a nap."

-32-
Sunny Day

This would be my first face-to-face with Ms. Sandra Day, though we'd spoken many times on the phone. It had always been brief, cordial, and unproductive. Not unlike our government officials meeting with Chinese officials over their cyber thefts.

"We had a frank discussion of the issues."

The New York firm of Wickerham and Snoot had set up its war room on the top floor of a downtown skyscraper, the mahogany-rich home of a Miami insurance defense firm. Officially, the local lawyers and the Manhattan big shots were co-counsel for Coach Coleman, St. Frances Academy, and the FHSAA. But it was clear to me that Sandra Day's clan of carpetbaggers prepared all the pleadings, motions, and memoranda of law.

How do I know?

The final product – the research, the reasoning, and the writing – was too polished for the local firm of Shamforoff, Suarez and Ruiz.

When I exited the elevator on the 48th floor, I had a lovely view of Biscayne Bay that was nearly obscured by two large men in front of the windows. They were security guards in gray slacks, blue blazers and earpieces, and one ran a metal detector over me. My cell phone beeped, and the guard asked me to hand it over.

"I have attorney-client communications on the cell," I explained politely.

"We won't disturb the phone," he said, "and I'm sure it's password protected."

"It is," I said, "and I'm sure your bosses could crack it like a crossword puzzle."

"We're sorry, sir," the second guard said, "but we need to ensure that visitors don't record conversations or take photos."

"Tell you what. I promise to follow the rules. But if you don't trust me and think you can take my phone away without suffering, at the very least, a fracture to a weight-bearing bone, come and get it."

They exchanged glances. One guard stepped back, turned, and spoke into his wrist, just like they do in the movies. After a few moments, a woman of about fifty, dressed for success in a double-breasted black tunic with red buttons and a matching skirt, headed for us with long strides. On the breast pocket of the tunic were two interlocking red "C's," which even I knew meant "Chanel." She was tall and fit with a strong jawline and expensively coiffed silver hair.

"At last we meet, Mr. Lassiter," she said, extending a hand, and waving the security goons away. "I'm Sandra Day."

"Call me Jake," I said, and we shook hands.

"I prefer more formality."

"Your call, Ms. Day."

"Shall we visit the conference room?" she asked pleasantly, as if I'd stopped by for tea and scones. We headed down the corridor, my phone still in my pocket.

"It just occurred to me," I said. "Sandra Day. Like Sandra Day O'Connor."

"No relation to the justice. My friends call me Sunny."

"Sunny Day."

"Exactly."

"Great name for a stripper," I said, without thinking, much like the time I jumped off Guffy Gorge 50 feet above the water.

"I beg your pardon."

"Or for a lawyer," I said, grasping for a life preserver. "Sunny Day. Great name for anybody. Sunny Day. Sunny Day. Sunny Day."

Her glare could have peeled paint. "Is this what you do, Mr. Lassiter?"

"Babble? Make a fool of myself? Sure thing."

"Use your size and your uber masculinity to intimidate women?"

"Aw, don't go there, Sunny. Sandra. Ms. Day. I'm pretty damn evolved."

"Really?"

"I've done meditation. Eaten kale. Attended Lilith Fair."

She showed me a patient smile. "Then I must assume you're under the influence of a good and patient woman."

"Under the influence? Hell, I'm plastered, dead drunk, stewed to the gills. Where my fiancée is concerned, I out-kicked my coverage."

We stopped in the open doorway of the conference room. Sandra Day said, "My people have done a deep dive on you, Mr. Lassiter, and it's most illuminating."

"Yeah?"

"You have a sketchy knowledge of the law. You have no partners, associates, paralegals, or assistants. No staff whatsoever, though you apparently have a retired homicide detective poking around at St. Frances. Your trial preparation is hit or miss, and you try cases by the seat of your pants."

"Have briefcase, will travel," I said. "Give me a blank yellow pad, and I'm ready to pick a jury."

"You frequently change strategy in the middle of trials."

"Like a savvy quarterback, I call audibles. You ought to try it."

"You've been held in contempt numerous times."

"As my pal Steve Solomon says, 'A lawyer who's afraid of jail is like a surgeon who's afraid of blood.'"

"Despite everything, you have an impressive record of victories in criminal court."

"Oh, don't sound so surprised."

"Most of your former clients speak highly of you, even those behind bars. As a younger man, you had a libertine lifestyle, but much like your incarcerated clients, your former lovers rarely speak ill of you."

"Perhaps because some fit into both categories," I suggested.

"Many of your trials have been televised. My people have watched and catalogued the videos, cross-referencing every objection you made, every exchange with witnesses, as well as your openings and closings. They also have read the transcripts of every case you've taken to trial."

"Your people must have a high threshold for boredom."

"They're *la crème de la crème*."

"I get that. My criminal clients are *la crème de la* crumbs."

"My people include psychologists, psychiatrists, and human factors experts. They look for tells just like the best poker players. Usually, they know within the first three questions just where a lawyer is headed on cross-examination. They've created algorithms for their predictions. But they say you're too unpredictable and that you're either a genius or an idiot."

"My people haven't done a deep dive on you," I said, "but my first impression is that you've got more than your fair share of *cojones.*"

"I'm choosing to take that as a compliment. Not every woman would."

We entered a corner conference room with windows looking east over the bay and south toward Coconut Grove. The table of dark wood was as long as a bocce court, and about a dozen folks who appeared to be lawyers occupied all but two of the leather and chrome chairs.

Behind the table, sitting in chairs against the wall were another dozen who were likely paralegals or assistants or just Sandra Day's "people."

She took the executive chair at the head of the table, and I sat next to her. I took a moment to inventory the roster. They were mostly well-scrubbed, well-groomed children – late twenties to late thirties – in conservative business attire. Many had the serious look of former federal law clerks who opted out of public service for the merciless grind and big bucks of private practice. If any of them had seen a courtroom, it would have been to carry Sandra Day's briefcase.

The younger ones were junior associates, bright-eyed and eager high achievers, over-confident in their legal abilities but proficient at brief writing and gold medalists at sucking up to partners in hopes of climbing the ladder to their penthouse world.

Think of the kids in junior high who did additional homework for extra credit and ran for student council.

The older ones were senior associates, most of whom would never become partners and would either be fired, kept on as contract workers, or farmed out to corporate clients for mind-numbing, in-house counsel jobs.

Think of palace eunuchs during the Ming dynasty.

"Mr. Lassiter, please let us know your grievances," Sandra Day said, "and my discovery team will see if we can meet your needs and avoid a contested hearing in front of the judge."

"I asked you to produce Rodrigo's helmet, and you didn't give it to me. It's a crucial piece of evidence."

At the far end of the table, roughly in Boca Raton, a young male lawyer piped up. "The equipment staff at the school inform us that, in the post-game chaos, the helmet went missing."

"Let me into the school, and I'll look for it."

Sandra Day raised a hand to keep junior from replying. "That's not how it's done, Mr. Lassiter. What else?"

"I asked for a copy of Coach Coleman's employment contract. Never got it."

"Relevance?" she asked.

"This is discovery. I'm not required to establish relevance. But I'll tell you anyway. I want to know what bonuses Coleman earns for winning the conference title or state playoff games."

"That's confidential. We'll brief the issue." Sandra Day nodded toward one of the older children at the table, a fellow with a reedy mustache and heavy black eyeglasses. "Myron?"

"There's a recent North Dakota case that goes our way," Myron said.

"While you're in Fargo, Myron," I said, "check out Canadian cases. Or just Canadian Club."

Sandra Day addressed the room. "People, pay close attention to Mr. Lassiter and the Everyman persona he cultivates."

"I don't cultivate anything other than mangoes on a backyard tree."

"Despite appearing to possess the legal abilities of a shopping-center shyster, a *Better Call Saul,* if you will," she said, "he is not the fool he may seem to be."

"I choose to take that as a compliment," I said. "Not every man would."

"W&S lawyers are most comfortable on a level playing field. One major law firm versus another," she continued, addressing her troops. "As Judge Duckworth might put it, heavy artillery followed by frontal assaults of infantry. But Mr. Lassiter's attacks may come from any direction with no warning or apparent preparation. He's a guerilla fighter."

"Rambo of the courtroom," I said. "And thanks for making me part of your training exercise."

"Never underestimate your opponent." She nodded to a young woman with a studious look and a gentle demeanor. The woman flicked what looked like a TV remote and a screen descended from the ceiling. Up popped a high school yearbook photo. *Mine! Eighteen years old with mile-wide shoulders, an unruly mess of sun-bleached hair, and a shit-eating grin. My nose not yet broken, I was a decent-looking dude with hell-raising in my eyes.*

"Naomi, would you please read the caption?"

"'Jacob (Jolting Jake) Lassiter. Football, four years. Captain of the Detention Squad. Voted most likely to do time,'" she recited.

A joke! Though I did get into a few scrapes and had a juvie record.

"Mr. Lassiter did not attend an Ivy League law school," Sandra Day said.

"University of Miami, night division," I said, proudly. "Top half of the bottom third of my class."

"What does this tell us about him?" she asked the group of eager beavers.

"Virtually anyone can become a lawyer," ventured the young woman with the remote.

"Mr. Lassiter's background is out of our frame of reference, and that makes him dangerous," said a young man in rimless glasses.

"Precisely, Gerald." Sandra Day turned to me. "Mr. Lassiter, would you be offended if I called you a throwback?"

"Not at all," I said. "I have old friends, old habits, and old values. You could even call me 'old school.'"

"Very well, then," Day said. "Shall we move on?"

I scanned the room again, and for the first time noticed a man in the far corner. Unlike the other male associates, all of whom were in suits and ties, he wore jeans, a brown suede jacket, and a western patterned shirt with a bolo string tie. He was also older, around 50, with a military salt-and-pepper brush cut and the telltale thick neck of a guy who pumps iron.

"Who's that joker?" I asked. "The one dressed like a color-blind cowboy on casual Friday."

She followed my gaze and said, "An observer."

"What's he doing here?"

"Observing."

"Is he with the Consortium?" I asked.

"What consortium?"

I tried to read her look but she was poker-faced. I glanced up, and the man was gone.

-33-
Law is a Contact Sport

My discovery conference with Sandra Day and her pack of jackals continued much as it had begun. I complained about their recalcitrance, and they made every excuse in the book and quite a few that had never been written down.

"I want a list of every injury suffered in pre-season practice by date and name of player," I said.

Myron of the black eyeglasses and mustache didn't even wait for his cue. "Confidential under federal law, specifically HIPAA."

"Anything else?" Sandra Day asked.

"My process server has been unable to serve a subpoena on Dr. Herlocher," I said. "Either tell me where you've stashed him or produce him for deposition."

After our one phone call, I'd been unable to locate the former team physician and suspected one dirty trick or another.

One of the senior associates, a young woman with a somber expression, said, "Dr. Herlocher has taken a sabbatical from his private practice and is treating indigenous people in the mountains of Chile. He's fulfilling a lifelong dream to do eleemosynary work."

"Commendable," I said, "unless it's total bullshit. My money's on a steer with diarrhea."

"We would share Dr. Herlocher's new address with you," Day said, "but he didn't give it to us."

If Day's plan was to aggravate me, it was working. Anger built inside me, a fireball in my gut. Then I realized something. No migraine. No tinnitus. No fuzzy thoughts. Not only that, those scary atrial fibrillations had taken a vacation. My heart wasn't beating out the wrong tune.

Maybe my brilliant fiancée was onto something when she said that the stress of a complicated task wasn't necessarily harmful. To the contrary, she figured there might be a jolt of beneficial hormones.

"Anything else, Mr. Lassiter?" Day asked.

"I want to take photos of the so-called 'Tunnel of Manhood,' but it's no longer on the practice field. Please produce it."

"The tent was donated to the Red Cross for use in disaster areas," Sandra Day said. "We believe it's in Puerto Rico now."

"Eso es maravilloso," I said. "Next item. All videos of practices, scrimmages, and team meetings prior to the game in which Rodrigo was injured. I've been requesting this since the lawsuit was filed."

Not to mention using a hacker to try and swipe them. Only today I received a text from Julian Martinez: "No news from Slovakia. But the bird is in the air." Meaning nothing yet.

"We've been through this," Sandra Day said, sounding put out. She turned to a young male lawyer halfway down the long table. "Winston, anything new to report?"

Winston stretched his neck and cleared his throat. He had wispy blond hair and WASPy good looks, and in an earlier era would have worn a three-piece suit with a pocket watch attached by a slender gold chain to his Phi Beta Kappa key. "The school's staff informs us that all video files are routinely deleted to prevent hacking by opponents," he said in a New England accent.

I pointed a finger at him. "The assistant coaches download all the videos onto iPads supplied by the school. Those can't all be erased."

"To the best of our knowledge, everything has been deleted," Winston said, a note of triumph in his voice.

"As my Granny would say, Winston, you ought not to fart near the gas range."

Winston's eyes went wide and he froze, open-mouthed, as if he'd just lost a point on the squash court thanks to a trick shot.

Sandra Day said, "Take it up with the judge, Mr. Lassiter, but do not dare berate my staff."

"Why? Will they faint?"

"There are rules, Mr. Lassiter."

"Oh, buckle your chin strap. Law is a contact sport."

"Need I remind you of paragraph five of the Preamble to the Ethical Rules?"

"Please do. I stopped reading at paragraph four."

A faint red blush crept up Sandra Day's neck. "I'll refresh your recollection. And I quote: 'A lawyer should demonstrate respect for the legal system and for those who serve it, including other lawyers.' End quote."

"Anything in those rules about lawyers who lie through their teeth?"

"That's quite enough, Mr. Lassiter. We're done here. You can take up these issues with Judge Duckworth."

"That's what she's there for. But before we go, one question. Do you know anyone who drives a shiny new Blackwing?"

"I have no idea what that is."

"A high-performance Cadillac."

"A Cadillac?" She made a scoffing sound. "My grandfather drove Cadillacs because his golf clubs fit in the trunk, but I don't know anyone these days."

"Sure you do," I said.

Looking up from his iPad, Myron peered through his eyeglasses and said, "Mr. Lassiter drives a 1984 Cadillac Biarritz Eldorado convertible with red velour upholstery that he once likened in an interview to the parlor of a New Orleans brothel. The car has a personalized license plate reading 'JUSTICE' followed by a question mark."

"Mr. Lassiter mistakes his irreverence for genuine wit," Day said.

"What can I tell you?" I said. "'SHYSTER' was taken."

"The Eldorado was previously owned by a marijuana dealer in Key West," Myron said. "Mr. Lassiter took the car as a fee after securing an acquittal on a possession with intent to distribute charge."

"Well done," I said. "Only thing you omitted, it took a year to get the smell of weed out of the trunk."

-34-

Blazing a Trail

"At ease, everyone," Judge Melvia Duckworth said, rather than, "Please take your seats."

All those years as a military judge had left their mark. A petite Black woman in her late fifties, she wore her judicial robes with a pink filigreed jabot at her neck. Her graying hair was styled in a mini-Afro, and stylish eyeglasses with orange frames were propped on her forehead. She had been one of the better judges in the criminal division before transferring to the civil division downtown.

We were in a sixth-floor courtroom of the ancient county courthouse. Dark wood beams rose from the walls and met at the center of the ceiling, resembling a giant rib cage and making me think I was in the belly of a whale. Sandra Day's infantry filled half of the gallery behind her. My half was empty. Fine. Outgunned but never outfought.

Peering down at me from the bench, the judge said, "I was hoping to simply have a status conference, but it seems we have discovery disputes. Mr. Lassiter, what's your beef?"

I ran through all my discovery requests and the stone wall the defense had erected, blocking every path. Sandra Day semi-apologized in the legal profession's approach to "sorry, not sorry," saying there was nothing she could do.

"According to my clients, nearly everything Mr. Lassiter seeks simply doesn't exist," she said. "My hands are tied."

"I'm sympathetic, Mr. Lassiter," the judge said, "but this is not uncommon in the civil practice. Defense lawyers are dependent on cooperation of their clients to comply with discovery."

"To be blunt, Your Honor, either counsel or her clients are not being forthcoming."

That's as close as I dare get to calling Sandra Day as crooked as a corkscrew.

"We'll be happy to supplement our written responses with affidavits attesting to our representations," Sandra Day said, in equally roundabout lawyer talk.

The judge turned to me. "Nothing more I can do, Mr. Lassiter. Ms. Day offers to swear by her statements, and she is an officer of the court."

"So was Torquemada," I said.

"Your Honor!" Sandra Day exploded in mock anger. "That's abusive."

"Well, that's just Mr. Lassiter's way." The judge turned to me once again. "But get yourself squared away, soldier. Is that clear?"

"Crystal, Your Honor."

"We're not down by the river," the judge said, meaning the criminal division in the so-called Justice Building. "It's more dignified and orderly here."

"I'll keep my boots polished and my bunk made, Your Honor."

"And your mouth zipped, except when I ask you to speak. As now. Status report, Mr. Lassiter."

"We'd ask Your Honor to set a trial date."

"Ms. Day?"

"As much as I'd relish trying this case against Mr. Lassiter, I doubt a trial date will be necessary. We'd ask for a full day summary judgment hearing at which time this case may be disposed of."

"I'll split the baby and set both," the judge said. "Want to give me a preview of your position on summary judgment, Ms. Day?"

"We'll shortly be filing numerous affidavits on both counts as well as extensive memoranda of law. The plaintiff is unable to make a prima facie case of gross negligence, and hence, count one must fail. The plaintiff's radical attempt to use the law of public nuisance to abolish high school football is contrary to law, and thus count two must fail."

"Your Honor, may I respond?"

"Keep your powder dry, Mr. Lassiter. I just wanted an overview."

"Respectfully, Your Honor, that's not an overview. That's Ms. Day jump-starting her argument on the motion."

"Stand down, Mr. Lassiter," she said, which was not the same as "sit down." More like "shut your trap."

I kept quiet and the judge turned to her laptop and scrolled through several pages. After a moment, she said, "Mr. Lassiter, count one is styled 'coaching malpractice.' Is that a tort?"

"It is if Your Honor says so."

"Uh-huh. And count two seeks to use the common law remedy of public nuisance to enjoin high school tackle football until the FHSAA can prove it's safe."

"Yes, Ma'am."

"Alternatively, you seek a lesser remedy. That I enact rule changes to make the sport safer, as if I'm Roger Goodell and the high schools are NFL teams."

"I wouldn't phrase it in precisely those terms," I said, "but yes, if we fail to meet the burden for injunctive relief, that is our alternative request."

"And what's your precedent supporting the relief you seek?" the judge demanded.

"Your Honor just said his name."

"How's that, Mr. Lassiter?"

"Commissioner Goodell announced this week that the NFL Pro Bowl will now be a flag football game," I said. "No more tackling. It's a safety measure, and if it's good enough for the NFL..."

"Totally irrelevant," piped up Sandra Day, the killjoy. "The NFL hasn't halted tackle football in the regular season, the playoffs, or the Super Bowl."

"Not yet," I said. "But this is historic. The Pro Bowl and its predecessors go back to the 1930's. Let's follow the NFL's lead."

"By precedent," the judge said, "I mean case law. Do you have any cases from any state or federal court to support your request to enjoin high school football?"

"I am pleased to say I do not."

"Pleased? To have no case law, no precedent, no authority of any kind?"

"I'm pleased that Your Honor will have the privilege of blazing that trail," I said.

THE TWITTERSPHERE

@Full_Metal_Jacket_9_Mil
Jerk Lassiter wants a nanny state to take away our football, our guns, and our porn.

***

@Life_is_a_Cab9
"And so it came to pass that Jesus loved football but hath reserved his wrath for those who punt on fourth and one." 2 Corinthians 13.

> **@Faithful_Flock87 Replied**
> I can't find the quotation in Corinthians.
>
> > **@ReverendHoops31 Replied**
> > I believe that was intended as satire.

***

@HistoryBuffer954
Very few boys die playing football, but if you listen to Lasteryear, you'd think it was a regular hollow cost.

***

@Pigpen3750
Commies hate football. Jackoff Lassiter hates football. Hugo, Lassiter is a commie.

> **@JucoEnglishProf83 Replied**
> It's "Ergo," you maroon!

-35-
Drinking Buddies

I was sitting in my usual booth in a dark corner of Keg South, minding my own business – the business of drinking my Australian lager – when the last person I expected to see walked in and took a seat across from me.

"Of all the gin joints in all the towns in all the world," I said, shaking my head.

Coach Monty Coleman's eyes darted from me to the patrons seated at the bar, to a couple guys playing darts, and back to me again. Handsome in a bland way, he looked tired around the eyes and had a nicked spot on his chin from a shaving miscue. He wore a navy blazer with an open-necked dress shirt and was deeply tanned from all those broiling practices under the Florida sun. With an American flag in one lapel and a St. Frances Academy pin in the other, he looked primed for a Kiwanis meeting.

"I can't talk to you," I said.

"I know. I know. Just listen, then."

"I can't do that either. You have counsel. It would be unethical for me to – "

"Please! Just listen."

I studied the red Budweiser sign on the far wall, the "U" blinking. A few feet away, two regulars played pool. "I don't know what you're up to, Coach. Maybe you're wearing a wire, and Sunny Day has cooked up a scheme to disbar me."

"She doesn't know I'm here. This is between us."

"What is?"

"I want you to see me as a human being. Not a name on a court pleading. Not a villain of this story you're telling."

I knew I should either walk out the door or throw Coleman out. But maybe he would say something useful. If violating a few Canons of Ethics would help Rod Pittman, well let's start burning the pages.

I said, "A prosecutor once told me that when she started seeing my clients – criminal defendants – as human beings, she'd have to quit."

"I get that. It helps you to demonize me. Maybe it's the only way you can rationalize ruining my life."

"Frankly, I don't give two shits about you."

Lourdes came by the table to see if Coleman wanted a beer, but he waved her off. "You think I'm a monster," he said.

"Nah. I think you're a coach. Army generals and football coaches have a lot of tolerance for other people's pain."

"I am filled with regrets, Mr. Lassiter."

"I'd love to hear them...in court."

"This is a tragedy for everyone."

"Especially Rod."

"Please tell him I'm sorry about everything. I'm torn up inside. I'm not sleeping."

"When you're paralyzed, it's also hard to sleep. Among other things, like breathe."

He put one hand to his face and massaged his forehead. Great, someone else has brutal headaches.

But hold on! It's another day without a headache or tinnitus or a racing heart. I'm in a zone. Feeling optimistic. Feeling strong. Now, what's this self-pitying jerk saying?

"All I ever wanted to do was coach. And do it the right way. I've paid my dues, from being a grad assistant at FSU to my first high school job where I mowed the grass and painted the yard lines."

"Spare me your life story. We'll have plenty of time to chat when I depose you."

Like why you didn't take Rod out of the game when his bell was rung and he thought you were his father!

"If this goes to trial," he said, "regardless of the outcome, I'll lose my job, and no one will hire me."

"You're right and you're wrong. When I prove everything you've done, even if I lose, St. Frances will can you. But there'll be lots of schools that'll like your style. Your next gig might be in West Texas, but so what? They love their Friday Night Lights. Now, are we done here because I'd like to order a Death Dog and some fries?"

"There's one more thing. I overheard Ms. Day on the phone talking about you."

"Oh, no. No, no, no. Unless she was hiring an assassin to plant a bomb in my hammock, I don't want to hear it."

"It's not bad. It's good, for both of us."

He didn't go on. Despite my better judgment, I chomped at the bait. "Okay, tell me."

"I will, but you have to hear me out first."

"C'mon. I got your message. You're a human being."

"I make six figures at St. Frances," he said, intent on saying his piece. "I'm expected to win. Playoffs are mandatory, state championships the goal."

It seemed like this was going to take a while. I signaled Lourdes for another beer and with a hand motion, told her to bring one to Coleman, too.

"I'm really good at my job," he continued. "But do you understand the pressure cooker that is my daily existence?"

I'll ask Dr. Stein, but I think I'm dealing with a classic narcissist here.

"Frankly, Coach, I don't give a damn."

"Kids enroll at St. Frances because they want the best coaching and the best route to a college program and ultimately the NFL. So all the parents think their kids should be starting. If the kid's on offense, they want more touches. If the kid's a linebacker, they want more blitzes. And if the parents are donors, they want to call the plays."

"Nobody made you take this job. It's your stepping stone to a college staff, so that's the shit you gotta put up with. Otherwise, hang up your cleats and sell pickup trucks in Sopchoppy."

Lourdes brought two beers, no glasses. I drained half of mine. Coleman didn't touch his.

"Have you seen how tough our schedule is?" he asked.

"I don't care."

"Last year, we played Austin Westlake on national television in Dallas. The number one team in the nation. If we'd lost, the parents would have gone after my job before the plane touched down in Miami."

"You don't see it, Coach, but you're helping my case. You're giving me the reasons you cut corners on player safety. The pressure to win overrides everything."

"Not true. I care about the players. I push them to go to class and study because so damn few will ever make a living at this."

He had finally run out of steam. The son-of-a-bitch had made a point. He probably was no different than most other high school coaches, which meant that the problem was the system itself, not Monty Coleman.

But I won't let myself feel empathy. Not when Coleman is the guy who's responsible for crippling Rodrigo.

"Okay, I heard you out, Coach. The big tease is over. Sunny Day said something that you're dying to tell me."

"They're going to make you an offer," he blurted out.

"Go on," I said.

"Ms. Day was prepping me for deposition, and she took a call. I stepped into the corridor, but the door was open, and I heard her part of the conversation."

"Yeah?"

"I don't know who she was talking to, but she said she would win the case on summary judgment, so why settle? She listened a bit, then said something like, 'It's a lot of money but it's your money. Do what you want.' And then, she said, 'Do you think he'll take it?' Of course, I couldn't hear the answer."

Odd, I thought. It's the insurance company who'd ask the lawyer, the person with boots on the ground, "Do you think he'll take it?" For Sandra Day to ask the question meant that the person on the other end of the line had a better read on me than she did.

Who could that be? And why authorize a settlement your trial lawyer doesn't ask for and apparently doesn't want?

"Why are you telling me this?" I asked.

"Because I'm hoping you'll take the offer, and we can all get on with our lives."

"First of all, Rod is never getting on with his life, at least not the life he had. Second, this vague conversation sounds like ninety-proof bullshit and one hundred percent wishful thinking. In your telling, it's an anonymous third party that will be making the offer instead of the lawyers, and that's not the way it's done. Unless..."

"Unless what?"

"Have you ever heard Sunny Day refer to the Consortium?"

He shook his head. "I've never heard her use the word."

"Did you hear her say anything else?"

He took a long pull on his beer, put the bottle down, and thought a moment. "She said something about Detroit."

"What'd she say?"

"I messed it up before. She didn't say, 'Do what you want.' She said, 'If that's what Detroit wants, do it.'"

Detroit!

I remembered my conversation with Judge Gridley.

"How do I find this Consortium?"

"You don't, Jake. They're headquartered in Detroit, but there's no listing. No phone, no office. You don't find them. They find you."

-36-
Why Number 58?

After fighting horn-honking traffic on South Dixie Highway for 40 minutes, I was sitting next to Melissa in Dr. Stein's office.

"I've long been interested in how partners from different backgrounds communicate and forge lives together," Dr. Stein began. "At our last session, which was cut short, we were about to discuss Jake's childhood," Dr. Stein began.

"Why me?" I asked. "Why not Melissa?"

"All right, we can start with Melissa."

"Or I can shortcut the whole deal," I said. "Melissa's upbringing was *Lifestyles of the Rich and Famous,* and mine was *Trailer Park Boys.*"

Dr. Stein shot me a look somewhere between chastisement and scorn. "Please let Melissa answer."

"We weren't famous, but there was generational wealth," Melissa said.

She modestly skimmed the surface of her family. Mother, an astronomer at Cornell, until they moved to New York for her father's job, an endowed chair and professor of humanities at NYU. Mother worked at the Hayden Planetarium. Home was a duplex on Central Park South, lots of activities in the Manhattan world of arts, academia, and culture. Then there was the getaway house in Greenwich with horse stables. Father spoke five languages, and Mother could tell you precisely when the universe will end, give or take a hundred billion years.

I let my mind wander as Melissa talked about her private schools before setting sail for Columbia, Yale, and Duke and all those degrees and fellowships. Yes, she's wicked smart, *summa cum laude* smart. Me, I graduated Penn State *summa cum luck*.

Who knows what magic in the cosmos brings people together? The initial spark that ignited the loins of our *Homo erectus* ancestors two million years ago still burns in us today. But that's only the beginning. What's the secret sauce for making a relationship work over time and through troubled waters? Shared values, surely. Mutual caring that goes far beyond the physical. Honesty and openness, as Dr. Stein has stressed. But the puzzle of relationships goes far deeper than the self-help table of your neighborhood bookstore.

"...so tragically, Jake," Dr. Stein said.

"I'm sorry," I said. "Could you repeat that?"

Apparently, Melissa had finished relating her happy and gilded upbringing.

"Could you describe your life before your father died so tragically?"

I shrugged. "Nothing special. Dad would come home from work at five-thirty every day, loosen his tie, kick off his black leather wingtips, and say, 'Honey, I'm home.' Mom would have a martini and a meatloaf ready and waiting."

"Ja-ke," Melissa said, in her storm-warning tone.

I exhaled a long breath and said, "Okay. When my father worked, it was usually on a shrimp boat. When he didn't, he was drunk. He was drunk a lot."

"Was he physically abusive to you or your mother?"

I swallowed once and caught myself biting my lower lip. "He never hit either of us with a closed fist."

"He slapped you, then. How did that feel?"

"How do you think!" I shot back.

Dr. Stein reached across her desk, picked up the damn horse, and squeezed three times. *"Neigh! Neigh! Neigh!"*

"You're being defensive, Jake. Another of the Four Horsemen that destroy relationships. Now, let's work through this. What do you remember about your father?"

I'd rather have a colonoscopy with a clumsy proctologist than talk about my childhood, but I promised Melissa I'd do this.

"Dad's hands were usually creased with dirt and motor oil. Calluses hard as clam shells." I exhaled a breath I didn't know I was holding. "And sure, he slapped me around. Mom, once in a while. It wasn't an everyday thing, and it's not like I lived in fear of him."

"Would you say you learned anything from your father?"

"Does siphoning gas from a tourist's motor boat count?"

I hoped that might end the inquisition, but Dr. Stein kept going. "Did your father spend time with you?"

"We'd toss the football back and forth in the trailer park."

"You lived in a trailer?"

"A double-wide 'til we were evicted. After that, we rented a detached garage and then lived in an old bait shop for a while."

"Did you enjoy playing football with your father?"

"It was okay."

"That sounds so noncommittal. Details, please."

"The trailer park didn't have a grassy field, but there was a gravel parking lot. He invented this game he called 'touchback.'"

"Touch football?"

"Not exactly. We'd stand 15 yards apart. He'd run straight at me with the ball, and I'd have to tackle him. If he got more than five yards, we'd do it again. If he didn't, he'd pass to me, and I'd become the runner. But he usually got more than five yards, with me hanging on to one of his legs. When I did carry the ball, he'd hit me with a forearm shiver to my throat that would knock my legs out from under me. I'd land in the gravel, and by the end of the day, I'd be bleeding from a dozen places."

"For a teenage boy, that must have been traumatic."

"Teenage? I was ten."

"Oh, my."

"I never cried. Wait, strike that. I cried once, and he called me a sissy and a bunch of names I won't repeat, but one rhymes with punt."

Dr. Stein steepled her fingers in front of her face and went into deep-concentration mode. She stayed that way for roughly two minutes, which at her hourly rate, cost us nine bucks. Then she said, "Obviously, you and Melissa come from far different backgrounds."

Oh, how wise and insightful. Is this what we're paying for?

"Do you think you played football to prove to your father that you weren't a sissy?"

"He was dead before I put on my first shoulder pads."

"The question stands."

"I played because I wanted a family. My teammates were the brothers I never had. My coaches were father figures. Plus, I loved hitting people."

"That's honest, open, and insightful. We're getting somewhere."

Melissa cleared her throat, signaling me to say something more, but I didn't know what. Feeling like a submarine captain about to be attacked by depth charges, I chose the safest course. I killed the engine and kept quiet.

"Jake, your jersey number," Melissa prompted me.

"What about it?" I asked.

She turned to the shrink. "In high school, college, and the NFL, Jake always wore number fifty-eight."

"So what?" I asked. "It's a linebacker number."

"Jake once told me that his father's favorite player was Jack Lambert, a linebacker with the Steelers. A player known for his toughness and violent hits. He wore fifty-eight."

"Again, so what? My old man loved the Steelers because they won four Super Bowls, and they had three great linebackers. Jack Lambert, Jack Ham, and Andy Russell, who, not coincidentally, were white, which appealed to a guy with a Confederate flag tattoo on his chest. But I see where you're both going. I'm messed up because I'm trying to win the approval of this mean, ignorant, alcoholic, and very dead asshole who had zero parenting skills."

"You're not messed up," Melissa said, "but your father is a ghost who haunts you."

"The truth is, I rarely think about the guy, but when I do, I make sure nothing I ever do will mimic anything he'd ever done."

"Even so, do you fear that a part of you is like the man you hold in such low regard?" Dr. Stein asked.

I reached deep into the wounds of my childhood for the truth. "I'm not like him at all. Except..."

"Yes?"

"Maybe I'm a little too quick to get angry."

Dr. Stein nodded. "You were reprimanded by the Florida Bar for assaulting a client."

"The guy insisted on lying under oath. Words flew. Then fists. I broke his jaw."

"And now you live with that regret?"

"Mostly that he had a weak jaw."

"So instead of managing your anger, you let your anger manage you."

That pithy little shrink-school aphorism didn't seem to contain a question, so I kept quiet.

"Just what do you want to get out of couples therapy, Jake?" Dr. Stein asked.

At last, an easy question to answer honestly.

"I'm here because I want our relationship to work. I'm trying every day to be a better person and a better mate. I want to make Melissa's good days even better and her bad days easier to bear."

"Commendable goals," Dr. Stein said.

"Our personalities were already formed when we met," I continued. "Our habits were ingrained. Our strengths and weaknesses were already on our scorecards, so we have to deal with each other as the finished human beings we are."

"And your weaknesses...?" Dr. Stein prompted me.

"One weakness – and you've jabbed at it – I'm afraid to show weakness. Like I said before, part of the reason I didn't tell Melissa about my A-Fib was because I didn't want to burden her. But there's also something ingrained in me about being stoic in the face of pain."

"Not crying when your father bloodied you."

"I guess. And I realize that I need to be open about my feelings and my fears, the things I keep bottled up. Which is what I'm doing now and why it feels like I just opened a vein. But so it's clear where I'm coming from..."

I turned and looked directly at Melissa. Those amber-flecked eyes appraised me, not sure where I was going. A slight smile played at her lips. Maybe she did know.

"...I love this woman. I feel blessed that some mysterious force in the universe made her feel the same way about me. Because I'm punching over my weight here, Doc."

"Punching?" Dr. Stein seemed puzzled.

"Melissa's out of my league. I'm second string on the Saskatchewan Rough Riders and she's the Super Bowl Champion in a ticker-tape parade. I want to be with her and hear those drums and bugles from now until the end of time."

"Melissa?" Dr. Stein said.

The love of my life kept her eyes on me and said, "We're on the same team, Jake, and we're in this together. We'll work through any issues that are causing problems. And we both know that every day can't be a parade with drums and bugles. I love a soft piano concerto as long as I'm sharing the music with you."

Dr. Stein said, "That brings us to your emotional bank accounts. Based on our last two sessions, you may have been making deposits without even realizing it."

The shrink told us the account was a mythical ledger of all the nice, little things one partner does for the other in a relationship. Turns out the Lassiter-Gold emotional bank account was overflowing with the currency of sweet, small deeds.

Melissa and I exchanged warm smiles. Dr. Stein closed her notepad and said, "Well, this seems like a propitious place to end the day."

-37-
Who Are Those Guys?

Ten minutes after leaving Dr. Stein's office, driving north toward Coconut Grove, I was happy, albeit $270 poorer, when my cell rang.

I picked up, and Julian Martinez sounded excited. "Got it, Mr. L. Everything you wanted."

"Great, Julian. Where are you?"

"South Beach, just getting into my car."

"I can come to you."

"Nah. I need to get out of here. Last night, a car was parked outside my apartment, two guys in it, sitting there for hours. I don't know if they were cops or –"

"Julian, was it a black Cadillac?"

"Yeah. Late model, temp plate."

Shit on a shingle!

"I just want to get the thumb drive to you," he said.

"What about your apartment? Is it copied onto any of your drives or your laptop?"

"No way. I don't leave evidence where it can stick to me. This is all there is. And the firewall slammed all the doors on my way out."

"All right, stay on with me as you cross the causeway."

"Oh, mother-fuster!"

"What, Julian? What?"

"The black car is right behind me."

I took a right onto Sunset Drive and pulled a stop. "Do you know where the Miami Beach police station is?"

"On Washington. I'm six blocks away."

"Drive straight there. Take the thumb drive in with you. At the front desk, ask for Detective Barrios. They'll tell you he's retired. You tell them he's on his way."

"Is he?"

"He will be."

I ended the call and rang Barrios. Thankfully, he answered on the first ring. "I was just gonna call you, Jake."

"Whatever it is, it can wait." I told him about Julian Martinez and the thumb drive and the phantom Cadillac Blackwing, and how this felt like *Butch Cassidy and the Sundance Kid*, a befuddled Paul Newman asking Robert Redford, "Who are those guys?"

Unperturbed, Barrios said he'd head to the cop shop and have a patrolman who owed him a favor escort Julian to my humble abode across the bay. Then he said, "Yesterday, I was poking around the school, and nobody's giving me as much as a *buenos dias*. When I get back to the parking lot, there's a black Caddy CTV-5 with dark-tinted windows. When I get to my car, it burns rubber pulling out of the lot."

"Sloppy," I said. "They can't follow anyone without being noticed. Julian. Dr. Herlocher. Me. And now you."

"That's not sloppy. If these guys are part of that Consortium you told me about, they're pros. They're not following you to find out where you're going. They want to spook you, intimidate you, let you know they're everywhere. Like the other Blackwing that was outside my house last night."

"What do you mean 'other'? How do you know it wasn't the same one?"

"Because I'm a detective. They were identical except the one at the school had forged aluminum wheels with low-profile tires. The one outside my house did not."

"So there are two."

"For a lawyer, you're excellent at math, but I'm betting on more than two. Besides the cars, they likely have some sophisticated techies and hackers, so you should take precautions."

"Like what?"

"I'd assume they can clone your cell phone, so toss it and use a different burner every day."

"Not practical," I said. "No one will be able to reach me."

"Just telling you what I would do. Dammit, Jake, do you even know what you're up against?"

"Of course I do," I lied.

-38-
Hey Hey, Sunny Day

Accompanied by a Miami Beach patrol car with no Blackwing in sight, Julian Martinez showed up at my house 20 minutes after I got there. He showed me how to upload the thumb drive to my laptop. Or maybe it was download. Either way, I was able to play the videos.

Thirty-seven hours in all!

Most of the practice footage had no audio. I fast forwarded to get an overall view. A lot of August practices shot from a tower, some at ground-level. A few team meetings, Coach Coleman laying down the rules familiar to anyone who's ever played.

Never be late for practice.

Keep your locker clean.

No drinking, no smoking, no drugs.

There were the usual coach-speak platitudes. "We're gonna play faster, hit harder, reach deeper into ourselves than our opponents."

The practices involved drills that brought back memories of stinking-hot, sweat-soaked days at Coral Shores High in the Keys where I never missed football practice and occasionally attended class. Gut busters, ball wrestling, squat thrusts, hand fighting, and the dreaded monkey rolls to get players used to hitting the ground and bouncing back up.

The St. Frances practices concluded with two dozen gassers, the dreaded forty-yard sprints repeated 24 times.

In full pads.

At full speed.

In the Florida sun.

When I played, we called the drill "Puke City."

Hell isn't fire and brimstone. Hell is August in South Florida.

On the video, several players didn't make it, falling to their knees and hurling, forcing other players to hop over the mess. I caught sight of Rod, who not only completed the drill, but led his group every time. The kid was in great shape, which only added to the gut-wrenching pain of seeing him now.

So young, so strong, so full of life. So much taken from him.

He would never sprint again, but I prayed he would someday walk and be able to brush his teeth and button his shirt and strum a guitar and kiss Kiara.

There were three scrimmages on the video but without kickoffs or punts, so Rod wasn't in them. The Tunnel of Manhood came near the end. Instead of the slick, professional look of the other videos, this was cell phone video, the tent illuminated only by hurricane lanterns, casting dark shadows.

They were running a pit drill. Whether it was called Oklahoma or Nutcracker or Blood Alley didn't matter. The NFL had banned the drills a few years ago, and more importantly, so had St. Frances's league.

The drill had a ritualistic aspect. Players on either side created a narrow corridor and screamed their guts out. One ball carrier and one tackler lined up in the corridor, facing each other. They took running starts and collided head-on like bighorn rams battering each other to win the heart of a lady ram. Here, the idea was to separate the guys who look good in shorts and T-shirts from the animals who paw the earth and claw, scratch, and chew their opponents to the bone.

Watching the moving shadows, I heard the shouts of their teammates mixed with the grunts and curses of the two boys in the pit. Likely the same sounds made by Roman gladiators fighting to the death.

Was the video admissible when Rod never participated in the drill? Sandra Day would contend that Coach Coleman could have beheaded players by guillotine inside the tent, but that was irrelevant to our case. I would argue that the entirety of Coach Coleman's conduct was on trial. How would Judge Duckworth rule? I had no idea.

I was stewing in this broth of uncertainty when Melissa came home, carrying dinner in cardboard boxes.

"I hope you're in the mood for maple orange salmon with a mango salsa," she said.

"Sounds great, thanks. I'm starving."

"And a detox bowl."

"Sounds like something from the bathroom."

"Carrots, broccoli, beetroot with turmeric to stimulate your liver."

I must have been exhausted, because I had no witty rejoinder. After dinner, Melissa curled up in an easy chair to read the latest issue of *Neuropathology*, and I returned to the videos, which were not turning out to be the treasure trove I had hoped. Coach Coleman didn't grab players by the facemasks and shake them violently to get their attention. He didn't deprive players of water until they fainted or suffered heat stroke. He didn't call his players "pussies" and spit tobacco juice into their faces as my high school coach had done. Coleman was the clean-cut CEO of a major high school athletics program and seemed damn competent.

Near the end of the videos, I found a polished six-minute piece with the production quality of ESPN's *SportsCenter*. Monty Coleman was the star. There were clips from team meetings, one-on-one quarterback sessions, and then at practice, he dashed from position group to position group, tooting his whistle.

At the end of the hagiographic video of the saintly coach, a caption on the screen read, "For more information, contact Bryan Sproules" with a phone number that had a 407 area code. Orlando, Florida. I googled the name. Sproules was an agent representing college football coaches.

So this is Monty Coleman's audition reel. He's looking for a college job and this is his sales pitch. So he has to win and win big.

Making me wonder:

What corners does he cut? And...

What does he tell the team when he's not performing for the camera?

Then it struck me. Coleman was miked on those full-contact scrimmages, so there had to be audio. I had missed that when I fast-forwarded through all thirty-seven hours. Now, I went back and started again. I found several clips with Coleman shouting very coachy instructions to the team. Nothing incriminating. Well, what could I expect? With the camera rolling, he wasn't going to offer hundred-dollar bounties for knocking an opposing quarterback out of the game.

It was around four a.m. when I found a full-contact scrimmage held just five days before the opening game. A wide receiver slicing over the middle juggled a pass and was a sitting duck for a defensive back who was closing fast and could have knocked him into next week. At the last second, the defender fell sideways, instead of smashing the receiver who surely would have dropped the ball.

Coleman sprinted toward them, blasted his whistle, and pointed at the defensive back. "Macklin! What the hell was that? You looked like a ballerina falling off the stage."

"Coach, I was coming in high, and it was gonna be helmet-to-helmet."

"Screw that, Macklin! Let me tell you something." Coleman looked straight at the camera and said, "Turn that off."

I heard a click, and the screen went black but flickered on two seconds later. The videographer must have screwed up and hit the button twice. Coleman was addressing the entire defensive squad. "Do I care if you pick up a targeting penalty? Hell, no. That'll make their receivers shaky coming across the middle. If you smash heads and the zebras throw a flag, you won't hear shit from me. If you're ejected, consider it your badge of courage. But don't curl up and die like Macklin just did."

He paused and lowered his voice as if he had a secret to share. "My high school coach used to yell, 'Be a headhunter!' The rule book says I can't tell you to do that. All I'll say is that college coaches are looking for guys who don't mind getting their hair mussed. They want to know just how tough you are. So, do some damage!"

Oh, yeah! If it's not a smoking gun, Coleman is at least sliding bullets into the chamber.

And what about his tricky use of "headhunter." He can't advise it? Hah. I have the audio from the radio station: "Then do it again, Rod. Be a headhunter. Stick 'em."

I turned off the laptop, retreated to the recliner, stripped down to my boxers, and dozed off. Just after sunrise, my cell rang. I checked the screen.

Now, what the hell does she want?

"Good morning, Ms. Day," I said. "How goes the abuse of widows, orphans, and paralyzed children?"

"You sound sleepy, counselor. Long flight home from Slovakia?"

It took me a moment. Oh, yeah. Julian said he'd be using a server in Slovakia. He'd also told me it would be impossible to sneak into the clouds without leaving fingerprints.

"No idea what you're talking about," I said, innocent as a parking meter burglar with pockets full of quarters.

"Computer hacking is a federal crime. Eighteen U.S. Code, Section Ten-Thirty."

"Go tell it to the judge."

"I shall. I'll seek sanctions against you that include jail time."

"I'll be ready. I never go to court without my toothbrush."

"I'll also file a motion *in limine* to exclude from evidence any items illegally obtained."

"I'll get back to you on that as soon as I learn a little Latin."

I waited, expecting her to raise hell about my meeting with Coach Coleman, a very big no-no in the ethics racket. But she didn't go there. Meaning Coleman didn't tell her, adding credence to his story that a settlement offer was coming, though perhaps not from Sandra Day.

"If that's all Ms. Day, I'm about to make some oatmeal with sliced papaya and chia seeds for my fiancée. I'd invite you over, but all I'm wearing are boxers with little Nittany lions on them, and I'm in dire need of a shower." I made a sniff-sniff-sniffing sound into the phone.

"You are a vile man, Mr. Lassiter, an embarrassment to the profession. I feel a personal obligation to drum you out."

In the old days, before I evolved, I might have said, "Better men have tried." But now, defanged of all sexism, molded by Melissa into the post-modern, state-of-the-art, woke bloke that I am, I merely said, "Is that the same obligation you felt when defending opioid manufacturers?"

Then I borrowed the tune from the anti-war chant of the Vietnam era, the one aimed at LBJ. "Hey hey, Sunny Day," I sang. "How many kids did you kill today?"

-39-
The Social Fabric of the Nation

I wasn't lying. I made a healthy breakfast and drank three cups of black coffee to compensate for my loss of sleep.

"You never made it into bed," Melissa said, studying me.

"Worked most of the night. But feeling fine."

"Are you remembering to take your heart medication?"

"Eating them like jelly beans."

"CTE symptoms?"

"No brass bands, no ice picks in my skull. No mood swings or confusion out of the ordinary."

She rewarded me with a smile. "I'm creating a sub-group within the study. Former players undertaking complicated tasks that require focus and concentration. Please keep doing your homework."

Meaning a daily chart of symptoms.

"Will do, doc."

She finished her breakfast, kissed me, and packed her briefcase for a day at the hospital. "Jake, do you promise to eat a healthy lunch?"

"A heavy lunch? Sure!"

"I give up." She raised her hands in surrender and headed for the door.

I spent the next hour going over my notes from the videos. Then my computer beeped with an incoming email. And another. And another. And another.

Sandra Day had filed her motion for summary final judgment. The motion was a slender seven pages long but was supplemented by roughly 1,200 pages of documents, and that was just on count two, the injunction request.

Included were 39 affidavits from coaches, human factors experts, sociologists, historians, economists, engineers, physicians, former NFL players, sports agents, NFL executives, and several PhDs in different disciplines. Then came the briefs in support of the motion, eleven in all, totaling more than 200 pages. And finally there was a document titled "Policy Arguments" that included 23 articles from various academic journals. The unwieldy caption of one treatise read: "Sociological and Historical Arguments in Support of the Proposition that High School Football is a Significant and Beneficial Component of the Social Fabric of the Nation."

Silly me. I thought it was just a game played with an inflated pig's bladder by boys who like to knock each other down.

This treatise alone ran a mind-numbing 211 pages. The intent, of course, was to paper me to death as punishment for storming the temple of the football gods. I jumped to the end of the document and found an appendix with the names of prominent Americans who played high school football. The list included Dwight Eisenhower, Robin Williams, and Ryan Seacrest. But not yours truly!

The motion for summary judgment on count one began with a clear-cut sentence: "Plaintiff is unable to point to a single act of Defendant Coleman that amounts to gross negligence, and therefore the claim must fail."

Unfortunately, Sunny Day was right about the first half of that proposition.

All we had locked down was one act of simple negligence: Coleman's failure to remove Rod from the game after the first helmet-rattling tackle. We needed more.

I called Solomon and Lord. With both lawyers on the line, I asked Victoria, the brains of the operation, the pressing legal question.

"To meet the gross negligence threshold, can I dump several acts of simple negligence into a pot with water and spices and make a stew of gross negligence?"

"A thought-provoking issue," Victoria said, sounding professorial.

"If the answer is 'no,' I'm going to lose before I even open my briefcase."

"If you have a briefcase, it must be to carry your lunch," Solomon said.

"Do these other acts of negligence all involve Rod?" Lord asked.

"Not specifically," I said. "That's why I called the count 'coaching malpractice.' I'm asking the judge to look at the big picture, how Coleman coaches the entire team."

Solomon made a scoffing sound. "The defense will argue that unrelated acts of simple negligence occurring at different times to different players can't amount to gross negligence involving your client. My gut tells me you lose."

"My brain tells me your gut is full of beans."

"Stop it, boys!" Victoria ordered. "I'll research the issue. Have you gotten anything in discovery that's useful?"

I'm not sure hacking the opposition's cloud storage is technically "discovery," but I'll go with it.

"Some ingredients for the stew," I said.

"What about count two?" Solomon asked. "You have any legal authority to destroy the American way of life?"

I considered telling him the truth but settled for a little white lie. "I'm getting there, Solomon."

"Hah! I heard you hesitate. Your song-and-dance might work in front of our two-digit IQ judges and our sleepy jurors, but you can't fool your best friend."

"Damn, that's depressing."

"What is, Jake?"

"That you're my best friend."

PART FOUR

"Two kinds of players aren't worth a darn: One that never does what he's told, and one who does nothin' except what he's told."

– Bum Phillips

"We work hard to achieve our goals, and when Saturday comes, we stand as a team. We look across at our opponents and say, 'come on, let's go, let's see how good you are.' We are ready. We play with enthusiasm and recklessness. We aren't afraid to lose. But win or lose, it is the competition which gives us pleasure."

– Joe Paterno

-40-
The Promised Land

I sat at the counter of a Cuban restaurant on Coral Way having my health-conscious lunch of a Cubano – the hot-pressed sandwich of pork, ham, cheese, pickles, and mustard – with a large order of fried plantains and a guava milkshake.

A man entered through the door behind me and took a seat on the adjacent stool, even though the place was half-empty.

"Is that your Caddy in the lot?" he said, gesturing over his shoulder.

"Yeah, did you crash into it?"

"Nah. Parked next to it."

I looked through the window and saw a shiny new Blackwing CTV-5 next to my 1984 Eldo. Gave the guy the once over. Jeans, boots, leather jacket, blue denim shirt with a bolo string tie. Military brush cut.

Yeah, him.

The "observer" from the day Sandra Day stonewalled me on discovery.

"For a guy who dresses like shit, you've got some wheels," I said.

"Not mine, but you probably figured that."

I had both hands wrapped around my Cubano, which kept me from clobbering the guy. "Are you the bastard who sucker punched me outside my house?"

"Different bastard."

Lourdes, the server, stopped by, and Bolo Tie said, "I'll have what he's having."

"So you're the other guy, the one I used for batting practice?"

He shook his head. "He's in an ankle cast. Helluva swing."

"I've got another bat in my trunk if you want to see it up close."

"You've got it wrong, Mr. Lassiter. I'm your new best friend."

I studied him a moment. Thick wrists, big hands, and a weightlifter's neck. A bland, forgettable face. I took him for ex-military, or ex-cop, or even ex-con.

"You have a name, friend?" I asked.

"You won't need it."

"I gather you work for the Consortium, and not Sandra Day."

"What Consortium?"

"Aw, give me a break."

"Officially, there is no such entity. But informally, yes, I work for what you would call the Consortium. And Sandra Day reports to us. To my superiors, actually."

"Define us."

"Bigwigs of major corporations."

I took a bite of the Cubano, cheese oozing from the sides. "Such as?"

"Sorry. Corporate membership is confidential."

"Like the Gambino crime family."

"The companies share common values. Rich, traditional American values, you might say."

"Obstructing justice does have a rich history," I agreed. "So what's the deal?"

"An omnibus settlement. Let's start with a very generous payout to the Pittmans on count one, a side agreement to take care of you, and, of course, dismissal with prejudice of count two with a few additional frills we can discuss."

"Why does 'side agreement' sound like a bribe and 'additional frills' like perversion of justice?" I said.

"Just hear me out. You have a 19 percent chance of surviving summary judgment on the personal injury claim. If you do, you'll have your paralyzed client next to you in the courtroom, and a sympathetic jury might ignore the judge's gross negligence instruction."

"Jury nullification," I said.

"Exactly. Then your chance of winning a verdict dramatically increases to close to 50 percent. Of course, Ms. Day will appeal, and she'll have a 45 to 55 percent chance of reversal, depending on the makeup of the panel in the Third District. Even if you win, your client won't see a dime for years. On your fanciful claim to halt high school football, you have a negligible chance – call it two percent – of surviving summary judgment."

"Where are you getting these numbers?" I drained my guava milkshake through a straw with a sucking sound. "Pulling them out of your ass?"

Lourdes brought his Cubano and all the trimmings, but Bolo Tie didn't take a bite.

"We've done thousands of simulations using sophisticated algorithms with proprietary software. The numbers are unimpeachable from a probability point of view."

"All of which leads us where?" I asked.

"To the promised land, Mr. Lassiter."

Lourdes brought a café Cubano without my asking, but it got cold as I listened to Bolo Tie. His employer — the Consortium, though he never used the name — would pay the Pittmans an immediate $6 million, what he called the "floor." When Rod reached maximum medical improvement, a legal term of art, a panel of two economists, two physicians, and a retired judge would determine the total payout with a cap at $24 million. Each side would choose one economist and one physician, and we'd have to agree on the retired judge. There would be no admission of liability, and we would be required to sign non-disclosure agreements.

He's not lying. It's generous. Lily and Tank will jump at it.

"To be clear, Mr. Lassiter, there's no settlement of the personal injury case without disposing of the count seeking to enjoin high school football. You will agree to the entry of a Summary Final Judgment with 17 findings of fact."

"Such as?"

"High school football has been made safer due to rule changes and improved equipment. The sport is an integral part of our schools, our communities, and American society as a whole. A court is powerless to grant injunctive relief because that would invade the province of the Legislature. That and 14 others."

"You want me to make it tougher for future lawsuits. You want me to cripple the cause I believe in."

"Don't you believe in medical research to make the game safer?"

"Of course, I do."

"You'll be the executive director of the brand new RHI Institute."

"Repetitive Head Injuries?"

"Focused on CTE suffered by athletes and military personnel."

"I'm gonna run a medical lab. Why? Are all the astronaut positions taken?"

"It won't be a lab. No bricks and mortar. It's a website where the Institute culls all the latest papers on CTE and organizes them by topic."

"So it's a sham. Nothing but a warehouse for other peoples' work."

"A content aggregator website. Once a year we'll publish a hard copy journal of the best content. No doubt they'll select some of your fiancée's cutting-edge work."

Sweetening the pot with that little bribe.

"What if I select an article that says the NFL falsified its medical research for years?"

He gave me a crooked smile and speared a sweet plantain with his fork. "First, you don't select anything. We have physicians on retainers for that. Second, nothing will be published that would embarrass any of our honorary members. That, of course, includes the NFL, the NCAA, the high school athletic associations, and specific industries such as helmet and equipment manufacturers."

"So what am I supposed to do in this job? Play pickleball with Roger Goodell?"

"Look good, for one thing. The executive director needs a presentable car." He slid a Cadillac fob across the counter to me.

"Your Blackwing? Seriously?"

"Not this one. Its twin brother is sitting in front of your house, part of your compensation package."

"Just curious. How many of these beauties do you have?"

"Four. And they only made 120, so you've got yourself a collector's item. How's your left knee these days?"

"Bone-on-bone that sounds like crickets at dusk, but it still works."

"The Blackwing has a six-speed manual with a clutch that'll stress your calf muscles and knee."

"Great, I'll do physical therapy so I can drive the car."

"It's got a whopper of an engine, 668 horsepower. Top speed is more than 200 miles per hour, but I wouldn't advise it."

"I'll remember that on I-95 in rush hour."

"It's tricked out to a $115,000 sticker price. Oh, almost forgot! Your pay. What do you think you're worth, Mr. Lassiter?"

"Not as much as the Blackwing costs."

"You're too modest. Imagine you're picked midway in the first round of this year's NFL draft."

"Quite a promotion. I was an undrafted free agent."

"Ancient history. Just pretend you're the sixteenth player taken. Jahan Dotson. Wide receiver..."

"Out of Penn State. I know. My alma mater."

"So how much will Mr. Dotson make in his first contract?"

"More than I made my whole career."

"To be precise, he signed a four-year rookie contract totaling just over $15 million. That'll be your pay from the Institute. Roughly $3.75 million a year for four years. And no one will clothesline you going across the middle."

A preposterous sum! I was right. It's a bribe and a perversion of justice.

"Why so generous?"

"That's not what it is. We're buying your name, your experience, and that lived-in face for a photo and bio on the website. You're the former player who wants to make the game safer. It's a compelling story, which one of our staff will write for you."

"So it's only a semi-sham institute but a totally sham job."

"The offer is open until five p.m. tomorrow. Call Sandra Day with your response. If we don't hear from you, well, as they say, we'll see you in court."

"That's what it's there for. But tell me this. Why make the offer today?"

"Why do you think?"

I didn't answer, and he brightened. "Oh, you think it's because you hacked the videos that make Monty Coleman look bad. We don't give a shit about him. He's collateral damage. We're doing it because it's a just result."

"Oh, spare me the bullcrap."

"Okay, how's this? Tomorrow is your client's birthday. Think of it as a present for him."

Of course they'd know Rod's birthday. The bastards probably know whether I'm wearing boxers or briefs.

"Still not buying it," I said. "Why pay me off if I've got less chance of winning than the Greeks at Thermopylae?"

He smiled at that. "Even outnumbered twenty to one, the Greeks – much like you – were a damn nuisance to the Persians."

"The Greeks all got beheaded for their trouble. But you're paying me millions."

"Would you feel better if we reduced your salary?"

"I'd feel better if I wasn't tempted by the money, which I am. And that makes me feel dirty."

"The NFL's paying Roger Goodell $128 million over the next two years. Is he worth it?"

I shrugged. "If the owners want to pay him that much, I suppose that makes him worth it."

Bolo Tie ate another plantain, then pointed his fork at me. "That's the second smart thing you said today."

I took the bait. "And the first?"

"When you said you were tempted by the money."

-41-
The Client is King

The Caddy in my driveway at home had 902 miles on the odometer and a transfer of title form on the front seat. It seems I already owned the black beauty. The prior owner was a corporation registered in Grand Cayman, doubtless one of the Consortium's shell companies. It pissed me off, just how damned confident they were that we'd take the offer.

I tried going over the file, looking for any evidence I might have overlooked. Searching for a magic bullet that didn't exist. My mind kept returning to the money. A handsome settlement for Rod and a princely sum for me.

Money, money, money. I could taste it!

I drove the Blackwing to Tank and Lily's house, parked in the driveway, and waited for them to come home from the rehab facility. I must have dozed off because just after eleven p.m., Tank jerked open the car door and hauled me out the driver's door by the scruff of the neck. I weigh 240 pounds, and my feet never touched the ground until he let go and I tumbled to the pavers.

"Oh shit, Jake! It's you." He bent over and helped me up. "Sorry. I thought you were the enemy. Did you steal their car?"

"Long story," I said. "Can we go inside? I brought some Pappy van Winkle."

Lily stood beside him, appraising me with wary eyes. We'd patched our relationship back together, but I'm not sure she would ever fully trust me.

Tank told me that Rod was improving every day, which I already knew from my many visits. Rod was in a pilot project using stem therapy and had regained much of the movement in his hands and was working on dexterity. And of course, busting his butt in grueling physical therapy. Next week, they would have him in that walking contraption he showed me, suspended by a harness over a treadmill.

Once in their living room, holding a tumbler of Pappy's bourbon, aged 15 years if anyone's counting, we drank a toast to Rodrigo.

"You'd be proud of your godson," Tank said, "how damn hard he's working in rehab."

"He takes after both of you. To Rod!"

I sipped at the luscious copper-and-gold liquid.

"Why are you here so late, Jake?" Lily said, her tone challenging.

I started by telling them about hacking the school's storage cloud and coming across Coach Coleman's blasé attitude about helmet-to-helmet hits and his startling "be a headhunter" diatribe.

"That's why he closed practices," Tank said. "He wouldn't want parents to hear that."

"Is that all?" Lily said.

I told them about their computer simulations, spitting out probabilities of our winning the case.

"Do those numbers sound right to you?" Tank asked.

I shrugged. "Algorithms can't measure love and loyalty and commitment."

"Meaning what?" Lily asked.

I repeated what I had told Melissa before filing the lawsuit. "The defense lawyers don't love the insurance company or the Consortium or Coach Coleman. I love the two of you and Rodrigo. I would do anything to get justice for you."

"Spit it out, Jake," Lily said. "What are you leading up to?"

I told them about the offer to settle Rod's claim with a $6 million floor and a $24 million cap, and Tank let out a long whistle and then wet his whistle with a long pull on the Pappy.

"You did it, Jake," he said, saluting me with his empty tumbler.

I told them there would be no admission of fault by Coach Coleman or the school, and we would all have to sign non-disclosure agreements.

"The legal fiction is that there's no wrongdoer and no settlement in the traditional sense," I said. "The documents will call it a 'beneficent contribution.' As if it's coming from the goodness of their hearts."

Tank shrugged his massive shoulders, signaling "no problem."

I said, "Plus, I'll have to agree to a consent judgment dismissing count two with a bunch of findings that will kneecap any lawyers who bring similar claims in the future."

"So your strategy worked," Tank said. "You bluffed them, you old rascal. Even if they think they have a 98 percent chance of winning the injunction case, they can't take the risk. That's why they're paying us."

I drained my bourbon. "Probably true, but that was never my strategy. I wanted to win both cases. This would be my last trial, and the most meaningful one of my life."

Lily scoffed. "All about you, and it always has been."

"Not fair," Tank said, jumping to my defense. "Look what Jake's done for us."

"He's not finished talking, you old fool! Can't you see he wants us to turn down the money?"

Tank shot me a look. "Jake?"

"I'm hoping you'll say, 'Let's go to trial. Let's prove what they did as a lesson to others to put safety first.'"

Lily jumped in and said, "You think you can win more money than they're offering?"

"I don't know. Maybe more than $6 million, probably less than $24 million."

"If we don't lose on summary judgment and get zero," Lily drilled me.

"It's possible."

"And the other count," Tank said. "You think the judge is going to abolish high school football?"

"The odds are against us."

Tank and Lily exchanged looks. "Yo, roomie," Tank said. "I hope you're more persuasive in court than you are here."

"I can't mislead you."

"We're taking the money," Lily said, with finality. "Right Langston?"

"Makes sense," Tank said.

"If you want to think about it overnight, the offer's open until five p.m. tomorrow," I said.

"We're done thinking," Lily said.

"Jake, you're on board, right?" Tank said.

I sighed and raised my hands in surrender. "The client is king. A lawyer has no discretion to go against the client's wishes."

"Then it's settled," Lily said.

"We'll celebrate tomorrow," Tank said. "Rod's birthday. We'll be at the facility by eight a.m. Will you be there, Jake?"

"I wouldn't miss it," I said, "though I might not be there exactly at eight."

-42-
Alligator Alley

I told the truth:

The client is king. And I will visit Rod in the morning. And I won't arrive at eight a.m.

The whole truth:

I'll get there an hour earlier than Tank and Lily.

But if I left something out, was it nothing but the truth?

Because I had a plan that might cost me my bar license, Tank's friendship, and maybe a couple broken bones.

But I wasn't sure I'd go through with it. I needed to examine my motivation.

"All about you, and it always has been," Lily had said.

Sure, I had told Melissa that this case would be my legacy. That in whatever time I had left, I wanted to do something worthwhile and lasting. As compared to my pre-Melissa days, my Cro-Magnon era, my unevolved man-child existence.

But does that make what I'm planning wrong? Maybe not morally wrong in the eyes of the universe. But probably unethical in the eyes of the Florida Bar.

Now, around midnight, I had no good reason to be on I-75, better known as Alligator Alley, heading due west across our

skinny peninsula in the Blackwing. I was doing 105 in fourth gear
– out of six – and the ride was creamy smooth, sweetly effortless,
and under control. The exhausts were singing opera at a roaring
fortissimo, which undoubtedly was intentional. The Big Daddy
Caddy's roar was meant to be heard. There was so little traffic the
night was black velvet with a million diamonds for stars.

I made three phone calls, apologizing each time for the lateness
of the hour. Kiara Parsons was wide awake, in the kitchen, baking
her first cake from scratch. For Rodrigo, of course. I told her I'd
pick her up at 6:30 a.m., and she was fine with that.

I called Victoria Lord who was working on her laptop in bed
while Steve Solomon snored happily next to her. Instead of telling
her that I was under orders to settle the case, I asked her what her
legal research had uncovered.

"Just found a Florida Supreme Court case you'll like," she
said. "*Faircloth vs. Hill*. It's old. Eisenhower was president, but
it's never been overruled. The Court held that several acts of
simple negligence can be combined to create a single act of gross
negligence."

"Great, Vic!"

"Don't celebrate yet. It's an auto-accident case, and the defense
will try to distinguish it on the facts."

"Please email the link, and I'll deal with it."

I called Melissa, whose nighttime reading was an article on the
neuropathology of stress in industrialized societies.

"Doesn't anyone go to sleep before midnight?" I asked.

"Where are you, Jake, and why is your car in the driveway?"

"Oh, that old thing."

I gave her the shorthand version of the day's events and said,
"I passed the Miccosukee reservation, so I think I'm in the middle
of the Big Cypress Swamp, but it's so dark out here, it's hard to
tell."

"What are you doing there?"

"Clearing my head, Mel." I glanced at the space-age dashboard display. "I'm going 112, but it doesn't feel like it."

"Jake! Please come home. Slowly!"

"Will do. Under the speed limit."

"I'll be in bed, naked when you get home."

"Forget what I said about the speed limit."

I saw the intersection of Route 29 ahead and told her I'd turn around and be home in a jiffy. We hung up, and I still wasn't sure what I would do in the morning.

I slowed to about 90 and thought I saw something in the road ahead. Just a silhouette slinking across the pavement. It stopped and turned toward me.

Two glowing green eyes! An alligator, maybe 10 feet long, fat and happy, and sitting motionless in my lane!

I slammed the brakes. The tires sang a song in a piercing falsetto, and the Caddy ground to a halt without weaving, fishtailing, or sliding into the canal just off the berm. Twenty feet in front of me, the alligator swung its tail and crawled ever-so-slowly across the road and disappeared into the sawgrass.

With no traffic in either direction, I eased into a U-Turn and headed east. Just then, my cell rang, and I answered, "Sweetheart, if you're still naked, I'm on my way."

"Ooh, sch-weet-heart," a woman's voice slurred. "I'm wearing the hotel bathrobe. Should I take it off?"

"Who is this?"

"And why, Jakey, are you in the middle of a swamp?"

"What? Sandra Day, is that you?"

"Do you like your new ride, you swamp rat? And your new wealth?"

The bastards put a tracking device on the Blackwing. I should have known.

"Ms. Day, what's up?"

"I am. In the Jacuzzi in my suite. With a bottle or two of Moët & Chandon. Aimeriez-vous Champagnie?"

I didn't answer and kept the Blackwing at a slow-pokey 85 as I headed back toward civilization, if western Broward County could be called that.

"May I be honest with you?" she said, slurring "hon-esht."

"Sure thing. I love new experiences."

"Deep in my heart of hearts, I hoped you'd reject the offer."

"I'm shocked. That you have even one heart."

"I knew your white-knight shtick was a crock of shit. A shtick shit and a shit shtick, and now you're driving a stick shift. Up to me, I wouldn't pay you a dime."

"Are you drinking in celebration or in self-loathing? Because the tiny part of your soul that you haven't already sold at a thousand bucks an hour seems to be plaguing you. Maybe you finally regret all the choices you made that created the beast you are today."

"Oh, you're one to talk, you phony Don Ho."

"Huh? The Hawaiian musician?"

"Don Keeyo."

"Don Quixote?"

"Him, too, you phony baloney Quixote. You're just a money grubber like all the rest. Line your pockets and to hell with your ideals."

I heard paper rustling from her end of the call, and then she recited, "Paragraph thirty-seven of your high-and-mighty complaint: 'The risks of serious injury and death outweigh any potential benefit of the game.'"

"I believed it then and I believe it now."

"Not enough to fight for it. All those words, buried with the detritus of good intentions. Enjoy your new car, shyster."

The line went dead, and I drove in silence. I slowed the Blackwing as I passed through Weston in Broward County. Forty-five minutes or so from home.

I thought over all the events of the day.

Bolo Tie. As slithery as the snake in the Garden of Eden.

Tank and Lily Pittman. I couldn't blame them for their decision, which was clearly logical.

Sandra Day. She wasn't evil, not in a biblical sense. She shared a trait with Coach Coleman. Each was the product of a system that rewarded victory at all costs.

My thoughts turned to Rodrigo, flat on his back in the rehab center, dreaming of walking and holding Kiara in his arms. I thought, too, of the other Rodrigos out there. The ones already crippled and the ones yet to be.

I knew what I had to do. There was a document to prepare. Then a couple hours sleep, and breakfast with Kiara and Rodrigo.

Sandra Day, you're right about one thing and wrong about another. I'm no knight. I fell off that horse long ago. But I still have my ideals, and they're worth fighting for.

-43-
"By and Through His Parents..."

Rod was already in his wheelchair when I showed up in his room at 6:40 a.m.

"Hey, you're early, Uncle Jake!"

"Happy Birthday, Rodrigo!" I sang out. "Your present's in the car."

"What is it?"

"A surprise, dude."

First of many today.

He lifted his right hand from the armrest. Slowly. But steadily. Then squeezed his fingers into a fist with his thumb extended.

Thumbs up!

"Love it!" I shouted. "You've been working hard."

"Are Mom and Dad with you?"

"They're coming later."

True enough, but we won't be here.

"Rodrigo, we need to get a move on, or we'll miss sunrise."

He looked puzzled. "We're going out?"

"For breakfast and not in the cafeteria."

"Did the doctors sign off?"

"C'mon, dude. When I broke curfew, I didn't get Coach Shula's permission."

"That's fire, Uncle Jake."

Still meaning "cool," unless teen slang had changed this week.

I wheeled him along the corridor to the oversized elevator at the rear of the building, and we descended to the loading dock. I guided the wheelchair down the ramp where the Blackwing was waiting, quietly rumbling.

The door opened and Kiara Parsons popped out. "Rod, baby!" she yelled. "Happy birthday!"

She leaned over and kissed him, then grabbed his right hand and gave it a gentle squeeze. He squeezed back, as best he could, and my heart felt the warmth exchanged between them.

"I baked a cake for you," she said, "my first one ever. It's a white cake with chocolate icing, your favorite."

"Thank you, Key," Rod said. "Love you."

"Love you back. The cake's in the trunk, along with Jake's present."

Rod shot a look at the Blackwing and whistled. "A new ride, Uncle Jake?"

"Therein lies a tale, kiddo. Therein lies a tale."

I hoisted Rodrigo into the front seat next to me. He wasn't heavy, having dropped weight in the hospital that he was just starting to gain back in the rehab facility. Kiara sat in the spacious back seat, leaning forward, twirling strands of Rod's hair around her fingers. I folded the wheelchair and put it in the trunk, and we were ready to go.

I turned off my cell phone. No way did I want to hear Tank Pittman calling me some colorful names for snatching his son. The engine was purring as I picked up I-95 in Overtown for the short drive to the Rickenbacker Causeway. Even at this hour, the expressway was jammed, commuters from Broward heading south, while suburbanites from the Gables, Kendall, and Pinecrest crawled north on U.S. 1.

"So what's going on, Mr. Lassiter?" Kiara asked.

"Yeah, Uncle Jake," Rodrigo said. "Spill the tea."

"Sunrise now, clarity later," I promised.

I swung onto the causeway for the quick trip to Key Biscayne. On the steep ascent, the Blackwing whispered, barely breathing in third gear. We passed a pack of early morning bicyclists chugging up the hill, all helmeted and spandexed.

At the top, I pulled over to the side so we could watch the sun peek out of the Atlantic, an orange fireball, setting the aqua water ablaze. It's illegal to park in the bike lane, but today would not be one for complying with rules.

"Wazow!" Rodrigo said. "I've never seen a sunrise like this."

"You're never awake early enough," Kiara said, laughing.

We were all quiet a moment, taking in the view. We watched a giant cruise ship chugging out Government Cut toward open water. The high-rises of Miami Beach were as white as polished pearls. As the sun gained height, it torched an ever-widening path through ocean and bay, the water sparkling as if electrified. To our left was the gleaming skyline of Brickell's high-rise towers, bankers and lawyers and brokers not yet banging their keyboards in the endless pursuit of money and status.

"I think I know why you wanted us to see the sun come up," Rod said.

"Yeah, Rod?"

"It signifies a new start. And new challenges."

"And new possibilities," Kiara chimed in.

"You two are so darned smart, I'm proud to be your chauffeur."

The bicyclists came up behind us and swung onto the roadway to get around the parked Blackwing. I expected them to shoot birds or shout at us to get out of the bike lane. But they simply waved. Maybe sunrise with an ocean view tempered the tension and anger of our roadways.

Back in the car, we hit dry land at Virginia Key, cruising past Miami Marine Stadium, once home to boat races and rock concerts, now an abandoned shell of splintered seats and crumbling concrete covered by graffiti. We passed the Seaquarium, where Judge Gridley tossed chunks of fish to the killer whale and tossed bullshit at me. We cruised through Crandon Park and turned right on Harbor Drive. I parked in front of the Harbor Donut Gallery, an old-school diner.

I pulled the wheelchair out of the trunk and the three of us took an outdoor table. The kids accepted my recommendation of Ted's Special: fried eggs with bacon, ham, cheese, and tomato on an English muffin. Plus hash browns on the side.

Rod could hold a fork, but his motor skills couldn't quite deposit the food into his mouth without spillage. He accepted Kiara's helping hand without embarrassment. After the first bite of the eggy mix, Rod smacked his lips in delight. "Man, that hits different than cafeteria food."

While the kids ate, I went back to the car, knelt under the rear bumper, and pulled the Consortium's magnetic GPS tracker from the chassis. A landscaper's pickup truck was parked nearby, its bed filled with palm fronds, so I tossed the tracker aboard.

Follow that truck, Sunny Day.

Back at the Blackwing, I grabbed the birthday cake with the chocolate icing and the birthday present.

Rod saw me coming and caught on immediately. He didn't have to be Sherlock Holmes to figure out his present. After all, I was carrying a guitar case.

"Uncle Jake! Is that a gypsy jazz guitar?"

"Either that or a machine gun, kiddo."

I opened the case and pulled out an acoustic guitar of blond wood.

Rodrigo beamed. "Sick! Uncle Jake, you're the GOAT."

The gift was a hit, I think.

Rod turned his head to look at Kiara. "It's a Dell'Arte Pigalle!"

"That's lit!" Kiara said.

I held the guitar so Rod could run a hand over its smooth top of polished spruce. Straining with effort, he plucked a single string with his index finger. Then, with more effort, he placed fingers on the second, third, and fourth strings and plucked again. It wasn't loud, but it was pure, and I felt the thrumming chord in my heart. Maybe there's been a more beautiful musical note somewhere in the world, but I haven't heard it.

"Can't wait to hear you play," I said.

"You will. I promise," Rodrigo said.

Kiara's eyes welled with tears. Happy ones, I thought. "You okay, Key?" Rod asked.

She sniffled and said, "Just lovin' seeing you cheesin'."

"Smiling?" I wondered aloud. "Like 'say cheese'?"

"Yo," Rod said, strumming several strings.

I let my imagination play with an image of Rod, months from now, playing Django Reinhardt's *September Song*.

After we polished off the eggs and potatoes and ordered three *café con leches*, Kiara cut the cake. And I told my tale. Beginning with yesterday's lunch with Bolo Tie. I told them that the defense's computer simulations gave us virtually no chance of winning the public nuisance case.

"On our damage claim," I said, "their simulations show one chance in five that we get past summary judgment, but if we do, a 50 percent chance of winning a jury verdict, and roughly the same percentage for losing the verdict on appeal."

"So roughly a five percent chance of winning the case at the end," said Rod, the math whiz.

I concluded by telling Rod about the offer: a $6 million floor and $24 million cap.

"Jesus Cristo!" His dark eyes widened.

"As part of the deal, we'd dismiss the injunction claim aimed at tackle football and agree to language that would make it more difficult for others to sue."

Then I told him about the first-round draft choice money they'd pay me for folding my cards, plus title to the Blackwing, which I called "the chocolate icing on my cake."

"Wow!" Rodrigo and Kiara said, in perfect synchronicity.

I waited while Rodrigo licked a piece of icing from the fork Kiara was holding. "What do Mom and Dad say?"

"They've told me to take the offer. But there's a wrinkle. Until this morning, the lawsuit was called 'Rodrigo Pittman, a minor child, by and through his parents.'"

"That's dinosaur."

"If that means antiquated, yeah, a lot of the law is like that."

"I see where you're going, Uncle Jake. Today's my eighteenth birthday. No more minor child."

My godson is sharp, no doubt about it.

"You got it, Rodrigo. Early this morning I electronically filed a document called 'Substitution of Party.' Your folks are off the paperwork. It's your lawsuit now."

"So I make all the decisions?"

"And I take orders from you."

"Do you want me to take the offer?"

"Part of me does. It guarantees your future and gives me a cushy landing spot for my old age. But part of me doesn't because it's a sellout. We don't get to prove what Coach Coleman did, and we don't shine a spotlight on the dangers of football."

"But you're not telling me what to do."

I sipped at the *café con leche.* "I'd rather just answer your questions and let you decide."

"If we turn down the offer, what happens?"

"If we lose summary judgment on count one, we go home empty-handed. Zero. Zilch. *Nada*."

"But if we get to trial..."

"If we present the case to a jury, I feel strongly that we'll win."

He nodded and thought it over. I could see the wheels turning. "More or less money than they're offering?" he asked.

"Somewhere between the floor and the cap. I wish I had a better answer."

"Are they right that the other count is a loser? That the judge will never abolish high school football?"

"Here's the thing, Rod. I'm not trying to abolish the sport. I asked for one of two alternatives. Either stop tackle football until the state association proves it's safe. Or, if the court doesn't want to go that far, ban kickoffs and punts and require the sensor helmets your Dad tried to get Coach Coleman to use. The court could enact lots of safeguards well short of banning the sport."

Rodrigo took a moment as Kiara lifted the coffee cup to his lips. "Do you remember when I asked you what it's like being a lawyer, Uncle Jake?"

"I said it's like playing poker with ideas."

"Then I asked whether you thought I could be a lawyer."

"And I said you'd be better than me."

"Did you mean it, Uncle Jake?"

"Damn right. You'd be a helluva poker player."

He was quiet again, so I waited. Finally, he said, "I don't know what to do. It's hard to go against Mom and Dad, after all they've done for me and all I've put them through."

"Talk to them. They're going to be furious with me, so you'll fly solo on that one. And whatever you decide is what we'll do."

My cell phone beeped with an incoming message. A "Notice of Production" from Sandra Day.

"Well, look at that," I said. "The defense finally found your helmet. They just filed a self-congratulatory pleading with all the hard work they put into finding it, and they graciously invite us to examine it."

A photo of a St. Frances helmet missing its face mask and chin strap was attached to the notice. Rod's number 11 was on the back.

Kiara cleared her throat and started to say something, then stopped.

I looked at her, and she said, "I hope you're not going to be angry with me, Mr. L."

"Why would I be?"

"That can't be Rod's helmet."

"And you know this how, Kiara?" I asked.

"Because I have it. I've had Rod's helmet since the night of the game."

-44-
Rodrigo Pittman, Esquire

On the causeway back to the mainland, Kiara told us what happened. On the second kickoff, she was on the sideline, lead cheerleader in the horseshoe formation, her back to the field, chanting "Go! Go! Goooooooo! Commanders!"

When the kick was in the air, she turned and saw Rod airborne, head-down, flying into that disastrous tackle. When he didn't get up, she ran onto the field but was kept away from him by one of the trainers. She saw Dr. Gupta and me kneeling over Rod and watched as we removed his helmet. Then, when the paramedics arrived, she picked up the helmet and kept it.

"I saw Rod could barely breathe when they put him into the ambulance," she said. "I was shook. I'm not sure why I kept the helmet, except...except I wanted something he had touched in case, you know. I'm sorry."

"It's okay, Key," Rod said. "Uncle Jake, could the defense have made an honest mistake?"

"Sandra Day doesn't make honest mistakes. She doesn't know we have the real helmet, so they created a phony one. If we were playing poker, I'd bet the farm that it's a smaller size than the one that flew off your head when you made the first tackle."

"They're cheating?" Kiara asked.

"Big time. They're fabricating evidence."

"That's so gnarly," Rod said. "You would never do that, would you, Uncle Jake?"

"I still believe the words carved in marble. 'Equal Justice Under Law.' For that to work, lawyers can't suborn perjury or fabricate evidence."

"If we don't settle, will they bring that phony helmet to court?"

"I certainly hope so."

Rod didn't ask why. I could tell he was trying to figure it out himself. After a moment, he said, "We lure them into the trap of hauling out the phony one first. And then ka-pow! We show the real helmet and prove just how sheisty they are."

"You're a quick study, Rodrigo Pittman, Esquire."

As I'd expect from a kid in Honor Society.

"Do you think they do crud like this in all their cases?" Rod asked.

"Every chance they get."

"Can't anyone stop them?"

"Beating their asses in court would be a start," I said.

Rod considered that a moment and said, "Like you said, I need to talk to Mom and Dad before deciding what to do."

The morning sun was high enough to turn the Brickell Avenue skyscrapers into a shimmering glare of mirrored windows from the causeway to the Miami River. I squinted, pulled down the visor, turned on my cell phone, and wondered how many times Tank Pittman had called me.

Nine! Each one progressively more belligerent.

"Yo, Jake. They say you took Rod somewhere. What's up, roomie?"

"C'mon, Jake. What stunt are you pulling here? Call me!"

"Hey, ass clown! Some dipshit from the Herald *just called and said you took Lily and me off the lawsuit."*

"Are you trying some flea flicker trickeration, you fumblerooski fool? Get your ass back here now!"

"If you turned down the settlement, I'm gonna kick your ass from here to Toad Suck, Arkansas, you brain-dead bastard!"

I stopped after the fifth message, which I could barely hear with Rod and Kiara laughing so hard.

"Never heard your father so salty," Kiara said.

"Dad gonna light your ass up," Rod said.

"Don't go all urban on me, Rodrigo. Doesn't work when you usually sound like Prince Harry."

"Big yikes!" Rod laughed, leaving me behind without a translator.

Once off the causeway, I swung the Blackwing onto the entrance ramp of I-95 and headed north. Twelve minutes later, we pulled into the rehab center driveway, and there was Tank Pittman, massive arms folded across his chest, waiting for his old roomie.

-45-
Tío Jake No Más

Rodrigo saved my life, or at least saved me from another broken nose. I pulled the Blackwing to a stop, and Tank opened the passenger door.

"I'll get you out, son."

"Don't be chapped at Uncle Jake," Rod said.

"He ain't your uncle, but he seems to think he's your father."

"Tank, I can explain everything," I said.

"Shut up and get the wheelchair. I'll deal with you later."

Tank reached into the front seat and gently lifted his son out of the car. He could have done it with one arm without straining.

"Dad, Jake's just trying to help us," Rod said. "Please don't whomp him."

From the backseat Kiara said, "He showed us the sunrise."

I got the wheelchair out of the trunk and set it up, then saw Lily standing near the front door of the facility. She glared at me with a look that could leave third-degree burns. Unwilling to face her wrath, I hurried back into the driver's seat.

Rod rolled toward the front door with his mother and Kiara alongside.

"I'll call you later, Jake," Rod said over his shoulder, following his father's instruction that I was *Tío Jake no más*.

Tank climbed into the passenger seat next me, ran his hand over the black leather dashboard and said, "If you've already turned down that offer we told you to take, I'm under instructions from Lily to spill some of your blood. You probably know she's still pissed at you for taking me to that strip joint in Buffalo."

I could have pointed out that was years before Tank and Lily met, and she never would have found out if he hadn't kept a garter belt embroidered with the name "Kandi Kane." Instead, I told him the offer was open until five p.m. today, and I hadn't tried to influence Rodrigo.

"I'm hoping the three of you agree on what to do," I said, "but if you don't, Rod's vote is the only one that counts."

He reached over and squeezed the steering wheel, which, had it been my forearm, would have splintered.

"You know what grinds my ass, Jake?"

I didn't answer, so he continued, "Rod idolizes you. Always has. Wants to be a lawyer because of you." He sounded dejected and exhausted. I could imagine his sleepless nights and tear-stained days, but there was no way to fully comprehend what Tank was going through. No way to feel a father's pain.

"Rod's really sharp," I said. "He'll be a success in any field he wants."

"Not football."

"The world's a helluva lot bigger than football, pal."

"I know. I know. I'm just thinking what kind of life he'll have."

"He's going to walk, He's going to play the guitar. He'll get through this with his inner strength and his parents' love. And he'll have a life."

"What about you and me, Jake? Lily wants to cut you out of our family."

"I was hoping we'd be friends in good times and bad. Just like always."

He took his left hand from the steering wheel and clasped it around my neck. Either he was going to strangle me or give me a good-buddy squeeze. He chose the squeeze. "I pretty much never say 'no' to Lily. But you and me, roomie. 'Til the end of time."

PART FIVE

"There are no one hundred percent heroes."
   – "Cinnamon Skin" by John D. MacDonald

"They don't call us sharks for our ability to swim."
   – Jake Lassiter

-46-
Cappin' and Creepin'

My neighborhood on Kumquat was quiet in the afternoon. I lay in the hammock in my backyard, swinging to and fro, and then to change things up, swinging fro and to. Melissa was at the hospital, so I was alone. I would have been listening to a clock tick away the minutes, but I don't have a clock that ticks.

Three o'clock came and went. Where...I wasn't sure.

Four o'clock did the same.

The Consortium's offer to settle, with all its goodies for me, would expire at five p.m. If I could travel at the speed of light, time would stand still, but not even the Blackwing could do that. So I waited for Rod's call with my instructions.

I was tempted to pass the time with a tumbler of tequila, but suspecting I might need a few watts of brainpower, I remained thirsty. I expected Rod to make a rational decision. An objective observer would surely tell him to take the cautious course.

"*Listen to your parents. Don't trust Wrong-Way Lassiter. Take the money and run.*"

Except Rod can't run.

I thought about my own skin in the game. What would I do with all that moolah? A big new house on a canal, Cocoplum maybe. A Bertram 50-footer with a dive platform, fighting chair, and two staterooms. No one would ever say, "You're gonna need a bigger boat."

Wait a second! That's not me. Those are the guys I ridicule!

At 4:45 p.m., my cell phone rang, and the little window said Langston Pittman was calling.

"Jake, you've got Rod and me on speaker," Tank said.

"Hey, guys."

"I have a question," Rod said. "If we go to trial, can you prove that Coach is cappin' and his lawyers are creepin'?"

"If that means 'lying' and 'cheating,' the answer is, yes, I think so."

Keeping my voice in neutral, no hitting the gas to push Rod one way or the other.

"And if we take their money now, we don't prove anything, right? They get away with it and can do it again and again."

"That's the nature of settlements," I said. "Especially with non-disclosure agreements."

"Is that common? To settle on secret terms?"

"It's done every day in courts from coast to coast."

"Does that make it right, Uncle Jake?"

Uncle Jake! *Tío otra vez.*

"I can't answer your question, Rodrigo. Sometimes, things are neither right nor wrong. They just are. I'm not going to tell you to lose your ideals. Not yet, anyway."

"If we go to court, what do I do?"

"You'll sit next to me. Second chair."

"You mean first wheelchair."

"Whatever you call it, you're going to help me."

"For real? Or do I just sit there to get sympathy from the judge?"

"Judge Duckworth is not big on sympathy. Solid legal reasoning, not emotion, appeals to her."

Tank said, "Be straight up, Jake. How can Rodrigo help?"

"He has great instincts. We have a situation I'll call 'helmet-gate,' and Rod instinctively knew how to handle it in court."

"Do you trust those computer simulations they gave you?" Rod asked. "That after appeals and everything, our chance of winning is only five percent?"

"All I can say is that judges and jurors aren't computers. They're human beings with emotions and feelings and, once in a while, brains."

"At first, the doctors gave me five percent chance of walking. Now, they say it's just a matter of when."

"Amen to that," Tank said.

They were silent for a long moment. It was a helluva big decision for a kid who turned 18 today.

"We're not going to settle," Rod said, with finality.

Wow. It's what I wanted to hear, but at the same time, I felt my chest tighten with the enormity of the responsibility.

"Tank, I'd love to have your blessing on this," I said.

"Not what I'd do, roomie. But like you said before, it's Rod's call. We're putting a lot of faith in you."

That hung heavy in the air like wet laundry on a flimsy clothesline. I needed to respond with something that was reassuring but also honest.

"I love both of you for your trust, and I'll die before I let you down."

***

At 4:55 p.m., I reached Sandra Day on her cell phone.

"I just emailed you the settlement papers," she said. "I hope you're not quibbling over language."

"You jumped the gun. We're turning down the offer."

"Very funny. You accepted last night, or should I say, early this morning when you called me and made inappropriate remarks.

Now, let's get this done so I can pack my bags and leave this humid hellhole."

"First of all, Ms. Day, you called me. And I thought you were my fiancée and were naked in my bed."

"Red light. Cease and desist! 'Naked' and 'bed' have no place in our conversations."

"Fine. Then I'll skip the Jacuzzi and the champagne. But rest assured, we never discussed the offer."

"You had just met with your clients at their home."

"As you know from the tracking device, which now thinks I'm at the county dump about to be turned into mulch."

"You must be insane. It's a ridiculously generous offer."

"Just following my client's instructions."

"You kept the car!"

"Fine, I'll re-title it back."

Wait a second. Why would I? I love that damn muscle car hiding under the Cadillac coat-of-arms.

She sighed and said, "While I'm surprised with your client's decision, on second thought, I'm rather pleased. This will be an excellent learning experience for my people. Nearly all our cases settle, so they see very few trials."

"Glad to be of use to Wickerham and Coot."

"Snoot!" she corrected me. "Do you hear that sound, Mr. Lassiter?"

Other than my tinnitus, nope.

"What sound?" I asked.

"Sharpening my knives. I'm going to slice you into pieces like the sushi chef at Nakazawa."

"And no doubt eat my liver with some fava beans and chianti. Bon appétit, Sunny Day."

THE TWITTERSPHERE

@Rambo_Rules132
Lassiter's pronouns should be "she," "her," and "tit."
> **@Juco_Prof_83 Replied**
> I think you mean "it."
>> **@Rambo_Rules132**
>> No, I mean "tit."

***

@SickPuppy305
Back in the day, I played junior varsity at Coral Gables High. Kid who tackles like that deserves to be paralyzed.
> **@Mom_of_Delray3 Replied**
> That's cruel, @SickPuppy305
>> **@SickPuppy305**
>> It's all about teamwork. My coach preached, "There's no 'I' in happyness."

***

@Jock_Jones_III
I heard Lassiter is dying. Well, I say good writtens.

-47-
A Life Sentence

Three Weeks Later...

"We had sex last night," I said.

"Oh." Dr. Rochelle Stein appeared puzzled. "And what was the problem?"

"No problem. Instead of starting with some hitch in the relationship, I thought I'd give you some good news."

"So the sex was satisfactory?" Dr. Stein asked.

"I'd choose a more exuberant adjective," I said. "'Volcanic' will do."

Melissa and I were in our usual spots in Dr. Stein's office. So was the little yellow horse.

"Jake has been feeling better," Melissa said. "More focused and fewer apparent symptoms. He's been warm and affectionate and..."

"Grrrr," I growled, in my best Tony the Tiger. "A maniac in the bedroom."

Dr. Stein smiled, blessing our coupling with her professional approval.

"There's a paradox here," Melissa said. "Jake is under a lot of pressure in the lawsuit. A lot of mental gymnastics, but instead of overwhelming him, it seems to have cleared his mind. I'm working on a new CTE study to probe deeper."

"Jake, it must be rewarding to know you may be able to help others with similar ailments," Dr. Stein said.

"I regret that I have only one brain to give to my country," I said.

We were all quiet a moment. Then, Dr. Stein asked, "Is there anything you'd like to discuss today that's causing concern?"

We both shook our heads, but I decided to cop a plea even when I hadn't been indicted. "I'm having an itty-bitty problem with anger."

"How so?" Dr. Stein asked.

"Not in the relationship, but in my outside life. I haven't punched anyone, but I have this fury building inside."

"Go on."

"In the case I'm handling, the other side plays dirty. Their investigators are really thugs who harass and stalk witnesses and tried to break into our house. I've been having fantasies about what I might do if I meet the bastards on the road or in a dark alley."

"Violent fantasies?"

"Broken bones and buckets of blood, so yes."

"Are they just fantasies? Or, given the chance, would you act them out?"

"I think I'd turn them into reality."

"Then your anger would be managing you, rather than you managing your anger."

Okay, another one of those shrink-school maxims.

"Irritability and temper issues are common among those with CTE," Melissa said. "But there are cognitive exercises to curb aggressive tendencies."

"Here's the thing. I don't want to curb or manage my aggression, if that means failing to do what ought to be done."

"Which is what, Jake?" Dr. Stein had just the hint of alarm in her voice.

"Like I said, these guys don't play by the rules. They'll cheat to win, the rights of my client and everyone else be damned. They simply don't give a damn."

"You didn't answer my question," Dr. Stein said. "Just what do you think ought to be done?"

I rubbed my chin with a knuckle, buying a moment's time. "If I remember the law of doctor-patient privilege, Dr. Stein, you can't repeat any admissions I make about past crimes I might have committed."

"That's true."

"But if I tell you that I plan to do something in the future like beat someone senseless with a baseball bat or run their car off the road, you have a duty to report me to the authorities."

"That's true, too."

"I think I'm going to keep my own counsel on this for a while."

"That's your choice, of course. But I do worry about you, Jake."

***

We spent the next 30 minutes going over our homework. Without sharing answers, we each had perfect scores on the Fondness and Admiration Questionnaire. If you asked me, I'd say the questions were too damn easy:

"I can easily list three things I admire about my partner."

Three? I could give you thirty-three!

"When we are apart, I often think fondly of my partner."

Duh. If not, why would two people be together?

"I'm very pleased with the two of you," Dr. Stein said, after looking at our scores. Then she closed her notebook and said, "You've both done an admirable job here."

"You've helped us," Melissa said. "A lot."

"Agreed," I said, meaning it.

Sure, I'd been skeptical. Some of the general principles seemed too obvious, too pat, or too cute.

Enhance your love maps.

Cherish your partner.

Nurture your fondness and admiration.

And, of course, avoid those damn Four Horsemen: Criticism, Contempt, Defensiveness, and Stonewalling.

Okay, so I was wrong! Therapy helped us. Of course, we started from a place of mutual love and respect and worked from there.

"It seems to me that the two of you have created shared meaning in your lives," Dr. Stein said. "You share goals and values and support each other's individual lives. I feel very good about the two of you as lifelong partners."

"Does that mean we get early release for good behavior?" I asked.

"Ja-ke," Melissa said in her chiding, yet playful, tone.

"Actually, Jake," Dr. Stein said, "I'm sentencing you to life. Together."

-48-
Locker Room Nostalgia

After we left Dr. Stein's office with a clean bill of relationship health, Melissa headed to the hospital, and I drove to St. Frances High School. It was deposition day for Coach Monty Coleman.

Bolo Tie, my favorite Consortium cowboy, in jeans and a shirt with pearly snaps, met me in the school's parking lot, just as I was getting out of my shiny Blackwing.

"Are you here to make sure I don't steal the chalk and erasers?" I asked.

"Good luck finding them, old-timer. It's all computer monitors and whiteboards."

Just then, my Blackwing's twin brother swung into the parking lot and squealed to a stop alongside us.

Its windows were tinted, illegally, a midnight black with a reflective glare. The passenger window rolled down, and a figure in a black hoodie and oversize sunglasses leaned out.

"The Unabomber a friend of yours?" I asked Bolo Tie.

"I owe you, Lassiter," the hoodie fellow growled. He shoved a crutch out the window and shook the rubberized tip at me. "And you're gonna get paid, big time."

The window zipped up, and the car tore out of the parking lot.

"Is that who I think it is?" I asked.

"We call them the Blackwing Brothers," Bolo Tie said. "That's Bones, and yeah, you broke his ankle with the baseball bat."

"Don't tell me the driver's name is 'Skull.'"

"Well, he does have a shaved head. He's not so bad, but Bones is an asshole. And stupid. Probably bluffing but don't be leaving any doors or windows unlocked."

Bolo Tie escorted me to the field house en route to the team's Booster Lounge.

"Let's take a shortcut through the locker room," he said.

The team was on the practice field, and the empty locker room had that familiar aroma of sweat and humidity, liniment and grass-stained socks. I could almost hear the *rip* of tape being torn from ankles and wrists, the splash of the showers, and the raucous, towel-snapping laughter of teenage boys.

We left the locker room and took an outside staircase to the second floor. We walked through a corridor lined with photos of teams from yesteryear. A few paces away was the Commanders Hall of Fame, the donors to the football program. Among the 8x10 head shots was Judge Erwin Gridley.

I pointed at the photo and said, "Gridley tried to scare me off the case, but you probably know that."

"He told me you were smarter than you looked," Bolo Tie said. "So I told Sandra Day you were a worthy adversary, and she said she wouldn't underestimate you, even though you wrote your legal briefs in one-syllable words with a crayon."

"She's done a deep dive on me. Knows every time I farted in court."

"Way more than that. Her team's behavioral psychologist created a flow chart predicting every move you'd make in response to various stimuli."

"Good luck. I don't even know what I'm doing next."

"This shrink advised the CIA in 2003 that Saddam Hussein was likely hiding outside a small town in northern Iraq and that when American troops came close, he would go underground. Which is where we found him, in a spider hole outside Ad-Dawr."

That stopped me. "When you say 'we,' do you mean you were there?"

"Not on Task Force 121, which pulled Hussein out of the hole. But yeah, I served in Iraq."

"So did our judge. Melvia Duckworth was in the Judge Advocate General Corps."

"Big Army, small world," Bolo Tie said.

On a loudspeaker, a female voice reminded students about a pep rally after final period Friday.

"So you told Day I wasn't a pushover. What can you tell me about her?"

"A lot. But I won't. Except she's smart and ruthless and seldom makes mistakes."

"Really? The day you made the offer, she called me after midnight dead drunk."

"Sandra Day doesn't drink."

"I suppose she didn't invite me to her hotel suite."

"Oh, she did that."

"Wait. You know? She told you?"

He didn't answer.

"She recorded it, didn't she?" I said.

Still no answer, and it took me a moment to put it together.

How the hell did I miss this? My instincts, once sharp as a stiletto, seem as dull and blunt as a prison spoon.

"She pretended to be drunk," I said. "If I'd shown up, she wouldn't be in the suite. There'd be a photographer, a dead hooker, and a pile of cocaine."

"A photographer. A live hooker. No cocaine."

"But why! What's her end game?"

"Think about it, Lassiter."

"On the call she said I was a phony who was going to take the money and run. And she really wanted to try the case."

"Reverse psychology. She wanted you to take it. She knew from the tracking device that you'd met with your clients. The psychologist told her that if you were settling, you would have gone straight home to celebrate with your fiancée. After all, you'd be newly rich. But if you went off to drink in a bar alone, or if you went for a long drive to nowhere, you were torn. You didn't know what to do."

Damn, their shrink nailed it.

We headed down the long corridor, and I said, "Why are you telling me this? You want Day to lose?"

"Oh, she's not going to lose. But I like watching a fair fight."

We entered the lounge, a long, rectangular room with open windows overlooking the practice field. Wearing a headset, Coach Coleman stood at the window in St. Frances sweats, watching his team working out below. After a moment, he spoke into the mic. "Kyle, tell Hamilton his job isn't just to shed blockers but to make tackles. He's staying engaged with the guard after the running back is five yards past him."

Speaking to an assistant. Coaches would yell instructions from their hospital beds if they had a live feed from the practice field.

Sandra Day and about a dozen of her associates lined one side of a conference table. The court stenographer sat at the end with her little machine. I exchanged curt hellos with Day and joined Coleman at the open window.

The field must have been freshly mowed, because I caught the scent of the grass. We were close enough for me to hear the *bleet* of the whistles, the *thwack* of the punter's foot smacking the ball, and the *thud* of pads on pads. Several players hurried along a sidewalk that ran between light towers, their cleats *clack-clacking* on the concrete. The sounds were a familiar symphony that evoked a thousand memories.

Across the field, the linebackers were shuffling through open spaces between three trash cans, then practicing their drops with forward and backward bursts. Closer to us, heavy-legged linemen were doing Gorillas, jogging in place, dropping belly-first to the ground, then hopping back up, over and over again. Grueling in the Florida heat.

"Remind you of anything?" Day asked from behind me.

"Only my entire life." I took my seat at the table. "I couldn't figure out why you scheduled the depo at a time the coach would miss practice. Then, you had Bolo Tie bring me here by way of the locker room. You're playing on my nostalgia."

"Am I now?"

"Do you think I'm going to fold my cards because I have fond memories of the game?"

"Not at all," she said. "But what do you think when you see all those young men gloriously happy to be working so hard, reaching deep inside themselves, learning self-discipline and sacrifice and teamwork?"

"I think if you could make the game safe, I'd be cheering for them and for you."

Oh, wait a second. That behavioral psychologist must have told her that I was the sentimental sort. Well, it's not working. Except that it is...in a way. From day one, I've known the benefits of high school football. But that won't hurt my performance in court. Or will it?

"I have a second reason for holding the depo here today," Sandra Day said.

"Of course you do."

"Would you agree that the setting is emblematic of high school football?"

"Sure. So what?"

"Would you consent to Judge Duckworth holding the summary judgment hearing in this room during a practice?"

Oh, that's rich. Maybe the band can strike up "America the Beautiful," too.

"On one condition," I said. "We'll do the first half of the hearing right here. And the second half in the ICU of the spinal cord center where we'll also show a videotape of the five-hour surgery on my client's neck. I made it through about fifteen minutes before hurling, but Judge Duckworth has seen combat, so she'll take every bloody close-up in stride."

"Touché, Mr. Lassiter. Let's swear in the witness and move on."

-49-
Evasion, Obfuscation, Amnesia, and Perjury

Coleman raised his hand and swore to tell the truth, the whole truth and nothing but the truth. Frankly, I would have been happy with a reasonable facsimile thereof.

Some lawyers take the primrose path method of deposing adverse witnesses. They start with a relaxing stroll, lull the witness into a false sense of security, then push the bastard into a punji pit filled with poisoned spikes. Me? I take the Luca Brasi approach. Nail the guy's hand to the table as soon as he settles his butt into the chair.

With no preamble, I said, "Before the second kickoff, when Rodrigo Pittman appeared woozy and disoriented, you sent him back into the game, did you not?"

"Objection to the form of the question," Sandra Day piped up. "Assumes facts not in evidence, and no foundation was laid. Further, it's argumentative."

"That's all?" I asked. When she didn't answer, I said, "Objections are reserved and needn't be stated on the record, Ms. Day. But you know that." I turned back to the witness. "Mr. Coleman?"

He looked toward Day who nodded. Then he said, "Rod didn't appear woozy or disoriented to me."

"When he made the tackle on the first kickoff, you saw him stagger when he got to his feet, did you not?"

"I don't think he staggered."

"Stumbled, then?"

"He might have slipped. I can't be sure."

"One way or another, he lost his balance?"

"I'm not sure."

"Rod's helmet collided with the returner's shoulder pad on that first tackle, correct?"

"The facemask of his helmet, yes."

"While Rod was running at close to full speed?"

"I can't swear to that."

"Isn't the returner, D.J. Arrington, at least 30 pounds heavier than Rod?"

"I'm not sure of Arrington's weight."

"Didn't the collision knock Rod backward and off his feet?"

"I'm not sure. It was difficult to see from my angle on the sideline."

"Rod's helmet came off making that tackle, correct?"

"Apparently, yes."

"And by rule, he should have sat out the next play?"

"Yes, but that was an official's error."

"An error you did not correct?"

"I also don't tell them when they miss a holding call on our grabby tight end."

That sly little remark drew smirks from Day's troops.

"Back to the helmet. It was too large for Rod, wasn't it?"

"No, sir. Our trainer has filed an affidavit regarding the helmet. Ms. Day also has made the helmet available to you for your inspection."

"So nice of her," I said.

"It's my understanding you have not sought to inspect it," Coleman blathered on, "so it seems to me you're giving up on that issue."

"Tell you what, Coach," I said, "you don't try to practice law, and I won't try to coach football. Deal?"

"Objection," Day said. "Argumentative."

I wondered what Coleman knew about the phony helmet charade, but this wasn't the time to find out. As Rod intuitively knew, that nasty bit of defense perfidy would best be unveiled in court in front of the judge.

"When Rod came to the sideline after the first kickoff, what did you say to him?" I asked.

"I can't remember exactly. I probably told him, 'good hit.'"

"In fact, you asked him if he was 'good to go,' did you not?"

He paused as if trying to remember. I've seen better actors in puppet shows. "Why, yes. Yes, I did."

"Asked him twice?"

"I believe, perhaps."

"Was he hurt on that first tackle?"

"No, I don't think so."

"So why ask if he's good to go?"

Coleman opened his mouth but nothing came out. His eyes darted to Day, then he said, "Rod had just run 60 yards to make the tackle. I wanted to make sure he wasn't winded."

"Oh, please! Rodrigo ran the 100 and 200 for the track team. In football practice, he always finished first in the gassers."

"Objection!" Sandra Day rang out. "Argumentative. And I can't find a question there."

"Okay, here's one. Mr. Coleman, are you familiar with the concussion protocol of your co-defendant, the Florida High School Athletic Association?"

"Of course. Every year, I take the refresher course."

"If a player suffers dizziness, he must be removed from the game, correct?"

"Yes."

"Or if he shows confusion?"

"Yes."

"Problems with balance?"

"That, too. Those are all in Policy 40.1 of the FHSAA," he said, showing off.

"When Rodrigo came off the field, after making a hard tackle in which he got knocked ass-over-elbows and his helmet flew off, and he either staggered or stumbled or slipped getting to his feet, were you concerned that he might have suffered a concussion?"

He paused a beat and then said, "I don't recall a specific concern, but generally I wanted to know if he believed he was okay for the second kickoff."

"Did you notice that Rod's eyes were glassy?"

"No."

"Did he have a vacant stare?"

"No."

"Did he seem disoriented?"

"Objection. Asked and answered," Day said.

"I just thought the coach's memory might have improved as he pondered his duty to tell the truth."

"Don't badger my client," Day commanded.

I ignored her and said, "Did Rodrigo seem confused before the second kickoff?"

"No."

I opened my laptop and said, "Let's have a listen." I hit a couple buttons and the audio played:

"You good to go?"

"I'm good, Dad."

"You okay?"

"I'm good to go, Dad."

I pushed the PAUSE button. "That's you and Rodrigo, correct?"

"Objection, and I instruct the witness not to answer." Day looked toward her foot soldiers. One of them, Myron of the eyeglasses and the reedy mustache, pushed a document across the table at me.

"Our motion *in limine*," Day said.

Two female associates also slid documents – as thick as hockey pucks – toward me. "Our supporting memoranda of law," Day continued.

"Could you briefly state your grounds to keep the audio out of evidence?" I gestured toward the three documents. "And by briefly, I mean less time than it would take to read that encyclopedia of legal mumbo jumbo you just hit me with."

Whoosh. More documents came my way. Judging from the first page, each was an affidavit.

"The audio tape has been tampered with," Day said. "So sayeth two expert witnesses."

"I'd like to cross examine them. So sayeth me."

"Fine. If you want to depose them, one is a professor of audiology at McGill University in Toronto. The other is one of the world's leading acoustical engineers. He's based in Samarkand, which, as I'm sure you know, is in Uzbekistan. We'll coordinate travel plans."

Her guys and gals tittered at that, knowing it would never happen.

"For the record," I said, "the audio has not been tampered with. It was enhanced to reduce ambient noise and to increase the volume of the voices."

"I assume you have an expert who will confirm that." Day had a lilt to her voice to suggest that she, in fact, assumed no such thing.

"Damn straight," I said. "I've got a pimply, pony-tailed guy at WQAM who worked part-time at Radio Shack when he was in high school."

"Mr. Lassiter, I will permit you to ask the witness what he recalls having been said, but only without reference to the tainted audio tape."

"Thanks, Ms. Day, for going to so much trouble, even framing my line of inquiry. Go ahead, Coach. Answer your mouthpiece's question."

Sandra Day shot me a lacerating look, and Coleman said, "I asked Rod if he was good to go, and best I recall, he said, 'I'm good, dammit.' Just to be sure, I asked him again, and he said, 'I'm good to go, dammit.'"

I gotta hand it to Sunny Day. When she preps her witnesses to lie, they turn out to be All-Pro Prevaricators.

"Just so it's clear," I said, "you're stating under penalty of perjury that Rodrigo said 'dammit' and not 'Dad,' correct?"

"Understand one thing, Mr. Lassiter," he continued. "I have a headset on, and my coordinators in the booth are yelling at each other and at me. The band is playing. The fans are screaming. So I'm telling you to the best of my recollection what I believe I heard."

"What did you say next?" I asked, evenly. This was not the time to argue with him. Nothing I could ask would make him depart from the script.

"Something to the effect of 'do it again.'"

I punched another button and the audio played: *"Then do it again, Rod. Be a headhunter. Stick 'em. Put a hat on a hat."*

"Same objection," Sandra Day said. "Don't answer any questions related to the audio. However, if Mr. Lassiter wishes to ask you, hypothetically, how you interpret the term, 'headhunter,' you may answer."

"If you're going to handle my side of the case, Ms. Day, please do a better job." I pointed an index finger at her. "Until then, I'll handle the questions."

"Be my guest," she said.

"Coach, isn't 'headhunter' an old football expression meaning to tackle high, going for the opponent's head?"

"Like a lot of football terms, it has several meanings. Hypothetically, if I said that, I wasn't telling Rod to attack the returner above the neck. In fact, Rod's tackle involved his helmet hitting the returner's thigh pad. Regardless what I said, he wasn't headhunting, as you have mistakenly suggested."

Sounding oh-so-rehearsed. Sunny Day and her lickspittles had work to do to make his testimony sound natural.

I hit a couple more buttons on the laptop and swung it around so Coleman could see the monitor. "This is your last scrimmage before the game in which Rodrigo suffered his catastrophic injury."

"Ob-jec-tion!" Sunny Day trilled. "This video was hacked in violation of the Computer Fraud and Abuse Act, and we are today filing a motion *in limine* with supporting memoranda."

Now, three of Day's associates rained a hailstorm of paperwork at me.

"Additionally, we will seek sanctions against you personally, Mr. Lassiter, and ask Judge Duckworth to refer the matter to the U.S. Attorney for prosecution."

"Then, I'll just play the video for my own amusement," I said, hitting another button. On the monitor, Coleman, believing the camera was turned off, barked at the defense after a player failed to make a tackle that would have involved a helmet-to-helmet hit.

"Do I care if you pick up a targeting penalty? Hell, no. That'll make their receivers shaky coming across the middle. If you smash heads and the zebras throw a flag, you won't hear shit from me. If you're ejected, consider it your badge of courage. But don't curl up and die like Macklin just did."

Then a pause and at a lower volume:

"My high school coach used to yell, 'Be a headhunter!' The rule book says I can't tell you to do that. All I'll say is that college coaches are looking for guys who don't mind getting their hair mussed. So, do some damage!"

"What damage did you want your players to do?" I asked.

"Don't answer that!" Sandra Day commanded. "Mr. Lassiter, my client will not answer questions based on tainted evidence. Move on."

"I'll move on when I damn well feel like it. Mr. Coleman, correct me if I'm wrong, but aren't you sneakily telling your players to be 'headhunters'?"

"Don't answer that," Day repeated, and her client kept quiet.

I tried similar questions to no avail. It was an issue I would raise later with Judge Duckworth.

Maybe I'd borrow Dr. Stein's horse and give a good 'neighhhh' in the courtroom. "Your Honor, they're riding the Four Horsemen of depositions: Evasion, Obfuscation, Amnesia, and Perjury."

"Mr. Coleman, are you familiar with the term 'rugby tackling'?" I asked.

"It's where the tackler slings the ball carrier down in the direction he's running, with the tackler's head behind the ball carrier."

"It's considered safer than the traditional helmet-to-chest, drive-him-backward method of tackling, correct?"

"I'd say it's trendy in some circles."

"Rod's father, Langston Pittman, a former All Pro defensive lineman, offered to teach rugby tackling, did he not?"

"Yes, and I turned him down. We'd give up an extra two yards on every play. We'd look soft, and we'd be soft. Our opponent's offense would be delivering the blows. You played defense, Mr. Lassiter. You're the guys who have to hit harder."

"You also refused to use those big rubber donuts for tackling drills, correct?"

"Same reason. If our defense doesn't run through ball carriers in practice, we'll get trampled in games. But I tell you what, Lassiter. I'll start using those rubber donuts the first time we play a team of truck tires."

He smiled at his little witticism and was becoming more relaxed and comfortable with each question. His lawyer had protected him, and I hadn't laid a glove on him.

The rest of the depo was similarly unfruitful. Coach Coleman fended off my questions with pre-packaged, slickly delivered answers:

– The team didn't use the sensor helmets Tank Pittman bought because they didn't work properly. "Bad technology," Coleman claimed.

– Nothing untoward happened in the "Tunnel of Manhood" tent. No illegal pit drills. Not the Nutcracker, Blood Alley, or Oklahoma drill. It was just a one-on-one tackling drill in semi-darkness with teammates screaming to simulate crowd noise at away night games. Oh...and the players loved it. Built camaraderie.

– Dr. Herlocher was responsible for securing a replacement team physician, and he was to blame for no one showing up. And no, the doc didn't resign because of anything that took place in the tent.

"So why did Dr. Herlocher abruptly quit?" I asked.

"He had an opportunity to fulfill a lifelong dream and do eleemosynary work with indigenous peoples," Coleman said.

Yeah, he used a ten-dollar word when the ten-cent word "charitable" would have worked fine. And sure, I remember one of Sunny Day's associates saying "eleemosynary" back at the discovery conference and also that this was Herlocher's "lifelong dream." So is there any doubt who's writing the script?

"And just where is Dr. Herlocher doing these good deeds?" I asked.

"In Patagonia."

The answer surprised me. So did Sunny Day's face, which froze for just a split second. In our discovery session, the same associate had said the sawbones was in Chile. Sure, part of Patagonia was in Argentina and part in Chile. Coleman just narrowed down his whereabouts, but that slip-up wasn't what surprised me.

Maybe I'd been too quick to conclude that the charity mission was fabricated. I thought they'd paid Herlocher to disappear on a luxury vacation. But the look on Sunny Day's face and the specificity of Patagonia told me something else. He really was doing charity work in Chile, and I might be able to find him.

"By Patagonia, I assume you mean the tip of South America and not the clothing store at the mall," I said.

"South America. Right."

"What city or town or village in Patagonia are we talking about?" I asked.

"Only if you know, Coach," Sandra Day quickly said.

"Dammit, Day!" I exploded. "Don't coach the witness! 'Only if you know?' Every damn question is 'only if you know.' That's such a cheap trick! You should be ashamed of yourself."

Sandra Day leveled her gaze at me, her face registering no emotion. "Don't you raise your voice to me," she said, *sotto voce*. "Don't use your bulk and your baritone to try and intimidate me. Don't put your manhood on display and use your toxic –"

"If you say 'masculinity,' I will damn sure put my manhood on display and piss all over every piece of paper you tossed at me today. And I've been sitting here so long, I might irrigate the practice field, too. Preferably from the window in this room."

That quieted her. One of Day's associates looked on the verge of swooning. I realized that I was standing. I'd gotten out of my chair, knocking it over without realizing it. My face felt hot, my mouth dry, and I could hear my heart beating in my ears. And not the regular pace, *tu-tump tu-tump tu-tump*. But racing at an irregular, jagged pace that frightened me.

If I'm going to stroke out, I can't let it be Sunny Day who sends me to an early grave. Damn, she baited me, and I swallowed it whole.

I picked up my chair, dropped back into it, and tried to regain some semblance of dignity as my heart kept zig-zagging.

Finally, Day said, "You are a vulgar and reprehensible man, a disgrace to an honorable profession. Perhaps it's time for the Florida Supreme Court to punch your ticket and not just spank you. Obviously, the court-ordered anger management counseling bore no fruit." Then, with a wicked little smile, she added, "Or are you still doing that in couples therapy?"

Okay, I get the point. You know every little thing about me, and you'll use it all. Winning is everything. Crush the opposition into dust. Why not? Maybe that's what gets you off.

I took in a long breath, held it, looked toward Coleman, and exhaled. "Let's circle back to the second kickoff in which Rod suffered his catastrophic injury," I said.

"No," Day said. "I will allow Coach Coleman to answer the pending question. Thereafter, this deposition is terminated due to your misconduct. Coach, do you remember the question?"

"Mr. Lassiter asked if I know where Dr. Herlocher is. What city or town in Patagonia?" Coleman shrugged and answered just as Sunny ("only-if-you-know") Day instructed him to. "Sorry. I don't know."

Neither do I. But I sure as hell would try to find out. My first call would be to the old gumshoe George Barrios.

I had hoped to dent the defense, if only a fender bender. But Monty Coleman was sharp, the very model of the modern football general. And damn well prepared by his squadron of legal eagles, sparrows, and hummingbirds.

Walking back to my Blackwing, weighted down by hundreds of pages of Sandra Day's paperwork, I knew I needed more ammunition to get past the summary judgment hearing that loomed on next week's calendar.

Just what can I find that would, to borrow Coleman's phrase, "do some damage"?

-50-
The Misery Rule

Two days before the summary judgment hearing, I was in the Blackwing – *my* Blackwing! – on my way to visit Rod at the rehab center when Rudy Schulian, my favorite obit writer, rang my cell phone.

"I'm still alive, but thanks for asking, Rudy," I said.

"Not why I'm calling, Mr. Lassiter. Our courthouse reporter says you won't return her calls, so I told her we were friends, and..."

"Friends, Rudy? I think of you more as my undertaker."

"Even so, with your summary judgment hearing coming up and everyone saying you're going to lose big time, I wonder if you'd like to comment."

"Sure, if you'll do me a small favor. The *Herald* had a photographer at the game where Rod Pittman was injured. The paper ran a photo of Rod sprawled on the field, motionless. I'm sure there are more. Probably a lot more."

"If it wasn't published, our policy prohibits – "

"Don't want to hear it. Get me those other shots, and I'll give you the best quotes of your life. I'll give you an exposé of conspiracy and fraud and dirty tricks that will leave your readers – the few you still have – breathless."

The line was silent a moment, and then he said, "I'll see what I can do."

***

Rod was sitting in his electric wheelchair when I entered the rehab center's sun-drenched day room, a spacious high-ceilinged space with skylights and 12-foot-high Kentia palms surrounded by green-and-yellow snake plants in large pots.

When he saw me, Rod raised both hands above his shoulders. It wasn't a smooth or quick motion, but his arms reached full extension.

"Touchdown!" I yelled.

"Watch this." Rod rotated his hands in the whirlybird motion of the line judge.

"False start! Five-yard penalty," I called out.

I took a seat next to his wheelchair and tousled his dark hair. "Spectacular, Rod."

"The rehab doctors say I'm way, way ahead of schedule."

A young woman in hospital smocks passed by the open doorway, saw us, and came into the sun room. "Rodrigo, *Cómo estás hoy?*"

"*Bien hasta que me tengas haciendo* leg lifts."

Spanglish, the language of Miami. A good-natured complaint about the difficulty of the leg exercises.

She laughed and said, *"Eres el mejor, Rodrigo."*

"Gabriella, say hello to Jake Lassiter," Rod said. "He's fam, my godfather."

We did our howdy-doos, and Rod said, "Gabriella is my favorite physical terrorist."

She laughed. "Rodrigo's my hardest working patient."

Gabriella moved on, and I emptied two trial cases on a long work table. Hundreds of pages of Sunny Day's defense motions, affidavits, memoranda, and briefs. I stacked my paltry paperwork alongside.

"So, Rodrigo," I said, "did you read that Florida Supreme Court case Victoria found?"

"*Faircloth vs. Hill.* Small negligent acts can be combined to create one big one of gross negligence."

"Excellent summary of the holding. What's the difference between that case and ours?"

"*Faircloth* involved a car crash," he said.

"So how do we use a case with such different facts?"

"By analogy. The driver did a lot of things wrong that caused a single accident. I'd call it 'driving malpractice.' Coach Coleman did several acts of 'coaching malpractice' that led to my injury."

"Nicely played. You're a natural."

"No cap?"

"Would I lie to my co-counsel?"

On the loudspeaker, a woman announced that an intermediate stretching class would begin in ten minutes.

"Now, did you read the documents I gave you on summary judgment?"

"Took me a week because I had to google so many terms."

"But you finished. Just like your leg lifts."

"To defeat their motion, we have to show there's a material issue of fact to be heard by a jury."

"Exactly."

"But I'm not sure what that means, Uncle Jake."

I considered how to explain the term to someone many years away from Civil Procedure 101. "Do you remember the Mercy Rule from Little League baseball?" I asked.

"If a team's behind by 10 runs after four innings, the game's over. They lose."

"Summary judgment's the same thing, although I'd call it the Misery Rule. The judge considers the sworn facts – affidavits and depositions – and the prevailing law. If the facts and law are insurmountably against us, and there's no way a jury could rule in our favor, the judge puts us out of our misery."

"Got it."

"Now, let's put a snowplow to this avalanche of paper."

We worked at the table for the next four hours. Every 20 minutes or so, Rod would brace his hands on the seat of the wheelchair and lift his butt to avoid the buildup of sores and to strengthen his arms.

Gabriella, Rod's favorite "physical terrorist," brought us sandwiches and drinks from the cafeteria. Without any help from me, Rod worked on his fine motor skills, hoisting ham-and-cheese into his mouth and not his ear. Hey, a dropped tomato wasn't going to kill anybody.

I organized our work the way I imagined Judge Duckworth would consider our case. We stacked our allegations against their sworn defenses and then considered our sworn rebuttals. If judged on size alone, we were Muggsy Bogues, and the defense was Shaquille O'Neal.

"Our smoking gun is Coach Coleman's failure to remove you from the game when you were so dazed you called him 'Dad,'" I said.

"Which he denies hearing. And the defense filed those affidavits saying the audio was tampered with."

"And I countered with the guy from WQAM and a speech professor who says that, even without the audio, he can tell that you used a one-syllable word, not two."

"'Dad,' not 'dammit.'"

"And we've got our first act of simple negligence."

We dug into hundreds of pages of documents. At every turn, our allegations were met with sworn denials and motions to exclude the evidence. Sandra Day's legal beagles were damn good at research and writing. Clean, concise prose supported by case law ranging from the newest Florida Supreme Court opinions to the Code of Hammurabi. Seems the ancient Babylonians had laws determining just how many shekels you'd have to pay for slicing off a man's ear.

As we worked, Rod thumbed through scholarly articles from academic journals the defense had attached to their affidavits. "Do you know a publication called 'Modern Tort Jurisprudence?'" he asked.

"I don't, but it's not my field."

"What about these? *Amateur Athletics Litigation. Twenty-First Century Developments in Sound. High School Athletics for Administrators.* They published a bunch of the articles cited by the defense."

I had seen that. And I'd been struck by just how on-point the articles were.

"Should High School Coaches be Immune from Tort Suits?"
"The Myth of Rugby Tackling in Youth Football."
"When Enhancing Digital Sound Distorts Rather Than Clarifies."
"Why Flag Football is More Dangerous than Tackle Football."

I figured that Sandra Day's library rats were just damn good googlers. But what did Rod see?

"What are you thinking, Second Chair?"

"I looked for the academic journals online."

"Make my day. Tell me they don't exist."

"I wish. They're published a couple times a year, and each one has editorial staff."

"Tell me the staff names are made up, or each journal has the same staff."

"That's what I was hoping, that they fabricated everything like they did with the helmet. But the staffs are real. And so are the authors. Some are distinguished professors at big-name universities."

"Professors can be prostitutes," I said.

On the loudspeaker, a woman announced that wheelchair basketball would be starting in ten minutes.

"There's just something about those articles," Rod said. "I can't quite put it into words."

"We're thinking alike, Rodrigo. The articles are almost..."

"Too good," he finished my thought.

"Right! You've got the skepticism of a born trial lawyer. You pick up enough rocks, you're damn sure going to find some snakes."

"I want to look deeper, Uncle Jake. But I don't have the computer skills to find everything that's in caches or in the clouds."

"Not a problem. I'll call Julian Martinez."

Just then, my cell phone hollered at me. Caller I.D. showed a bunch of digits beginning with 56. An international call.

I know 55 is Brazil from having gone to Rio a few times for Carnival. I know 52 is Mexico from having a few clients jump bail and flee. But 56? Could it be...Chile?

"Mr. Lassiter, this is Dr. Herlocher."

"Bless you, doctor. Barrios didn't tell me he'd found you."

"He hasn't, but he's been calling every medical facility in Patagonia, and word got to me."

And you're calling to help! Please let it be that.

"As I told you in our prior conversation, I feel terrible for Rod, and I have an affinity for your lawsuit."

Oh, no. I heard a "but" coming the way a dog hears the mailman.

"But I can't help you. That's all I can say."

"Wait, wait, please don't hang up. You already helped by pointing me to the videos in the clouds. But now, we're in desperate need of an affidavit. You don't have to come to court. Just tell us about the pit drills inside the tent and why you quit."

"I can't do that."

"Okay, something less accusatory. You gave Coach Coleman three days' notice, but he failed to have a replacement physician on the sidelines. C'mon, that's true."

"It is, but I signed an affidavit taking the blame for that."

"You can correct that."

"I can't. I signed an NDA. that has a penalty clause – $5 million – for any disclosures. I'm sorry."

"Why would you do that?"

"Ms. Day's clients are funding my work with the Onawo people. An entire medical facility in the mountains. Do you know how much a single MRI machine costs? I'm doing good things here. I'm sorry, Mr. Lassiter. Very sorry."

The line went dead, and I was left listening to an electronic buzz that might as well have been the medical examiner's saw biting into my skull.

PART SIX

"C'mon, you're the Jakester. You may be the lion in winter. Your fur may be matted, your gait unsteady. But Jake, you are still the lion."
    – Raymond (Sugar Ray) Pincher

"Waves can wash away the most stubborn stains, and the stars do not care one way or the other."
    – "A Deadly Shade of Gold" by John D. MacDonald

-51-
The Power of Positive Thinking

The following day, I was back at the rehab facility working with Rod. We spent most of the afternoon and evening going over the paperwork yet again. Our last chance to prepare for tomorrow morning's live-or-die hearing. I took notes in the margins of dozens of documents and tried to organize my thoughts. Rod had regained enough use of his hands and fingers to use his laptop, and he pecked away on his own mission.

"I'm feeling good, Uncle Jake," he said. "Buzzing like before a game."

Which is more than I can say for myself.

I was filled with self-doubt and the gut-stabbing fear that I would let down the people I loved. Early on, both Melissa and Victoria had told me not to take the case. But I didn't listen.

Ego! Arrogance!

Sure, they both came around, but what if their gut instincts were correct?

And what about my conduct? Pulling that stunt to go around Lily and Tank and get the birthday boy to turn down the settlement?

Hubris! Stupidity!

The news media and their bastard children, the social media, were agog with courthouse rumors and predictions. Basically, no one expected me to win. That is, no one expected the lawsuit to live to see Thursday morning.

If that's not bad enough, my damned heart just decided to do jumping jacks.

Did I take my medication this morning? My fuzzy brain couldn't remember.

My cardiologist had told me to head to the E.R. straightaway the next time I felt those fibrillations. They'd jolt me with electricity – cardioversion – to shock my heart back into rhythm. And if that didn't work, there was always an ablation procedure, burning or freezing areas of the heart with the out-of-tune rhythm.

No time for any of that fun today.

So, beat yourself to a frenzy if you want to. Yeah, lately I'd taken to talking to my heart.

"So how's it going with those scholarly articles the defense filed?" I asked.

"I have a theory but no proof."

"Welcome to my world, Rodrigo."

He smiled and said, "I think the defense showed our lawsuit to these experts and secretly paid them to write articles about hypothetical situations that matched the facts of our case."

"And somehow backdated the articles to appear they were published years ago," I said. "Could Julian confirm it?"

"Not yet. He found the articles in the cached website files on the dates where they belonged. The thing is, unlike the other articles, they have their own funky codes for firewalls, and Julian can't get through them."

"What do you think it means?"

He shrugged, something he couldn't have done two months ago. "I'm just a noob."

Meaning "newbie."

"But I'm thinking we were right," Rod continued. "Their tech people uploaded the articles into older journals as if they'd been there all the time, then created new firewalls to cover their tracks."

"Great theory," I said. "The only problem is..."

"We can't prove it unless Julian blasts through the firewalls."

"In the next 12 hours, give or take," I said, looking at my watch.

I was growing tired, but Rod, bless his heart, just kept on trucking. He read and re-read the key documents and showed the enthusiasm of a coach giving a pep talk.

"We're gonna kick their ass, Uncle Jake."

I believe in the power of positive thinking.

And I believe in the power of a righteous cause.

So now, despite all the evidence to the contrary, I acted as if I believed I could rescue the case, rescue Rod, and rescue myself.

"You bet we are, Rodrigo," I said.

-52-
Skull & Bones

Just before ten p.m., I left the rehab facility and headed south on LeJeune Road in light traffic, intending to cross Dixie Highway straight into Coconut Grove. I needed a belt of Jack Daniel's and a few hours' sleep before tomorrow morning's hearing.

I heard the blare of a car horn, checked the rearview, and saw my Blackwing's evil twin in the lane to my left. We both caught the traffic light at Bird Road, across the street from Coral Gables High School. I was in the right-hand lane, and the Blackwing Brothers directly to my left. Their passenger window slid down, and I waited for a hooded head or a crutch or an AK-47 to pop into view.

Instead, Bones, the guy in shades and a hoodie from the St. Frances parking lot, leaned out and said, "Listen to this, asshole." He turned toward the driver and said, "Turn it up, Skull."

I caught sight of the driver's shaved head as he leaned forward. A second later, a voice came from the Blackwing's speakers.

"To be honest, Uncle Jake, I can't think of anything Coach did that was so bad."

Rod's voice! What the hell!

I tried to remember just when he'd said that.

The hospital room!

Like the player who taunts an opponent crossing the goal line and has the touchdown called back, Bones just stepped in his own crud. He'd let me know that Mary Mallon, the phony nurse, wasn't just listening to us. She'd been wearing a wire.

Now, what can I do with this tidbit of info?

Skull and Bones had the recording and who knows what else in their Blackwing? My gas tank was three-quarters full. I had my emergency, auxiliary backup Louisville Slugger in the trunk.

Then another familiar voice from their car.

"To meet the gross negligence threshold, can I dump several acts of simple negligence into a pot with water and spices and make a stew of gross negligence?"

My voice! And then...

"A thought-provoking issue."

Victoria Lord. Our phone call of weeks ago. Dammit! Barrios had told me the Consortium probably had techies who could clone my cell phone. He advised using a different burner every day. But I didn't want to risk people not being able to reach me, so I did nothing. Another act of stupidity!

Now, Bones leaned out the window and grinned at me. The toothy smile of a shark appraising a grouper. "I'm gonna miss you, asshole."

The light had turned green, and two drivers behind us were leaning on their horns. Skull edged his Caddy from its lane into mine, creeping in front of me.

Twenty feet away. In their car. Evidence of illegal wiretaps, and who knows what else?

Their Blackwing burned rubber turning right onto Bird Road. Instead of going straight – toward home – I peeled out behind them. They had followed me.

Let's see how they like it. And let's see what else they have in their fancy car.

As soon as he made the turn, Skull showed off the car's explosive acceleration, hitting 70 in seconds before tapping the brakes and swinging left across traffic onto the entrance ramp for the Palmetto Expressway headed south. The ramp also connected with the Don Shula Expressway, so I couldn't be sure where they were headed. Didn't matter. I was right behind them.

Skull bore right – the Shula – heading into southwest Miami-Dade, but why? It was just suburban sprawl for miles.

Are they luring me somewhere? Is there a trap waiting with Bones getting his promised revenge?

Their Blackwing was doing 90 as we crossed the Killian Parkway, and I was four car lengths behind. As Bolo Tie had warned me, the clutch stressed my left knee, but my adrenaline was pumping, and I didn't care about the ice-pick stabs of pain. My heart was still doing its raggedy calisthenics, but I had other things on my mind.

Brake lights winked at me as they slowed. Were they going to take the 128th Street exit? And why?

Wait! Miami Executive Airport is on 128th just past the Tamiami Pinelands.

What did Bones say? "I'm gonna miss you, asshole."

The Consortium has a Lear or a Citation waiting for these two and whatever trove of goodies they're carrying.

Sure enough, they took the next exit, an elevated ramp that traversed the Florida Turnpike and emerged on 128th Street. I was close behind. It was a street of muffler shops and warehouses and low-end strip malls. Dead and dark and no traffic at this time of night.

We passed 122nd Avenue doing a pleasant 75, and then I eased forward, tailgating them. Closer and closer. I got to within two feet of their rear bumper, and there was a sudden flash, Bones hitting me with a spotlight that momentarily blinded me.

I blinked several times and shot them the bird but stayed on their tail. Bones leaned out their passenger window, and a second later, a beer can exploded against my windshield, splashing my black beauty with brew.

What to do? I could kiss their rear bumper in the bump-and-run technique favored by stock car drivers, but I wasn't trying to pass them. I wanted to stop them.

Once past 127th Avenue, I pulled into the lane alongside them, my front bumper aligned with their rear bumper. To the right was a pinelands nature preserve, a dark forest surrounded by a chain-link fence. I'd try the PIT maneuver, the fancy Pursuit Intervention Technique George Barrios showed me years ago when we'd both owned cars with too much horsepower and had consumed too much beer.

The idea was to ram my right front bumper behind their left rear tire, turn hard right, and accelerate into their vehicle. Their rear tires would lose traction and go into a counterclockwise skid, coming to a halt facing the other way.

We were only one mile from the airport, so it was now or never. I gently turned the steering wheel right, my front bumper one foot from their left rear tire. Bones leaned behind Skull at the wheel and hit me with another blast of the spotlight. I blinked and squinted and eased off the gas. They pulled ahead of me, and I accelerated to align my front bumper correctly. I spun the steering wheel to the right, angling into their car...just as Skull hit the brakes.

Instead of turning them around with leverage, I sideswiped them, scraping their car's entire left side with the shriek of metal on metal. My Blackwing bounced left and theirs veered right. Tires screaming, their car skidded off the street, bounced into a gully and flipped end-over-end, coming to rest upside down atop the collapsed chain-link fence that surrounded the nature preserve.

I got my Blackwing under control, slid through a 180, and drove back to where theirs was upended like a capsized turtle, its tires still spinning. I slid to a stop, hopped into the gully and crawled up the broken fence. It took about a minute, as I twisted a knee, cut my left hand, and pulled a muscle in my neck doing a clumsy gymnastics move to open the rear door on the driver's side.

Both men were suspended, upside down in their harnesses, their faces smushed into the deployed air bags.

"Are you dipshits okay?" I asked.

"I got whiplash and can't move, you fucktard," Skull whimpered.

"Broke a friggin' kneecap, asshole," Bones whined.

"Get us down," Skull said.

"Too dangerous. Paramedics will do it. Now, where are the recordings?"

"Screw you!" Bones said.

The ceiling of the car was now the floor. I took inventory. Two suitcases, one garment bag, several unopened cans of beer, two cell phones, two wallets...and a boxy leather briefcase with a telescoping handle, the kind favored by airline pilots and trial lawyers. The briefcase was on its side and open, its contents scattered on the roof, now the floor, of the Blackwing. I grabbed several folders. Each was neatly labeled: "Phone Conversations." "Hospital Transcripts." "Surveillance Photos." "MP3 Files." "Herlocher NDA." "Helmet Specifications." Loose on the floor was the phony hospital I.D. of Mary Mallon.

Oh, Typhoid Mary, you are gonna be a great Plaintiff's exhibit.

I opened the wallets and found driver's licenses for Skull, who was Simon Crankshaw from Las Vegas, and Bones, James Bonegar from Dearborn, Michigan. I used my cell phone to photograph the licenses, then slid them back into the wallets.

"Here's the deal, guys," I said. "I'm taking this stuff. I know who you are, and I have proof of your felony wiretapping and assaulting me outside my home. If you or any of your pals threaten me or anyone I care about, you're going away for hard time. As for this accident, you didn't see the make or model of the car that hit you."

"Take it all," Skull said. "Won't help you in court 'cause you're a field mouse and Sunny Day is the python who's gonna squeeze the living piss out of you."

Fifty feet away, on the street, a pickup truck came to a stop near my Blackwing.

Shit! A lousy time for a Good Samaritan.

I saw the silhouette of a husky man get out of the truck. "You need help up there?" he yelled.

"Everybody's fine. But why don't you call 9-1-1 for us and report it?"

Because I don't want my cell number on the call.

"Glad to help." He got back into his truck.

Two minutes later, I was back in my wounded chariot, the entire right side scraped and gouged. I was heading east on 128th Street with a full briefcase when the police and paramedics, sirens wailing, passed me going the other way.

-53-
Tailed Me, Tapped Me, and Droned Me

"Are you okay, Uncle Jake, 'cause you look tired?" Rod asked.

"I'm good."

I was operating on two hours' sleep and four cups of coffee. We were in the back of the rehab center's wheelchair van, parked in a handicapped space in front of the courthouse on Flagler Street. The driver had departed to get breakfast, and we had about an hour before the summary judgment hearing.

"Why's your hand bandaged?" Rod asked.

"Car repair gone bad."

Rod didn't probe further, and I kept quiet about my late-night encounter with Skull and Bones. Moments later, Julian Martinez joined us in the van.

"Bingo!" Julian said, smiling. "Banged through the firewalls on those academic journals last night." He handed me a stack of photocopies. "These are the real tables of contents, the original ones, as they appeared a few years ago. The articles they hit you with weren't there. They were created later and inserted into backdated copies of the journals they programmed to look original. The old ones – the real ones – were in a treasure chest behind a series of firewalls."

"Great work, Julian. I can use this."

After Julian left, Rod asked a smart question. "When's the best time to show the judge all the crud we've got on the defense?"

"We don't do it in dribs and drabs. We wait for the opportune moment."

"Which is...?"

"I won't know until it happens. Then, as Judge Duckworth might say, we carpet bomb them."

Fifteen minutes later, I was walking from the elevator to the courtroom, carrying Skull and Bones's trial bag and an easel covered by a blank sheet of paper with numerous photographs underneath.

Yeah, an old-school tripod easel and hard-copy photos. No high-tech exhibits for me.

Next to me, Rod buzzed along in his electric wheelchair. Sandra Day's people – at least a dozen young lawyers – sat on benches or slouched against the wall outside the courtroom door.

"Bunch of tools," Rod whispered to me.

"They make me big mad," I said, trying to be hip.

Rod laughed and said, "That's so cheugy, Uncle Jake."

"Whatever," I said, as we entered the courtroom.

Sandra Day sat alone at the defense table, a rainbow of color-coded files spread in front of her. She acknowledged me with a curt, "Mr. Lassiter," then smiled at Rod. "Welcome, Mr. Pittman, and good luck today."

He thanked her and motored to a spot next to me, ready for battle.

"Uncle Jake." Rod pointed to a large, thick envelope on the floor, propped against one of the legs of our table. My name was on it along with a red-inked: "LEGAL AND CONFIDENTIAL."

"Is this from you, Sunny?" I asked, picking up the envelope.

She glanced over, pretended to look puzzled, and said, "No, I hadn't noticed that."

Whatever was in it, she wanted to watch me open it. She likely enjoyed seeing spiders eviscerate flies. I tore the flap off the envelope. Inside were perhaps two dozen 8x10 black-and-white photos. Surveillance shots.

First up, a couple long-lens photos of Judge Gridley and me at the Seaquarium. The time stamp was, of course, the day our lawsuit was filed. So it appeared I was unethically trying to *ex parte* the judge, even though he's the one who called the meeting to feed Lolita.

Talk about a killer whale!

Next was a photo from inside Judge Gridley's chambers, taken by a hidden camera the very next day. This time, I looked angry. Several sheets of paper were paper-clipped to the photo, a transcript of my conversation with the judge. I skimmed to the juicy part:

"You'll recuse yourself, sua sponte, *today or I'll take you down hard and go after your pension."*

Oh, great. Prima facie evidence of extortion. What other treats were in store?

An affidavit of Dr. Brian Herlocher, the beneficent sawbones who was nonetheless willing to throw me under the bus.

"Affiant states that Jacob Lassiter called my office under false pretenses, pretending to be Milton W. Sanborn, Jr., attorney with Wickerham and Snoot..."

A Bar violation to be sure, but pale in comparison to extorting a judge.

The next few photos puzzled me. How the hell did they get shots of Julian Martinez and me in his broom closet of an office at the cruise ship terminal? It took a moment for me to realize they were taken from outside, looking through Julian's third-floor window.

Drone shots!

The bastards had tailed me, tapped me, and droned me.

Next came several photos of Julian working at his computer at home. Another puzzle until I realized they'd been taken by his own computer. The Consortium had turned Julian's artificial brain into a traitorous machine. A series of screenshots from Julian's computer followed. Snippets of the St. Frances files he'd found hiding deep in the clouds.

No doubt about it, my hacker has been hacked.

But they saved the best for last. Oh boy, did they ever.

A series of photos taken last night from Skull and Bones's Blackwing.

First was a shot of me tailgating them, one hand on the steering wheel, the other shooting them the bird. My mouth was curled into an angry sneer, my eyes squinting against the glare of the spotlight Bones was holding. I looked homicidal. If I'd been wearing a poncho and smoking a slim cigar, you'd have thought I was Clint Eastwood about to splatter blood and guts with my lever-action Winchester.

In the next several photos, my Blackwing was alongside theirs, dangerously close. My eyes were wild, my grin demonic. Basically, I looked batshit crazy.

Rod had been watching me silently. Now, he braced his arms and lifted himself from the chair, both for his exercise and to get a better look. "Jeez, you're like totally postal."

Oh, how they've nailed me. Let me count the ways.

They had me on extortion, conspiracy to violate state and federal computer hacking laws, assault with a motor vehicle, hit and run, and let's not forget larceny for stealing the briefcase and its contents. If they wanted to swing for the fences, or in this case, a downed chain-link fence, attempted murder.

I kept calm and called out to Day, "This all you got, Sunny?"

She didn't answer, so I carried the photo of me looking the most maniacal to the defense table. "Love it," I said. "I'll take a dozen 8x10s."

"Perhaps one is for Mr. Schulian for your obituary?"

Letting me know she's heard my phone calls.

"Okay, enough sparring. How did you know I'd follow Skull and Bones last night?"

"I never give away our tradecraft."

Maybe so, but Bolo Tie had said something that stuck with me.

"Her team's behavioral psychologist created a flow chart predicting every move you'd make in response to various stimuli."

"I can guess, Sunny. You asked your in-house shrink what I would do if Bones taunted me with those tapes."

She stayed quiet a moment but couldn't resist the urge to tell me just how damned smart she was, and how I was dumb as an ox. Lowering her voice to a whisper she said, "Our Dr. Fortunato said there was an 83 percent chance you'd respond emotionally and follow the Blackwing."

"Aw, c'mon. The shrink couldn't have known I'd force Skull & Bones off the road."

"True. He predicted there was only a 32 percent chance you'd resort to violence. He is not infallible."

I waited for more, but she wouldn't spill the tea, as Rodrigo might say. I thought it through. And there it was.

Skull and Bones weren't taking a flight out of town.

"You just wanted me to chase those guys all night," I said. "They were leading me somewhere or nowhere or anywhere. It was just sport for you, having me lose a night's sleep before the hearing."

She shrugged. "One of my people suggested we siphon your gas tank, have you hit empty on Tamiami Trail near the Everglades. I nixed that as excessive."

"How semi-ethical of you."

"The photos were a welcome surprise. Sometimes you go fishing for bluegill and catch a shark."

"So what's the deal, Sunny Day?"

"It's quite simple. If you attempt to use anything from the briefcase you purloined, we will have no choice but to seek your indictment for multiple felonies."

"Oh, you're good, Sunny. Dishonest, soulless, and evil to the core, but damn good at what you do."

"Spare me the moral condescension. It's not a good look."

The door opened, and Tank and Lily Pittman entered the courtroom. Alongside was Kiara Parsons, carrying a canvas bag.

My people.

I needed to show them to their seats, in front of the bar and just behind my table.

"What you don't understand, Mr. Lassiter," Day continued, "is that I'm going to win today, not because I'm a better lawyer than you, though I certainly am. I'm going to win, not because the facts and law are with me, though they surely are. I'm going to win because there is nothing I will not do to ensure that I win."

PART SEVEN

"If the machine of government is of such a nature that it requires you to be the agent of injustice to another, then I say, break the law."
— Henry David Thoreau

"Make crime pay. Become a lawyer."
— Will Rogers

"Make sure when anyone tackles you he remembers how much it hurts."
— Jim Brown

-54-
Sunshine State or Nanny State

We all rose from our seats – other than Rodrigo – when Judge Duckworth climbed the three steps to the bench, her black robes sailing, a pink filigreed jabot at her neck. Slipping on her orange-framed eyeglasses, the judge said, "Good morning, everyone."

We weren't in first grade, so no one said, "Good morning, teacher." But we did sit down in unison after the judge sank into her cushy, high-backed chair. She surveyed the courtroom, taking in two dozen associates, paralegals, and factotums from Wickerham and Snoot, several rows of reporters, bloggers, kibitzers, tweeters, instagrammers, and social media influencers. One television camera was manned by a Channel 10 crew, and Rudy Schulian was perched in the front row with Angel Castillo, a *Miami Herald* photographer.

"I see the Plaintiff is here," Judge Duckworth said. "Welcome to my courtroom, Mr. Pittman."

"Thank you, Your Honor." Rod nodded, sounding like a veteran warrior of the justice system.

"All right then, here's the order of battle. We're going in reverse order today. We'll start with count two, injunctive relief, then move to count one, the personal injury case. No speechifying, no repeating your paperwork. I've read it all, from the defense's massive assault on our forests to Mr. Lassiter's rather spare documents."

"I always took the word 'brief' literally, Your Honor," I said.

"Fair enough. Ms. Day, it's your motion. Forward march."

Sandra Day glided around the defense table and stopped 10 feet in front of the bench. She wore a double-breasted navy blazer over a matching below-the-knees skirt. The only frills were a simple strand of pearls and twin rows of gold buttons on the blazer. Her shoes were no-nonsense navy pumps. Her silvery hair came down past her ears and curled toward her face three-fourths of the way to her chin.

"May it please the court," she began, the traditional supplication of peasants to the Crown. "Neither the law nor the facts support the plaintiff's extraordinary demand that you destroy an American institution. There is simply no precedent for such a radical remedy, and we are confident that Your Honor will not pull the plug on Friday Night Lights."

She paused long enough to let the scribblers and laptoppers jot down what was obviously the theme of her case.

"However, I agree with plaintiff's counsel about one important point," she continued. "In high school football, even if coaches and administrators exercise reasonable care, a player still may be seriously injured or even killed. Why? Because there are dangers inherent in football that cannot be eliminated."

She turned toward me with a look of supreme confidence. "The FHSAA states exactly that in the consent form signed by the parents of every player. This stark warning allows parents to make informed decisions, and many choose not to have their sons play a sport where violent collisions are part of the game. In fact, participation in high school football has been declining each year for more than a decade, and that's fine with us. Yet despite the known risks, despite the fear of injuries, about one million boys continue to play high school tackle football. A great number are from underprivileged backgrounds, and for many, football is their free ticket to a college education."

"Many" being two percent.

"The question today," she continued, "is whether one injured plaintiff and one lawyer with a personal grievance against the sport should be able to light the wildfire that burns this American institution to the ground."

Another line intended to be quoted hither and yon.

"Mr. Lassiter is going to tell Your Honor that there are 80,000 concussions in high school football each year."

I love it when opposing counsel makes my arguments.

"There are nearly 50,000 deaths in auto accidents each year, but we don't ban cars. We've made driving safer with seat belts and shoulder harnesses and air bags. Likewise, the high schools and equipment manufacturers have made football safer with better helmets, fewer full-contact practices, rule changes, and courses on concussion protocols for coaches. Football should not be banned. It should be improved."

Face it. She's good on her feet. A Broadway star performing for us yokels in the sticks.

"Mr. Lassiter has chosen the wrong forum," she continued. "To declare high school football a public nuisance, he must turn to the Florida Legislature. In Chapter 823, the Legislature has banned activities that are deemed too dangerous or antithetical to the public good. Gambling dens, brothels, derelict boats, and discarded refrigerators are all considered public nuisances. If Mr. Lassiter wishes to outlaw high school football, he should go to Tallahassee and petition his state representative."

"Fat chance," I whispered, loud enough for Day to hear.

"But Mr. Lassiter won't do that because he knows he cannot succeed. The elected legislators will never turn the Sunshine

State into a nanny state. They know we cannot place teenagers in a bubble to protect them from all of life's risks. Neither the Legislature nor any court will give high school football the death penalty that Mr. Lassiter seeks."

I bounced to my feet, both because my lower back was stiff from last night and because I needed to interrupt Sandra Day's flow. "Your Honor," I said, "Counsel misrepresents the relief we seek. We have not sought the death penalty. We seek a temporary ban until the FHSAA proves tackle football is safe. Alternatively, we ask that Your Honor order the elimination of kickoffs and punts plus other safety measures."

"I wonder," Judge Duckworth mused, "if those lesser remedies might be even more problematic for the court. You're asking me to be the commissioner of football for hundreds of high schools and thousands of players."

"Someone has to do it," I said, immediately wishing I had a better answer.

"Not only that," Day said, piling on, "but the so-called temporary ban is a misnomer. If I'm a tenth grader and the court bans football for three years, well that's the death penalty for me, isn't it? Further, curtailing high school football will destroy college football, which in turn, will destroy professional football."

Ah, there it is. The Consortium getting its money's worth.

My thoughts were interrupted as the courtroom door opened, and I glimpsed two men walking down the center aisle. One was dressed in a chauffeur's uniform. The other was a walking skeleton in a charcoal three-piece suit and an orange tie with leaping silver foxes. At least six feet five, skinny as a snake with a shiny bald dome, pince-nez spectacles, and a complexion as pale as ice, he supported himself with a cane. His age? From appearances, he could have voted in the Eisenhower versus Stevenson election. Both times.

Moving slowly, he came through the swinging gate at the bar, stopped and scanned the courtroom. He took his time, as a rancher might as he counted his cattle.

His gaze took in the gallery, the judge on her raised bench, the clerk at her table, the court stenographer at her little machine, Sandra Day and her Ivy League assassins, and Tank and Lily Pittman behind the plaintiff's table. Finally, his eyes landed on Rod, and then after a quick appraisal, on me. From his scornful look, if I were one of those cattle, I must have had anthrax.

He cleared his throat, wheezed, and remained standing.

Okay, I give up. Who the hell are you?

-55-
Duke of Wellington, Ike of West Point

"Your Honor," Day said, "May I present Schooner Wickerham IV, chairman emeritus of Wickerham and Snoot?"

The judge nodded. "I believe it's Colonel Wickerham, is it not?"

"Retired." His thin lips crinkled into a smile. "Captain Duckworth, yes?"

"Also retired," the judge said. "Your family's military tradition is well-known, going back to the Civil War."

"General Wickerham. Held the high ground at Gettysburg."

"Cemetery Ridge," the judge said, almost wistfully.

"Is that a West Point class ring I see on your finger?" Wickerham asked.

Oh, please! Unless he borrowed the telescope from his childhood friend Galileo, Wickerham could not have spotted the ring. Obviously, Sandra Day scripted this touching moment of common – and hallowed – ground.

Judge Duckworth held up her hand, revealing a hefty ring of black onyx and gold. "Class of 1987," she said.

"I'm a little before that." Wickerham's chuckle produced a wet cough.

"Hoo-ah," I whispered to Rod.

Rod leaned over to me and said, "How old is that dude?"

"Somewhere between 90 and hell," I said. "Closer to hell."

"Your Honor," Day said, "Mr. Wickerham joins us today from his home in Palm Beach. He wishes to observe the proceedings."

"Honored to have you, Sir. Your reputation precedes you. "

Judge Duckworth saluted the old coot as if he were her superior officer. His return salute was a mere wave of his cane, and he eased his old bones into a chair just behind Sandra Day.

I wanted to get the show moving. I was exhausted from so little sleep, and my gut was roiling from black coffee on an empty stomach. The first flickers of a hot migraine were beginning to singe the back of my skull, and my heart was still racing off the road.

"Ms. Day, please continue," the judge said.

Day spent the next 20 minutes dissecting the few cases in existence that sought to ban tackle football in Pop Warner leagues, junior high, and high school. Every case favored the defense. Then Day launched into an assault on the notion that concussions cause CTE.

"Plaintiff alleges that high school football is life-threatening because of concussions and even sub-concussive impacts. He then attempts to link concussions to CTE, and that brain disease to death. However, despite the hullabaloo in the news media..."

Did she just say "hullabaloo"?

"... science has yet to establish a definitive link between concussions and deaths decades later."

Judge Duckworth lifted her chin and seemed to silently ask Day to explain.

"The problem," Day continued, "is that studies cited by counsel in his rather skimpy paperwork show a correlation between football and CTE but not causation. We know that not every football player who suffers a head injury develops the brain disease. In fact, very few do. And because CTE can only be diagnosed after death, it's impossible to link an injury from decades earlier to the disease that ultimately causes death. Any study that purports to do so must be dismissed as junk science."

Thump. Thump. Old man Wickerham banged the cushioned tip of his cane against the floor in approval, much like Members of Parliament exclaiming, "Here! Here!"

As Day continued yammering, I grew fidgety, one of my knees bouncing as if I were the lead guitarist in a rock band. "You got ants in your pants?" Granny Lassiter would have said. That old devil migraine became a swirling maelstrom, moving across my frontal lobe like a waterspout across the bay.

Day cited several affidavits of physicians, statisticians, and medical researchers that supported her position on concussions. Turning toward me, she said, "Mr. Lassiter suggests that high schools should replace tackle football with flag football. We have filed the study of Professor Morgan Charleston, document 37-A, to the effect that flag football is the more dangerous sport."

Bull's-eye! One of the backdated articles. I was tempted to interrupt, but I chose to let Sunny Day run with the line like a streaking bonefish while I sat in my skiff, watching my reel unspool.

"Players in flag football collide at full speed, just as in tackle football, but because they don't wear pads or helmets, Professor Charleston has found they are at greater risk of injury."

Professor Charleston is a paid prostitute, if that's not redundant. Go on, Sunny, keep swimming the flats. I've got plenty of line.

"Additionally," she continued, "Florida high school players with only flag football experience will never be able to compete at the college level. Thousands of families would leave Florida so their sons could play tackle football in other states."

Great! Maybe there would be less traffic on I-95.

Day summarized a dozen affidavits from professors of humanities, economics, and philosophy. The gist was that high school football was deeply ingrained in the history and culture of the good old USA.

But so was dueling with pistols at dawn.

"Your Honor, the Duke of Wellington famously said that the Battle of Waterloo was won on the playing fields of Eton," she said. "I wonder if D-Day was won at Abilene High School in Kansas where General Eisenhower played football."

"And at West Point!" Schooner Wickerham piped up, though no one asked him to. "Ike played at Army. Lost to Jim Thorpe and the Carlisle Indian School in 1912, helluva team."

Judge Duckworth peered at the old coot, but instead of chastising him, said, "Coached by Pop Warner."

Damn, I'm getting some Army home cooking, and I don't mean MRE chicken burritos with a 25-year shelf life.

Wickerham tapped his cane again, *thump-thump.*

"Finally, Your Honor," Day said, "I must share a thought about my opposing counsel."

Uh-oh. Those thoughts probably come in four-letter words.

"Mr. Lassiter is a local hero."

Really? I never intended to become a hero, and I succeeded.

"After a hard-scrabble upbringing in the Keys, he gained fame in the realm of sports and then built his reputation in the arena of the law. These days, his struggles with brain disease are well-known. I cannot help but wonder if it is Mr. Lassiter who is the true plaintiff on count two, and if this is his battle, though he fights in the name of his client."

If I tried a cheap trick like that, Judge Duckworth would throw me in the stockade.

I got to my feet, about to object, but didn't need to.

"Please move it along, Ms. Day," said the judge, expressing minor disapproval.

I dug into my forehead with my knuckles, trying to massage away the pain. I blinked a few times, and when I opened my eyes, there were two Judge Duckworths and two Sandra Days. I last had double vision when Sugar Ray Pincher caught me with a three-punch combo – left jab, right cross, left hook – that knocked me goofy.

"I'll conclude with this, Your Honor," one of the Sandra Days said. "A week ago, I received a phone call from a former professor of mine at Harvard Law. The man has taught for 40 years but has never been to a Harvard-Yale game. Not exactly a football fan. He said, 'Sandra, I've read about your case in the *Times*. Fascinating. All those young boys running around in plastic hats and knickers, bouncing off each other. Kind of frivolous, isn't it?' Before I could disagree, he said, 'But it's really part of the social fabric of America, isn't it?'"

I'd like to take this professor's deposition, because I'm pretty sure he's a product of Sunny Day's insidiously clever imagination.

"Your Honor, I couldn't have said it better." Day paused, perhaps congratulating herself for that touching note of legal fiction. "In conclusion, Plaintiff fails to meet his burden, and there is no material issue of fact to be tried by a jury on count two."

"Thank you, Ms. Day," the judge said. "Mr. Lassiter, let's cut to the chase. Can you point to any precedent that would compel me to grant the rather extreme relief you seek?"

I got to my feet, looked toward the dark beams that rose from the walls and curled toward the high point of the ceiling. And that's when the courtroom started to spin.

-56-
Fighting for the Future

I placed both hands on the table to steady myself and inadvertently knocked a file folder to the floor. The headache pounded at my temples. I tried to focus my vision on the sign above the judge's bench: "We Who Labor Here Seek Only the Truth." I never liked the sign, and now there were two of them.

Just don't fall!

The storm in my brain was competing with another sound. What the hell? Who was talking to me?

Judge Gridley.

"Put a lid on the lawyering, boyo. Your case is a loser."

And Joe Paterno.

"Eyes to the sky when you tackle!"

And Don Shula.

"Why? Because I said so, Lassiter! Dammit, you're just like Buoniconti, another lawyer for the defense."

"Mr. Lassiter," the judge said, looking concerned. "Would you like a short recess?"

"What? No. Ready to rock."

"No, coach, I'm fine. Just got my bell rung is all."

"Then, please proceed," the judge said.

"Before I answer Your Honor's question about precedent, my client has something he'd like to say."

Unorthodox? Sure, but at least Day wouldn't have had an algorithm that predicted it.

Rod braced both hands on the defense table and slowly rose from the wheelchair. All those hours in the gym had rebuilt his arms to perhaps half their prior strength.

"Oh, Mr. Pittman, there's no need to stand," the judge said.

"Begging the court's pardon, there is," I replied. "It's important to Rodrigo."

Judge Duckworth looked at me quizzically.

"We could've rolled Rod in here today in a bed with oxygen clips in his nose, a nurse and doctor at his side. We could've played up the fact that the surgeons originally gave him a five percent chance of ever walking again."

"Many plaintiffs' lawyers would do precisely that," the judge said.

"But Rod has worked his tail off every day," I said, "with the best doctors and the best therapists. He's a brave, smart, and honest young man. And when he told me he had something to say and would show Your Honor respect by standing, I wanted to honor that wish."

"I admire that," the judge said, a note of compassion in her voice. "Please proceed."

Rod shakily got to his feet, reaching his full height and keeping his balance by gripping my shoulder with one hand. His navy blue suit hung loose, and his neck swam inside his shirt collar.

"May it please the court," Rod began, just as I'd taught him. "When I was transferred from the hospital to the rehab center, I made three promises. The first was that I would go to court with Uncle Jake. Mr. Lassiter. And I would stand up and thank Your Honor for hearing our case. So, regardless how the case turns out, thank you for your time and expertise."

"You are quite welcome." Judge Duckworth smiled warmly. "May I ask about the other two promises?"

"Sure. I would learn to play the guitar in rehab. It's great therapy for my hands, and I always wanted to play. And the last one, someday soon, I'll walk out of the rehab center. With no crutches, no cane, no one holding me up. That's all, Judge."

"That's a lot," she said. "You're a determined young man, and I am confident you will succeed. Thank you."

Behind us, I heard Lily Pittman sniffling. Behind the defense table, Schooner Wickerham made a scoffing sound, or maybe he was just clearing phlegm.

I held Rod's upper arm and eased him back into his wheelchair. Buying time with Rod pinch-hitting for me was working out. In my skull, the storm subsided from a small-craft warning to simply a breezy day, and now only one judge was perched above us on the bench.

"Mr. Lassiter," the judge said, "do you have controlling precedent that would compel me to rule that high school tackle football constitutes a public nuisance?"

"Your Honor, there's no case directly on point either for or against that proposition," I said. "We can, however, reason by analogy to cases that have declared public nuisances to exist far beyond those expressly forbidden by statutes. The doctrine of public nuisance has existed for a thousand years, finding its way into English Common Law in the 1100s."

"The time of the Vikings," Schooner Wickerham grumbled.

"You oughta know," I fired back at him.

"Mr. Lassiter," the judge said, "please address your remarks to the Court."

"Will do." I paused a moment to remember where I was. "Ms. Day told Your Honor that one million boys play high school football. That's 1,500 boys for every player in the NFL.

We're all concerned about concussions suffered by NFL players. Where is the concern for all those boys who will never make a dime playing the game? As a society, we've banned bullfighting and dog fighting and cockfighting because we protect animals from abuse. What about teenage boys? Today's high school players are bigger, stronger, and faster than those from earlier eras. Even with rule changes and limited contact scrimmages, the collisions have become more violent, just as we are learning more about the dangers of repetitive head injuries."

I looked down at the table where Rod scrawled on a legal pad: "On a roll, Uncle Jake!"

"And your case law?" the judge prodded me. "The ones you wish to analogize?"

I spent the next fifteen minutes summarizing cases I had gathered with Victoria Lord's research and analyzed with Rodrigo pitching in.

"Activities that lawfully existed for decades or centuries can still be found to be public nuisances," I said. "Most notable are the asbestos and tobacco lawsuits, which resulted in billions of dollars of payouts. We've cited the cases in what Ms. Day called our 'skimpy paperwork,' and we suggest that Your Honor can rely on them for precedent."

"Understood, Mr. Lassiter," the judge said, "though I'm not sure I agree. But please continue."

"The theory of public nuisance has been used against both the Boy Scouts and various archdioceses for covering up thousands of cases of child abuse. Recently, the theory has been the underpinning of verdicts against the opioid manufacturers for creating a public health crisis by playing down the dangers of the drugs."

Day hopped to her feet. "Counsel's argument is quite misleading," she said. "The opioid cases have dramatically different results across the country, and many of the cases lost by the industry at trial are on appeal. I am proud to say that Wickerham and Snoot secured reversal of a $465 million public nuisance judgment in Oklahoma."

"The Snooters must have had a great victory party," I said. "Too bad the 70,000 people who died of opioid overdoses last year couldn't attend."

"That's enough, Mr. Lassiter," the judge said. "Let's consider asbestos, tobacco, and opioids. They've killed millions over the years. On the other hand, deaths in high school football are extremely rare. Now, concussions are another story. Defense counsel concedes there are 80,000 per year. However, she cites the affidavits of numerous physicians to the effect that there's no definitive proof of a causal link between concussions and brain disease."

Ready for that counterpunch, I said, "Plenty of doctors testified under oath that coal mining didn't cause black lung disease, asbestos didn't cause mesothelioma, smoking didn't cause lung cancer, and opioids weren't addictive. I would ask Ms. Day's doctors, 'How much were you paid?'"

The judge nodded, which I took to be a good sign. However, I wasn't overjoyed with being grilled after she let Sandra Day preach from her pulpit without interruption.

"Are you contending that medical science has reached a consensus on the long-term effects of concussions?" the judge asked.

A damn smart question. The direct answer, unfortunately, is "no."

"The research is ongoing," I said, waffling. "We're making advances in both brain imaging and CTE research, but in the meantime, should our teenage children be the lab rats for experiments on the effects of repetitive head injuries?"

"You answered my question with a question," the judge said, pointedly.

"Did I?"

Judge Duckworth shot me a scolding look.

I considered just what to say. A lawyer is an actor on a stage who must not appear to be acting. In Shakespeare's day, audiences at the Globe tossed oyster shells at performers who displeased them. In my day, I've had judges hurl insults as deadly as axes. Now, Judge Duckworth was putting pressure on a weak link in our case.

"I'll put it this way, Your Honor. I would rather be early to address this problem than late. I'm fighting for the future of these boys' lives."

"I'm still looking for a concrete answer, Mr. Lassiter."

I gave it one more try. "The cumulative effects of repeated impacts to the head with the brain sliding inside the skull like Jell-O in a bowl are known to be dangerous. The only thing unsettled is the scope of that danger. The FHSAA admits this in its consent form provided to parents."

"Go on," the judge said.

I walked to my tripod easel, peeled back the blank page to reveal a poster-board enlargement of a paragraph from page two of the form. Then, I read aloud:

"'Preliminary evidence suggests that repeat concussions, and even hits that do not cause a symptomatic concussion may lead to abnormal brain changes known as Chronic Traumatic Encephalopathy, which can only be seen on autopsy.'"

I let that sink in a moment, then said, "With that breathtaking admission by her client, it's disingenuous of Ms. Day to take a contrary position."

I took down that poster, revealing one underneath. "And here's the very next sentence of the defendant's consent form: 'There have been case reports suggesting the development of Parkinson's-like symptoms, Amyotrophic Lateral Sclerosis, severe traumatic brain injury, depression, and long-term memory issues that may be related to concussion history.'"

Again, I paused before speaking. "It's far too late in the day to suggest that tackle football is not dangerous."

"Got it, Mr. Lassiter," the judge said. "One last question. In your complaint, you concede that high school football has many benefits for student athletes. Do you stand by that today?"

"I do, Your Honor, along with the next sentence." I thumbed through my file, found what I needed, and read my own words aloud: "However, tackle football stands alone as an inherently dangerous sport.' We contend that the risks of serious injury and death outweigh the benefits of the sport."

"That's the balancing act, and I'll take all the guidance you can give me."

"Your Honor, when I see a few dozen boys on a team enduring countless violent collisions while a few thousand others simply watch from the stands, I wonder if there might be a better way. I'd much rather see varsity teams playing flag football against other schools. Intramural leagues, too. Boys and girls at both levels of competition."

I paused to gather my thoughts, which gave Day a chance to pop out of her chair. "Respectfully, Your Honor, the question isn't what Mr. Lassiter would 'much rather see,' but whether he has met his burden to survive a motion for summary judgment. Because the science is unsettled, and for all the policy reasons we discussed, we would suggest he has not."

"All right, I've got it," Judge Duckworth said. "I'll defer ruling until after we hear the defense motion addressed to count one. Let's recess for an hour and resume after lunch."

The judge stood, and so did we. Rod, whose energy was fading, made an effort to stand, but I put a hand on his shoulder, and he settled back down. Just as she reached the stairs to descend from the bench, Judge Duckworth stopped and turned toward me.

"Mr. Lassiter, may I ask you one final question?"

"Of course," I said.

As if she needed my permission!

"If you had it to do all over again, with the knowledge you have now, would you still play football? Starting in high school, through college, and the NFL?"

I glanced at Tank sitting behind our table. He gave a little shrug.

"Your Honor, I've never lied to the Court, and I won't start today. But I must ask the relevance of that question."

Judge Duckworth pursed her lips and thought it over. "Mr. Lassiter, I take your point. You don't have to answer the question."

"Oh, I think he just did," Sandra Day said, with a triumphant smile.

THE TWITTERSPHERE

@JavierTuco23
Sr. Lassiter tiene razón. The judge should balance the benefits of tackle football against its risks.
> **@Miamuh_for_Miamians Replying**
> Go back to Cuba and cut sugar cane!

***

@TheGoodBook666
Jake Linkletter is the alter eagle of Satan.

***

@Bitchin_NonStop2
Newspaper says Lassiter is a criminal lawyer. So why isn't he in jail?

***

@USA_Luv_or_Leave
Abolishing football is a conspiracy of Freemasons, Knights Templar, and international Zionists. And I am not anti-semantic.

-57-
What Else Do You Have?

Tank and Lily took Rod to lunch, and I spent most of the hour in the lawyers' lounge, sitting at a small table, going over the items I'd liberated from Skull and Bones's briefcase.

What's my best evidence of the defense's duplicity and deceit? Something tangible?

I'd seen a lot of dirty tricks played by lawyers, but the phony nurse wearing a wire...well, that was a new one. I slid her laminated ID badge – Mary Mallon – into my suit pocket, unsure how I could use it without copping to various crimes myself.

I tried to think strategically. If I got into a mud-slinging match with Sandra Day, who would look dirtier to the judge? I remembered Dwight Eisenhower's explanation for not responding to Joseph McCarthy's deranged allegations:

"I won't get into a pissing contest with that skunk."

Of course, Ike was a five-star general, not to mention President, so he could stay above the fray. I was a private fighting in the trenches, running out of ammo, so I didn't have that luxury.

Ten minutes before we were due back in court, Tank limped into the lounge, bringing me a greasy, lukewarm double cheeseburger and a 24-ounce Coke. I gobbled the burger in three bites and washed it down just as quickly.

"I don't give two shits about shutting down high school football," Tank said, taking a seat next to me.

"I know," I said, between burps.

"But this morning gave you a chance to warm up, work out the rust."

"How'd I do?"

"You were okay, Jake. But that lady lawyer. Jeez, she's damn good."

"As good as anyone I've been up against," I agreed, "and totally without scruples."

"Just tell me that you're gonna win on count one. That we're not getting our asses kicked out of court."

I waited for two lawyers from the county attorney's office to get up from an adjoining table and head out the door. "I've got some very powerful evidence, Tank, but the way I gathered it is a bit ticklish."

"How'd you gather it?"

"In a word, feloniously."

"So, can you use it or not?"

"The trick is to get the judge angry at me but not at Rod, and angrier at Sandra Day than at me."

***

Except for the judge, we were all in our places, including Schooner Wickerham IV, seated behind Sandra Day. His bony fingers reached into his vest pocket and took out a gold watch, possibly given to him by Abraham Lincoln. I doubted Wickerham had another appointment. Maybe it was just time for his midday prune juice.

Judge Duckworth hurried into the courtroom from the rear door and bounded up the steps. We stood but she waved, signaling we should put our butts back into our chairs.

"We'll hear the defense motion for summary judgment on count one, the personal injury claim," she began. "I've read the paperwork and have some inquiries of counsel. Mr. Lassiter, would you agree that because of the signed waiver, you need to make a showing of gross negligence to survive the motion."

I got back to my feet and said, "That's the case law, Your Honor."

"So, what's the act of gross negligence that you believe will get you to trial?"

"Acts, plural. Coach Coleman's multiple acts of simple negligence can be combined to constitute a course of conduct that a jury could find constitutes gross negligence. As authority, we cited – "

"Faircloth vs. Hill, the Florida Supreme Court case," the judge said. "Got it, and I've read your memo of law equating what you call 'driving malpractice' in that case with what you call 'coaching malpractice' in your case. I'm not sure about those labels, but you've convinced me that *Faircloth* is controlling."

Score one for Rod!

"Now, be specific," the judge continued. "What are these multiple acts of negligence you can prove at trial?"

"First, Coach Coleman failed to place Rod into concussion protocol, despite just having made the head-first tackle on the first kickoff. His helmet flew off, and he staggered getting up, then stumbled off the field and was so dazed he mistook the coach for his father."

"I listened to the audio you submitted on that point. The original is difficult to make out, but on the enhanced version, the Plaintiff clearly says 'Dad.' Next?"

Sandra Day was on her feet. "Your Honor, we have a *motion in limine* that seeks to exclude the enhanced audio as unreliable."

"Sit down, Ms. Day. You'll have your chance. Mr. Lassiter, please continue."

"Coach Coleman failed to have a physician on the sideline, as required by league rules," I said. "A physician would have taken Rod out of the game."

"Got it," the judge said. "But the team physician who retired, Dr. Herlocher, essentially took the blame. He signed an affidavit saying it was his responsibility to secure the replacement."

"First, he didn't retire," I said. "He quit in disgust at Coach Coleman's rule-breaking. Second, the defense bribed him to sign a false affidavit and leave town so he couldn't testify. He told me as much on the phone."

"Objection!" Sandra Day bounced up again. "Counsel is testifying, and I must protest..."

"Protest later," the judge said. "Mr. Lassiter, please move on."

"Coach Coleman conducted illegal pit drills in a secret 'Tunnel of Manhood' tent on the practice field," I said.

"Which the defense denies," the judge said, "and you have no direct evidence to support your claim. What else, Mr. Lassiter?"

"On the sideline, Coach Coleman encouraged Rod to make an illegal tackle when he said, 'Be a headhunter. Stick 'em. Put a hat on a hat.'"

"And the defense claims that 'headhunter' is simply hyperbole and 'hat on a hat' refers to blockers each picking up the right defensive player. The defense also argues that your client wasn't injured in a helmet-to-helmet collision, rendering the coach's instructions irrelevant. Anything else, Mr. Lassiter?"

"Coach Coleman also refused to teach rugby tackling and refused to allow his players to wear sensor helmets provided free of charge by Rod's father, my former teammate, Langston Pittman."

The judge frowned and said, "Neither is required by league rules, so let's just move on."

"We've submitted a video and transcript of a St. Frances full-contact scrimmage in which Coach Coleman again encourages illegal tackling techniques."

"Watched it," the judge said, "though it's also subject to a defense motion to exclude from evidence. As I recall, the coach berated a player for failing to make a tackle, saying he looked like a ballerina falling off the stage."

"Then the player said he was coming in too high and wanted to avoid a helmet-to-helmet collision."

I waited for Judge Duckworth to thumb through the transcript of the coach's exchange with the player. "And what did Coach Coleman reply?" she asked.

I read from my copy of the transcript. "'Do I care if you pick up a targeting penalty? Hell, no. That'll make their receivers shaky coming across the middle. If you smash heads and the zebras throw a flag, you won't hear shit from me. If you're ejected, consider it your badge of courage. But don't curl up and die like Macklin just did.' Then after telling the team that his high school coach told his players to be 'headhunters,' Coach Coleman concludes by saying, 'Do some damage.'"

Judge Duckworth was quiet a moment, so I filled the void. "In a nutshell, Coach Coleman instructed his team to violate the targeting rules that are designed to prevent head and neck injuries."

"But, Mr. Lassiter, isn't all that just coach-speak?" the judge said. "Don't coaches frequently use exaggeration when they exhort their players to be aggressive. 'Knock their blocks off,' or something similar?"

"The video is just one piece of the mosaic, Your Honor. When all the pieces are put together, they show a pattern of misconduct that we call coaching malpractice."

"I just wonder if that's a bridge too far. Your client doesn't appear on the video in which the coach is speaking. Also, he wasn't injured in a helmet-to-helmet collision, so there's the question of relevance. On that secret tent you mention, you don't claim that your client took part in the allegedly illegal pit drills. The failure to have a doctor on the sidelines seems to be the result of an unfortunate miscommunication between the departing team physician and a new one. And again, rugby tackling and sensor helmets are not required. That leaves you with the one event that directly involves the Plaintiff. What did he say, and what did Coach Coleman hear on the sideline before the second kickoff?"

The judge paused, and the courtroom was silent, except for Schooner Wickerham IV's snoring. I glanced at Sandra Day. She was suppressing a smile. And why not? My case was crashing and burning.

"So let's unpack this," the judge said. "I'm denying the defense motion to exclude the sideline audio, as there's no showing that enhancing the sound distorted it. On the enhanced audio, the Plaintiff said, 'I'm good to go, Dad.' Said it twice. However, I must consider Coach Coleman's sworn testimony that he heard, 'I'm good to go, dammit.'"

I waited. We could go down in flames any second.

"The coach had to make a split-second decision in the heat of battle. Just as in the military investigations where hindsight is 20-20, it's nearly impossible to comprehend the situation in real time. That's a lesson I learned in the Judge Advocate General Corps. So here's Coach Coleman who has his assistant coaches jabbering in his headset and fans cheering, the band playing, and the chaos of the first football game of the season. It's not unreasonable to believe that the Plaintiff said 'Dad' and the Defendant heard 'dammit.'"

"It's also not unreasonable to believe that the coach is lying," I said.

"I'm not finished, so stow it, Mr. Lassiter," the judge chided me. "Coach Coleman also testified that the Plaintiff did not appear to be dazed or confused. But under the rules for summary judgment, I must view the facts in a light most favorable to the non-moving party, the Plaintiff, and draw every reasonable inference in favor of that party. So, Mr. Lassiter, for today, I consider the coach's failure to remove your client from the game an act of simple negligence."

"Thank you, Your Honor." I exhaled a long breath.

"However, on what you have presented so far, I see no additional acts that, when taken together, amount to gross negligence. Prompting me to ask in the plainest of terms, 'What else do you have?'"

-58-
Helmet-Gate

Judge Duckworth waited for me to answer, and I did my best to make it concise...and to bait Sandra Day.

"Coach Coleman, his training staff, and St. Frances are jointly liable for providing Rod with a helmet that was too big for him and came off during Rod's tackle on the first kickoff."

"Perhaps I can speed this along," Sandra Day said, getting to her feet.

I kept quiet. I knew exactly what she was going to do, and it had nothing to do with speed. She was pushing me off the path into what she thought was a pit of quicksand, and I knew was a warm bubble bath.

"After an exhaustive search, my people found the Plaintiff's helmet and offered it to plaintiff's counsel for inspection." Day motioned to Myron, her bespectacled, mustachioed associate, who opened a large trial bag and came out with a St. Frances helmet missing its facemask and chin strap. "Mr. Lassiter declined, and I will understand if he likewise declines today's offer to have his client try on the helmet."

"We'll take up counsel's generous offer." I reached the defense table in two strides and snatched the helmet.

Day's eyes widened in surprise. Schooner Wickerham IV gave me a sideways grin of yellowed teeth and whispered, "Nincompoop."

"Is this your helmet, Rod?" I asked, back at our table.

"Sure looks like it," he said, just as we'd rehearsed. "Has my number 11 on the back. Scuff mark on the front."

Using two hands, I gently worked the helmet onto Rod's head and tugged at the earholes. "How's it fit?"

"Perfectly," he said.

"So, Mr. Lassiter," the judge said, "are you withdrawing your claim about the helmet?"

"We'll see." I slipped the helmet off and handed it to Rod who peered inside. "Rod, what else do you notice about that helmet?"

"It's not mine."

The reporters and social media gadflies buzzed in the gallery. Sandra Day got to her feet but was momentarily speechless. I turned to Kiara, sitting behind us. She pulled another helmet out of the canvas bag she was holding. It looked identical to the first one, right down to the number 11 on the back and the scuff mark on the front.

"Let's try this one," I said, slipping it on Rod's head. I placed two fingers in the ear holes and slid the helmet back and forth.

"It's too big," Rod said.

"But is it yours? The one you were wearing when you were injured?"

"Objection, Your Honor," Day said in a moderate tone, betraying no fear. "The Plaintiff is testifying while not under oath, and in any event, this is not an evidentiary hearing."

"Overruled. You opened the door to this, Ms. Day, when you offered the helmet for an in-court demonstration," the judge said.

Hands just a bit shaky, Rod removed the helmet and looked inside. "This helmet is definitely mine."

More buzzing from the gallery.

"How do you know?" I asked.

Rod reached inside the helmet, his fingers stretching for something in the top webbing. His face was pinched with the effort, but I made no move to help him.

Let the judge see his determination and just how difficult simple tasks can be.

He drew his hand out of the helmet with a photograph gripped between two fingers.

"What's that, Rod?" I asked.

"A picture of my Dad in his Dolphins' uniform."

"May I approach?" I asked, and the judge waved me to the bench, Day nimbly following, a fox trailing the hound. I handed the photo to Judge Duckworth.

Tank Pittman. Big old number 77 in a four-point stance, a posed shot for a team media guide of yesteryear.

Rod turned in his wheelchair and pointed at Tank. "That's my father, Your Honor. Langston Pittman. And my mother, Liliana Santiago-Pittman."

Tank looked at Rod, eyes brimming with tears, and patted his chest just over his heart. Lily dabbed at her own eyes with a handkerchief.

"By any chance, is your father named after the poet Langston Hughes?" the judge asked.

"Yes, Ma'am," Rod said. "He had me memorize *Let America Be America Again* when I was five." In a melodious voice, Rod recited, "'Let America be the dream the dreamers dreamed. Let it be that great strong land of love.'"

The judge smiled warmly, then said, "Mr. and Mrs. Pittman, you've done a wonderful job raising your son."

They nodded their thanks in unison.

I headed back to the plaintiff's table, and Day moved back to the defense table. Wickerham leaned forward toward Day and said, "What'll she do next, give them reparations?"

As the judge made a notation on her legal pad, Day said, "We move to strike all references to the second helmet and the photograph of Plaintiff's father in that counsel has made no showing of chain of custody. For all we know, Mr. Lassiter inserted the photo into the helmet last night."

"I'll make a proffer," I said. "The helmet has been in the custody of Kiara Parsons from immediately after the injury when she picked it up from the field until she handed it to me in court today. If Your Honor wishes, I'll put her under oath to establish that. As for the photograph, we have independent proof that it was in the helmet at the time of the injury."

The judge lifted her eyeglasses until they were perched on her forehead. "And how can you possibly prove that, Mr. Lassiter?"

I moved to the easel, removed the poster board of the consent form, and uncovered an enlargement of a photo, a black-and-white shot of Rod lying on the field on his side, one leg atop the other, as if sleeping. His helmet was still on his head.

"The *Miami Herald* photographer who covered the game is in the gallery today," I said. "His name is Angel Castillo, and he can authenticate the photos."

A dark-haired man in the front row of the gallery hoisted his camera and smiled.

"Proceed, Mr. Lassiter," the judge said. "What do you have?"

I uncovered the next photo, a shot of Dr. Gupta, the St. Peter's team physician leaning over Rod. Then, one of me removing Rod's helmet. The next photo was just the helmet on the ground, the opening facing the camera.

"The final photograph is an enlargement looking straight into the helmet at ground level. While the photo is a bit blurry from the magnification, you can clearly see the photo inside the helmet with a portion of the number 7 on the jersey as well as part of Mr. Pittman's big belly."

"I see the photo and the number, Mr. Lassiter," the judge said. "Please tie it all together on this issue."

I moved back to the Plaintiff's table and passed close enough to Schooner Wickerham IV to hear him mutter, "Cheap vaudeville trick."

"It's twofold," I said. "First, the defendants provided my client with an ill-fitting helmet. Second, defense counsel or her agents fabricated false evidence and attempted to perpetrate a fraud on the court."

"We did nothing of the kind," Day shot back, "and I resent the implication."

"There's no implication," I said. "I smacked you right in the kisser."

"Your Honor, we're at the mercy of our clients," she said, the first note of desperation in her voice. "The helmet was provided to us by the school, and we produced it in the ordinary course of discovery."

"Whoa, Judge," I said. "Fifteen minutes ago, Ms. Day clearly said 'my people' found the helmet."

"A figure of speech," Day said. "Our hands are clean."

"Ha! Out, damned spot, says Lady Macbeth," I said.

"No *ad hominem* attacks in my courtroom, Mr. Lassiter," the judge warned.

"Sorry, Your Honor." I studied my shoe tops for a second, not one bit sorry. "But we're talking about Helmet-Gate. Just how far up the chain of command does this perfidy go?"

Judge Duckworth leaned back in her cushioned chair and seemed to study the ceiling, maybe looking for celestial help. Like most jurists, she didn't want to believe that lawyers who toiled in her courtroom had the ethical standards of card sharks.

"I am troubled by the defense producing the wrong helmet," the judge said in the mildest of tones.

"Troubled?" Why not enraged? "Wrong helmet?" Why not fraudulent evidence?

"However, Ms. Day, an officer of the court, has denied any knowledge, so I'm accepting that," the judge said.

What the hell! The hand grenade I'd tossed into the defense bunker was a dud.

"Anything else on the merits, Mr. Lassiter?" the judge prodded me.

"I would urge Your Honor to consider the helmet issue much more seriously. The defense took a smaller helmet, scuffed it up to look like Rod's, placed his number on it and removed the facemask and chin strap. This is a blatant act of fraud, not an innocent mistake."

"Even assuming that's true, how does it affect the merits of the case?" the judge asked.

"Simple. If the helmet don't fit, the defense is shit."

Whoops! That wasn't planned.

The gallery erupted in laughter. Reporters elbowed each other in glee. Tweeters tweeted. TikTokers ticked and tocked. Instagrammers grammed. Behind me, Tank Pittman guffawed as only a man topping 300 pounds could. Sandra Day kept her poker face, and her "people" stifled their smiles.

Schooner Wickerham IV stood and raised his cane over his head, looking like Moses, or rather Charlton Heston, bringing the word of God down from Mount Sinai. "What kind of circus you running here, Captain?" he croaked at the judge.

Judge Duckworth didn't respond. She was busy glaring at me with a look she must have used as a military judge when sentencing miscreants to Leavenworth.

-59-
A Bag of Dirty Tricks

Judges almost never bang their gavels.

Oh, sure, on television and in the movies, they do it all the time. Hollywood scribblers love both the visual effect and the sound – a rifle shot! – to put an exclamation point on the scene. Judges also rarely shout, "Order in the Court!"

Judge Melvia Duckworth didn't bang her gavel or holler. Rather, she aimed the gavel at me like a military policeman with a Sig Sauer.

"Ja-cob Lass-i-ter," she said in the same tone my Granny used when she caught me poaching lobsters. "There will be decorum in my courtroom. There will not be scatological language or playing to the gallery. Is that clear?"

"Perfectly."

"Let me ask you a direct question, Mr. Lassiter. Do you have any expert testimony that the oversize helmet caused or contributed to your client's fractured vertebra or bruised spinal cord?"

"Neither of our two neurosurgeons can say to a reasonable degree of medical certainty that the helmet contributed to Rod's injuries," I said.

"Thank you for your candor. So the relevance of the oversize helmet is what?"

"It's yet another negligent act, another boxcar in the long freight train that rolled onto the tracks in summer practice and ended with the second kickoff of the first game."

"A freight train hauling unrelated items of cargo," the judge said.

"Respectfully, the acts are clearly related. They show a pattern, a continuum that amounts to coaching malpractice."

"A tort you have created and named and now ask me to recognize as the law of Florida."

"Ten years from now, they'll be writing law review articles about Your Honor's foresight," I said.

"Either that, or ten months from now, the Third District will reverse me in a scathing opinion. Now, Mr. Lassiter, do you have anything else in support of your personal injury claim?"

"I need a moment, Your Honor."

Maybe two moments. One to figure where to start, another to calculate my chances of going to prison.

I leaned close to Rod and whispered, "I told Melissa I would win this case because I love you and your parents, and the defense lawyers don't love the company that pays them."

"Yeah?"

"Now, I have to prove it."

"I know we're losing, Uncle Jake. Is this where you throw the Hail Mary?"

I winked at him. "You just gave me the starting point. Mary Mallon."

"I remember. Typhoid Mary. I googled her."

I stood and spoke to the judge in the most gentle tone I could manage. I wanted to sound regretful to be making such incendiary allegations. "The Plaintiff moves, *ore tenus*, to strike

the defendants' pleadings and for sanctions against Wickerham
and Snoot on grounds of fabrication of evidence, subornation of
perjury, repeated violations of discovery, obstruction of justice,
invasion of the attorney-client privilege, illegal wiretapping, and
non-consensual wire recording."

Murmurs swept through the courtroom, and the judge
silenced everyone with a wave of the hand.

"That's a heavy ammo can you're toting, Mr. Lassiter," the
judge said. "For your sake, it better have live rounds. Now, why
didn't I hear about this until today?"

"I would have made the motion earlier and in writing, but
I only acquired the necessary proof last night. It's a bag of dirty
tricks that has no bottom. It started with the phony helmet and
then became a web of lies and deceit, a conspiracy to thwart justice
at every turn."

I could hear the clicks of keyboards in the gallery, reporters
and social media influencers banging away. At least, I still knew
how to say a quotable sentence or two. For whatever reason, my
morning headache had faded away. There was no double vision.
All was clarity.

I opened the briefcase I'd taken from Skull and Bones's
Blackwing, just as Sandra Day hopped to her feet. "Your Honor,
Mr. Lassiter committed several felonies, including assault and
theft, in obtaining this alleged evidence, so we would ask – "

"How do you know what Mr. Lassiter has in that briefcase, his
metaphorical bag of dirty tricks?"

"Well, I assume..."

"Did he take it from you or your staff?"

"No, no. Not at all."

She sounds flustered, not a Sunny Day trait.

"Apart from how it was acquired, do you know what's in that
briefcase?"

"Well, not precisely, but..."

Sunny Day was stumped. If she said too much, she would tie Skull and Bones to the law firm and to her. From the look on her face, she was violating the first rule of football and lawyering.

Never let them see your fear.

Schooner Wickerham IV was *rap-rap-rapping* his cane against the back of Day's chair. "Say something, woman!"

Didn't he get the memo? Women don't need to be told when to speak and when to be silent.

Wickerham wasn't helping. Day stood frozen in place.

"All right, Mr. Lassiter," the judge said. "Empty your rucksack and let's see what falls out."

I held up the phony hospital ID badge of Mary Mallon and briefly told the judge how she entered Rod's hospital room and secretly tape-recorded our conversation. Then I read from the transcript of the recording I'd gotten from Skull and Bones as the judge listened raptly, her eyes wide.

"A two-bagger of criminality," I summed up. "A non-consensual and therefore illegal recording and a breach of the sanctity of attorney-client communications by an agent of the defense."

"Quite a serious allegation," the judge said. "As serious as I have ever encountered against a member of the Bar."

"For the record," Sandra Day said, regaining her composure, "I did not hire this Mary Mallon, and I have never even met her."

"The real Mary Mallon was known as Typhoid Mary in the early 1900s," I said.

"Before my time." Day forced a smile, trying to make light of the moment. "I have never heard the name."

"Uncle Jake," Rod whispered. He held up his cell phone and showed me what his googling had found.

I checked the screen, then spoke to the judge. "In 2021, an article appeared in the New York State Bar Journal entitled: 'Covid

Query: Could Mary Mallon be Forcibly Quarantined Today?' The byline on the article is 'Sandra Day.'"

Whispers flowed through the gallery, rippling like a river sluicing over boulders. This time, the judge made no effort to stop the noise.

"Mr. Lassiter obviously doesn't understand how the top law firms operate," Day said.

"And how is that?" the judge asked, her tone challenging.

"I have scores of associates. They often write articles that appear under my name. It's an accepted practice."

Judge Duckworth stared at Day with what I hoped was skepticism. Still, giving nothing away, she turned to me, "What else, Mr. Lassiter?"

"If Your Honor would examine the folder entitled 'Helmet Specifications,' you'll see the blueprint for reproducing Rod's helmet in a smaller size. It's the smoking gun that proves the defense fabricated false evidence."

"Let me see everything from that briefcase," the judge ordered.

I complied, and the judge took several minutes to comb through the folders, poker face in place. Then, she said, "Breaching the sanctity of the attorney-client relationship and fabricating evidence. Two rather breathtaking acts of malevolence. I shudder to ask if you have anything else."

I summarized the rest. Illegal wiretaps of my phone conversations. Coercing Dr. Herlocher to sign a false affidavit taking the blame for failing to get a replacement physician, then bribing him to skip town for Patagonia. Backdating articles paid for by the defense but made to look like impartial scholarly research pieces. Stalking, intimidation, and threats by Crankshaw and Bonegar, the guys I call Skull and Bones. Trespassing on my property and assaulting me, though I left out that I'd clobbered Bones first with the baseball bat.

When I was finished, Day said, "I am not aware of any of that, and I'm quite sure I never met anyone named Crankshaw or Bonegar."

"Your Honor, those two crumbs work for the Consortium and do Wickerham and Snoot's dirty work," I said. "It's quite possible they kept a wall of deniability between themselves and Ms. Day."

The judge seemed perplexed. "Ms. Day, what is this Consortium?"

Day shrugged. "I'm not sure, though I have heard the name."

"Like Hitler heard of the Gestapo," I said.

"A word of advice, Mr. Lassiter," the judge said. "When you're about to plant your flag on the enemy's mountain, try not to shoot yourself in the foot."

"I apologize, Your Honor."

The courtroom was silent a moment, except for the gasps and sputters of the ancient A/C system.

"Ms. Day, what's your response to the rather startling evidence of misconduct Mr. Lassiter has presented?" the judge asked.

"Your Honor," Day said, "I implore you to ask Mr. Lassiter just how he acquired this alleged evidence. And if he invokes his Fifth Amendment rights, I have several photographs from last night that reveal the nature of his criminal conduct."

"No need," I said, grabbing the photo that showed me with a maniacal grin, just before sideswiping Skull and Bones's Blackwing. I held the photo so the judge could see it.

Crisis Management 101: When your opposition has the goods on you, it's better to tell your story first.

"Last night, I followed Crankshaw and Bonegar, the men who stalked me, assaulted me, wiretapped me, and were the phony nurse's accomplices and getaway drivers. We had an accident. Their car flipped over, and when I went to render aid, I found the evidence in their car."

"To render aid!" Day exploded. "He did no such thing. He intentionally ran them off the road. He illegally seized this so-called evidence, which must be excluded by this Court."

Judge Duckworth peered through her eyeglasses and said, "This isn't a criminal case, so there's no Fourth Amendment issue and no exclusionary rule. The defense motion is denied, and I will consider everything in that briefcase."

"But Your Honor..." Day began, and stopped. She was flummoxed.

"If you believe Mr. Lassiter committed a crime, feel free to take it up with the State Attorney," the judge said.

"Raymond Pincher?" She made a scoffing sound. "My people tell me he's one of counsel's closest friends. Mr. Lassiter even calls him 'Sugar Ray.'"

"As do I, Ms. Day. Sugar Ray and I are both members of the African Missionary Baptist Church, and casting doubts on his integrity holds no water with me."

"I only meant that..."

Ah, Sunny. We all know what you meant. Again, she was speechless.

"Mr. Lassiter," the judge said, "you've asked for the extraordinary remedy of striking the defense pleadings and leveling sanctions against defense counsel. Just what do you have in mind?"

Sanctions, right. It's not something that ever came up in my criminal practice. So, just what the hell do I have in mind?

Schooner Wickerham IV stood and cleared his throat, the sound of a garbage disposal chomping chicken bones. "May I be heard, Your Honor?" he bellowed in a baritone that belied his frail frame. He bowed from the waist, his head dipping so low that if he'd been a British barrister, his powdered wig would have slipped off.

At the defense table, Sandra Day grimaced and said under her breath, but loud enough for me to hear, "Oh, sweet Jesus, what now?"

-60-

The Price of Pork in Poughkeepsie

"Mr. Wickerham, what's on your mind, Sir?" the judge asked.

"Your Honor mentioned the word 'sanctions,' and I believe it is my duty as chairman emeritus of the firm my great-grandfather and Hiram Snoot founded to briefly respond."

Five-to-one he won't be brief, because in his heyday of fountain pens and leather-bound ledgers, no one interrupted the bastard.

"When I was four years old," he said, "my father introduced me to Oliver Wendell Holmes, Jr. who was 92 and retired from the Court, but still sharp as a bayonet. In the Civil War, Holmes was a brevet colonel and my great-grandfather, the first Schooner Wickerham, was a major general, both with Massachusetts regiments. This cane was carved from the limb of an oak tree that took several bullets for Schooner at Chancellorsville, where both men fought."

He held up his cane and his knees wobbled. "After the war, Schooner was instrumental in forming the Tenth Cavalry Regiment."

"The Buffalo Soldiers," the judge said.

"Called the 'colored cavalry' by the redskins in the Indian Wars," Wickerham said.

Judge Duckworth shook her head but said nothing. At the defense table, Day's eyes squeezed shut. Next to me, Rod said, "Rude dude."

"Now, what's all this have to do with the price of pork in Poughkeepsie?" Wickerham asked, in the mother of all rhetorical questions.

No one took a stab at it, so Wickerham continued, his tall, frail form leaning forward, one hand gripping his cane. "I've been around the Maypole a few times, and I have never seen such a spectacle in any courtroom as I have witnessed today. I have never heard such poppycock and balderdash as put forth by Plaintiff's counsel. He is a pestilence, a carbuncle on the soft underbelly of our noble profession."

Rod stifled a laugh. "He's dissing you big time, Uncle Jake."

"Mr. Wickerham, please refrain from personal attacks on counsel," the judge said, calmly. "Do you wish to address the issue of sanctions?"

"Yes indeedy-do. In the 152 years of Wickerham and Snoot, not once has the stain of sanctions sullied our hands. Not when we represented John D. Rockefeller in price collusion. Not in the Panama Canal kickbacks case. Not in union-busting from Boston to Kansas City, our Pinkertons carrying truncheons instead of briefcases. To put a fine point on it, I fear sanctions would put me in an early grave."

Rod snorted. "Dude's a zillion years old."

I shot a look at not-so-Sunny Day. The color had drained from her face, and she chewed at her lower lip. If she could get her hands on General Wickerham's cavalry sword, she would willingly fall on it.

"Now, I see what's going on here," Wickerham said. "Notwithstanding my feelings about Plaintiff's counsel, his client is quite appealing. Engaging and winsome. Your Honor cannot help herself."

"How's that?" the judge asked.

"You cannot help but to have empathy for a young mulatto of such charm and intelligence."

The judge seemed too shocked to utter a word.

Day exhaled a sound as if she'd been kicked in the gut by an Army mule.

Rod whispered, "What's a mulatto?"

"Later," I said.

"Sounds like a drink at Starbucks," Rod said. "Gimme a Frappuccino and a double mulatto."

"The Plaintiff is a fine lad," Wickerham blathered on, "a credit to his – "

"School!" Day shouted, leaping to her feet. "And his family."

Startled, the old codger pointed his cane at Day's empty chair. "Sit, woman!"

"Mr. Wickerham, get to the point," the judge demanded in a tone as firm as concrete. "What legal argument are you making?"

"Only this. Any mischief in discovery or alteration of exhibits or overzealous investigative techniques cannot be laid at the feet of my firm. There is a Chinese wall between our partners and the group known as the Consortium."

"So you know of the existence of this Consortium?" the judge said.

"Know of it? I started it with several captains of industry."

Oh yeah? I didn't know that. Do tell.

"The Consortium renders valuable litigation support in our major cases. But we do not control its actions, and we are not liable for its conduct."

"You can't insulate your firm when your lawyers use the fruits of the poisonous tree you planted," the judge said. "I've heard enough. Please take your seat."

"Now, see here! I outrank you, Captain."

"Not in my courtroom, you don't!" The judge leaned forward over the bench and pointed a finger, like a stiletto, at the old man. "Now sit your bony ass down because you're flirting with contempt."

Wickerham rocked back as if he'd been slapped in the face by General Robert E. Lee's white gloves. Wordlessly, he folded himself back into his chair, then whispered to Day, "Looks like we're getting some home cooking. Collard greens and cornbread."

"Mr. Lassiter, when last we spoke, you were going to tell me what sanctions you sought against the defendants and their law firm," the judge said.

I stood and felt a sharp pain in my jaw and a compression in my chest. My hands were clammy, and I felt short of breath.

Heart attack? No, not now! Not when I'm on the verge of a great victory. Even the messenger in ancient Greece who ran from Marathon to Athens got to deliver the good news before dropping dead.

"Mr. Lassiter?"

I should ask for a recess. And an ambulance.

But maybe it's just stress and a sleepless night and those muscles I strained climbing the fence into the Blackwing.

"Your Honor," I began, "as for the motion to strike and for sanctions against Wickerham and Snoot..."

My mind froze. Just like that. My ears were ringing like church bells.

"Uncle Jake, we talked about this," Rod said. "Remember? A virulent cancer?"

"Mr. Lassiter, I'm waiting," the judge said.

"Shr-tri-ke pleadings, Rod," I mumbled to my client. "Do it the way we sht-alked."

"Are you faking, Uncle Jake?"

"Jush-t do it."

Rod boosted himself from the wheelchair with both hands and unsteadily got to his feet. "Judge, based on the retail misconduct of defense counsel..."

"Whole-sale!" I said.

"The wholesale misconduct of defense counsel," Rod began again, "is a virulent cancer that has infected every pleading as well as every affidavit and exhibit filed by the defense. We ask on count one that you strike all defenses and find for the Plaintiff...that's me...on liability."

Rod had run out of ammo and looked at me.

"And...and sh-et a jewelry trial...that is, a jury trial on damages, Your Honor," I said. Thankfully, the pain was abating, and I no longer felt like a defensive lineman was sitting on my chest.

"Are you all right, Mr. Lassiter?" the judge asked.

"Dine and fandy. That is, fine and dandy."

"We have the motion to strike the defense pleadings. Please speak to the issue of sanctions against their counsel."

My tongue was having trouble getting out of the way as I tried to speak. "Moe-ney. Mu-nay."

Did I just have a stroke?

"Are you saying 'money,' Mr. Lassiter?"

I nodded vigorously.

"And as for the amount?"

Again, Rod came to my rescue. "We look to the punitive damages statute for guidance. Florida Statute Section..."

Rod couldn't remember, but somehow it stuck in my brain, just like those gunky tau proteins. "Sexy-shifty-eight," I said.

"Sexy what?" the judge asked.

Rod said, "Judge, it's Section 768.73. Punitive damages are limited to half a million dollars in most cases and $2 million in certain others. As punishment for misconduct, we ask the court to award a sum against Wickerham and Snoot in whatever amount it sees fit between those numbers."

"Let's take a 15-minute recess," the judge said, "and I'll issue my rulings. Mr. Lassiter, do you need a glass of water or aspirin or anything?"

"Two-keel-uh."

"To kill what?"

I concentrated on the word and said, "Tequila."

-61-
Horrific and Reprehensible

"Are you okay, Jake?" Tank Pittman asked.

I was bent over the sink in the restroom, the primeval plumbing groaning while it delivered a trickle of water that I splashed on my face. "Tip top, Tank. Wow, your son. He's something, huh?"

"He's great, Jake, but I'm worried about you."

"My transmission got stuck between gears. Fine now. And we've got the judge. At least, I think we have."

"Let me get a look at you."

I glanced at myself in the mirror. I hadn't gotten any better looking, but at least I wasn't drooling, and my mouth wasn't hanging open. I turned and let Tank study me.

"When you were talking gibberish, it reminded me of my Momma when she had a stroke," he said, "but you look okay. Not great, but okay."

"Lassiter and Pittman," I said, trying to change the subject.

"How's that?"

"My new law firm. Rodrigo will be a helluva trial partner."

"He just turned 18, Jake. Can this wait 'til he graduates from high school?"

"But you saw his potential, right?"

He ignored my question. "Rod said you were faking it. You put the ball on the ground in the old fumblerooski so that he'd have to pick it up and run with it."

"Rod said that?"

"Told me it was part of your strategy. Some sneaky lawyer shit to give him more face time with the judge."

"Such a smart kid. That's exactly what I did."

I looked back in the mirror, expecting my nose to have grown a foot, but no. Just the same old bump. However, I wasn't lying about one thing. Rodrigo Pittman would make a helluva good lawyer. Prompting one more thought before heading back into the courtroom.

I hope I'm still vertical when they swear my godson into the Bar.

***

I wrapped an arm around Rod's shoulder as I took my seat next to him. "Whatever the judge rules," I said, "it's been one of the great honors of my life representing you."

Rod looked at me with his large dark eyes that might have shimmered with a tear or two.

"Just as we did this morning, we'll start with count two," Judge Duckworth said to the packed courtroom. "The Plaintiff emphasizes that he seeks, not to abolish tackle football, but to put it on hold until the FHSAA can prove it's safe. That could be one year, two years, or forever. Mr. Lassiter, your heart is in the right place. But your head is..."

Up my ass? Please, not that.

"...in the clouds. Now, you have clearly demonstrated that tackle football is a dangerous sport. You rightly point to the extraordinary language of the consent and waiver that all parents must sign."

She adjusted her eyeglasses and looked down at her file. "Even if there's no negligence, and I'll quote, 'Your child may be seriously injured or killed because there are certain dangers inherent in the activity which cannot be avoided or eliminated.'"

The judge looked up and seemed to address the entire courtroom, not just counsel. "Now, there's a warning that will make parents think twice. Which, of course, is its purpose. That and immunizing everyone from the principal to the janitor from negligence claims. Now, if you saw that language on a power mower or a tire jack or a parachute, you might not cut the grass, change a tire, or try sky diving. And, as defense counsel has pointed out, participation in high school football has been decreasing for several years. So that waiver serves a salutary purpose."

The judge paused, and the gallery was hushed, awaiting her decision.

"Counsel, my ruling will not please either one of you. Mr. Lassiter, while you have made a case that the sport could be made safer, you have not met the burden on your request for an injunction. Ms. Day, you've made an excellent case about the rich tradition of the sport and that some measures have already been taken regarding safety. Still, you're not going to get summary final judgment, at least not today."

Splitting the baby? Just how will that work?

"I'm deferring ruling for a period of nine months and ordering the FHSAA to report to me what additional steps are being taken to make the game safer. I will send out a detailed bill of particulars with guidelines as to the issues that concern me. We'll re-convene in nine months to assess the report and determine what else, if anything, remains to be done."

Sandra Day stood and spoke softly. "Your Honor, earlier today you indicated it would be problematic for the Court to be, in essence, the commissioner of high school football. But isn't that what you're doing?"

"A lot has happened today, and none of it reflects well on you or your firm, Ms. Day. If you don't like my ruling, the doors of the Third District are always open." The judge's tone was unusually brusque.

Day sank back into her chair and pinched the bridge of her nose between two fingers.

In the gallery, there was an insistent clicking of keyboard keys, two dozen chickens pecking at the ground. As the judge began to speak, I leaned forward and listened as intently as a safecracker straining to hear the clicks of the dial.

"As to count one, I will skip the adjectives such as 'horrific' and 'reprehensible,'" the judge said, not skipping them at all. "I will simply say that Typhoid Mary has infected this case, and that was only the beginning of the defense's maleficent actions. The Court grants Plaintiff's motion to strike all pleadings and defenses of the Defendants on account of wholesale – and retail – violations of the Florida Rules of Civil Procedure and the criminal law. Additionally, the Court grants Plaintiff's motion for sanctions and awards $2 million which shall be paid not by Defendants or their insurance carriers but rather by the law firm of Wickerham and Snoot."

Your Christmas bonus, Sunny? Forget about it!

"The Defendant's motion for summary judgment on count one is denied. Inasmuch as all defenses have been stricken, the Court will set a trial by jury solely on the issue of damages. And I think that's quite enough for today."

Judge Duckworth stood, and so did we. Before heading down the steps, she paused a moment, as if something had just occurred to her. "Let's expedite this. I encourage counsel to meet and discuss an appropriate sum to settle plaintiff's claims. Should that fail, we'll pick a jury two weeks from today."

The judge exited the rear door of the courtroom, and I stood still. Rod gripped my forearm with more strength than I knew he had. I clasped a hand on top of his. Neither of us said a word. The respect and love and joy were understood. I felt a jolt of pain in my neck, but it was only Tank Pittman giving me an affectionate squeeze.

Lily stood and leaned close to me. "I'm glad I didn't shoot you, Jake."

***

That night, when Melissa got home from the hospital, I had the champagne already chilled. She jumped into my arms and wrapped her legs around my hips, and we kissed, long and deep and slow. I twirled around as if we were dancing, and she rested her head on my shoulder. We stayed that way a long, warm minute, and I knew that at this moment, I was the luckiest sumbitch in the world.

She purred like a cat and said, "You are such a big, strong, virile man."

"If you're objectifying me...please don't stop."

"I'm so happy for Rod and Lily and Tank," she said, "but I'm also overjoyed for you. It's a new beginning."

"So you're not opposed to me going back into private practice?"

"Not at all. The case breathed new life into you. New clients will be lining up. You're the lead story everywhere tonight."

"And tomorrow they'll have another one. But it feels damn good to help people I love."

We downed the bubbly on empty stomachs. Well, maybe Melissa's stomach was empty.

"Are you hungry?" she asked.

"Starving," I said, stifling a burp.

"What did you have for lunch today?"

"The usual. Kale salad with shaved carrots and a celery juice."

"Uh-huh. I guess that's why your breath smells like roadkill racoon."

"I might have added some protein along the way."

"I love you, Jake Lassiter, you big galoot."

"And I love you right back. Now and forever."

-62-
Consorting with the Consortium

Three days after the hearing, I was sitting in my reserved booth at Keg South minding my own business when I heard a voice that sounded familiar.

"Is that your Blackwing in the parking lot?"

"Why? You hit it?" I looked up and saw Bolo Tie.

"Who could tell the difference?" he asked.

"Been too busy to take it to the shop."

"I've seen you on the news, counselor." He slid into the booth across from me. "It's true what they say about the camera adding 20 pounds."

His salt-and-pepper brush cut was a little longer, and he still wore his usual uniform of jeans, western shirt, and string tie. He scanned the menu and said, "How are the Death Dogs?"

"Memorable. In the middle of the night, you'll still be thinking about them."

I signaled Lourdes to bring the frankfurters and two Australian lagers. After a moment of silence, I said, "Okay, I give up. What are you doing here?"

"You heard the judge suggest that the parties meet to settle your damage claim."

I looked past him toward the door. "Is Sunny Day joining us?"

"I fired her," Bolo Tie said.

"*You* fired *her?*" I said.

"The Consortium hired her, and I fired her. I have broad discretion where the group's procedures and personnel are concerned."

"And its checkbook?" I asked.

"We'll see."

At the nearby pool table, someone whooped with joy, and money changed hands.

"I feel like I've gotten to know you, Lassiter," Bolo Tie said.

"How so?"

"I've been watching you since that discovery conference with Sunny Day and her over-educated twits."

That made me smile. "I remember seeing you in the back of the conference room. You stuck out like a trout in a bowl of shredded wheat."

"And I remember Day telling her underlings not to underestimate you, but that's just what she did. Not your legal acumen, but your willingness to risk everything for your client. Your *cojones.*"

"Sometimes, they're all I've got."

"Don't underestimate yourself. The way you suckered Day into producing the phony helmet, well that was a thing of beauty."

That brought back a memory. "The day of the coach's deposition, you gave me some inside information about Day. I asked why, and you said you liked to see a fair fight."

"Yeah?"

"But that wasn't it, was it?"

He scratched his chin with a knuckle but didn't answer, flicking a glance at Lourdes who delivered the brewskis and the cheese-slathered frankfurters.

"The last few years," he said, skeptically eyeing the Death Dogs, "I've been gunning for Day and the guys you call Skull and Bones."

"Did you fire those knuckleheads, too?"

"Shut down their entire unit. No more breaking the law to win court cases. Without knowing it, Lassiter, you helped me clean house."

"Glad to be of service."

"Now, let's see if we can resolve your case without the judge having to empanel a jury."

"If you're serious about that, it would be my pleasure to consort with the Consortium," I said.

"I've gotten numbers from our economists and medical experts, and here's how I'd like to do this. Secret ballots. We'll each write a settlement number on a napkin. There's a floor of $8 million. Neither of us can go below that number. If the higher number is 20 percent or less in excess of the lower amount, we'll settle on the higher number. If more than 20 percent, we'll settle on the lower number."

I took a sip of the beer to figure it out. "I never heard of anything like this."

"It's in the beta stage," he said. "It worked fine the first four times. This is the fifth."

"I'm trying to do some math in my head."

"Let me help," he said. "Let's say you demand $13 million, and I offer $10 million. The case settles for $10 million because your demand is more than 20 percent higher than my offer. But if you demand $13 million, and I offer $11 million..."

"We settle for $13 million. Okay, you're trying to keep me from going too high. I get that. But what's to keep you from going too low and stealing the pot?"

He gave me a long, steady gaze.

"Your good faith," I said, answering my own question. "That it?"

"It's about time you started trusting me, Lassiter."

I asked Lourdes to bring us some napkins that weren't covered with melted cheese and soaked in beer. She brought them along with two pens.

I watched Bolo Tie's face as he scribbled on his napkin. I'm trained to distrust people, but something told me he wouldn't turn skinflint to save the Consortium a million here or there. I decided on a number, then increased it. Maybe too much? I didn't know. I wrote the number on the napkin right under the Keg South logo. The number? Let's just say it would buy a lot of beer.

Bolo tie unfolded each napkin, then smiled. "This is a new one. We both wrote the exact same number."

"Fierce!" I said. "That's what Rod would say."

"Deal," Bolo Tie said, reaching across the table to shake my hand.

We shook, and I said, "Hey, I'm picking up the lunch tab."

-63-
From May to December

Two months later...

I'd been feeling fatigued the last few days, which was odd, because I was sleeping well and hadn't exerted myself, except to hoist several margaritas as soon as the sun was over the yardarm, or at four p.m., whichever came first. Melissa and I were taking a week off. She needed the break, and I was happy to provide sunrise beach walks and sunset siestas – and fiestas – in the cushy bed of an oceanfront suite.

We were at Cheeca Lodge in Islamorada. I grew up not far from here geographically, but a million light-years away economically. The rusted-out trailer park I remembered as a kid had been replaced by a waterfront development with pint-size, million-dollar condos.

Some nights at Cheeca we dined at the resort's fancy flagship restaurant. Other nights, we gobbled lobster mac and cheese and conch fritters, washed down by tequila at the oceanfront tiki bar. Walking the beach on our second day, I became short of breath but didn't mention it to Melissa. Same with the migraine that flared on the third day and the racing, erratic heart later that evening. I'd had the fluttering heart off-and-on for a year now, so the symptoms no longer frightened me. Still, I was glad I remembered to pack my medication, the blood thinners and beta blockers prescribed by my cardiologist.

Under the theory that nothing should interfere with a good vacation, I ignored my symptoms and enjoyed every minute of our getaway. When we checked out of the hotel, sunbaked and weary, I was chomping on a frozen Key lime popsicle and feeling better. Sure, there was a bit of tinnitus, but not an ear-banging brass band. More like Jimmy Buffet searching for his lost shaker of salt.

We headed north on the Overseas Highway, my shiny, repaired Blackwing thrumming contentedly. This was Rod's day to come home from the rehab center, and we couldn't be late. Melissa dozed off just as we hit the Florida Turnpike, whose signs alerted me to the exit for the Don Shula Expressway.

Maybe it was the coach's name that triggered it, but a memory came back then. That cemetery where I'd seen my own name in those scary nightmares. Now, fully awake, I saw the names on the other graves. Six of them.

Nick Buoniconti. Jim Kiick. Jake Scott. Bob Kuechenberg. Bill Stanfill. Earl Morrall. All Miami Dolphins on the undefeated 1972 Super Bowl team. Each one dead of CTE. I've said it before, and I'll say it again. "Perfect season, my ass!"

I chased the memory and motored on. Thirty minutes later, I pulled into the parking lot of the rehab center, and Melissa woke up, yawning as I parked the car.

"Hello, Sleeping Beauty," I said.

"Hmm," she said, stretching her arms over her head. She leaned over and kissed me, then drew back. "Why are you sweating, Jake?"

"Guess I don't have the A/C on the right temp."

"And you're a little pale under your tan."

We got out of the car and headed toward a small park with picnic tables adjacent to the center's driveway. The facility's staff, which had come to love Rod, had set up a white U-shaped wooden trellis with the name "Rodrigo" made of red roses, arcing across the top. Bottles of champagne and sodas chilled in coolers, and a lunch of sandwiches and salads awaited us.

Rod had told his parents to wait for him outside the facility. That went for Melissa and me, too, though girlfriend Kiara was exempt from the order. The kid wanted to make an entrance, or an exit, as the case may be.

Tank approached, kissed Melissa on the cheek, then bear-hugged me. "Love you, brother," he said.

"Love you back, you big tub of guts."

"Thanks for being here, Jake," Lily said.

"Are you kidding me? This is the greatest day ever."

From the little park, I could see inside the glass doors of the lobby. As we waited, I felt the first flames of what I thought was a migraine. But this one was different. Just a dull ache in the back of my head and neck that seemed to move to my jaw.

At high noon, the door opened, and we could hear the applause from the lobby where physicians and staff were lined up, a gauntlet of well-wishers on either side of Rod, who was walking under his own power with a smiling Kiara alongside.

He walked slowly and deliberately. But not wobbly. And without crutches or a cane.

Life is good. I feel blessed to see this moment with the people I love.

Rod walked across the driveway toward us, his gypsy jazz guitar slung around his neck, and we started applauding. And crying. Lily, Tank, Melissa, me. A flood of joy.

Rod's dark hair had grown longer, and a forelock fell across his forehead, reminding me of a young Elvis Presley, guitar and all. He smiled broadly as he reached the park. Rod and Kiara sat on two high stools that were perched on the edge of the grass. Then, as he promised months ago, Rod began strumming *September Song* on the guitar, as he and Kiara sang a duet:

"Oh, it's a long, long while from May to December...
But the days grow short when you reach September."

I turned toward Melissa who had her eyes on me. I saw all the warmth and love in the world in those eyes. I thought again about just how damn charmed a life I've led.

"When the autumn weather turns the leaves to flame...
One hasn't got time for the waiting game."

I looked at the trellis, which blurred, and suddenly the roses that spelled out "Rodrigo" rearranged themselves. Now, withered and unkempt, petals falling to the ground, they spelled "Jacob."

What the hell is that?

Oh, a faded funeral wreath.

My mouth felt dry and my jaw ached. Not a toothache, but something deeper. I looked at Melissa, whose eyes widened in alarm.

"It's okay, Mel," I said. "I've never loved like this before."

"Jake...Jake!"

I heard her voice, but my eyes must have been closed, because I couldn't see her. I felt my knees give way, but I didn't fall. Tank Pittman, that mountain of a man, a friend to the end, caught me and was carrying me somewhere. I don't know where because I didn't get there.

I heard Melissa one last time. "Don't let go, Jake. Stay with me. Stay..."

And then it all went dark and silent, and my last thought was that I was a very lucky man and that nothing hurt at all.

###

BOOKS BY PAUL LEVINE

JAKE LASSITER SERIES

TO SPEAK FOR THE DEAD: Linebacker-turned-lawyer Jake Lassiter begins to believe that his surgeon client is innocent of malpractice . . . but guilty of murder.

NIGHT VISION: After several women are killed by an Internet stalker, Jake is appointed a special prosecutor and heads to London and the very streets where Jack the Ripper once roamed.

FALSE DAWN: After his client confesses to a murder he didn't commit, Jake follows a bloody trail from Miami to Havana to discover the truth.

MORTAL SIN: Talk about conflicts of interest. Jake is sleeping with Gina Florio and defending her mob-connected husband in court.

RIPTIDE: Jake Lassiter chases a beautiful woman and stolen bonds from Miami to Maui.

FOOL ME TWICE: To clear his name in a murder investigation, Jake searches for buried treasure in the abandoned silver mines of Aspen, Colorado.

FLESH & BONES: Jake falls for his beautiful client even though he doubts her story. She claims to have recovered "repressed memories" of abuse . . . just before gunning down her father.

LASSITER: Jake retraces the steps of a model who went missing eighteen years earlier . . . after his one-night stand with her.

LAST CHANCE LASSITER: In this prequel novella, young Jake Lassiter has an impossible case: he represents Cadillac Johnson, an aging rhythm and blues musician who claims his greatest song was stolen by a top-of-the-charts hip-hop artist.

STATE vs. LASSITER: This time, Jake is on the wrong side of the bar. He's charged with murder! The victim? His girlfriend and banker, Pamela Baylins, who was about to report him to the authorities for allegedly stealing from clients.

BUM RAP: Defending Steve Solomon in a murder case and fighting his growing feelings for Victoria Lord, Jake find a missing witness—a stunning Bar girl—before she's eliminated by the Russian mob.

BUM LUCK: "Thirty seconds after the jury announced its verdict, I decided to kill my client." Is Jake suffering brain damage from all those concussions? And will he really resort to vigilante justice?

BUM DEAL: Appointed special prosecutor in a high-profile murder case, Jake vows to take down a prominent surgeon accused of killing his wife. There's just one problem...or maybe three: no evidence, no witness, and no body.

CHEATER'S GAME: Lassiter puts the college admissions process on trial when he defends his brainiac nephew Kip who's caught up in the true-to-life scandal that led to more than fifty federal prosecutions.

EARLY GRAVE: When his godson suffers a catastrophic injury in a high school football game, Lassiter sues to abolish the sport and becomes the most hated man in Miami. Still battling CTE, Lassiter's relationship with fiancée Dr Melissa Gold hits a rocky patch and they head to couples' therapy.

SOLOMON & LORD SERIES

SOLOMON vs. LORD: Trial lawyer Victoria Lord, who follows every rule, and Steve Solomon, who makes up his own, bicker and banter as they defend a beautiful young woman, accused of killing her wealthy, older husband.

THE DEEP BLUE ALIBI: Solomon and Lord come together—and fly apart—defending Victoria's "Uncle Grif" on charges he killed a man with a speargun. It's a case set in the Florida Keys with side trips to coral reefs and a nudist colony where all is more—and less—than it seems.

KILL ALL THE LAWYERS: Just what did Steve Solomon do to infuriate ex-client and ex-con "Dr. Bill"? Did Solomon try to lose the case in which the TV shrink was charged in the death of a woman patient?

HABEAS PORPOISE: It starts with the kidnaping of a pair of trained dolphins and turns into a murder trial with Solomon and Lord on *opposite* sides after Victoria is appointed a special prosecutor, and fireworks follow!

STAND-ALONE THRILLERS

IMPACT: A Jetliner crashes in the Everglades. Is it negligence or terrorism? When the legal case gets to the Supreme Court, the defense has a unique strategy: kill anyone, even a Supreme Court justice, to win the case.

BALLISTIC: A nuclear missile, a band of terrorists, and only two people who can prevent Armageddon. A "loose nukes" thriller for the twenty-first century.

ILLEGAL: Down-and-out lawyer Jimmy (Royal) Payne tries to reunite a Mexican boy with his missing mother and becomes enmeshed in the world of human trafficking and sex slavery.

PAYDIRT: Bobby Gallagher had it all and lost it. Now, assisted by his twelve-year-old brainiac son, he tries to rig the Super Bowl, win a huge bet . . . and avoid getting killed.

BOXED SET

SHATTERED JUSTICE: Four of the author's best-loved best-sellers: "Solomon vs. Lord," "The Deep Blue Alibi," "To Speak for the Dead," and "Illegal."

PRAISE FOR PAUL LEVINE

TO SPEAK FOR THE DEAD

"Move over Scott Turow. *To Speak for the Dead* is courtroom drama at its very best."
—Larry King

"An assured and exciting piece of work. Jake Lassiter is Travis McGee with a law degree . . . One of the best mysteries of the year."
—*Los Angeles Times*

"Paul Levine is guilty of master storytelling in the first degree. *To Speak for the Dead* is a fast, wry, and thoroughly engrossing thriller."
—Carl Hiaasen

NIGHT VISION

"Levine's fiendish ability to create twenty patterns from the same set of clues will have you waiting impatiently for his next novel."
—*Kirkus Reviews*

"Sparkles with wit and subtlety."
—*Toronto Star*

"Breathlessly exciting."
—*Cleveland Plain Dealer*

FALSE DAWN

"Realistic, gritty, fun."
—*New York Times Book Review*

"A highly entertaining yarn filled with wry humor."
—*Detroit Free Press*

"A dazzler, extremely well-written and featuring so many quotable passages you'll want someone handy to read them aloud to."
—*Ellery Queen's Mystery Magazine*

MORTAL SIN

"Take one part John Grisham, two parts Carl Hiaasen, throw in a dash of John D. MacDonald, and voila! You've got *Mortal Sin*."
—*Tulsa World*

"Recalling the work of Carl Hiaasen, this thriller races to a smashing climax."
—*Library Journal*

"Wonderfully funny, sexy, and terrifying."
—Dave Barry

RIPTIDE

"A thriller as fast as the wind. A bracing rush, as breathtaking as hitting the Gulf waters on a chill December morning."
—*Tampa Tribune*

"A tale involving drug smuggling and murder, windsurfing and murder, multi-million-dollar thievery and murder. The action never stops."
—*Denver Rocky Mountain News*

"One of the best mystery writers in the business today. The story fairly leaps with enthusiasm toward the finale. *Riptide* is Paul Levine's finest work."
—*Ocala (FL) Star Banner*

FOOL ME TWICE

"You'll like listening to Jake's beguiling first-person tale-telling so much that you won't mind being fooled thrice."
—*Philadelphia Inquirer*

"A fast-paced thriller filled with action, humor, mystery and suspense."
—*Miami Herald*

"Blend the spicy characters created by Elmore Leonard with the legal expertise and suspense made famous by John Grisham and you have Paul Levine's *Fool Me Twice*."
—*Lake Worth (FL) Herald*

FLESH & BONES

"The author keeps the suspense high with innovative twists and touches of humor that spice up the courtroom scenes."
—*Chicago Tribune*

"Filled with smart writing and smart remarks. Jake is well on his way to becoming a star in the field of detective fiction."
—*Dallas Morning News*

"A well-focused plot that stresses in-depth characterization and action that is more psychological than macho. The author keeps the suspense high with innovative twists."
—*Atlanta Journal Constitution*

LASSITER

"Since Robert Parker is no longer with us, I'm nominating Levine for an award as best writer of dialogue in the grit-lit genre."
—*San Jose Mercury News*

"Lassiter is back after fourteen long years—and better than ever. Moving fast, cracking wise, butting heads, he's the lawyer we all want on our side—and on the page."
—Lee Child

"Few writers can deliver tales about sex and drugs in South Florida better than Levine."
—*Booklist*

STATE vs. LASSITER

"Blend the wit of Carl Hiaasen with Elmore Leonard's dialogue and throw in John Grisham's courtroom skills, and you have State vs. Lassiter."
—Amazon Review

"Lassiter's narrative, which oscillates between self-deprecating and wiseass, is so entertaining and the story so deftly plotted that you will want to read more of his adventures even before you are through."
—*Bookreporter*

"Lassiter is likeable and a character that stands tall like Jack Reacher, Travis McGee or Spenser. Levine's only problem is he isn't prolific enough. I want more Lassiter!"
—*Pick of the Literate*

BUM RAP

"The pages fly by and the laughs keep coming in this irresistible South Florida crime romp. A delicious mix of thriller and comic crime novel."
—*Booklist* (starred review)

"Levine effectively blends a puzzling crime, intelligent sleuthing, adroit courtroom maneuvering, and a surprising attraction between Victoria and Jake in this welcome-addition to both series."
—*Publishers Weekly*

"Ebulliently seamless melding of Levine's two legal-eagles series."
—*Kirkus Reviews*

BUM LUCK

"A one-sit, must-read novel full of memorable characters and unforgettable vignettes. Levine's pacing is perfect as always, and the pages just fly by, even as he juggles multiple plots with his own unique aplomb."
—*Bookreporter*

"A gripping and often quite an amusing thriller with a surprising climax, all of which is built around an intriguing cast of characters as it achieves an almost flawless rhythm."
—*Book Pleasures*

"Paul Levine continues his trademark brisk pacing with timely storytelling and well-placed humor. 'Bum Luck' is elevated further by teaming Jake with Steve Solomon and Victoria Lord. The trio make an unstoppable team—concerned about the law, but even more about people."
—*South Florida Sun-Sentinel*

BUM DEAL

"Any book with Jake Lassiter is a drop-everything, read-it-now for me—and this one has Solomon & Lord too. Bum Deal is fantastic."
—Lee Child

"Fascinating, fully developed characters and smart, well-paced dialogue keep the pages turning. Levine manipulates the expectations of the reader as skillfully as Jake manipulates the expectations of the jury"
—*Publishers Weekly* (starred review)

"Bum Deal is the real deal. Jake Lassiter at his smart-talking, fast-thinking best. A funny, compelling and canny courtroom thriller, seasoned with a little melancholy and a lot of inside knowledge."
—Scott Turow

CHEATER'S GAME

"A riveting legal thriller that Grisham fans will love."
—*Blue Ink* (starred review)

"One of the best legal thrillers of the year."
—*Mystery Scene*

"Clever, funny and seriously on point when it comes to the inequities of society and the justice system, Cheater's Game is top-notch stuff from Paul Levine. His Jake Lassiter is my kind of lawyer."
—Michael Connelly

SOLOMON & LORD SERIES

SOLOMON VS. LORD

"A funny, fast-paced legal thriller. The barbed dialogue makes for some genuine laugh-out-loud moments. Fans of Carl Hiaasen and Dave Barry will enjoy this humorous Florida crime romp."
—*Publishers Weekly*

"The writing makes me think of Janet Evanovich out to dinner with John Grisham."
—*Mystery Lovers*

"Hiaasen meets Grisham in the court of last retort. A sexy, wacky, wonderful thriller with humor and heart."
—Harlan Coben

THE DEEP BLUE ALIBI

"An entertaining, witty comedy caper with legal implications . . . sparkles with promise, humor, and more than a dash of suspense."
—*Blog Critics*

"A cross between *Moonlighting* and *Night Court* . . . courtroom drama has never been this much fun."
—*Fresh Fiction*

"As hilarious as *The Deep Blue Alibi* is, it is almost possible between the cleverly molded characters and sharp dialogue to overlook that the novel contains a terrific mystery, one that will keep you guessing."
—*Bookreporter*

KILL ALL THE LAWYERS

"A clever, colorful thriller . . . with characters drawn with a fine hand, making them feel more like friends than figments of the author's imagination. Levine ratchets up the tension with each development but never neglects the heart of the story—his characters."
—*Publishers Weekly* (starred review)

"Levine skillfully blends humor, a view of Miami, and the legal system into tidy plots."
—*South Florida Sun-Sentinel*

"Another successful fast-moving, highly entertaining mystery. Irreverent to juveniles, judges, and the judicial system, but does it all with a wink. Encore . . . encore."
—*Reviewing The Evidence*

HABEAS PORPOISE

"Steve Solomon and Victoria Lord are smart and funny and sexy in a way that Hollywood movies were before comedies became crass and teen-oriented."
—*Connecticut Post*

"A *Moonlighting* crime novel. Great fun."
—*Lansing State Journal*

"Entertaining and witty with lots of laughs."
—*Mysterious Reviews*

STAND-ALONE THRILLERS

IMPACT

"A breakout book, highly readable and fun with an irresistible momentum, helped along by Levine's knowledge of the Supreme Court and how it works."
—*USA TODAY*

"Sizzles the Supreme Court as it has never been sizzled before, even by Grisham."
—F. Lee Bailey

"A masterfully written thriller, coiled spring tight. The plot is relentless. I loved it!"
—Michael Palmer

BALLISTIC

"*Ballistic* is *Die Hard* in a missile silo. Terrific!"
—Stephen J. Cannell

"It's easy to compare Levine to Tom Clancy but I think he's better for two simple reasons—he's a better storyteller and his characters are more believable, good guys and bad guys alike."
—Ed Gorman

ILLEGAL

"Levine is one of the few thriller authors who can craft a plot filled with suspense while still making the readers smile at the characters' antics."
—*Chicago Sun-Times*

"The seamy side of smuggling human cargo is deftly exposed by the clear and concise writing of the Edgar Award–nominated author. *Illegal* is highly recommended."
—*Midwest Book Review*

"Timely, tumultuous, and in a word, terrific."
—*Providence Journal*

PAYDIRT

"In the tradition of Harlan Coben's thrillers, Paydirt is a sizzling caper with spine-tingling suspense, laughs, thrills, some football, and a touch of romance!"
—*The Daily Review*

"This book is great for mystery lovers, suspense lovers, and even those loving the good ol' All-American pastime and those who play while being true to themselves. A heartwarming story with lots of twists and turns."
—Amazon Review

"Paydirt is one of those books that has characters that stay with you long after the book is finished. The story was a fast and engaging read. I loved the way Levine built up the suspense about the Super Bowl while still keeping the story believable."
—*Vine Voice*

NUMBER ONE BESTSELLING AUTHOR
PAUL LEVINE

Photo by Doug Ellis

Paul Levine is the Amazon Number One Bestselling Author of the "Jake Lassiter" and "Solomon vs. Lord" series. Levine won the John D. MacDonald Fiction Award and has been nominated for the Edgar, Macavity, International Thriller, Shamus, and James Thurber prizes. A former trial lawyer, he also wrote twenty episodes of the CBS military drama "JAG" and co-created the Supreme Court drama "First Monday" starring James Garner and Joe Mantegna. The international bestseller "To Speak for the Dead" was his first novel and introduced readers to linebacker-turned-lawyer Jake Lassiter. "Bum Rap," which brought Lassiter together with Steve Solomon and Victoria Lord, was an Amazon #1 bestseller. His latest book is "Early Grave" in which an ailing Lassiter sues to establish high school football as so inherently dangerous as to constitute a "public nuisance" that should be abolished. For more information, visit the author's website at www.paul-levine.com or follow him on Twitter @Jake_Lassiter.